THE
ALLURING
TRAVELER

Kathleen Garnsey

Paperback-Press
an imprint of A & S Publishing
A & S Holmes, Inc.

ISBN 13: 978-0692740422
ISBN: 0692740422

DEDICATION

I would like to dedicate this book to my dear friend, Norma Eaton. She has encouraged me from the moment I met her, and has continued to be there for me. Her professional advice is always welcome and needed, but her friendship is irreplaceable. Thank you Norma for being my friend and colleague.

ACKNOWLEDGMENTS

Many thanks to my friends Norma Eaton, and Sharon Kizziah-Holmes of Paperback Press. Both kind ladies have provided me with excellent advice and encouragement. Without them I would be lost. Thank you both for the fantastic jobs you do for me.

CHAPTER ONE

"He'll die within twenty sun-cycles."

"You're sure?" The doctor nodded and Jorell Sutone's heart sank. She could not believe someone poisoned her father. Unconscious and pale, Alextor Sutone, ruler of Sector-Three, lay on his deathbed.

"Your father is the sole reason peace reigns on Okeron. We both know chaos will erupt in all three sectors if he dies."

"Which is why we must keep his condition secret. The citizens of Sector-Three will panic and chaos will break out, plus his enemies will take advantage any way they can."

"I care deeply about your father. You have my loyalty and sworn oath, Jorell."

"I know, and I thank you." Jorell looked into Doctor Roan Willock's sympathetic eyes. She'd known him her entire life, and he was a dear friend to her father. At least she had one person she could trust. "I'm scared. The moment he dies the Tri-Planet Treaty will be void, and all three sectors will engage in war—a war we cannot stop."

The doctor put the scanner in his bag. "I'll spend every moment in the lab looking for an antidote. But, I *must* warn you, it doesn't look good. My top researchers are working on it sun-cycle and moon-cycle."

"They must never know why they're working so hard."

"Stop worrying, they've been told it is for the military, an antidote for military chemical warfare."

"How can I not worry when my father lies closer to death with each breath he takes, and the planet moves toward war? Be serious, Dr. Willock, how could I not worry?"

He patted Jorell's back. "How many times must I tell you to call me Roan?"

"Sorry, habit I suppose."

"Stay calm. I'm on your side, but if you keep going this way you'll be a patient yourself. Rest assured, whether you're here, or attending to other matters, I'll check on him regularly and insure his comfort."

"Thank you." She fought her emotions. "I'm not sure what to do, nor do I know who to confide in." With the back of her hand she wiped tears from her cheeks. "I can't do this alone."

"There is someone who can help, but you won't like it."

"Do I have a choice?"

"I know a man some call a miracle worker, but he's known as *The Traveler*."

She took a step back. "You don't mean that scoundrel who moves through time wreaking havoc wherever he goes?"

"There isn't time to recount all the feats he's accomplished, or to tell you how wrong all those rumors are. But I can tell you I have firsthand knowledge."

"You? When?"

"It's a long story, but I hired him to take care of an incident in my past. He was worth every credit I paid him."

"I've heard nothing but negative about him."

"Have you ever heard those comments from someone he's worked for?"

"No, but..."

"You're wasting time. If you've heard the stories, you know he's solved all his cases successfully." The doctor sighed. "People love to gossip, especially about things they don't understand." He picked up Jorell's hand in his. "I happen to know where he's at this very minute, and if I hurry, I might be able to set a meeting for you this moon-cycle."

She took a deep breath and considered her options. There were none. Doctor Willock was a good man, and more important, her father trusted him. She used her mind probing ability to read the good doctor's thoughts. She sensed only deep frustration, along with a need to heal his patient. "Fine. Set it up."

"Right away. Be ready when I call, *The Traveler* doesn't stay around long."

Roan smiled at her and she returned the gesture. She knew in her heart he'd never steer her wrong. "I'll be ready." She watched the older man leave her father's private quarters. Could some time traveler bring her father back from the brink of death? The idea was crazy.

There was no doubt the poisoning was political, and that left a planet-wide list of suspects. The doctor was right, there was no time to waste. She knew her father's wishes, since she'd worked by his side for eight annual-cycles. As the last living signer of the Tri-Planet Treaty, he wanted the three Sectors to remain separate as the treaty required.

To fix this mess *The Traveler* would have to be a wizard straight out of a storybook, and she doubted a man like that existed. What she'd heard about him left her more than skeptical. From his hideous looks to his despicable behavior, he slipped in and out of time taking what he wanted, not caring who got hurt in the aftermath. The door opened, then closed and she knew without looking who walked toward her.

"Jorell?"

"What?" She turned toward the familiar voice and found Rand standing before her. He was handsome, well-dressed, hair combed to the side with a perfectly straight part that began over his right eyebrow, and of course, not one hair out of place. She could not believe this fine specimen of a man was to be her life-mate in less than half an annual-cycle.

Rand was thirty-five, which made him only two annual-cycles older than her. They'd worked together as a team, he with his political advice, she with her intuition and people reading abilities, had paired successfully.

Rand cleared his throat. "How is your father? Any change since I left?"

"Doctor Willock was here, but there's no change." Rand was strong and she needed his support now more than ever. Of course she wasn't weak, it was just nice to lean on someone once in a while, especially since her father's condition remained secret.

"I see." Rand crossed his arms over his chest.

"Have you addressed the council yet about my father's sudden absence?"

"I told them what we agreed on, that he took leave to visit his seriously ill sister. I did not tell them when he'd return."

"Were they satisfied with that?"

"For now." Rand dropped his arms and shrugged his shoulders. "Since there's nothing I can do here, I'm going to my quarters."

He leaned toward her, kissed her on the forehead, then turned and left the room. She wished he'd stay to keep her company. A warm shoulder to lean on had just turned cold, but Rand never showed much emotion. At least he volunteered to cover for her father's absence, and to assume her duties so she could stay close to him.

She walked over to the large, upholstered chair beside her father's bed and sat. To keep her father alive she was willing to take risks. She slouched down and laid her head on the soft, fabric of the arm, the same as she'd done for the past three moon-cycles.

Sadness held her in its ugly grasp. What would she do if he died? His mortality never crossed her mind since he'd been so physically active, and one of the best rulers Okeron had ever known.

Only the doctor, Rand and two other long-time staff members knew about her father's condition, but they were all extremely devoted and trustworthy. Working in politics had taught her not to trust anyone. However, at times like this a few people had to be trusted. No one person could pull this off.

Her father ruled with a calm, peaceful hand, but he'd been under severe stress since Marto Braxton, ruler of Sector-One, died in a tragic air-trans accident nearly an annual-cycle ago. Plus, it had only been forty sun-cycles since Trom Carsun, ruler of Sector-Two had been found dead while on vacation. The news reported Trom's death as a hiking accident, but she doubted that since he gave up hiking many annual-cycles ago. What bothered her was how quickly both sector rulers had been replaced with new, younger men, as if no one even cared that the previous rulers were gone.

Politics *was* the root of all evil. Ever since she could understand, she'd seen and heard enough lies and sinister plots to last a lifetime. Since the deaths of the two sector rulers, she'd talked to her father about being more cautious, but he insisted there was nothing to worry about. She strenuously disagreed.

For the first time in her life, her father was wrong. One glance at his lifeless body and ashen skin confirmed her worst fears. He should have listened to her, but would it have mattered? All he'd done was attend a formal dinner, his regular bodyguards and security in place.

Since Doctor Willock was skeptical about a cure, her only option was to hire an unsavory character who claimed to do the impossible. Her eyes burned and she blinked. Maybe a little sleep would clear her thinking.

A gentle ring sounded. She sat up straight, fumbled with the folds of her gown, then pulled her com-pod from her pocket. "Yes?"

"*The Traveler* is waiting to meet you in the east garden."

"Thank you, Roan. I'll be right there." She checked the time, surprised she'd slept for two time-units. She slipped the device back into her pocket and rubbed her sore neck. Chairs were not meant for sleeping.

She laid her hand on her father's forehead. It seemed strange his skin was cool when he was covered to his neck with a therma-shield. She hated to leave, but this meeting could be his salvation, so she stood and walked toward the door that automatically opened at her approach.

After she stepped into the hall, the door closed and locked behind her, part of the security system. If security was excellent in the capitol building, how had someone managed to poison her father? She shook her head and concentrated on the task at hand.

The Traveler's profile had not been available on her com-unit, and in every story she'd heard, he was described vastly different. Either the reports were about several different travelers, or he was a master of disguise. She didn't really care what he looked like as long as he was capable.

The door to the east garden opened just as she reached the glass barrier. She stepped into the cool, brisk air of the moon-cycle and walked toward the far corner where two male figures stood under a tree. They must be somewhat competent since they picked the only place the security vid did not accurately reach. One man was tall, one medium, but she couldn't see details, only shapes. She hurried closer, anxious to meet a miracle worker.

She stopped in front of the two men and worked hard not to let her jaw drop. The shorter, middle-aged man had bushy, blond hair with a nasty looking scar on his right cheek. The taller one had long grey hair topped by a strange, floppy hat, his face badly wrinkled by age, and his body reflected too many meals. She concentrated in an effort to get a mental feeling from them.

Confused thoughts came at her from the shorter man, but his demeanor read happy and peaceful. From the larger man she picked up nothing. Some people she could only read periodically, and there were a select few she couldn't read at all. Psychic gifts weren't *always* reliable. The shorter man stepped forward and began to speak.

"Princess Jorell, I'd like to introduce *The Traveler*."

The grey-haired man took off his hat and bowed slightly. She couldn't miss the moonlight that bounced off the top of his shiny, bald head. Now that his face was no longer shaded by the brim of his hat, his pale skin nearly glowed in the dark, and probably would have if it weren't for the deep-set wrinkles that seemed to be everywhere.

He wore typical attire for the elderly, but his shirt and pants were very worn, and his ragged coat should be burned. He looked more like an indigent than time-traveler. "Nice to meet you. But I am *not* a princess."

The shorter man bowed. "To me you are." He straightened. "You're too beautiful not to be a princess."

She held out her hand in greeting, and the blond man accepted, but the old man just stood, his back hunched by age, both hands holding his ancient hat, looking frail and useless. She couldn't read him, but at least she didn't detect fear, or evil. She retracted her handshake offer. "Okay, we can play it your way."

"Good. Don't waste my time. State your need."

"At least you can talk." He made an ugly face at her, which for an old man like him was not hard. She thought she heard him growl. Her answer may have been curt, but he deserved it. It was odd how his voice sounded like a much younger man's. "My father has been poisoned and there is no known cure. He's currently lying unconscious, and will die within twenty sun-cycles unless we go back in time and prevent him from receiving this lethal chemical. Is this within your power to accomplish?"

"Possibly."

"What does that mean?" He stared at her with dark brown eyes that seemed to look through her. She tried hard to get a reading on him. Not an emotion, not a thought, not anger, greed, or anything else came through to her. It seemed he'd erected a mental wall, but she sensed he wasn't what he appeared to be. One question nagged her; was this man capable of what she asked? "Well?"

"First, I have a policy not to become involved in politics. Second, you must understand how time travel works, and the consequences of meddling in the past."

His stern stare did not make him pleasant to watch, and now it seemed his crotchety personality went hand in hand with his disheveled appearance. This meeting made her very uncomfortable. "Please explain both of those two rules."

"Many people have asked me to change politics for their personal reasons, and I have refused them all. No potential customer is worth the repercussions that could come from changes that would financially benefit some, but make others very angry."

"I understand that reasoning, but I'm asking to save my father's life, and to prevent a planetary war. If my father dies, so does the Tri-Planet Treaty. Do you know what that means?"

"I do, and it's the only reason I'm talking to you now. But you must understand the ramifications of manipulating something in the past."

"I'm sure altering history can have a definite effect on today, and the future." She had the feeling she'd said the wrong thing when he shook his head at her.

"Think about this scenario. I go back in time and kill your mother before she gives birth to you. That means you would not be talking to me, you would not exist. Or, if I had life-mated your mother instead of your father, you could be *my* daughter."

"That's a terrible example."

"Then I've made my point. Change one thing and it multiplies exponentially, whether you want it to or not."

"My father must live."

"Give me one good reason."

"I love him, and...he's ruler of Sector-Three. He's a fair and honorable leader, and peace will die with him. Surely you know that." She wished his expression would change, he looked...spooky.

"At least you gave the right answer."

"Will you help me?" He stared at her as if she were an alien with green horns, foaming at the mouth. The way his gaze bore into her, she'd swear he was trying to read her. Then his mind touched hers like the tickle of a tiny feather, but it was so fast she couldn't sense a deep, core feeling from him.

"As soon as my fee is transferred."

"Payment is not a problem. What's your price?"

"Fifty-million credits."

"Are you insane?"

He smiled. "Most would agree with that assessment."

His request was completely outrageous. She needed to sit and digest this for a moment. On her first step toward the bench, her toe fell into a divot in the grass and her ankle painfully turned. She tried to catch herself, but it was too late.

Before she hit the ground, the old man reached out and scooped her into his arms. She wrapped her arms tightly around his neck, and the strength of a warrior radiated through her. The man who held her was definitely not soft, or old. He carried her to the nearby bench and set her down. When he pulled his arms back her fingers touched some kind of metal arm braces under his clothing.

The old man's arms and chest were rock hard. His oversized waistline was padded, along with several other places. He'd carried her as if she weighed next to nothing. He was not what he pretended to be. "Thank you."

Sector-Three's treasury could well afford to pay him, but she needed to decide if it was a wise decision. She had the authority to make the transfer, but she'd have to cover her tracks so no one realized who she paid, or for what. The more she thought about it, the more she realized she had no choice. She had no other plan, and before anyone noticed fifty-million credits had been spent, her father would either be dead, or back as ruler. The decision was simple.

He sat next to her and stared, his arm resting casually along the back of the bench. Instead of feeling put off by an old wrinkled man, a twinge of attraction coursed through her. That thought shocked even her. "Who are you?"

"They call me *The Traveler*."

"I know that much. You must have a name. Everyone has a name."

"We don't know each other well enough for me to tell you my name. Traveler will be fine."

"I suppose in your line of work, you can't be too careful." She detected a small, repressed chuckle. What she'd said must have struck home, even if she'd meant it more as a warning, he did not seem the type of man who needed to be warned. Based on his reputation and how long he'd evaded publicity, he'd have to be the most careful man on the planet. "How soon can you start?"

"As soon as possible. Your case will have a lasting effect on the citizens of Okeron." He stood and began to pace. "Many lives, other than your father's, depend on our actions. We have research to do before we can simulate an effective plan. As you say, your father is a fair and just ruler who puts his people's best interests ahead of his own, so we must proceed in the same manner."

"Thank you."

"I still don't think you understand the full scope of *my work*." He pulled a card from his pocket. "Here's the account number. When the credits are deposited, we'll meet again to finalize our agreement. Until then."

The man half bowed, turned on his heel and disappeared into the thick foliage of the garden. The bushy-haired man had remained silent, but he bowed, then waved before he too blended into the tall greenery. How could she describe *The Traveler*? He was arrogant, but there was always a thin line between arrogance and confidence. His payment demand reflected an overdose of superiority, or was it plain greed? *The Traveler* would be worth every credit if he succeeded. She refused to think of any alternative outcomes.

If it hadn't been for the dark, baggy coat, she might have noticed the man's build before he took her into his arms. She needed the most competent person in the galaxy, if she were to save her father. She suspected that under the 'old man' guise he was exactly the man she needed.

CHAPTER TWO

Kane peeled off the components of his disguise one painful strip at a time. He hated the old man ruse the most because of all the glue and all the facial pieces. Dobie's disguise took glue too, but not as much, even though he complained twice as loud.

He had to admit, he enjoyed watching Jorell Sutone interact with an old man, at least until he carried her. She'd squeezed his neck and shoulders tightly several times, and when a deep, questioning look crossed her face, he knew she'd figured it out.

When he'd held her in his arms, he sensed a strong connection to the feisty, First-Advisor. Fire-red hair always attracted him, but with Jorell, it was far more than her hair. He'd never met her before, yet it seemed like he knew her. Since she was the only daughter of Sector-Three's ruler, she'd been in the media her entire life, which was the likely reason she felt familiar.

"Chief?"

His friend entered their hidden warehouse base on the south edge of city limits, where deserted buildings were the norm. They had many locations, but this was the most secure and centrally located for the majority of their activities. "In here." He turned and looked at his friend. "Did you get our stuff?"

"Yeah." Dobie dropped a cloth sack on the floor. "It was where we left it." He moved closer to Kane and laughed. "Sorry Chief," he held up one hand. "But you always look goofy with red marks all over your face."

Kane lifted one eyebrow at the only man who dared tease him.

"Until you find better glue, I'm going to look like this for a few time-units."

"The princess is quite a looker, isn't she?"

"I suppose. It was too dark to tell. And she's *not* a princess." He wasn't about to admit he'd been enamored by their new client, not to mention the emotional and physical attraction she'd stirred in him. He'd always remained immune to feminine charms, yet Jorell shredded his private vow, and that bothered him.

"And I suppose it was too dark when you picked her up and carried her. You two were looking eye to eye—literally!" Dobie nodded several times.

"It doesn't matter what she looks like. She's just a client, and if all goes well, our last client."

"I couldn't believe you asked her for fifty-million credits. That's a lot of credits on any planet. Do you know what we could do with all that?"

"Don't get excited until you see it in our account."

"When we do, we could buy that fancy—"

"Dobie!" His partner sat on a wooden barrel close to his chair at the make-up station and made one of his stupid faces. "We've had fun, and we've accomplished what others only dream of, but–"

"What about all those disasters we averted?"

"My point exactly. We need to retire while we still can."

"Well, Chief, I guess we've seen about everything behind us and in front of us, so we might as well settle down in the 'now' and see what kind of trouble we can make."

"I thought you were sweet on that blonde from twenty annual-cycles ago." His friend smiled broadly and Kane knew exactly where his mind had drifted. They'd met a lot of people during their travels, and every once in a while there was someone special they'd get close to, and for Dobie, it was that blonde.

"I've tried to forget about her. Maybe we should retire in 2227. It was a good annual-cycle, don't you think?"

Kane had given a lot of thought to retirement. He was tired of playing with people's lives. All he wanted was a normal life like every other citizen. "What's wrong with staying in the here and now?"

"I think you're too fond of someone you just met." Dobie laughed.

Kane shook his head. Dobie was closer than he knew to a correct assumption. Dobie gave him a big grin, the one that said just kidding. "Quit laughing, and take off your face, including that awful scar you're so fond of."

"It makes me a tough warrior, like I earned it the hard way." Dobie hopped off the barrel. "You just want to laugh at me when I take this off. I know you."

"I certainly hope you do." His partner knew him like no other living person ever had, or would. His profession left no room for close relationships. All they had was each other, and they both knew why.

Dobie started yelling, moaning and groaning while he removed his hair and make-up. Having a friend like him was a pleasure, even if his behavior often went over the top. He acted stupid and fooled everyone he met, but under his comic routine and infectious laughter was an extremely intelligent man with a true heart. He was an honorable friend who *never* let him down. When you trusted someone with your life, you had to be sure.

Kane pulled off the last strip of wrinkles then removed his old man wig. He ran his fingers through his hair and scratched his scalp. "I won't miss this part, that's for sure."

"What do you think about the new job? Could be an ugly pit of snaketors."

"Whenever you deal with politics you find the worst of human nature mixed in with a few who actually care."

"Yeah, and it's hard to tell the difference. That's more your expertise than mine. I just entertain them."

Kane grinned. "You *are* the most entertaining person I know."

"Oh, Chief, what a nice thing to say; especially when you only know one person!" Dobie laughed. "Now, tell me what you think of the red-headed princess."

He kept his head down and cleaned up the mess he'd made on the small counter in front of him. "She's just a client."

"Really? I didn't know you'd gone blind and stupid. I thought you were a genius, with common sense and good judgment, but if you don't have anything to say about the most beautiful woman we've seen in many a decade, forward and backward, then–"

"Okay!" Kane lifted his hand up in surrender. "She's beautiful, I noticed, and she's built nicely."

"I'd say that's an understatement. However, if she's our client, you'll spend more time with her. Maybe then you'll notice all of her attributes."

"Why are you so infatuated with her?" He turned and stared at Dobie. "She's engaged to be life-mated soon, so it doesn't matter what she looks like, or how nice she is—she's taken."

"I know, I just thought–"

"Quit thinking. We have work to do." If he didn't know better, he'd swear his friend was matchmaking, but he wasn't interested. It made him wonder why Dobie wanted to push Jorell at him when he'd never done it before. He turned back toward the counter, picked up the brush and ran it through his hair. "Let's move to our mountain place. I think better there."

"Fine by me, Chief. I haven't had a chance to play with all the new toys you bought me."

"I wish your *toys* weren't so expensive." Kane put down the brush, stood, then walked to the door. Dobie picked up the bags they'd packed earlier and followed behind as usual.

"Nothing but the best modern technology for us, Chief."

Dobie set the security system and the locks slid firmly closed behind him. Kane pulled his com-pod from his pocket, entered the key number and the doors to his two-seater air transport opened. He jumped behind the controls, strapped himself in, and waited while Dobie took his place in the passenger seat, which he always claimed was for the navigator. Dobie liked talking in 'antique terms' as he called them. He was a mixture of the old and new, all in one crazy package.

The doors closed, the engine roared to life and he pulled back on the throttle so the craft lifted straight up. Air-traffic was heavy at this time-period, which made it easy to blend in with other vehicles and not draw attention. He made a point to follow every fly-rule while in city air-space. "Tell me partner, where should we start?"

"We could go forward and see who grabs the power, or backward to see who poisoned him. Your choice."

"My thoughts exactly. There's the usual pros and cons for both. The question is, which direction would be faster? Time is crucial."

"The only good news is that time passes differently while we're gone."

"We should get at least seven sun-cycles there for one here."

"Probably, but you know how that goes." The passage of time from one place to another varied, depending on when they left, how long they were gone, how far back they went, or how far forward. It wasn't an exact science. Mistakes happened regularly, like landing in the wrong place, or the wrong time, or in the middle of a major event or celebration. But this assignment was life and death with no room for error.

Kane veered off toward the mountains, away from the everyday city routes he hated, and straight toward his secluded home. It wasn't long before he sighted the disguised building peeking out from the sheer mountainside. Their work often required complete privacy, and the remote setting served them well. He parked the transport on the pad and waited while it lowered the vehicle into the underground depot.

Once they were securely inside, he moved the transport off the pad, parked it, then opened the doors and looked at Dobie, who was not fond of being underground for any reason. "You can open your eyes now." He didn't dare laugh. They both had their weaknesses. They teased each other about a lot of things, but they'd agreed long ago their fears were off limits. "Let's get inside and you can warm up your toys."

Dobie got out and hurried to the lift. He always led the way down here, especially since he couldn't wait to get topside. Claustrophobia was Dobie's biggest fear, so Kane quietly followed. The door closed and up they went, then the lift stopped and opened into the main area. Once Dobie was in the living room, Kane walked into the galley, pressed the button on the in-wall dispenser, and ordered two cups of koffa. He carried the hot, aromatic drinks to where Dobie was already busy at work. He handed one cup to his friend, then looked out the picture window between the galley and the screen. The view from here was breathtaking, from the tree-covered countryside all the way to the distant lights of the city. It's why he built here.

After several sips of koffa he sat in the chair next to Dobie. "So, what have you found?"

"First I gotta say, I love the new system, and the wall screen is fantastic!"

"Glad you like it. Cost me more credits than I want to think about."

"The decorator we hired did a great job. She even listened to me when I suggested burgundy furniture, and touches of gold and black. I like it." Dobie slapped Kane on the back. "Thanks, Chief."

"You're welcome. I'm glad we finally got to see it completed. I was afraid she might take the credits and run."

"Not with what you paid her."

"Credits talk, that's for sure." Kane sat down next to Dobie. "Now, let's get to work."

Dobie nodded. "In the upper left corner of the screen you have the ruler of Sector-Three, Alextor Sutone, the last living signer of the Tri-Planet Treaty. Next to him, you have the recently deceased ruler of Sector-Two, Trom Carsun, and next to him, his appointed replacement, Nazar Ferris."

"Nazar! We can't seem to get away from that son-of-a—"

"Easy Chief. I know you've wanted to kill him since you first met, and I don't blame you, but you can't do it right now."

Kane stared at Dobie and restrained a frustrated groan. Nazar was an ass, there was no other description for him. He was despicable in The Academy, and was probably worse now. One day the nasty bastard would get what was coming to him.

"Chief, are you listening?" Dobie waited for a nod then continued.

13

"Next to them you have the other recently deceased ruler of Sector-One, Marto Braxton, and his appointed replacement, Ramon Coster."

Kane shook his head. "All we're missing is Alextor's replacement and our picture would be complete."

"From the looks of the current Sector-Three's hierarchy, it would appear that Rand Arroray would be voted leader upon Alextor's death. Even though Jorell is first advisor and technically second in command, there has never been a woman leader." Dobie signed. "So that essentially leaves Rand to be ruler."

"Isn't Rand a recent addition to the government?" He watched Dobie nod and point to the stats on the screen.

"Seems he was teacher's pet, and managed to get all the attention and kudos. Plus he got the women, the awards, and every break possible—just like our favorite classmate, Nazar."

"No wonder I already dislike Rand. The only difference between him and Nazar is that Rand went to another academy.

"It appears Rand's been a busy boy." Dobie pulled up more information. "He graduated from the best Conservatory on Okeron, served in the military for four-annual-cycles, began his work at the capitol of Sector-Three as a junior advisor, moved rapidly to senior advisor, next to Jorell, and he's also engaged to her. That sets off sirens for me." He looked at Kane. "How about you?"

Kane took a long drink of koffa and let its warmth trickle down his throat. "Absolutely. Don't trust him even in your sight." Kane shook his head. "What's the background of the Sector-One replacement, Ramon Coster?"

Dobie read the screen for a moment then turned to face Kane. "Coster and Rand were classmates at academy, and they served together in the military. Coincidence?"

"There's no such thing. The explanation is conspiracy."

CHAPTER THREE

Jorell paced the confines of her father's bedchamber to ease the pain in her back. Spending the night in a chair beside the bed was taking its toll, but she did not want to leave him, not now.

The door chime sounded. She'd set the lock to high security which meant she had to open it herself. She walked to the small wall screen and saw Rand, tapping his toe and checking his wrist-device. She touched the pad and the door opened. Rand marched in as if it were his personal residence, and he had complete control.

"My dear." Rand stepped in front of Jorell, gave her a kiss on the cheek, then stepped back. "How are you?"

"You mean, how is my father?"

"No, I meant, how are *you?* I'm worried about you. You look tired, and a bit haggard."

Haggard? She walked to the mirror on the opposite wall and looked at herself. Rand was right, her lack of sleep, and worry showed all too well on her face. "I apologize for my appearance."

"Apology accepted." Rand walked past Jorell. "How is your father?"

She followed Rand while he marched into her father's sleeping chamber. Why did she play his game? He expected everyone to look and act as perfect as he thought he was, and anything less required an apology. She was too tired to argue, or fight his indignant attitude. That's why she apologized, even if she shouldn't have. Rand's conceited manner rubbed her the wrong way, but she'd pick her fight when she had more energy. "No change."

Rand put his arm around her shoulders, but she did not feel any warmth or comfort. Maybe she was beyond help. "Doctor Willock was here earlier, but was called away. They're still working on an antidote."

"Any success?"

Jorell shook her head. "They won't give up." Rand pulled his arm back, then he walked toward the window past the foot of the bed and took a seat at the small table. He looked even more arrogant than a few moments ago.

"Have they identified the poison yet?"

"They've narrowed it down to three remote possibilities."

"That sounds totally incompetent."

She walked over to the chair across from him at the table and sat down. "Why would you say that?"

"Time is of the essence, my dear. And, the council must make preparations for a vote."

"First of all, the council does not know there's a problem yet, so there is currently nothing they need to prepare for. Second, I know time is short, and I don't need you to remind me." She turned her gaze to the window beside her and looked out over the grey, depressing view, which mirrored the way she felt. Rand was not helping.

"We need to be ready, just in case."

"No!" She jumped up and walked out of her father's room. She crossed the living area and stepped out on the observation deck, hoping it would calm her temper. She knew the moment Rand stepped onto the deck behind her, his negativity permeated the space. "The council is *not* to know about my father's condition."

"You can't keep this secret forever, and the moment they know, they'll take a vote to replace him."

She turned and stared into Rand's dark brown eyes. Where had his softer side gone? When had he become so hard and uncaring? Why was she only now seeing his *new* personality? If she confronted him about his attitude, he'd accuse her of losing her mind rather that admit he'd lost all emotion. A fact that scared the Diabolus out of her. "What gives you the right to dismiss my father, the ruler of Sector-Three so easily? Is that how you truly feel?"

Rand reached his hand out toward Jorell. "Of course not, my dear." He laid his hand on her shoulder. "The government must go on. As Senior Advisor, you know protocol as well as I do. You need to prepare yourself, Jorell."

She met his gaze, but his eyes appeared blank. She'd seen that look before, a signal she'd lost the argument. "It just hurts to talk about my father as if he were already dead." She shook her head. "If and when the time comes, I will do what is necessary."

"You're upset." Rand pulled his arm back. "I didn't mean to add to your suffering, just prepare you for the inevitable."

Only anger held back her tears. Rand made it quite obvious he had no feelings for her father. She doubted he had compassion for his own family since he'd yet to mention them to her for any reason. Either he wasn't close to them, or he didn't have any. Either way it did not bode well for their relationship.

Rand had no idea how watching her father edge closer to death's door every sun-cycle tore her to pieces. He was supposed to be the man she'd spend the rest of her life with, yet they only grew farther apart. She'd worked hard to love the man her father had picked for her, but he'd become unlovable.

"Do you understand what I'm telling you, Jorell?"

"Perfectly. You think I'm a child that needs everything explained." Rand may be staunch on procedures, but this time he was way off, and she would not allow him to bully her, or make her act prematurely. "Rand, you need to give this situation more time. Plus, it's *my* decision, not yours. He could recover and return to his position."

"Or he could die. Then what?"

"Until he's dead, the Council members are to be told he's away on a family emergency. No one is to know about his current condition, and I expect your full cooperation and loyalty in this matter. I am *not* too emotional to be rational, and as First Advisor, I am next in line to rule."

"You, above all others, know there has *never* been a woman ruler."

"I plan to be the first." Jorell watched him take a deep breath, as if he were trying to lower his anger before he let loose on her. She suppressed the urge to punch him. She looked over the fifteen-story balcony and pushed an ugly thought from her mind.

"Jorell, you don't understand."

"I understand perfectly. You think I'm a child. I do not need explanations or guidance, and I will not allow you to bully me into acting prematurely." She took a deep breath. "*We* will wait to make a decision."

"Is there anything I can do to help?"

That was the last thing she'd expected. Unfortunately, his tone did not match his words. "Cover for me when I'm not available. But before *any* vote is taken I'm to be informed."

"Of course." Rand turned and walked to the entryway, then stopped and looked back. "If there's any change in your father's condition, you'll let me know?"

"Certainly." She watched Rand leave, and when the door closed behind him, she released the breath she'd been holding, relieved he was gone. This sun-cycle Rand proved once again how aloof and irritating he could be, and she was tired of being complacent about his bad behavior.

Times like this made her wish she had a brother, or sister to lean on, but there was no one to confide in, nor a shoulder to cry on. She returned to her father's bedchamber where he lay like a statue; still, quiet, his skin devoid of color.

Maybe some music would calm her nerves. She touched the entertainment pod on the table beside her and her favorite song softly filled the space. Complete silence made her feel lonely, but music was always a welcome companion.

Friends were in short supply. Because the demands of her job required security, and the necessity of government secrets, she could not easily form friendships. In her youth, she'd been kept isolated, tutored within the capitol building's walls, including advanced Academy. When she graduated, she began working at her father's side, which created continued isolation.

When Rand arrived he'd been a breath of fresh air. They shared the job and the stress it brought. From the beginning, he'd shown a special interest in her, with flowers and gifts on appropriate occasions. He was handsome, available, and accessible. Her father saw him the same way, and chose him for her life-mate. What more could she want? What she did not have—true love.

The ring of her com-pod interrupted the calming music. She'd anxiously waited all moon-cycle, and half this sun-cycle to hear from *The Traveler*. Every time-unit that passed left her with deeper apprehension about her choice. She sat on the bench at the end of the deck before she answered. She was so nervous she feared her knees might buckle and she'd end up on the floor. "Greetings."

"First Advisor, Jorell. *The Traveler* has received your transfer of funds, and will meet with you immediately if you're available."

"Name the place."

"Come alone and use the private, Ruler's escape exit. You'll be picked up outside the exit door."

"How do you–"

"It's our job. A small air-transport will be waiting."

"When?"

"Now." The call abruptly ended. How could they possibly know about the secret escape exit? It proved *The Traveler* was careful, which should make her feel better about him. Instead, she wondered even more who he was, and how he knew so much about the capitol.

Her father maintained that only the ruler and his family knew about the hidden escape tunnel. Her father wasn't a liar, but it was now obvious others had knowledge of the secret. She stood, made her way into her father's massive walk-in closet and grabbed the bag she left there. Since she had no idea where she was going, and did not want to be recognized, she pulled out pants and boots.

If anyone did see her they'd think she was simply a common woman. She could count on one hand the number of people who'd seen her dressed casually since it was not proper for her position. It took no time at all to pull off her gown, hang it up, then put on her pants. She picked up the tunic and slipped it over her head, then down into place.

The silver-toned, sash-like belt in the bag caught her attention, so she grabbed it and tied it loosely just below her waist. She stepped in front of the full-length mirror on the back wall and decided she liked the look.

She put the com-pod in her pants' pocket, then walked to her father's bed. When she touched his hand, it seemed cold. She moved her hand to his forehead, which was cool and clammy. She pulled the thermal-cover higher and gently moved his arms under the warmth, careful not to tangle the various lines connected to him.

It amazed her how tubes and liquid pouches kept him alive, but she was grateful they could. She turned and hurried toward the galley. After crossing the length of the room she opened the door to the walk-in pantry and made her way to the back corner. This exit was meant only for the ruler and his family to escape should there be a need.

The need had arrived.

CHAPTER FOUR

Kane waited outside the hidden, royal escape exit. It was well concealed behind trees, shrubs and rocks. He doubted it had ever been used, since there wasn't a visible crack in the rocks where an exit could be. Dobie had gone to great lengths to find a floor plan of the capitol building of Sector-Three. In fact, he had to hack into the original architect's private system, since all files outlining the exit were long ago destroyed.

The beautiful Advisor should arrive any moment. He'd never admit it to Dobie, but he had noticed everything about her from the moment she stepped into the dim light of the garden. Even in the darkness that moon-cycle, she'd been gorgeous from the top of her flaming red hair to the tips of her petite little toes. Most women failed to impress him, but Jorell Sutone was an exquisite exception. She set every inch of his body on fire just by being close.

Jorell was the kind of woman a man could not stop looking at, or thinking about. His thoughts must have made her materialize, because Jorell poked her head around the large rock door. The door itself was a giant rock with no visible signs of hardware, and no apparent way to open from the outside.

He was taking a huge leap of faith, meeting Jorell as himself. A feeling of nakedness flooded over him. Normally he wore a disguise no matter who he met with, or how many times. How else could he remain elusive? However, this was his last, and most important mission. If he couldn't trust Jorell Sutone, who could he trust?

A quick check of his wrist-com affirmed he'd waited nearly a full time-unit, but Jorell was worth the wait. He stared at the rocks and tried to discern exactly where she would appear. As if on cue she appeared, tight white pants were barely visible above knee-high, turquoise leather boots that matched a long sleeved tunic that stopped about mid thigh. What he liked most was the V-neckline that showed a hint of cleavage he'd love to explore. The only excuse he had for such a tantalizing thought was the simple fact he was male, and Jorell was far too much female to go unnoticed.

When she turned her gaze on him and looked him over from head to toe, he couldn't miss the look of shock on her face. "Jorell Sutone."

"Who are you?"

She walked up to him, the breeze gently blowing her long, curly red hair away from her face. Her expression remained serious, but under the circumstances, he expected nothing less. He'd trained himself to notice everything, to read people by their expressions, body posture, and thousands of other little tell-tale signs that indicated if they were happy, lying, impatient, or bored.

Jorell's gaze fixed on his hand-carved metal, Raviat Cuffs around his wrists and part of his forearms that showed since he'd rolled up his long sleeves. "I'm here to pick you up." She glared at him in confusion. "Please, follow me."

He led her through the landscape to where he'd parked the air-transport. The door opened when he hit the button on his pocket-pod. He stood in the opening and motioned for her to enter. She stepped inside, moved to the front, and took Dobie's usual seat. Watching her from behind was every bit as tempting as the view from the front.

"Can you tell me where we're going?"

Kane shook his head. "*The Traveler* is a careful man and doesn't want any complications." He took his seat, powered up the engine, then removed a blindfold from a storage compartment in the console and handed it to Jorell. "Please, put this on."

"Is this really necessary?"

He nodded and she took the black cloth from his hand. Her soft fingers brushed against his, but when she pulled back he caught a slight tremble in her hand. She sighed deeply, then tied the cloth at the back of her head. He watched her adjust it several times while he buckled her harness, then his. He pulled back on the control stick and they lifted straight up. Air traffic over the city was heavy, as usual, but the more vehicles there were, the less people noticed.

To maintain anonymity he engaged the sunshield he'd spent far too many credits to install. The system had saved his life several times. It not only shielded him from roving eyes and photo devices, it also deflected most all weapons capable of taking out a transport-craft. Amazing what credits could buy.

The actual distance to his mountain home wasn't that far, but taking her on a long, windy route, with lots of twists and turns would convince her they were at a very remote location.

Considering the amount of credits she deposited in his account, it would not make sense for her to sabotage *The Traveler*. During his annual-cycles of working he'd learned one thing, the knife in the back always came from the person you least expected. It was unfortunate it had to be that way, but who was he to question human nature?

"You never told me who you are. Do you have a name?"

She had no idea what a leading question that was. He normally went by *The Traveler* and never gave his name to clients. For some reason, he didn't feel the need to withhold information from Jorell. He'd worry about the back stabbing later. "Kane."

"Where are you taking me?"

"We'll be there shortly." He'd been circling their destination for a while, but this pass he cut speed and landed on the platform that would take them into the transport storage hanger below. He shut the engine down and removed his safety belt while the vehicle slowly descended. The overhead door closed over them automatically while they moved further under the surface. He reached over and untied the blindfold, his forearms and fingers brushing against her soft hair.

She unfastened her safety-belt and surveyed her surroundings, curiosity and awe evident in her expression. He stood and stepped back into the craft's central area to open the hatch. Once he stepped out, he offered his hand and helped her disembark. He escorted her to the lift at the north corner of the garage. They stepped inside and quickly ascended to the main level. The clear doors opened and she stepped off first.

He followed Jorell into the main room that lay in front of them. She turned to face him, and her beautiful green eyes penetrated the barrier around his heart. He wasn't prepared for such an intimate feeling of closeness. She stared at him as if she were memorizing every detail of his face.

An overwhelming urge to reach out and touch her consumed him. He wanted to smooth the loose curls that were out of place, to feel her skin against his, but he thought better of it. Dobie entered the room and rushed toward them. The short, but enjoyable link they'd shared instantly severed.

"Chief! Glad you're here. And Princess Sutone," Dobie bowed from the waist, then straightened, "so nice to meet you."

Jorell looked at Kane. "Are you going to introduce me?"

"Jorell Sutone, this is Dobie, friend extraordinaire, and trusted partner."

"It's nice to meet you Dobie. And please, call me Jorell, I'm not a princess."

"Jorell, love it! Can't wait to get started. But, don't be offended if I call you princess from time to time. It suits you so well." Dobie spun around and rushed toward three stools sitting in front of the command console. "Please, Jorell, have a seat."

When Jorell smiled at Dobie he looked very pleased with himself, and nodded for her to proceed. She sat in the center seat and Dobie took the stool to her left. He slid onto the last empty seat to her right.

"Is there someone else you'd like me to meet?"

Kane liked the sassy twinkle in her eyes. "Who would that be?"

Jorell smiled. "You know, that cranky, wrinkled old man that met me in the garden last moon-cycle? I believe he's called, *The Traveler*?"

It was difficult to keep a straight face when she put it that way. "He's not important."

"Oh, I think he is." Jorell reached out and placed her palm on Kane's cheek.

Immediate warmth surged through him. He never expected such a dramatic reaction to a simple gesture, nor had he experienced one before. He should gently remove her hand, but he liked it--too much. Besides, she was smart, and not easily fooled.

Then her hand moved to his shoulder then down his arm. She knew. Mischief twinkled in her eyes, and a slight smile pulled at the corners of her kissable lips. Her exploration stopped just above his cuff, where she paused and gave a slight squeeze.

"Is there something you'd like to tell me?"

Jorell had decided he wasn't an old man when he'd carried her to the bench in the garden. He answered with a shrug.

"I think we all know who you are." She glanced at Dobie. "Don't we?"

Dobie nodded. "He's actually hundreds of people, and you met only one of them. Wait until you see him dressed as--"

"Dobie, I don't think First Advisor Sutone is interested in the characters I play, so if we could just get on with this."

"Okay Chief." She raised one eyebrow at him, as if she were coaxing him into a deep confession, but he had to keep his different identities confidential.

"Princess," Dobie cleared his throat, "if we make any mistakes, or wrong assessments, please correct us immediately."

Jorell turned her gaze on Dobie. "I will."

Kane tried to concentrate on the wall-screen, but even though

Jorell's interest moved to the work at hand, he sensed a mind probe. Her familiar tickle moved around his mind and tested for an opening. She was one beautiful, highly skilled woman, and it was his fault she'd seen through his disguise. He needed to understand her thought patterns, and her special abilities.

This was a first, her trying to read him, while he tried to read her. From what he found, she was the real thing; Advisor, daughter, mind reader, and he noted another connection, which had to be her fiancé.

Dobie pointed to several places on the wall-sized screen then smiled. "There, grid nine. The Tri-Sector Treaty clearly states that upon the death of all three signers, the treaty becomes null and void, and a new treaty must be drawn, passed by their respective councils, and signed by all current rulers--as required by law.

"It details how the Sectors were divided from four to three, the same as we learned in school. Each Sector was awarded the exact amount of land, and the exact same amount of control over Okeron's single water source. Each sector is required to have fifty council members, elected by the people of each designated area of the Sector, but the Ruler is elected by the council. The result is that all three have equal say in the singular water supply of Okeron."

Kane leaned closer to the screen.

"Problem, Chief?"

"Just checking the fine print."

Jorell cleared her throat. "There's no need. Dobie summed it up accurately. Believe me, I've lived with that agreement as if it were a family member."

"It ended an ugly war, and has held together all these annual-cycles." Dobie scratched his head. "So why head for another war now? If they continue, it will happen."

"We don't know that, Dobie." Kane stood and walked around the counter to closely study the screen.

Dobie leaned his head closer to Jorell's ear. "That's how he thinks, ya know? He paces and stares, but stays quiet until he's done."

Jorell smiled. "Thanks. I wondered what he was doing."

"How did your father react when Ruler Trom Carsun of Sector-Two was found dead on that mountain?" He watched a lone tear fall from her right eye, roll down her cheek, and land on her striking blue tunic. Then she took a deep breath, tilted her head back and looked at him with hypnotic green eyes. Diabolus! Jorell was hauntingly beautiful, and that description was for her alone. She was truly one of a kind, striking, and too damned appealing.

"My father was devastated. He had a very close relationship with

Trom. They met often, and not just for business. They often met for a recreational trip. They liked to hunt. They called it 'their outdoor thing'. He was a good man and a devoted friend."

Kane watched more tears escape from her eyes. He hadn't expected this discussion to be so difficult for her. She needed a drink. He walked into the galley, opened the wine cooler concealed in the wall, and pulled out a bottle of his favorite vintage from the rack. He grabbed three glasses and returned to his seat.

"Good thinking, Chief."

Kane opened the bottle, poured a glass full for Jorell and handed it to her, then filled two more. She immediately took a long drink. The woman didn't just look tired, she appeared exhausted, mentally and physically. He sat down next to her and sipped his wine. "I know you're weary, but we have a few more questions, if you're up to it." She took another sip, then turned her gaze on him.

"I'm fine." She held her glass up a bit higher. "Thanks for the wine, it's very good."

He smiled. "You could say it was a very good year." A quick glance at Dobie and he knew his friend was thinking about that adorable, little blonde in Sector-Two that was very sweet on him, especially after they shared a bottle of this same wine.

"What kind of comments did your father make about the accident? Anything you remember could be helpful." The wine seemed to have the desired effect on Jorell. Now that she was relaxed she would feel free to talk.

"I assume you want the unadulterated truth?"

"Absolutely." Kane refilled her wine glass in hopes he could loosen her tongue even more. "We need to know everything before we attempt interfering with the past. Even the slightest detail can mean something when we put the whole picture together."

Jorell nodded. "When my father received notification that Trom was dead, he became extremely angry. More angry than I'd ever seen him. He immediately contacted Gesel Carson, Trom's life-mate. They had a long, private conversation. When I saw him again, he was raging, and acting like I've never seen him." She looked into Kane's eyes. "All he could say was that Trom was murdered. He insisted his friend was too smart to get himself lost on some mountain--alone. Trom wasn't a young man. He'd been a hiker once, but he gave up the sport long ago. And even if he had gone hiking, he never went by himself."

"Did the investigation reveal anything?" Kane watched her shake her head and gaze at the floor. "Do you know anything more than reported in the media?"

"Things progressed rapidly. First the funeral, with all the pageantry due a ruler. Then the council convened, a vote was taken, and Nazar Ferris became the new ruler of Sector-Two."

"Did your father know Nazar prior to his election?" Dobie held his glass out and Kane refilled it.

"He'd met him several times on trips to see Trom, and he'd seen him during the quarterly Tri-Sector meetings. He didn't have private conversations with him, if that's what you mean."

"What was his opinion when they elected him Ruler?"

"It was an intense time. My father confided to me he didn't care for the man, nor did he trust him. Nazar is about our age, and I assumed his resentment was because he lacked experience."

Dobie finished his wine and set his glass on the counter in front of him. He put Nazar's picture on the screen. "What do *you* think of him, princess?"

"I never got a reading on him, but when he spoke I sensed what he said was *not* what he was thinking. However, I get dishonesty from most politicians and council members. I hate it. I really do, but it's normal in politics."

"Why?" She turned her gaze on him. Had he hit a nerve? Jorell's mental-wall held tight, she managed to ward off all his usual mind probing tactics. He twisted his left wrist cuff and wondered why she still stared at him so intently. At least she wasn't a fan of Nazar. It was best he kept his past experiences with the man quiet, at least for now. This wasn't about anyone but Jorell and Alextor. "Don't the colonies elect their own representatives?"

"They do, but it seems once they move into the capitol world it becomes all about the politics and greed, the people they're supposed to represent become forgotten." Jorell looked into Kane's eyes. "They lie to get what they want. Laws, policies, re-election, and personal gain. They may not be greedy when they arrive, but soon they willingly embrace all the dirty deals that go down in the halls. They often negotiate behind the statues of our founding fathers who created a free-will planet, an astonishing accomplishment when so many are not." Jorell set her empty wine glass on the counter. "I digress. I'm sorry."

"Don't apologize for the way you feel, or for what you see. I prefer honesty. I've never understood why anyone would rather hear a lie than the truth. Our existence would be vastly different if we all lived in honesty."

"I'm glad to see we agree, at least on that issue."

"I believe we agree on a lot of issues." Kane studied Jorell and couldn't deny that he liked what he heard, and thoroughly enjoyed what he saw. She didn't fit the usual female mold--just another pretty face without a mind of her own. She had substance, and ethics.

Kane shook his head. "Honesty is the key to saving your father's life. Before we tamper with the time continuum, we need as much background information as possible. And you, being his daughter and advisor, would know far more than anyone else."

"Ask me anything." Jorell turned in her chair to face Kane. "I don't know what information you need."

"That makes two of us." Kane combed the hair back from his forehead with his fingers. He couldn't help notice the enticing cleavage when she leaned toward him the way she was. This kind of problem was new to him. He had never worked for a woman he desired, but Jorell, well what could he say? "Who might want to take power from your father?"

"I don't really know. There's always those few who would challenge as a way to move up the ladder. I have no names."

"Who are his worst enemies?"

"You're kidding, right?"

"I have a sense of humor, but I'm not using it right now." He leaned closer to her. "I'm serious." She stared at him with mesmerizing, emerald-green eyes, and he was immediately seduced. A unique intimacy and connection sparked between them, but her gaze did not waver. She dug deeper into his soul, as if looking for buried secrets.

Jorell straightened in her chair and turned her attention to the wall-screen. "No matter what decisions he makes, there are those who disagree. But I wouldn't exactly call them enemies."

"Anything you want to add, Dobie?"

"Well, based on my research over the past few sun-cycles, I agree with Jorell. No real enemies surfaced in the surveillance data. It appears Alextor Sutone is beloved by his people."

"He has at least one enemy--whoever poisoned him. I keep wondering why he wasn't killed instantly, like the other two Rulers?"

"Good question." Dobie leaned forward and looked at Kane. "If there's a connection in the system, I'll find it."

"If anyone can find it, you can, so keep looking." He turned back to Jorell and found tears rolling down her cheeks. "I'm sorry if this upsets you, I really am, but if we're to save your father, what you know could be crucial." He wiped tears from her cheek with the palm of his hand.

"I'm sorry, but as an advisor, I'm not allowed to reveal Sector secrets."

"This is no ordinary situation. Your father will die if we don't find a way to save him. Anything you tell us is confidential. If you don't trust us to help you, we'll stop right here and return every credit you paid." He picked up the bottle, refilled all three glasses, then handed one to her.

"You're right. I'm sorry. I'm not thinking straight." She took a sip of wine. "I believe you and Dobie are honest, it's just difficult for me to trust," she looked into Kane's eyes, "anyone. My father has been burned by those he calls friends too many times. You never *really* know who your friends, or enemies are."

"Dobie and I have met those same people." He laughed, and tilted her chin up with this finger. "But, there are good people in all three Sectors. And I can honestly say, I've met them also." Finally she smiled. He didn't like to see her upset, especially when she had a smile that could light the entire room. "That's better. Now, when was the last time you slept?"

"I dozed for a bit in the chair."

"Why don't you take a nap. Our questions can wait." Kane walked around the counter, took her hand and helped her stand. He led the way through the living area and down a hallway. "You can use this guest chamber."

He opened the door and led Jorell inside. He let go of her hand and gestured toward the bed. "Make yourself at home, and if anything comes up, I'll come and get you."

"But Doctor Willock doesn't know where I am."

"Dobie has his ways of keeping track of the doctor, and his patient. So, don't worry. If there's any change, I'll let you know immediately."

"Promise?"

"I'm a man of my word." She looked at him with raised eyebrows. "Don't make me put you in that bed." He was afraid if he picked her up to lay her down he'd find himself beside her, or in an even more intimate position. The woman did stir his desires, and he was not used to the feeling.

She sat, then reluctantly laid on the bed. "I'll leave now. Dobie and I have work to do." He left and closed the door, which proved more difficult than it should have been.

Kane returned to his seat next to Dobie. "Jorell was no help. We're no closer now than before." He ran his fingers through his hair. "Let's start at the beginning."

"Which beginning, Chief?"

"The Tri-Sector Treaty. Think logically. Two of the three original signers are dead, and the third is barely alive."

"Someone wants war?"

"More like control. If the general population were protesting and making noises, I'd say war was brewing, but I think it's about power, even if we don't have credible proof yet."

"Do you have a hunch who could be behind a so-called power grab?" Dobie scrolled through files on the screen.

"If I had one guess, it would be Pakar Moran."

"Seriously?" Dobie stood, walked into the galley. He returned with another bottle of wine, which he held up for Kane to see. "This calls for more." He refilled their glasses and handed one to Kane. "You're serious, right?"

"Very. Look at the events. Two new leaders were chosen, both younger men, both placed in their respective government positions swiftly with no complications, both have the necessary education, and neither of them have close family ties."

Dobie shook his head. "And that all adds up to?"

"We know Nazar well enough to know he can be bought." Kane took a drink. "And I'll guess Ramon Coster is a lot like Nazar."

"If that's true, Pakar had to buy over half the council members in both Sectors to assure election results."

"I'm sure he enjoyed corrupting the Council." Kane laughed and Dobie joined him. They both knew too much about Pakar, and what made him happy.

"Pakar is one slick, and demented snaketor. But how did he get back to Okeron without being detected?"

"We've always operated in disguise, so the detection issue is explainable. He probably bought a new face as well." Dobie gave him a frustrated grimace. "I know. We have more questions than answers, and it's only a theory. However, I'd like you to look for anything that leads in that direction."

"Okay." Dobie ran his fingers over the board.

Kane took a deep breath while Dobie flashed up one file after another, yet nothing related to Pakar. His partner was correct when he called him a snaketor, and that's the nicest thing that could be said about the evil man.

"Chief, I can't find anything in the official, or the unofficial records. It's like the sneaky-snaketor disappeared from the face of the planet, never to be seen, or heard from again. The only remaining information about him is war related, or pre-war issues. We all know he started the war between the four Sectors by taking over the only water supply on Okeron, and withholding water from the other three Sectors. He controlled everything on the planet back then."

"Surely you can find something we weren't taught in school."

"Everything on Pakar stops the day he was deported. Nothing after that. I would have thought they'd keep him under surveillance."

"Guess they didn't. Out of sight, out of mind."

CHAPTER FIVE

Jorell opened her eyes and looked around the strange room. Where was she? Not one thing clicked in her mind as familiar. She shook her head and sat up. It all rushed back. Reality was like a slap in the face. She slipped her com-pad out of her pocket and made a call.

"Doctor Willock. Is there any change in my father's condition?"

"I'm afraid not, but he's resting well. Something you should be doing."

"I'm at a friend's house, and I just had a rest. I was planning to stay here a little longer if everything is okay."

"I'm glad you got away. Stay as long as you like. I'll let you know if there's any change. I promise,. Just relax and rest."

"I'll try."

The doctor laughed. "Don't try. Do it. Signing off now."

The good doctor had been right about one thing, *The Traveler.* Did he know what Kane really looked like? He was the most handsome man she'd ever seen. When Kane carried her in the garden, his rock-hard arms supported her, and his strength radiated through her.

She knew the moment she touched him he was not an old man, but she never planned on him being absolutely gorgeous. She'd thought the new Sector-Two ruler, Nazar was an attractive man, but next to Kane he paled in comparison.

Nazar and Kane shared a few similarities, but there was a unique feel to Kane that she'd never experienced around Nazar, Rand, or any other man for that matter. She liked Kane's longer dark hair, and the way it brushed his shoulders. Not all men looked good with a longer style;

however, Kane pulled it off with class, and it suited his personality. Then there was his body, and what a body it was. His build was pure, primitive warrior. Nothing about the man was ordinary.

Kane had a deep, soothing voice she could listen to forever. Dobie was such a contrast to his partner. Dobie was cute with bushy blond hair, and boyish features that made him look younger than Kane, even though they were the same age. She was engaged and should not be noticing other men, yet she couldn't help herself from wanting Kane to hold her in his arms and tell her everything would be fine.

With a sigh she stood, straightened the bedcovers, then walked to the door, which opened on her approach. She hurried down the hall toward the sound of Kane's voice. Neither man turned when she walked up behind them, but she knew they were both aware of her presence. "I'm ready to help."

Kane turned his gaze on her and her knees instantly went weak. She was pathetic, allowing herself to be intrigued and attracted to a man she'd just met, yet the giddy feeling was nice. Why hadn't Rand ever stirred the reactions Kane did? One reason, Rand was her father's choice, not hers.

If she were truthful, she'd accepted Rand's proposal to placate her father. He'd let her make the final decision, but he silently pressured her by talking and acting as if Rand was her choice. she'd gone along with her father's wishes--the way she always did. She'd assumed her attraction to Rand would grow with time, but the one thing she hadn't planned on was Kane—the one man who made her question her decision.

"How are you feeling, princess?" Dobie turned in his chair and smiled.

"Much better, thanks."

"I'm glad, because we have plans to make." Kane turned in his chair and patted the seat beside him. "Please, join us."

She took the seat next to Kane. "Have you learned anything new?" She hoped he'd answer soon because she was all too aware of the warmth of his body next to hers. They may not be touching, but they certainly shared an intense heat.

"We believe there's a conspiracy to unseat your father, which would give someone the ability to gain power."

"Are you talking about Rand? The Council would vote him Ruler, even though his position is under mine. We all know there's never been a woman Ruler, and I doubt they would start with me." Tears burned her eyes. They were talking about her father's death. She took a deep breath.

"I wasn't thinking about Rand exactly, but he could play a part."

Dobie turned his head toward Jorell. "Right now my choice would be the two new rulers, Ramon Coster and Nazar Ferris. But they're too obvious, so I've been looking deeper."

Dobie's smile was warm and happy, so she couldn't help smiling back. "Please explain."

"Well, it's usually never the most obvious, although it can be. So we look deeper to see who's behind it all, then we often have to go back to the top where--"

"Dobie!" Kane looked at Jorell. "He gets carried away. What he means is, we haven't narrowed it down yet. We're simply investigating, using the age old formula of, 'follow the money'. The most obvious is a good starting place."

"I agree." She studied Kane while he worked on the keyboard. His shirtsleeves were slightly rolled up and she saw the wide metal bands that started at his wrists and ended mid forearm.

The feel of those bands remained fresh in her mind, but now she studied the intricate designs that enhanced the shiny titanium. Kane didn't seem the type to wear jewelry, unless it served a useful purpose. On him, they looked appropriate. They were like the ancient battle cuffs she'd seen in history books, worn only by the most elite warriors.

"I think you should start with Nazar and Ramon." Jorell watched Kane and Dobie nod. "They're both power hungry, both approximately thirty-five annual-cycles, which means they can enjoy their newfound power for a very long time. However, what they do want, and are extremely fond of, is credits. Everyone knows that rulers write their own tickets and have the Sector's wealth at their disposal."

"She's good, chief."

"I'm impressed, but I expected you to be good. After all, you're the top advisor to Sector-Three's ruler."

"Yup, Chief, or you could say she's number one for number three! Kinda of catchy, don't ya think?"

Jorell laughed. "I think I'm going to like working with you, Dobie."

"Me too. But what about the Chief?"

When she turned her scrutinizing gaze on him he immediately hid the smile that already tugged at the corner of his lips.

Dobie laughed. "I haven't seen him be funny yet, and I like funny people."

If she read him correctly, he just gave her a seductive smile. He must have forgotten she was engaged to Rand. No matter the situation, she could not become involved with someone she hired to work for the government, it was bad business.

Kane cleared his throat. "I can be funny, but this is not the time." Kane leaned back in his chair. "Tell me, First Advisor, besides Nazar and

Ramon, who would you suspect?"

"Whoever is closest to them I suppose."

Dobie cleared his throat. "Who else is closest to your father on a regular basis?"

"Rand Arroray, my father's other advisor, and," she took a deep breath, "my fiancé."

"We know about Rand. He's been in his current position a little over three annual-cycles, before that he worked with several different council committees. He's had noteworthy success in his professional life," Kane turned his head to look at Jorell, "and in his personal life as well."

Kane's comment sent instant heat to her cheeks, and she could only pray he did not see her blush like a schoolgirl." Do you suspect Rand of something?"

"We're just hypothesizing, nothing more. We're not attacking your fiancé."

"Good." She could not tell them what she thought about Rand. In fact, she could not explain her feelings right now. Was Kane the reason she suddenly felt so separated from Rand? "When will you travel back in time and fix the problem?"

"I wish it were that easy." Kane glanced at Dobie. "Over the annual-cycles we've learned to be sure we're going to the right time and place. Otherwise it's, pardon the pun, a waste of time."

"I'm sure you're right, but I'm not into waiting right now. My father has very little time left." She hung her head. "I care deeply for him."

Tears rolled down her face. Why was it so difficult to control core emotions, especially when a parent was involved? All she wanted to do was cry her eyes out, but she certainly did not want to show weakness to Kane and Dobie. She was simply too tired to deal with everything.

Kane slipped his finger under her chin and tilted her head up. "Jorell, we understand the urgency, and sympathize with your distress. We will do everything in our power to remedy this. Our success rate is phenomenal, but there have been a select few cases that experienced less that positive results. I'd be doing you a disservice if I told you everything will be perfectly fine."

"Is that your way of saying your client died?" Kane chucked at her question, which made her want to slap him.

"To date, we've never lost a client. A satisfactory conclusion can mean a multitude of things." He handed Jorell a tissue. "I'm trying to explain that when you deal with time, space, people and fate, you walk an extremely tight rope."

She held up her hand. "I'm an educated woman, and I have a logical mind, so I understand all too well what you're saying. My father may die no matter where you travel, or what you do." She thought he'd say something, instead there was a tickle in her mind, then she heard his voice. He asked permission to mind-meld with her.

Of all the times she'd read people, only two others could mind-meld with her, and both had been women. Kane gently sent mental requests for her to open to him. Mind-melding with *The Traveler* scared her, yet it excited every cell in her body.

She answered his request by giving him the permission he asked for. A weak feeling consumed her entire body. She shivered slightly while the commanding man entered her mind. The earlier tickle became a warm, comfortable feeling, and that surprised her a bit. Mind-melding was a very intimate experience, and with Kane she'd expected it to be tense, instead it was indescribably alluring.

"Don't be afraid. I will not invade your private space. I'm surprised we can mind-meld. It's so rare."

"*I agree.*" He looked at her with his gorgeous blue eyes, and butterflies tickled her abdomen. The connection between them was far more than a simple meld. This was deep, as if they were long lost lovers.

"Do you know what this means?"

She had no idea what he was asking, or what kind of an answer he expected. "*I don't.*"

"It's not important. One step at a time."

Dobie stood and stared at Kane and Jorell. "Well now. Aren't we playing nice together?" He stepped in front of Kane. "For some reason, I'm feeling left out of this little chat."

"Ignore him, Jorell. He's jealous."

"*Of what?*" Kane smiled at her and she thought her heart would melt. If it were possible, his devilish expression made him even more handsome.

"Our mind-meld. He's tried and tried, but he's never been able to meld with me, but he can sense emotions."

"I see."

"Dobie is a very kind hearted man, who hides behind his looks and humor. He tries to act like he doesn't care." Kane leaned closer to Jorell. "I'd tell him he's a terrible actor, but I'd hate to see him cry."

The twinkle in Kane's eyes said he was joking. After a quick glance at Dobie she returned her gaze to Kane. "*I agree. Dobie crying his eyes out could get ugly.*" Kane laughed and she joined the merriment.

Dobie straightened. "Is someone going to tell me what the joke is?"

"Sure," Kane stood and slapped Dobie on the back. "Jorell was worried you might get lost when we travel back."

"I never get lost, Princess. So don't worry your pretty little head about me. Now," Dobie returned to his chair, "we have some planning to do."

CHAPTER SIX

Jorell looked up when the doctor entered her father's room. She waited impatiently on the chair while he performed his various tests. She rubbed her neck. Sleeping in chairs was not restful. The doctor shook his head with a scowl on his face. All her hopes were once again lost, and her heart sank. "How is he?"

"The same. His body struggles to stay alive, but the poison still works against him. I've never seen anything quite like this before." The doctor looked at Jorell. "What I mean is, I've faced many types of poisons, but none that take so long to kill a man."

"I suppose that's the good news?"

"It would be if we had the cure, or even knew where to find it, but that's not the case."

Dr. Willock hadn't told her anything she didn't know, yet the news still shook her to the bone. "Haven't you learned anything from your research?"

The doctor put the scanner in his bag, closed it and grasped the handle. "The only thing we've determined is that the poison is biological, and it originates in a living organism. We're working diligently to learn the source, and it's complicated because it could be imported from another planet." He rubbed his forehead. "You understand how difficult this is, and how badly I want to save Alextor."

"Of course I do, the same as you understand how much is at risk here."

"I do." The doctor shook his head. "I've been friends with your father since our school days. He insisted I bring you into this world, and I gladly did. So you see, this is very difficult for me as well." He looked at his wrist-piece. "I must get back. It's early. There's still hope to make a break-through this sun-cycle."

She stood and stepped closer to Doctor Willock. "Thank you for staying with him as much as you have. I truly appreciate everything you're doing."

The doctor put his hands on Jorell's shoulders. "Take care of yourself before you drop to the floor in exhaustion. That's doctor's orders, young lady."

The doctor pulled her to him and gave her a hug, the same as he'd done all her life. He'd been like a second father to her, and she understood his close friendship with her father, and how this affected him. "Thank you."

"You know I'd do anything for you and your father." He wiped a tear from Jorell's cheek. "You look tired. I prescribe more rest for you."

She smiled at him. "It's been hard, and—"

"I get it, but you won't be much use to anyone if you're run-down and sick."

"I promise I'll get more sleep."

"See that you do." He picked up his bag. "By the way, how are you getting along with The Traveler?"

"Fine. Thanks for putting me in touch with him. One question though, what did he look like when you saw him?" She walked with him to the entry door where they paused while the door slid open.

"He resembled the primitive-natives who live toward the bottom of Okeron." He kissed her on the cheek. "Good-bye, my dear. Rest well."

She watched him walk down the hall, then she turned and returned to her father's beside. Tears spilled down her cheeks when she looked at a once virile ruler, who now lay hauntingly placid and pale. Not long ago he rushed from meeting to meeting, giving commands to his staff as he walked so fast she could barely keep up. For an older man he remained physically fit, and mentally alert. No one ever put one over on Ruler Sutone. Until now.

It amazed her how quickly life could change. When she looked at him now, it seemed she were in a mausoleum paying her last respects. One glance at the time-display and she realized Kane and Dobie would arrive any moment as planned.

She went to the private door in her father's study that led into his office. It was to her advantage that her office adjoined his, and her living quarters also adjoined her office. Since her father's poisoning it was crucial she not be seen entering his residence, using his office and staying so long. She could not afford to raise suspicion, everything must appear normal.

It didn't take long to make her way through two offices and into her quarters. Once inside, she shed clothes on her way to the lav. She turned the shower on and stepped inside the large, marbelus enclosure. When hot water trickled over her body she sighed. Life had been so simple, a fact she'd not reflected on. Before she'd thought things were hectic, with no time to think. Now she feared the future.

If her father died, she'd be devastated, but that would be nothing compared to the chaos that would erupt across the entire planet of Okeron. The everyday peace and carefree lifestyle everyone enjoyed would change forever, and that was unthinkable.

She stepped out of the enclosure and the water automatically stopped, then the comforting warm breeze of the body-dryer came on. It only took a moment to dry off, but she always lingered because it was so relaxing.

Her closet was full of beautiful long gowns, or as Dobie would say, "Princess-proper attire." Today she wished she could wear a worn tunic and pants, but her meeting with Kane required proper attire. She stepped out of the shower and walked into her closet. She removed a gown in her favorite color, light blue. It may be silly, but she wanted to look her best for him.

After her undergarments she slipped the gown over her head. It fell into place with a few adjustments, and she fastened the shiny, gold belt around her waist. While she brushed her hair she thought about her mind-meld with Kane. It was very intimate, exciting, and oh so tempting. She pulled her hair up high on her head and used a gold fastener to create a sleek up-do. She applied her make-up as always, but took greater care this sun-cycle. Her building desire to see *The Traveler* again made her feel more feminine than she had in a long time.

Most of her sun-cycles were filled with business meetings, and her moon-cycles were occupied with boring, formal Sector dinners. If she'd stayed more alert she might have noticed a conspiracy against her father forming, but it was useless to dwell on things she could not change.

After one last look in the mirror, she walked to the private entrance to her office. She stopped and took a deep breath. It made no sense to be so nervous. She was used to mingling in large crowds, and speaking to them. Entertaining visiting dignitaries was her job, but Kane had an extraordinary effect on her. Just the thought of seeing him sent an anxious tingle down her spine.

CHAPTER SEVEN

"Ya know boss, our little princess must be quite the business woman. Look at all the toys *she* has to play with!"

"Down Dobie. She might let you touch them when she gets here."

"What exactly was going on between you two last moon-cycle?"

"You could say...we connected." He knew Dobie's skeptical expression all too well; eyes squinted, forehead wrinkled, and lips pursed. He was funny, and that was one of the reasons he enjoyed his company. Dobie then sent him his pretending to be jealous look.

They'd been together so long he knew Dobie's thought processes as well as his own. Dobie was the brother he never had, and they shared more experiences together than anyone would ever guess. They trusted their life to each other, and there was no higher honor. "Don't touch anything until Jorell gives you permission."

"I know, I know, but I like what I see." Dobie stepped closer to Jorell's desk. "This is one big office. Sure puts most of ours to shame."

"That's because she has one, and we have too many."

"I'd settle for one if it looked like this."

Kane resisted laughing at the faces Dobie continued to make, and the way he rolled his eyes. "You missed your calling, my friend."

Dobie groaned. "Really? What would that be?"

"Being a clown in the Intergalactic Circus." Dobie rushed toward him, but before they got physical the door opened. Jorell stepped into the room and her presence immediately filled the space with feminine energy that reached out to him.

"Good morning, gentlemen. I hope you haven't been waiting long."

"We'd wait all sun-cycle for you, Princess." Dobie glanced at Kane. "Wouldn't we, Chief?"

"She's paying, so I suppose we would." He wanted to tell her how fantastic her blue gown made her beautiful red curls look, but this was not the time to be intimate. They were here to work, but it would be difficult with a distraction like Jorell.

"I am paying you *extremely* well, I might add." Jorell sat in the chair behind her desk, then motioned toward the two chairs in front of it. She waited for Kane and Dobie to take their seats. "You asked for several of our security recordings. I've arranged for you to have access to any and all security vids. I'm sure Dobie can find what he needs, and I'm here if you need help." She glanced at Dobie. "If I'm not mistaken, I believe you might like to use the equipment?"

Dobie stared at Jorell. "I knew it was love at first sight."

"By all means, go get started."

Kane wanted to laugh at Dobie's half-walk, half-skip movements which quickly moved him to the vid center. He sat on the upholstered bench in front of the equipment, but remained silent and still. He turned his gaze back to Jorell. "I believe he's beginning to purr like a lyenick."

"I'm glad I could bring a little pleasure into his otherwise mundane existence."

He laughed. "I knew there was a sense of humor in there somewhere." His statement brought a smile to her lips, which made her look too kissable. For the first time in his career, his thoughts about a woman overtook his passion for his work. He reminded himself sternly about the pressing job at hand.

"This is great!" Dobie yelled. "But I have one question, Princess. How is your system set up?"

"You mean security?"

Dobie nodded. "Is it set up to trace users?"

"Of course, but my father and I have uncensored, untraceable access."

"Fantastic, oh beautiful one!"

Kane shook his head. "You must excuse my colleague. He tends to get carried away."

"So I noticed." She smiled at Kane.

"He can be amusing." Jorell stared at him, her gaze unwavering. He couldn't take his attention off the neckline of her gown, which she filled out very nicely. She glanced at Dobie then back at him, a perfect smile on her flawless face.

"Amusing? That's putting it mildly." She leaned her forearms on the desk and clasped her hands.

Kane detected a teasing quality to her voice, along with genuine concern. He could only wonder what she was like when she wasn't under so much pressure. "I'd like to see vids of the last Sector Meeting."

"Of course." She rose from her chair, walked over to Dobie and took a seat next to him. "Show Sector Meet fourteen-thirty-nine."

The computer responded to her mellow, sexy, voice and brought up the requested meeting. He stood, walked over to Jorell and sat next to her, inhaling her light, floral scent. What was it about this woman that appealed to him so much? She looked fantastic, sounded great, and smelled even better. Stupid question considering the answer was everything.

"Chief?" Dobie leaned forward, extended his arm in front of Jorell and waved a hand up and down in front of Kane's face. "Okeron calling Kane."

"I was thinking."

"Dangerous. You looked very far away, Chief."

"You have no idea."

"Shall I move so you two can talk?"

Dobie laughed. "Definitely not. I like you in the middle, but I don't know about him."

"I'm not sure about either one of you."

He might have worried about her comment if she hadn't smiled so playfully. Unfortunately, her smile faded, and her serious, troubled look returned. "Jorell, can you please identify all the people in the vid?"

"I'll try. There are some names I don't know, but I know which delegation they're with."

"That will suffice." Jorell began naming all the people she knew, all of which were female. Not that a female couldn't be deadly dangerous, but he suspected power-hungry men in this case, and his hunches were usually correct.

Jorell's lovely voice kept reciting names and short backgrounds of the people at the meeting. No one but those invited had attended, and everything appeared copasetic.

"Chief, I don't see or hear any alarms." Dobie leaned forward and stared at Kane. "Should we go to another vid?"

Kane rubbed his forehead. "Yeah. Whatever the plan was, it took place before, or after this meeting." He looked at Jorell. "Did you know the servers?"

"Not well, but they're familiar to me since this meeting was held here. I can't say the same for meetings in the other Sectors."

He stood, stepped behind the bench and began to pace. There were times he had to walk to think, especially with Jorell so close and tempting.

"So?" Dobie rose and joined Kane. "What do you think?"

"It's obvious nothing happened at this meeting." He glanced at Jorell. "Can we see vids of previous Sector Meetings?"

"Of course. Show Sector Meeting fourteen-thirty-eight."

When she began reciting names again, he mentally sensed her frustration. What surprised him was being able to read her thoughts and emotions at times, even when she did not cooperate or send him anything. "Is there anyone present at this meeting that shouldn't be there?"

Jorell stared at the screen. "I don't see anyone." She turned her gaze on Kane. "This was the last meeting with Trom Carsun in attendance, and it was only a few sun-cycles later he was found dead on Sotra Mountain."

"You mean murdered?" She nodded her agreement, and he watched her blink back tears. "Did you notice anything suspicious? Like someone acting nervous, or different than normal?"

She sighed and rubbed her chin with one hand. "I probably should have noticed something, but off hand, I can't think of anything, or anyone that seemed out of the ordinary."

"Well Chief, looks like it's going to be the hard way, as usual."

"From the sound of it, I doubt I'll like it, but what does Dobie mean?"

Kane sat down next to Jorell. "My esteemed colleague means that conspiracies are rarely caught on vids. Think Jorell, if you were planning to overthrow a ruler by some form of murder, would you take the chance of being caught on vid?"

"Of course not, but nearly everywhere is covered by vid."

"But not all vids include sound, and there are places where one can obtain privacy."

"True. So where do we go?" Jorell crossed her legs and straightened the skirt of her gown.

"We?"

"Yes, we. You don't think I'm going to let you and Dobie go without me, do you?"

"Of course I do. You're our client, and clients don't get involved in-

-

"Illegal activities?"

"No. Dangerous situations."

Dobie stood and stared at Kane and Jorell. "Do I need to separate you two?" He laughed, then returned to his seat. "Now, our first priority

is to keep Jorell's father alive. Second, we need access to off-limit areas that only Jorell can enter. So, Chief, you might want to consider her request."

Kane walked to the window and gazed out over Capitol City. Unfortunately, this case might prove to be worth every credit he'd charged. "The only thing worse than political schemes, is dealing with politicians."

"Well said." Jorell smiled.

"And I thought you enjoyed it." Dobie laughed. "Do you remember that one Councilwoman from Sector--

"Enough, Dobie. I don't think the First Advisor wants to hear about that."

Jorell stood. "Don't be so sure, Kane."

Dobie looked first at Jorell then at Kane. "You're right, Chief. We don't discuss cases with anyone other than the client."

It was Jorell's turn to laugh, and he loved the sound of her voice. Her face lit up when she was happy, but he knew this moment would be short lived. "If, and it's a very big if, I let you travel with us, you must promise to do exactly as I say. Can you do that?"

"I can."

"Chief, I'm not sure it's possible to take her along."

"Neither am I, but there's a first time for everything."

Dobie grabbed Kane's arm and walked him to the far side of the room. He put his mouth to Kane's ear. "You know I was teasing you before about her traveling with us, but we can't risk anything happening to her. I'm shocked you'd even consider it."

"If we don't succeed, Ruler Sutone *will* die. If he dies, this entire planet will erupt in war, or worse."

"What's the 'or worse'?"

"You're aware of a certain type of weapon that could be used, but it's too early to speculate."

"You really think she should go?"

"We need her unlimited access, and knowledge of the important people in all three governments, so I say, yes."

"Chief, do you know how it works?"

"You have to open your mind to me before we can transport. If you could mind-meld it would be easier, but it works as long as we're physically joined." Kane glanced at Jorell. "I believe she can mind-meld with me."

Dobie stepped back and slapped his forehead with the palm of his hand. "I should have known. That's what was going on between the two of you last moon-cycle, isn't it?"

Kane nodded and his friend's expression turned to complete disappointment. "Until now, how many people do you know that have mind-melded with me?"

Dobie tapped his temple with his index finger. "Aah, I think the number is…zero."

"Correct, so don't feel so left out." He never mentioned how Eunis used to reach him, but she was gone, so there was no reason to bring it up.

"I know. Sorry. It's a sensitive subject for me." Dobie looked Kane in the eye. "I've tried so hard, yet--"

"You haven't failed, never think that. I'm still closer to you than anyone--ever. You're the brother I never had. You're irreplaceable. Remember that, my friend."

"I will." Dobie glanced around the room then back at Kane. "I'll go check more vids."

Kane slapped Dobie on the back. "You know what to look for." He repressed a laugh as he listened to Dobie mumble to himself while he walked back to the wall-screen. Dobie was always sensitive, but that was due to his past. When they met in Academy, they were both orphans with no one to lean on but themselves. Their friendship quickly became deep and enduring, and they shared a rare honesty most people never experienced. The Boys Academy was full of two types of kids; the rich kids not wanted at home, and orphans with no home, which created a volatile mix.

He watched Jorell stand and move behind her desk. She took a seat in her tall, wide-backed chair, but she looked mentally far away. Then he felt her tickle his consciousness a moment before her message permeated loud and clear.

"I'm going with you."

He needed her to go, but his reason had turned personal. Kane walked over and sat in one of the two chairs in front of her large, hand-carved, kria-wood desk. She glared at him with a determined look that altered her beautiful features." *Since you now have the ability to mind-meld, have you tried to contact your father since he's been unconscious?"*

"I'm not sure how to answer that, since you're the first person I've ever melded with. I usually only ascertain general meanings, but I can tell if they're lying, and that's what my father wants to know."

"*I see.*" He leaned back in the chair and tried to decide what there was between them that allowed such a complete meld. What the implications were, he wasn't sure, but taking her along would be wise. Or was it what he wanted to do? *"Do you realize the risk of time travel?"*

CHAPTER EIGHT

"I think so, but tell me anyway."

"There's always a chance we'll arrive somewhere in time and never get back. We could completely miss our target date and end up in the middle of something we never planned on." He took a deep breath and let it out slowly. "It's an imperfect science."

"Seems more like magic than science."

"It's magic all right." He was aware of Dobie working on the computer system behind him, but he couldn't take his eyes off Jorell. Her shiny red hair curled invitingly on her shoulders, and the dip of her neckline revealed intriguing fair skin he'd love to explore.

"When do we leave? And how long will we be gone?"

"Soon, and I don't know." Kane stood. "I'd like to see your father now."

"Of course. I should check on him anyway."

"Dobie, you coming?"

"I'd like to stay, if it's all right."

"Fine. You have access to everything, and no one will bother you. If you need anything, just push that contact button on your left."

Dobie pushed keys and lit up the display panel." Got it, Princess."

Kane stepped clear of the chair. "Ready?"

Jorell stood, walked around the desk and headed toward the door on the far side of the room." Follow me."

He'd gladly follow her anywhere she wanted to go. She carried herself regally, like the woman she was, head held high, back straight, shoulders back, and she walked with a purpose to her step. It was obvious why her father relied on her.

Even wearing fashion-heels, Jorell moved quickly across the large room. How any woman could function in such uncomfortable shoes, walking on tip-toes he'd never know, but the view from this angle was certainly worth it. He should be ashamed of himself, but he was a man who loved women, and Jorell's cute little wiggle hypnotized him.

He'd do well to maintain a professional relationship. He had an unbroken rule; never sleep with a client, but he'd yet to find a rule that couldn't be broken. Besides, Jorell Sutone, second in command of Sector-Three, was off limits to commoners like him. Then again, there was a first time for everything.

Jorell stopped in front of the end wall and reached out to straighten a beautiful, large picture of the cityscape. When she moved the frame about an inch the wall opened and she stepped through, then indicated for him to follow. "I'm impressed."

"I thought you might be. This is a secret not even Rand is aware of, but I'm sure you won't mention it to anyone."

"Dobie and I know how to keep secrets." He smiled when she turned to look at him. "We have many ourselves."

"I'm not surprised."

The wall closed and he found himself inside Jorell's office. She led the way across the room, through another room, then into a large walk-in closet. The back wall opened and they stepped through into another, even larger closet, and finally emerged into Alextor's private quarters via the pantry.

"Would you care for some koffa before we see my father?"

"That would be good." He watched her order from the insta-serve. "This is quite the place."

Jorell smiled. "Suited for a ruler?"

She handed him a gold rimmed, royal blue cup, with a gold handle. Their fingers brushed, which caused their eyes to meet. She was beautiful, and he could not stop himself from staring. "I expected a servant."

"I've awarded all father's personal staff an extra twenty sun-cycles paid vacation. I told them he wanted to reward them for all their hard work and loyalty while he was away."

"Didn't they ask questions, or see him in his present condition?"

"Only his personal valet saw him looking a bit sick. Luckily his shift was over before father fell unconscious. I assured him I'd watch him, and that he'd be fine in the morning." She took a sip of koffa. "I called the entire staff to my office for a meeting, which is not unusual. I told them he left for an extended political meeting, and from there he'd planned a short vacation. They were all happy to receive additional paid leave."

"You're very efficient."

"It's my job." Jorell picked up her koffa and took a sip. "I've made alibis for him many times when he needed a bit of personal time. But this is far different."

She walked toward the arched doorway, koffa in hand and he did the same. When he reached her side she turned and stepped into the ruler's bedchamber. When he entered, a strange sensation rippled through him. It was a vague uneasy feeling, but at the same time, he sensed an energy struggle within her father's unconscious body.

Jorell stared at him, a questioning look on her face. When she stepped closer to the bed a visible change took place, and it wasn't good. Her focus moved past him as if someone were standing behind him, yet no one was visible. She appeared haunted and empty. "Jorell?" He grabbed her shoulders with his hands. "What's wrong?"

"You feel it, don't you? I see it in your eyes."

Her voice sounded too calm, animated, and void of emotion. She looked and acted surreal, as if an outside force invaded her mind and body, causing this reaction. He slid his hands down her arms and took her hands in his. Her skin was cold, and she failed to grip his hands in return, she just let him hold hers as if they were objects not attached to her.

There was only one way to end this. He closed his eyes and concentrated. A very ominous energy wanted to consume them both, and it was difficult to maintain the mental wall he created to stop the evil invasion. The unseen entity wanted to steal every ounce of energy they possessed, and would probably consume their very souls if permitted.

He felt as though his heart were in a vice and someone kept tightening it. Soon it became impossible to breathe, the force pressing hard against his lungs. He strengthened his resolve by concentrating on benevolent energy. He called upon light to come to his rescue and consume the darkness. Slowly the paralyzing cloud began to lift, the hold on his heart loosened, and after several deep, fortifying breaths, he returned to normal.

Eunis always warned him about Energy-Lamias. She'd explained it as the dark arts, and that nothing good ever came from contact with a Lamia. Now he understood.

With his mind he sent Jorell healing energy and called her name over and over. Her eyes roamed the room, but she was still in some sort of trance. *"Jorell, concentrate on what I'm saying. Concentrate on me. Jorell."* He pressed his forehead to hers. *"Answer me, Jorell, before it's too late. Jorell!"*

She shook her head. "Why are you yelling at me, Kane?"

"Sorry. I think we should go back to your office now." He'd expected her to mind-link with him, but she'd spoken out loud. Whatever kind of entity had been there had nearly taken her over. He escorted her to the doorway, her hand still in his, only now she squeezed tightly. He didn't let go, afraid she could fall prey once again.

Jorell simply walked to the door, looked in the scanner, then walked into the hall. She paused while the doors closed behind her, then she turned her gaze on him. This time her eyes spoke volumes, and he sighed in relief. She was back.

"Kane, tell me what just happened."

"Let's take a walk in the garden." She picked up on his unspoken meaning and began to walk fast down the empty hall. In her haste her heel caught on the carpet and she faltered. He slipped his arm around her waist so quickly she gasped, her gaze directed on his.

Her grateful glance told him more than she knew while they made their way to the door at the end of the hall. She looked into the security scanner and the doors opened into the Royal Gardens.

Once outside, the doors shut behind them. While she moved along the path, using him for support, she began to tremble. He pulled her off the walkway into the shadows, picked her up in his arms and carried her to the bench at the far end of the garden where the security cameras did not focus well.

He gently set her down, then made himself comfortable beside her. She shivered. He put his arm around her shoulders and pulled her body against him for warmth, even though she shook from nerves rather than the cool evening air.

"Thank you. I don't know what came over me." She looked into Kane's eyes. "I've never experienced anything like that."

"Nor have I."

"Who, or what was that? It felt evil, with a hunger to possess."

"You're right on both accounts." With his fingers he tucked a few stray hairs behind her ear. "You just experienced the dark arts at work. There's at least one entity behind that evil energy. There could be several."

"How does it work, and how close is this person?"

"The entity could be next door, or in another Sector. He, or she, operates using energy-transference. It's similar to time travel, but instead of his or her body traveling through time and space, they send their energy to attack their chosen target."

"I'm not sure I understand."

Kane was surprised when she rested her head on his shoulder, but he liked it there. "That entity was here for your father. It's called remote energy theft. The actual term is an *Energy-Lamia*. Many people do it subconsciously on a minute basis. Haven't you noticed that just being around a certain person makes you tired? They literally suck all the energy out of you, then move on to the next victim, that's what keeps them going."

"Of course my father can't defend himself when he's unconscious."

"Actually, I sensed him fighting against the dark energy. Of course he was too weak, but it's a good sign. While I helped him fight off the dark energy, I learned your father is strong willed, honest, and works for the good of his people, not for political, or financial gain." She smiled at him and her eyes sparkled. Her love for her father was obvious, as well as her desire to save him.

"How were you able to do that? I've never been able to read him, and I read nearly everyone."

"You're too close. We all face failure when we use our minds to help those we're closest to." She raised her head from his shoulder and rubbed her eyes.

"So what do we do?" Jorell looked Kane in the eye. "When do we start?"

"We've already begun." She squinted and wrinkled her nose at him, a gesture she seemed to make every time she had more questions than answers. "Dobie is working the technical stats as we speak, and, as we've just learned, whoever is behind this is either involved in the dark arts himself, or using someone who is an expert at it."

"And I suppose you're going to tell me not to rush into anything until we have all the facts?"

He chuckled, amused that she hadn't known him long, yet she knew what he was about to say. "I sensed you were a fast learner."

"You're laughing at me."

"I'm laughing at myself. It seems I've been too predictable lately."

"I just hope you're as predictable in my father's case as you've been in your previous ones." She rose from the bench and stood in front of Kane. "Is there a case you haven't been able to solve?"

He stood and faced her, then took her hands in his. "You're still shaking."

"I have good reason."

"So you do." He smiled. "I've successfully completed all my cases, but there's always a first time, everyone knows that. But I swear to you, here and now, that I'll do everything possible to save your father." He lifted her left hand to his lips and gently kissed her fingertips. "I give my word." He lowered her hand.

"That's all I can ask."

Tears rolled down her cheeks and he gently brushed them away. "Good." He glanced around the deserted garden. "Let's walk as we talk." He stood, then helped her up. She slipped her arm through his and they stepped onto the path. The world seemed right with Jorell at his side. "Who are the people closest to your father on a daily basis?"

"His personal valet, Beron Potom, myself, his advisor, Rand Arroray, Nica Ballie, his personal housekeeper, and Doctor Willock." She glanced at Kane. "He encounters a lot of people on a daily basis, but not many in a close, personal way."

"That I expected, which makes this so difficult. As of right now, everyone on the planet is a suspect."

"Couldn't we narrow that to Sector-Three?"

"Absolutely not. Sector-Three is the last Sector necessary to void the peace treaty, but they could be from any Sector, with their own agenda. Someone wants your father out of their way."

"I thought maybe I was making more out of his condition than I should, but..."

"In this case it's not possible."

"You're serious, aren't you?"

He nodded and stared at her for a moment. "Dead serious."

"I'm glad you're thorough."

The gentle breeze blew her hair back from her face and she looked like a goddess in the bright moonlight. She was tempting, and *engaged.* He had to remain impartial and uninvolved. In all the annual-cycles he'd been in business, he'd not broken that rule, but Jorell could make him break it for the first time. "Do you know any energy workers that could stay with your father in your absence?"

"I've worked with several over the annual-cycles, but there's only two I really trust. Should I contact them?"

"Your father needs someone capable of fighting an Energy-Lamia with him at all times. He needs protection. A lot of harm can be done when he's weak and unconscious."

"Is that a nice way of saying he could die from an attack?"

He stopped walking and so did Jorell. He took her hand in his and sighed deeply. "I believe you prefer honesty, so the answer is, yes. However, a Lamia may only want to influence his behavior in some way." Jorell started to protest so he placed a finger on her lips. "We know we can protect him, as long as we catch the attack at inception."

Jorell shook her head and blinked back tears. "How do you know we can protect him? It was only by accident we were there this time."

"First, there are no accidents. Second, have faith. We stopped this one, and we'll stop the next, should there be one. Now, you need to set a meeting with your trusted energy workers so I can instruct them."

"Actually they're twin sisters, both gifted, and I trust them."

"Do you trust Dr. Willock?" She nodded and he wiped a stray tear from her cheek. "He should be there also." He waited for a moment while she gathered her thoughts. "Always show your strength, because the enemy is always looking for your weakness." She looked at him as no other woman ever had. He couldn't explain the mental and physical connection with her. Although the bigger question was, why?

CHAPTER NINE

Jorell paced while she waited for everyone to arrive. The chime sounded and she rushed to open the door, stunned to find Kane looking tall, masculine, and far too appealing. She took a deep breath to steady herself. "Please, come in. You're a bit early. Would you like a cup of koffa?"

"That would be nice. Thank you."

She went into the galley, requested two cups of koffa, then carried them into the parlor where Kane waited. He took the cup from her and she thought he winked at her, but she was so tired she probably imagined it.

"Were you with your father all moon-cycle?"

"I slept in the chair by his bed, but nothing happened."

"From the way your eyes look this sun-cycle, I'd say you didn't sleep much."

"Your assumption is correct." She set her koffa on the table in front of the sofa. "I still can't believe someone would do this to him. He's loved by everyone in Sector-Three, and the other Sectors as well."

"Jorell, it's not about how people feel about their leader, it's about some 'one' wanting control of Sector-Three, and most likely the entire planet. And they don't care if it requires a war, genocide, or worse to achieve their goal."

"I hope you're wrong."

"So do I. Also, don't tell anyone I'm *The Traveler*. I can better serve you if I remain anonymous."

"I agree. And I assume it's best not to reveal any plans of leaving the capitol?"

"Correct. The less anyone knows the better. Dobie and I don't usually involve clients in our work," Kane looked into Jorell's eyes. "But this case requires your expertise."

The chime rang and she returned to the door. When it opened she greeted the twins and the doctor. "Welcome. Please, take a seat."Her guests walked past her, each of them glanced at Kane with suspicion. Her gaze moved toward Kane who took his place beside her. "I'm happy you're all here. Let's get started."

The twins and the doctor took seats in the parlor, their attention on Kane, who had a commanding aura about him. He appeared relaxed, as if he were in his element. He looked amazing in the dark-blue, designer suit and light blue shirt, obviously expensive and worth every credit. He had no right to look so temptingly handsome.

"I'd like to thank you for coming on such short notice." She heard Kane in her mind. *Introduce them.* She immediately replied out loud, "Kane, I'd like to introduce you to my dear friends, Alesa and Ariel Drumond," she waited while they gave a nod to him, "and Doctor Willock." The doctor tipped his head in greeting as did Kane.

"I'm glad to meet you, although I wish it were under different circumstances."

Whenever she was close to Kane she sensed nothing but goodness and honesty in his aura. If all the other people she had to read were more like Kane, the government would be much better.

"Someone wants Ruler Sutone dead, and will go to any lengths to accomplish the deed. Right now he lies in an unconscious state from an unknown poison. He has sixteen sun-cycles of life remaining, and that's if Doctor Willock's estimate about the poison is correct." Kane looked at the doctor. "I am not questioning your expertise in any way."

Doctor Willock nodded. "No offence taken, I assure you."

The twins' gasp didn't surprise her since they were both close to her father, and respected him as their leader. They hung their heads for a moment then returned their gazes to Kane. This was not an easy meeting for her, especially since she was tired and prone to emotion.

"Steps are being taken to counteract the poison. However, a new threat has surfaced, which is why you're here. Ruler Sutone is under psychic attack by the dark forces."

The doctor cleared his throat. "Ruler Sutone will more than likely die from the poison. Why should we worry about these so-called, dark forces?"

"That's a good question. I've seen psychic attacks on healthy people, and after several attempts the victims died."

The doctor shook his head. "I don't especially believe in the dark arts, or any of the mind games I've heard about. But I am concerned about Alextor's physical health."

"Doctor, we don't know each other, but I hope you'll trust me when I say, if the psychic attacks on Alextor aren't intercepted by us, there will be no physical health left, he *will* be dead."

Jorell watched the doctor rub his forehead, but Kane did not take his gaze off him. "Kane, what do expect the doctor to do?"

"Just be aware of this threat." Kane sat next to the doctor on the sofa. "I wanted you to hear about this so if you're ever alone with Alextor, and you notice, or feel anything strange, you'll call for help."

"I don't understand all this crazy stuff."

"Kane," Ariel began, "maybe I can explain it to the doctor." She turned her gaze on Doctor Willock. "You know Alesa and I, and you know some of the work we do, right?"

"Yes, but you and your sister are different. You do good work, you help people."

"We do, but there are those who work for personal gain or control, and they use the dark arts. Surely you understand that."

"I've always heard the dark arts existed, but I never gave them any thought, nor did they ever interfere with my work. This is new to me." Doctor Willock looked at Kane. "I'll do what I can. I may not understand it, but I'm smart enough to know I don't have to understand to help. So tell me what to do, and I'll do it."

"That's all I ask. Let me explain. The first sign an attack is underway is that you'll feel strange, like someone you can't see is watching you. That feeling may come over you in the form of a chill, or a shiver, but you'll know it when it happens.

"Then you might experience a tapping sensation in your mind, a gentle nudge for entry, like the brush of a feather. You'll also notice an energy that isn't right, it will feel negative, and it will envelope you. It's goal is to invade its victim. And this mysterious '*it*' is what some call evil."

Kane took a deep breath. "This evil force has one purpose here, to invade Alextor Sutone, and it won't stop until it's successful."

Alesa stood and walked over to Jorell. "What do you need us to do?"

"I need you, or Ariel, to be with my father around the clock. One of you must be at his bedside at all times. I trust you both will know what to do if another attack happens. His life will be in your hands."

"Do you know any secrets to stopping them?" Alesa asked.

Kane stepped closer to Alesa, "You and your sister work with positive energy, also called light energy, or love energy. Light and love is the only shield against the dark, evil energy. Once you're aware of that, you can concentrate on sending nothing but positive energy at the unseen force, and it will retreat. But that doesn't mean it's easy, or that it won't keep trying."

Ariel turned toward Jorell. "Where will you be?"

"I have government business to attend to, and I may have to travel to the other Sectors for a short time." Jorell stood and put her hands on Alesa's shoulders. "I'm relieved you both will look after my father."

"You have our word. We'll protect him." Alesa turned her attention to Kane. "What else can you tell us?"

"Just project positive energy at all times. I'm sure you've felt negative energy before." Kane paused and the twins nodded. "You'll know what to do."

Ariel took her sister's hand, and Jorell's hand. "We're in this together."

Jorell fought back tears. "I'm so grateful for friends like you two."

"Ladies," Kane began, "I'm sure you're up to the job, but *never* underestimate the power you're up against."

Alesa stepped in front of Kane. "No harm shall come to Alextor. You have our word."

"Trust no one with this information. The perpetrator could be anyone, including someone you know."

"I'm sure it's not anyone we know."

Kane shook his head. "Really? Are you *sure*? Do you know something I don't?"

Ariel bristled and both sisters looked insulted. Jorell put an arm over each of their shoulders. "What Kane is trying to say is that it could be anyone. We don't know who wants my father dead, so everyone is suspect."

Ariel took Jorell's hand and gave it a squeeze. "What about Rand. Do we allow him in?"

"I think…I mean he knows, but…" She looked at Kane and hoped he'd answer the question for her. How could she say she didn't trust her own fiancée in front of three people she cared about?

"The fewer people involved the better. Rand included. He may know Alextor is ill, but it's best to keep him at a distance.

"Exactly. My apologies if I insulted your powers or intentions. I'll check on Alextor now." Kane turned and walked to the bedroom.

"I know all this comes as a shock. It's still hard for me to digest. Kane may be blunt, but he's very honest. What he's told you is fact. My father will die in sixteen sun-cycles if we don't find an antidote." She knew better than to tell them she was about to be whisked through time by '*The Traveler*' himself to learn who wants her father dead, and what kind of poison he used. It would be the trip of her life to save her father. She prayed for success.

Her back suddenly went hot and tingly. She turned and found Kane staring at her. Now her face was hot. Damn the man! He had a way about him she found seductive and sexy, all wrapped in a muscular body that surpassed every man she'd ever seen, including Rand.

"I'll get you two a drink." She excused herself to escape from Kane's scrutiny before her body overheated to the point of combustion. He'd distracted her train of thought and made her...no! She refused to think about him in those terms. She was engaged to Rand and had no business feeling anything for Kane. He was here to do a job that required his extraordinary abilities, and she'd do well to remember that. She ordered two fruit-aids and carried them back to the twins.

"Thanks." Alesa took them both and handed one to her sister.

"Shall I send someone to pick up your bags?"

"That would be nice," Ariel said.

"Consider it done. I'll have them put in the guest room."

"Jorell?"

"Excuse me." She wondered what Kane wanted that was so important he called for her. She walked across the parlor and into her father's room to where Kane stood. "Yes?"

"You're about to call a page? Or a servant?"

She nodded at his question, but didn't understand the disgruntled look on his face. "Yes. Why?"

"Think, Jorell. Your father is gone on business, so no one would be in his quarters. Servants talk. Why would they bring the twins luggage to the ruler's quarters?"

How could she have made such a mistake? "I'm sorry, Kane. I won't make that mistake again." She turned and sat on the chair by the table. He sat on the seat across from her.

Kane reached out and took her hand in his. "You're used to having people do things for you, and under ordinary circumstances that's not a problem. It's a habit, and habits are hard to break. You need to go into survival mode and carefully consider every order and command."

"My apologies. You're right. I haven't been thinking like a ruler. I've been acting like a private citizen, and a distraught daughter. I'm quite aware how secrecy is tantamount to our mission." She drew in a deep breath, then sighed. "It will not happen again. You have my word."

"You're a daughter desperately trying to save her father's life."

Kane tilted her chin up with his finger. "If you think it's difficult here, traveling through time presents even more complex problems. If you forget in the future, it can be fatal." Kane shook his head. "I'm responsible for your life, and your father's, and I take that responsibility to heart."

Kane's voice was firm, yet kind, and for that she was grateful. He was testing her, and so far she'd failed miserably. Lately, nothing had gone as planned. Hopefully, the future would bode better.

"Now that Alesa and Ariel are here you need to get some rest. You can't help if you're exhausted. Today is an example of how difficult things become if you're not ready."

Jorell nodded at Kane's wise words. "You're absolutely right, and I'll gladly take your advice."

Kane stood. "I have plans to coordinate, and even I need some sleep. I'll contact you in about ten time-units." He walked to the doorway and turned. "I'll take care of the twins' bags."

"Thank you." When Kane turned and left the room her gaze followed the subtle movement of his backside. He was fine. Kane appeared muscular, intimidating and dangerous. Rand was built similar to Kane, but she wasn't drawn to him the same way. Maybe it was the danger of falling for Kane that tempted her. Whatever the reason, she had to ignore Kane if she wanted to stay engaged.

CHAPTER TEN

Kane slapped Dobie on the back and laughed. "Thanks, I needed that, my friend. You've always been good at lifting my mood. Guess that's why I keep you around."

"Boy you're slow. I've always known that!"

When Kane pretended to hit him, his friend ducked and laughed. It was good to forget, just for a moment, that the planet's problems rested on his shoulders. He had a hunch this case would be the most difficult of his career. He'd solved many murder cases, lots of cheating life-mates looking for proof to dissolve the union, and more theft cases than he could count. But the assassination of a ruler? Actually, it would be three rulers if Alextor died.

"Boss? Which way? Forward, or backward?" Dobie scratched his head. "Planet Okeron calling Kane."

"Sorry, I was thinking."

Dobie rolled his eyes. "I won't ask about who."

"Good. Now, what's your vote?" He waited. "What's the matter? Panator got your tongue?"

"Don't joke about Panators. You know they scare me."

"You're stalling."

"Right. Considering time is the enemy, I say go back. The poison was given to him within twenty-four time-units of the Sector Meeting. So we go back and become his shadow for that time period. If we watch everyone who comes in contact with him we might prevent the poisoning."

"True, but we haven't narrowed the field of suspects so it could be anyone, and we still have no idea what kind of poison it is. There's an overwhelming risk of failure."

"Chief, it's always a gamble when we travel."

"If we went forward first, we could learn who's behind the conspiracy so we'd know who to look for in the past."

"Do you think there's time?"

Kane carefully considered Dobie's question. He wished he had a private portal into the future and the past so he knew the outcome of everything. His only problem was being human. Some might argue due to his special abilities, but he was just as human as the next man. "I don't know, but going back to stop it in the first place is probably the most logical and time smart plan."

Dobie walked to the galley-serve and ordered wine. He took the bottle, grabbed two glasses and went back to sit by Kane.

He watched his partner open the bottle and pour two glasses. "Is it time to celebrate?"

"No. But it might relax you so you can get a few time-units of sleep before you meet up with Jorell. She's quite the looker, isn't she?"

He studied his wine silently for a moment. "I hadn't noticed."

Dobie shook his head, looked to the ceiling and held up his arms. "By the planets! My partner has gone blind and stupid! Help him, please!"

He squinted and groaned. The attempt to convince Dobie he was oblivious to Jorell's charms had obviously backfired. "Did you learn anything from Jorell's computer?"

"I'd like to say yes, but I didn't find anything out of the ordinary. The delegations kept to themselves; a bit of debate took place, but there were no angry words or fights. I couldn't even find much interaction outside of the main floor."

"Sounds boring."

"You have no idea. The only high point was a motion by Ruler Sutone to officially investigate Sector-Two for violating water laws. Unfortunately, Sector-One voted against him, and the issue was dismissed. So, basically it was one Sector against two."

"I'll have to ask Jorell about that. Every war on this planet has been over water."

"Yeah, it's a necessary commodity to every living thing. And since there's only one source, whoever has the source has the control."

"We both know what that means." Dobie looked at him and nodded his complete understanding. "Okeron's history is about to repeat itself, and it's up to us to stop it."

"Easier said than done, Chief."

"I don't want to see planet-wide war any more than you do. The weapons are bigger, better, and more destructive than before. There would be devastating mass annihilations, to say the least."

"Okeron, as a planet, could even be destroyed." Dobie stood and stretched. "I don't want to think about the consequences if we fail."

"Neither do I, my friend, neither do I."

CHAPTER ELEVEN

Jorell stared at Dobie and Kane sitting across from her in her living area, both men on the edge of their chairs. "I know a little about the water situation. What do you want to know?"

"What incident spurred your father to request that Sector-Two be investigated?" Kane set a stack of papers on the floor beside him.

"It wasn't one incident, the problems have mounted over time." Jorell clasped her hands in her lap. She hated talking about her father as if he were gone. He should be speaking for himself. "As long as Marto Braxton was ruler, there were no problems. When Ramon Coster came to power, the problems began. He refuses to respect the current equitable split. He's out for himself, not his Sector."

"We're relying on your *unbiased* opinions concerning the political problems. But of course, you can't divorce yourself from your loyalties." Kane sat back in his chair.

"No opinion is 'unbiased', but I'll try." She crossed her legs and took a deep breath. "I assume you both understand the original agreement, where all three Sectors were given equal access and voting abilities concerning the disbursement and control of water to each Sector?"

Jorell paused a moment while Kane and Dobie nodded. "Almost immediately after Marto Braxton's death, the new ruler, Ramon Coster, upped the amount of water for Sector-One. He claimed his people needed it, but he's no more a man of the people than Pakar Moran. Pakar and Coster both claim Sector-Three took more than their share and they were just getting even. Their claims are fabricated lies."

"Do you have proof?"

"How do you prove a lie propagated against you, especially when both Sectors back the lies?" She stared at her hands in her lap. "They can easily forge paperwork to say anything they want." She looked up. "It's our word against theirs."

"Dobie and I aren't here to judge. We're on your side, remember?"

"I know. The last meeting was the first time we were accused of stealing water. We haven't stolen anything, and it infuriates me to be accused of something we did not do!"

Jorell sighed, then looked Kane in the eye. "Sorry. I did not mean to raise my voice." Kane appeared sympathetic, and she sure could use a big dose of it right now. "My father is an honest man, as were Marto and Trom. The three of them ruled peacefully for over twenty-five annual-cycles."

"Let's go back to the Origin-War for a moment. We all learned in school how there were four Sectors and they all fought over the water, hence the war. They ended the war, and ended Sector-Four at the same time. Therefore, three Sectors and peace. What I'm curious about, is if your father confided any secrets about that time with you?"

"He told me more than what's in history books, if that's what you mean, but I'm sure he left out as much as he told. What exactly are you looking for?"

Kane settled against the back of the chair. "What really happened to Pakar Moran?"

"History books say he was spared death, and his punishment was deportation from Okeron. My father said he was sent to Larent."

"That planet is on the far side of our galaxy."

"Exactly. Only criminals reside there. You'd better enjoy total lawlessness if you plan to survive. However, no one there asks questions, so it's the perfect place for a leader to collect a so-called army, and about anything else he wants. There's no law, and no government. So, whoever has the guts can claim the power, and can rule until he loses his followers to a new leader."

He shook his head and glanced briefly at Dobie. "We've been there, and you're exactly right. Some criminals enjoy living there since there's a lot of money in sex, drugs, and weapons. If they hadn't mastered it before their sentence, they perfected it there." Kane shook his head. "Did your father ever speak about Pakar's son?"

"He said Pakar had twin sons born in 2214. One died, and no one knows what happened to the surviving son, including his name."

"That's my supposition as well. Tell me everything your father said about Pakar."

"Forgive me, Kane. But what does Pakar have to do with my father's poisoning?"

"Either nothing, or everything."

"I'm confused." Either Kane was a genius, or certifiably insane. "What you're suggesting is so far removed from logical explanation that it's simply ridiculous."

"I understand your skepticism, but hear me out. Pakar was angry. In his eyes he was wronged, and his pride demolished. Of course he would never show it, but he wanted to kill those who deported him from Okeron and said he'd be executed on the spot if he returned. So what does a man like that do? He takes his time planning revenge, then returns to Okeron with a vengeance, and doesn't quit until he's punished everyone responsible for his demise."

"I never gave Pakar a thought. You could be right. By the planets, I should have seen this coming."

"Princess," Dobie began, "don't blame yourself. Men of power must always have power, and if they lose control, they'll do anything to regain it."

"Dobie is right. Pakar is driven by revenge and the need to regain power."

"I do understand. I've been surrounded by power hungry men my entire life. They don't all exhibit the ruthless pursuit, but they are victims all the same. Until now, we've had safeguards against an overthrow of the system, but now, with two leaders dead and my father incapacitated, those safeguards are gone—possibly forever."

Kane stood and began to pace. "This plot is deeper than anyone suspects. If it's Pakar, the reason is simple; to right a wrong. If it's not him, we'll have to dig deeper. Either way, we'll need to jump back in time. Our first target will be the last Sector Meeting, held in Sector-Two."

She sighed. "How long will we be gone?"

"When you time-travel, time passes differently. Even if we stay for a week, we may miss only a sun-cycle or two. Sometimes only a few time-units." Kane returned to his seat.

"I've heard the time-bending theories, but never put much stock in the idea."

Kane squinted at her, but appeared to be very deep in thought. "Are you sure about this?" She waited for his reply, but he simply stared; not at her, something in the distance, but it seemed like he wasn't in his body. "Kane?"

"Sorry Princess, he sometimes does that. But only when he's deep in thought, or possibly in another room."

"What?" Dobie gave her a smile that said he'd protect Kane with his life. Where had the handsome Traveler gone? Could he astral travel at will? If he had time traveled, his body would not be here. "Explain yourself, Dobie."

"Well, you see, he kinda goes..."

Jorell gasped when Kane tilted his head back then brought it forward to focus on her, as if he just reentered his body and came back to life.

"I'm sorry. I didn't mean to ignore you. I heard something and wanted to check it out. I'm here now. What did you ask me?"

"I asked if you're sure of our destination?"

"I'm never sure, nothing is for sure. Let's just say it's a place to start." Kane stood and walked around the room.

"Father always says you can't finish if you never start. So, when do we leave?"

"Don't be too anxious. There are rules you must learn before you leap." Kane paused his steps in front of Jorell.

"You look nervous. That's not giving me confidence for my first jump." Kane ran his fingers through his hair. She liked men with longer hair, it was far sexier than the short styles that were so popular. Kane didn't seem the type to worry about what others thought of him. Too bad Rand couldn't take a lesson from Kane. Rand cared about every speck of lint on his clothes, and he'd refuse to go anywhere if he didn't look perfect.

"I've never taken anyone but Dobie with me before. I'm worried about..."

"My safety? Don't be. If you can't save my father, they'll come after me next anyway. I prefer my chances with you."

Dobie jumped to his feet. "Don't say that, Princess!"

"It occurred to me while we discussed this possible conspiracy theory you've presented. At first I didn't believe a word of it, but it's making sense...too much sense." Kane turned his gaze on her, and with each breath he took, blue eyes turned darker. He made her feel so self-conscious.

"Princess, you can't be serious!"

Kane walked over to Dobie and put his hand on his shoulder. "She's absolutely correct in her assumption, my friend, and you well know it."

The interplay between Kane and Dobie was interesting and quite unique. They communicated through facial expressions. One would nod, the other lift an eyebrow, and that went on until they both nodded.

"Sorry, Princess." Dobie walked over to Jorell. "If you'll excuse me, I have some calculations to make."

She watched while Dobie left, then her office suddenly seemed small now that she was alone with Kane. Why he set her body on fire she couldn't explain, especially since she was betrothed.

Her connection to Rand did absolutely nothing to quell her urge to kiss Kane. It didn't say much about her character to want another man, but no matter how hard she tried, her attraction to Kane grew stronger and her will to be with Rand diminished.

"Jorell, I must ask you one last time. Are you sure you want to risk your life to time-travel with us?"

"I'll tell you one last time, yes. It's my father's life, and possibly mine on the line as well, so how could I make any other choice?"

"You win. But I want you to remember, I'm not sure it will even work."

"If you can take Dobie, you can take me."

Kane laughed. "If I didn't know better, I'd swear you've seen us while we were taking off, or landing."

"And why would that be so funny?"

"Let's just say we don't always land where we think we will, or in good condition."

"Explain what you mean by good condition?"

"Most of the time our clothes go with us, but there are times we arrive without them."

Heat rushed to her cheeks while her mind went places it shouldn't. "You're not serious."

"I wish I weren't. But don't worry, we've had much more success lately." He walked up to Jorell, took her hand in his and lifted it to his lips.

Lightheadedness struck and she thought she might pass out. Her stomach fluttered. He kissed the back of her hand then slowly lowered it, his gaze focused on hers. Kane was a charmer, and she suspected he'd had a lot of practice. That still didn't explain why he caused her heart to race so fast she could barely catch her breath.

"Are you all right, Jorell?"

"I'm fine." He finally released her hand, and after several deep breaths her breathing returned to normal. "I should have eaten this morning."

"I doubt you ate last night either."

"I thought I...you're right, I didn't." She stood and walked to the window. Something about Kane pulled her to him. The sensation was indescribable, something she never experienced with Rand.

Her relationship with Rand seemed more business than romance.

That often happened when two people worked together. Rand was different from most men she knew. He concentrated so much on business he had little energy left for romance. Her father had pushed her relationship with Rand, and he believed that since they were a compatible match, Rand would take excellent care of her. Their only shared interest involved politics, and the sad truth about Rand was that the only person he loved was himself.

Kane walked up behind her and she sensed his heart beating a bit faster than normal. Was he having a reaction to her? Probably not. Her imagination often participated in wishful thinking. She still had hope that she'd life-mate for love, even though most couples never accomplished a love match. "Would you like to join me for lunch, Kane?"

He nodded. "We have much to discuss."

"We do?" Kane put his hands on her shoulders and turned her to face him.

"We leave this moon-cycle for our first jump."

CHAPTER TWELVE

Kane paced the back corner of the garden where he'd first met Jorell. He'd never been this nervous about a job before, but he'd never tried to save an entire planet before. If he thought too much about every ramification based on Ruler Sutone's life he'd lose his mind. If the Ruler died so would the freedom of every inhabitant. And his worst fear would materialize—Pakar Moran.

If that wasn't enough to worry about, he held Jorell's safety in his hands, literally. He'd learned how to jump through time and take Dobie with him, but were his powers strong enough to transport three of them?

There couldn't be a worse time to experiment. He should stick with the tried and true; *The Traveler* and Dobie. However, he needed Jorell's political connections and savvy. At least that's what he told himself. He and Dobie had learned how to adapt to any circumstance. They'd become experts on how to change their appearance, yet he doubted it would be enough this time.

"Chief, why don't you sit down and relax. Jorell will be here soon. We're early, ya know. We always are."

"If that's true, why do I feel too late for this jump?"

"Probably because we've never had such limited time to deliver a giant miracle."

"That must be it." Dobie stood, jumped in front of him and grabbed his shoulders to stop him from pacing. "Dobie, do you understand what we're up against? This isn't like finding stolen art, or long lost relatives. This is life and death. The survival of our entire planet!"

"You're making me worry, and that's not good. I'd rather not have one of my spells right now, if you don't mind."

Kane smiled at his friend, thankful he was here. "I've seen your spells, and they're not pretty."

"My point exactly!" Dobie let go of Kane.

"What's keeping her? What if her father—"

"She'll be here. I'm sure of it."

He laughed. Dobie loved to turn the table on him. When they began working together he had to teach Dobie the art of patience. Now it seemed he needed that lesson himself.

When he turned toward the building the door opened and a trim, black-clad figure emerged. The lights highlighted shiny, red hair and he immediately knew it was Jorell. She walked toward them with obvious determination in every step she took. He was surprised she wore pants instead of her normal long gown attire. Gowns looked remarkable on her, but those tight pants revealed the princess in a whole new light.

Jorell strode up to him and stopped, her gaze unwavering, her jaw clenched. She tried to appear confident, but fear consumed her emerald eyes. "Did anyone see you leave?"

"Only Alesa and Ariel know I left. By the time anyone realizes I'm gone, we'll be back."

"I hope that plan works." She looked at him with at least a hundred questions written all over her face. "How is your father doing?"

"No change."

Dobie put a hand on Jorell's shoulder. "Look on the bright side, Princess, he's still alive, and we're here to help. It'll all work out. I promise."

Kane cleared his throat. "What Dobie means is we promise to do everything within our power."

"I understand you cannot make promises." Jorell hung her head and stared at the ground. "Can we go now?"

"Of course." He stared at Dobie and motioned for him to step back a bit. "What I need you to do is concentrate on the day before the last meeting at Sector-Two. The object is to arrive the day before at an inconspicuous location. Do you know of one we could all focus on?" He watched the myriad of expressions dance on Jorell's face. She was obviously considering her options, which pleased him. Careful was the keyword here.

"Behind the royal family's living quarters it's like a park. There's a wide expanse of grass, trees, bushes, and a very realistic man-made waterfall with a hidden cave behind it. I played there as a child."

"Great. We'll plan to land on the grassy area and picture a waterfall in the distance. The target date will be S2-196-2247."

Jorell looked at Dobie then back to Kane. "Tell me what to expect."

"You'll feel lightheaded, and it will seem as if everything is spinning around you. You'll want to panic, but resist that urge. You'll experience total darkness, then lights will swirl around you. Just hang on to *me. Don't let go*, no matter what happens."

"He's right, Princess. You don't want to get lost in time. It's not a friendly place, and you'd be hard to find." Dobie shook his head.

"Did Dobie mention he has firsthand knowledge? It took me half an annual-cycle to find him once."

"Chief, I'm not sure you were looking all that time."

"He's right. I needed a vacation, so I took my time." Kane laughed. "I don't think you should scare Jorell right now."

"Fine. Just don't lose me again."

"You're lucky, my friend. It's the longer trips that get you in trouble, but we aren't going that far back."

"Good. So, how are you going to take us both?"

"Dobie take your usual position." Dobie stood and faced him at arm's length. "Jorell, step in between us, facing me." While she took her position he rolled his sleeves up to his elbows so his cuffs were free of obstructions. "Now, put your arms around my neck. Dobie, grab my shoulders like always."

Kane put his hands on Dobie's shoulders. "Let's see if this works." It was difficult to concentrate with Jorell's breasts pressed firmly against his chest, but he had to focus on their destination. The only hope he had to take her along was to mind-meld with Jorell. By joining their thoughts and energies he would gain the extra strength he'd need. He'd tested the universe the first time he took Dobie, and he was about to test it again. *"Jorell, can you hear me?"*

"Yes."

Her reply was short, but comforting. *"Good. Keep your mind open to me. I'll guide you."* He also had to speak to Dobie in order to guide him. "Dobie. Relax. Go with the wind, hold on tight. All is well. Relax. Think of the waterfall and the grass. You want to go there."

Kane felt every muscle in Jorell's body tighten. "Jorell, concentrate on the exact location you mentioned. It's where you want to be. It's within your reach.

He tightened his hold on Dobie's shoulders, a move that always helped ease his friend's fears. He had lost him in time once, and did not want a repeat instance when the stakes were so high. "Close your eyes. The date of impact is S2-196-2247, the sun-cycle before the collective Sector Meeting in Sector-One."

The ever-present wind of unseen universal forces began to swirl and encompass everything. All he saw were the arms of darkness swirling and grabbing him. Dobie and Jorell's bodies both shook. Dobie was experienced, but Jorell was a virgin at time travel.

The tri-metal that covered his wrists and forearms began to glow and grow warm. Light bounced off them like lightning bolts. The sensation of being lifted into space took over, and he knew they were on their way. Dobie's grip tightened, and Jorell's hold around his neck was close to strangulation.

He heard panic in her mind. *Jorell, relax, the floating sensation is normal. Go with the energy, it's benevolent and only wants to guide you. Don't fight it. Put a circle of love around us that no evil can breach.*

Her rapid breathing caused her breasts to rise and fall against his chest. *Keep your eyes closed and remain focused on the waterfall, grass, and the date. Concentrate Jorell, it's imperative.*

He sensed Dobie's growing fear. "Dobie, concentrate. This is no different than any other jump. Jorell is fine. You're fine. We're moving toward our destination. Breathe, my friend."

Dobie squeezed his arm in a reassuring gesture. Jorell's arms around his neck shook, then the rest of her body joined in, and he sent pure energy to her. She shivered like a naked woman in snow. *Hang on, Jorell. You're doing fine. I'll keep you safe.*

Kane, I'm scared.

Focus on the destination place and time. Think of nothing else. Her head fell against his chest. The swirling increased to the point of no return. They whirled through time and space at a rate the mind could not comprehend. Then Jorell appeared in his mind, waiting for instructions. *Hold tight, it's almost over.*

The Raviat Cuffs Eunis put on him protected him against the flowing energy that pulled at them while they traveled. Sparks bounced off his cuffs, and they began to glow, burning the skin beneath the metal. He should have anticipated the heat due to having Jorell with them. Extra energy, extra heat.

"Kane, you're on fire!"

"I'm fine."

"I'm scared!"

"Concentrate. Hold me tight. I'll take care of you." He knew what was going through her mind, everyone experienced a jump differently, yet the fear remained the same. Sparks continued to bounce off the metal around his forearms, the building heat searing his scarred skin yet again, but without the Raviat Cuffs he could not time travel.

Round and round he twirled on the magic layer of time, Jorell's arms tightly around his neck, Dobie's fingers digging into his shoulders so hard he'd have bruises. He repeatedly sent messages to Dobie and Jorell to focus on their destination. Dobie knew the process, but this was Jorell's first.

Loud, howling winds rang in his ears. The stronger the wind, the closer to entry they were. *Hang on Jorell.* Dobie's grip tightened. "Easy, my friend."

White, flashing lights consumed them, then the familiar humming noise took over and grew so intense it shook his body, along with Dobie and Jorell's. *Hang on, Jorell. We're about to land.* She squeezed his neck in acknowledgement since she was scared out of her mind, and speechless. He sent another message, but she'd shut down the mind link; a normal response for a panicked person.

"Jorell, answer me. Jorell, can you hear me?" He waited for her reply. Then her arms were pulled from his neck and he lost touch. He reached out for her, but she was gone. He lost his grip on Dobie's right arm, and he couldn't find it again in the blinding light. He and Dobie fell so quickly he knew the landing was upon them.

Cold washed over him and his tenuous hold on Dobie immediately severed. Dobie had been ripped from his grasp, but that was normal to them, it was Jorell he worried about. Water. They'd landed in water. His feet hit the bottom of whatever water source he was in and he pushed up. *Jorell, swim up!* Dobie, push to the surface. *Jorell, follow the bubbles up.*

His head cleared the surface only to encounter water falling from above. He swam to the right and found himself in a large, cavernous room. Dobie popped out of the water in front of him, a big smile on his face.

"We made it, Chief!"

"Where's Jorell?" Dobie shook his head, which was the answer he'd feared. He dove under the surface and swam in a big circle around their landing spot. Churning water made visibility poor. It was nearly impossible to see anything. He dove deeper and finally found her body-- motionless on the bottom.

In near panic he swam to her, grasped her around the waist and pulled her to the surface. She had to be alive. It would be his fault if…. A moment later he surfaced and made his way to the rocky ledge where Dobie helped lift her out. She lay lifeless on the cold stones, and he began mouth-to-mouth resuscitation. He gave her his breath and pressed on her chest several times. He would not give up on her. He tried again and again. He rolled her on her side, relieved when she spit up several mouthfuls of water.

Finally she opened her eyes and coughed up the last of the water she'd swallowed. He thanked his lucky stars the glow of life had returned to her beautiful green eyes. He slipped his arm behind her and helped her to a sitting position. Water trickled down her face, her clothes clung to her body. She never looked more seductive. "How do you feel?"

"Wet, and embarrassed. I was dizzy and disoriented. I'm sorry, I...."

"You have no reason to be embarrassed or sorry." When she smiled at him his heart beat faster, which made him feel like a schoolboy once again.

"Thanks for saving me." Jorell took several deep breaths.

"You're welcome." She blushed, but she didn't look away this time. Her innocence glowed, and he could only hope Rand appreciated his fiancée for the unique woman she was.

"Princess, I've never been happier to see you!" Dobie stood. "You had me scared there for a while."

Kane nodded. Actually, she'd terrified him, but he did not dare tell her that. Jorell was his responsibility and he'd nearly lost her. "Feeling better now?"

"I'm a bit cold with all these wet clothes clinging to me."

"We'll take care of that. And Dobie, do me a favor, don't strip down like you did before."

"Of course not." Dobie wrung out the bottom of his shirt. "There's a lady present."

"I've noticed." He turned toward Jorell unable to take his gaze off her. She may be soaked to the bone, but she was still more beautiful than any woman he'd ever seen. It would be impossible for her to look bad since she was a natural beauty. "How do you feel, physically?"

"I'm not sure since I don't know how I'm supposed to feel."

Jorell stood with her shoulders back, her wet clothes molded to her every curve, looking more enticing than it was safe to look in front of a man. Now that her breasts were clearly visible since the soaked material had become a second skin, he realized they were bigger than he'd thought. Not that it mattered, but he smiled at the pleasant surprise.

Kane stood, unable to take his gaze off Jorell. She presented a very unique picture. Wet, red hair dripped down her perfect face, and wayward curls framed her cheeks. He mentally shook himself. If he wanted to complete this mission he needed to channel his thoughts away from Jorell. He turned his gaze on Dobie, who looked pathetic in wet pants that were even baggier than they were dry. One look down at himself confirmed he didn't look much better.

Kane, Dobie and Jorell all laughed, releasing the stress and frustration that always accompanied a jump through time. "We all look pretty sorry. There's one thing for sure, we landed right on target."

Laughter mingled with the soothing sound of the waterfall echoing off the rock walls of the cavern.

"Well *Traveler*, what's our next move?" Jorell pulled wet fabric away from her skin.

"We need to confirm the date and time."

Jorell smiled. "I can do that."

"You're at greater risk here than we are since your other self is already here for the meeting. Dobie and I can slip in and out without detection since no one knows us. We make great waiters, don't we Dob?"

"The best. We've had lots of practice."

"That we have."

"I'm happy for you both, but my teeth are chattering from the cold."

"Right. Let's get to our place first. We can confirm the date there and make our plans." Kane ran his fingers through his hair to get it off his forehead.

"Your place? How is that possible?"

"We've purchased several places at various times, in various locations, so no matter where we go, or when, we have a place available to us."

Jorell shrugged her shoulders. "I guess it's important to have a place of your own."

"Even if we're lucky enough to arrive with the clothes on our backs, there are special requirements, depending on the job, but we need a place to store supplies."

"I see your point. So, let's go, I'm freezing."

"Sorry." He put his arm around her, "Do you know a good way out of here? We don't want to be seen."

Jorell wrung out the ends of her hair. "Follow me."

Kane did like following her, especially in water-drenched, skin-tight pants. She offered fantastic scenery. He heard her in his mind asking if he was trying to tell her something. "I'm making plans, you must have picked up my thoughts." She was better than he thought, and he needed to be more careful. Most readers couldn't read him so he wasn't used to maintaining a protective wall at all times.

When she contacted him mentally, her soft touch gave him a warm, happy feeling he liked. What reaction would she have if she knew exactly what he was thinking? That he wanted to feel her bare skin against his, to touch her curls, and caress her body. He wanted her in his bed, and he didn't give a damn about her fiancé.

CHAPTER THIRTEEN

Jorell wandered around what Kane and Dobie called "our place" in amazement. It was some type of warehouse they had converted into storage, office space, and quite lavish living quarters. The huge storage area held everything to enable both men to be someone different thousands of times over.

The storage aisles held shelves full of hats, shoes, boots, suits, formal wear, along with some clothes fit only for beggars, thieves and clowns. One aisle caught her eye because it held attire that would be considered 'old man attire', which she guessed was Kane's favorite disguise.

She smiled when her memory conjured Kane as an old man in the garden. She never would have guessed his age was so different from his appearance. When he'd carried her in his strong, muscular arms, holding her close, even the padding under his clothes could not dispel a rock hard physique. That was the moment she knew he was not what he pretended to be.

A bit further down the main aisle she came to a section full of women's clothing. Why would they have such a complete selection of feminine attire? Kane could never pull off dressing as a woman, but Dobie could. She pictured Dobie wearing a formal gown and had to laugh. Dobie was small enough to get by with a masquerade like that, but he certainly would never win a beauty contest.

Kane's and Dobie's voices echoed and bounced off the building's high domed ceiling. She wasn't close enough to distinguish words, but she knew they were discussing future plans and she wanted to give them time alone.

The warehouse was an astounding place with everything a person needed to play any sport, or to participate in any activity on the planet. How many times had they merged into situations without anyone noticing? They really were professionals, but were they good enough to save her father?

The place grew silent and she immediately hated being alone so she hurried back to the living area. Dobie was gone, but Kane stood in front of the huge view-screen, so focused he didn't even notice she stood behind him.

"What did you find, Jorell?"

How wrong she'd been. When he turned to face her she could not calm her rapidly beating heart. "I found a lot of interesting things, but I'm waiting for you to tell me the plan. Who shall I be? A young socialite, or an old man?"

Kane laughed. "Who do you want to be? You've attended countless Sector Meetings, how could you best garner information?" Kane turned back toward the screen.

"I could be an OA."

"Who would you be an Official Assistant to?"

"If I had the uniform, I could move freely anywhere, and I'd never be questioned. Assistants wander in and out of the meetings, they're everywhere seeing to the needs of all three Sectors."

"And what will you do when you run into yourself at the meeting?"

Jorell stepped closer to Kane. "That's what you're for, to tell me what to do. We share a mind-link and we can freely converse during the meeting." She smiled.

"Princess, always remember the first rule of time travel; change one tiny thing and you alter the future. It's tricky business. One wrong word can set events on a different path. Are you prepared for that?"

"I pray that I am. I must save my father. He isn't lying in an irreversible coma because of anyone's good intentions. I presume that as long as the future is changed for the positive it will work out. Right?"

"In a manner of speaking, but it will change many other things as well. Time magnifies actions and words. They take on a life of their own, and once that happens, you can't control the end result."

"Then I suppose you just travel back a bit further and fix what you messed up. Right?"

"Wrong. It's not that easy. You can turn a bad situation into a full-blown disaster."

"You know more about it than I do, so I'll take your advice. I promise."

"That's all I ask. Dobie and I have learned to proceed with extreme caution."

"I shall do the same."

"I know your intentions are honorable, and you only want to change your father's health. But I wouldn't be doing my job if I didn't warn you that it's never as easy as you think, and there could be complications from *any* action you take."

She studied Kane's features and found only concern and honesty. In her heart she knew she'd chosen the right man to help her, and she thanked her lucky stars.

"So, who do you want to be?"

"If I were an Official Assistant assigned to one of the Sectors, I'd be privy to conversations, and various information pertaining to their Sector."

"Sounds logical. You know what they do, and what you might learn."

"What about you and Dobie?"

"I thought we'd hang around the food and drink areas. Someone slipped your father poison; maybe we can prevent it from happening. Plus, servers love to gossip."

"You must have done the waiter thing before?" She watched Kane nod. "Does the help really gossip that much?"

"Fortunately, or unfortunately, yes."

She sighed and sat on one of the stools in front of the media screen. "I never realized they talked so much."

Kane sat on the seat next to Jorell. "It's the way of things. It's been that way since the beginning of time on nearly every planet in the galaxy. It may be cliché, but it's the age old battle of the haves versus the have-nots. And you would never hear them due to your position, and the fact they're probably talking about you."

"I suppose." She looked into Kane's eyes. "And I suppose it's also easy to hire an assassin if the credits are high enough?"

"Absolutely, that's how it works, and if we're lucky, it will happen in front of us so we can stop it."

Jorell looked away from Kane's handsome features and stared at the screen in front of her. "Have you or Dobie found anything new?"

"Not really. We've watched tomorrow's meeting several times, but nothing new. We have time to prepare."

Jorell twirled damp hair around her finger while she thought about what was to come. They were about to interfere with the Sector-Two meeting. She'd been to the actual meeting, but now she felt like a spy. Nothing mattered except to keep her father alive.

"Jorell? What is it?"

"I was thinking how strange this is. You and Dobie are used to tampering with time and people. I'm not, and the reality just sank in."

Kane took her hand in his. "I'm glad it did. You'll do fine. If I didn't think you could handle it, I wouldn't have brought you."

"If you're trying to make me feel better, don't. My father is dying, and I'm somewhere in the past trying to...to..."

"Help him. Jorell, you're not wasting time, you're playing with it to save his life. There *is* a difference."

She refused to show weakness. "I'm sorry. I don't mean to be emotional, it's just that I'm..." She looked at Kane, relieved not to see judgment in his eyes.

Kane stood, took both her hands in his and pulled her to her feet. He wrapped his arms tightly around her and she laid her head on his broad shoulder. It had been a long time since anyone had shown her sympathy and solace in their embrace. It was good—too good.

Kane ran his hands up and down her back in a soothing motion she hoped would go on forever. He made her feel safe, and she had no urge to move. The warmth of his body and the strong rhythmic beat of his heart against her ear had a peaceful, calming effect on her frayed nerves.

"Hey, Chief! I need..."

She immediately pulled herself away from Kane, turned her back on Dobie, and pretended to concentrate on the view-screen.

"Dobie, what can I do for you?"

"Sorry, I didn't mean to interrupt."

Kane leaned toward Jorell. "I'll be right back."

****

"Sorry Chief, really. I didn't mean to interrupt anything. If I'd have known you two were aah...aah...."

"It's okay, my friend. She needed a shoulder to cry on and I was there. End of story."

"I see." Dobie cleared his throat. "Actually, I thought it would be nice if you two were to get together. I think you have a lot in common, and I know you're both attracted to each other."

Dobie stopped talking, gazed up at the ceiling and started to whistle. Kane walked over to his friend, put his hand on his shoulder and guided him down the hall. "I get the implication, but I have no intention of getting close to Jorell. This is business, and that's how it must stay."

Dobie chuckled and shook his head.

"It's not funny." Dobie laughed harder. "I meant what I said." He stared at the only man who knew him well. Of course he'd see the attraction, he hadn't done a very good job of hiding it. Jorell was a little more difficult to read, but she had not shied away from him. She seemed to enjoy his embrace when she was crying, but she was vulnerable right now.

"Sorry. I was half-teasing, but not about the chemistry. A blind man could see that!"

"I hope you're exaggerating because we have to work together in public, and I wouldn't want anyone to see an attraction that could blow our cover."

Dobie slapped Kane on the back with his hand. "I only saw it because I know you, and I was also fishing to see how hard you protested."

"And what did you learn?"

"That if things were different you'd be interested in her, but they're not, so you're not. Right?"

"Something like that. Now, let's get our wardrobe in order."

"Who are we?"

"First we'll set Jorell up as an Official Assistant to Sector-One. She could be recognized by someone in Sector-Two since she was close to the ruling family. You, my friend, will also be an Official Assistant, or OA as they're called, and you will be assigned to Sector-Two. I'll be a floor supervisor for the serving staff. I need more freedom than a waiter has so I can check the galley area as well as the serving stations."

"Good plan. I'll collect what we need. You should get back to Jorell. I'm sure she'll need some coaching, especially when she meets herself for the first time."

"Right. I'll head back. Don't forget to make her about fifty pounds heavier, at least, and go for dark hair, really dark, and we may have to give her a scar."

"And a few wrinkles?"

"I like it. She'll look so unlike herself no one would ever recognize her."

"I'll see you when you're done." Dobie nodded and took off to plunder the warehouse. He turned and headed back to the main area. Jorell had a lot of adjustments to make. He and Dobie had done undercover jobs for over fifteen annual-cycles, so adjusting to the look and feel of glued on skin and extra weight had become second nature. Jorell was about to have a very eye opening experience, one she'd never forget.

He entered the open area and found her studying the meeting they were soon to attend. She appeared to be at home with Dobie's complex system. "Have you learned anything?" She turned her gaze on him and he immediately found himself lost in the depths of her mesmerizing green eyes. He was slipping; no woman had ever hypnotized him the way she did.

"The meeting is exactly as I remembered. Nothing out of the ordinary. The motions were orderly, everyone seemed content and calm. Except when Nazar proposed the water rights be renegotiated. There were a few protests, but nothing violent or threatening."

"Tell me about the past meetings when the three original rulers attended."

"All three originals are, or should I say were, passionate men. At times issues turned emotional, voices were raised, and on a couple of occasions one of them would leave. But they shared a mutual respect and always managed to solve their differences amicably."

"What's different now?"

"Everything. My father still looks out for the people of Sector-Three, while Ramon Coster and Nazar Ferris are emotionless robots, only looking out for themselves and their credits. There's no respect on their part, nor do they care about their constituency."

"Respect and friendship takes time to achieve. Maybe it's just too early for such feelings."

"I doubt they're capable of feeling anything. I don't trust them, and neither does my father. We talked about this exact same thing, and my father admitted that Ramon and Nazar scared him. He also had a feeling they'd come after him next, and that's proven true."

"We don't know that, Jorell."

"We know it, we just don't have proof."

"Then we'll find proof." A loud crash sounded behind him. Jorell hopped off her stool and started running toward the sound and he followed right behind her. They entered the warehouse and rushed down the second aisle toward the scraping noises.

Dobie sat in the center of the walkway, a lady's scarf covering half of his head, and a purple feather boa lying over his left shoulder. Women's underwear covered the rest of him, which made him quite a sight. He moved his right arm and another box of frilly white garments spilled across his lap. "What happened, Dob?" He looked up at him and grinned the way he always did when he had no definitive answer.

"Remember when you told me the boxes weren't stacked securely? You were right."

Kane offered Dobie a hand up. "So, did you find everything we need?"

"I think so, as soon as I find it under this mess I'll bring it to you."

"Need help?" Kane stacked a few boxes on top of each other.

"If you want to carry this box, you can." Dobie handed a large box to Kane. "This is for Jorell. You can explain it to her."

"I'll be happy to."

"I'll be there in a minute. You two go on."

"Okay." He glanced at Jorell who turned and began to walk back. Following Jorell always provided an extra bonus. She had the cutest little wiggle when she walked, and he took great pleasure watching her every step.

"I assume we'll have to be at the meeting early if we're supposed to work there."

"Three time-units early."

"I had no idea the help arrived that far ahead of us."

"They do, and you'd better get some rest. I'll show you to your room. He led her back to the living area, then down a hall. When he reached the end he tapped a floorboard that slid back, looked down into the eye scanner and waited. The floor closed and the heavy metal door opened. Once they stepped through the open doorway the metal made its usual clicking noise when it locked behind them.

"I'm impressed."

He watched Jorell's gaze move wall to wall, and ceiling to floor. "We have excellent security here, so you can sleep well."

"You and Dobie have worked wonders." She ran her hand up and down the wall to her left. "I love the terrain finish on the walls." Jorell took a few more steps then stopped. "Do you and Dobie live here?"

"That depends on what time we're in, but we do stay here when we can." He stepped closer and tucked a stray hair behind her ear. In the recessed perimeter lighting, her red hair took on a golden hue, but it also allowed him to see the beautiful aura about her. "We've used this place a long time."

"I can tell." She smiled. "It's so…you." She took a step back. "I mean, you and Dobie."

He opened the last door on the left, then stepped aside. She strolled in, her mouth half open while she walked across the room and ran her hand over a marbelus statue of a very large bird.

"You have expensive taste."

"In some things." He loved it when she smiled the way she was at this moment. It was sexy to be sure, with a hint of mystery and surprise. She was so seductive because she had no idea what effect she had on him. That made her the most dangerous kind of flirt.

"These quarters are elegant, and well appointed. Even better than in my sector."

Kane chuckled. "You expected less?"

"I'm not sure what I expected, but this wasn't it."

"I'm glad you approve." Kane gestured toward two upholstered chairs. "Please, have a seat. I'll get you a glass of wine before you retire." She nodded her consent with a cute little smile. If she wasn't taken he'd kiss that smile off her face and turn it into desire.

Instead of luring Jorell into his bed, he poured two glasses of red wine and returned to where she waited, looking more appealing to him than when he left. He handed her the glass, took his seat, and watched her gaze methodically wander around the room before she turned it on him. How he loved those mesmerizing green eyes.

"What do you want to tell me?"

"I didn't say I wanted to tell you anything."

"You don't think you're easy to read, and you forget I'm in that business. It's what I do for my father, read other's emotions, intentions, and thoughts if I can."

"Sorry, I'm not used to working with anyone who has your level of talent." He took a deep breath. "I wanted to warn you about running into yourself tomorrow."

Jorell took a sip of wine. "Hmmm, that's an excellent point." She focused on Kane. "Okay, what happens if I run into myself?"

"Avoid touching yourself. If you do, there will be a painful transference of energy. It could possibly paralyze you, if not kill you."

"You're serious, aren't you?"

"Absolutely. And it can happen by accident. Let's say you're taking a message to yourself as an OA, and when you hand it over she touches you. It happens easy enough. Break the contact immediately and you'll only sustain a minor shock, but if the hold is not broken...let's just say it gets worse."

"Has it happened to you?"

"Once. I literally bumped into myself, half out of curiosity, but I regretted it. Now I make sure it never happens."

"You're a careful man. I like that. I'll heed your warning."

"You too are careful, and successful. It's one of the reasons I agreed to work for you. Plus, I have a few bones to pick with Nazar Ferris. So if this assignment allows me to inflict a little pressure on him, all the better."

"Dare I ask what happened between the two of you?"

"I'll tell you, but not tonight. It's a long story and you need your rest." More like it was a painful story, one he really didn't care to share. He stood and walked to the center of the room.

"This will be your room. It can be locked from the inside for your safety and no one can get in. Dobie and I will be down the hall. My room is on the right, his on the left. Just in case you need anything, there are three intercom positions." He pointed to the table next to the bed, then to the door, and then toward the bathroom. "Press D for Dobie and K for Kane. You are G for guest."

Kane walked to the wall next to the bed, pressed a button and a table slid out. He pressed a button and the curtains on the far wall opened and a beautiful beach scene appeared, the sound of surf gently caressing the shore, and a slight breeze began to circulate the air in the room. "If you don't like the beach there are several others you can choose, or none at all."

"You've thought of everything. I'm impressed."

"Good moon-cycle." He walked to the door, opened it and reluctantly left her alone. He could not violate his own rules, or interfere with her engagement.

One question bothered him. Would he tell her the truth about himself and Nazar Ferris, or would he maintain the silence he'd kept all these annual-cycles? Dobie didn't even know the whole truth, he knew just enough to understand the situation.

He'd told Dobie a story about how Nazar cheated during his military training. He had to tell him something since they'd all been together in the Academy, but he'd never revealed to anyone what he'd seen Nazar do in a dark alleyway one moon-cycle. He wished he'd been able to stop it, but he'd been too late. Old hatreds grew stronger with time, but so had he. Soon he'd settle the score. Soon.

CHAPTER FOURTEEN

Jorell stared in the mirror unable to recognize the woman looking back. She had short, black hair styled close to her head, a small scar on her left cheek and several wrinkles that made her look at least thirty annual-cycles older. The extra weight provided by padded under-garments was not appealing, but it did make her look like a typical, middle-aged worker with plain features, creases, and no make-up. It was laughable that it took tons of make-up to look this bad.

Dobie and Kane were fantastic at becoming different people. She'd never have believed such transformations were possible, but the three of them were living proof.

Kane had become a middle-aged, pot-bellied supervisor. His uniform gave him credibility, and the light-brown wig looked so real she'd swear he'd cut his hair short and colored it. Dobie looked like her counterpart, dressed as an OA, except his uniform was the dark-blue of Sector-Two while hers was Sector-One's signature, deep-green.

Dobie actually looked cute in his red wig. His normally unruly, curly, bushy blond hair was a stark contrast to the smooth, well-manicured style he sported this sun-cycle. She really liked Dobie, he was easy-going and fun, the opposite of Kane, who was the epitome of a highly skilled warrior, muscular, serious, and too ruggedly handsome. Why did opposites attract?

Kane and Dobie finished closing up the warehouse and setting the security system. Her heart beat faster at the thought of the task at hand. Her father's life lay in their hands, and their lives might also be forfeited if the wrong people found out what they were up to. The conspiracy theory was real, and nearly complete.

"Princess?"

She turned at the sound of Dobie's voice. "Is it time?"

"For the fun to begin?" Dobie laughed. "I know what you're thinking, but you're wrong. We care very much about your father. I was referring to our acting. It's an art, you know?"

"Not really, but I'm about to find out."

"That's the spirit." Dobie walked toward the main door. "Come on, Princess. You don't want to miss your ride."

She walked toward Dobie, but sensed Kane behind her. The familiar tickle in her mind did not surprise her. It was Kane's way of getting her attention so she could receive a telepathic message. *"Kane?"*

"I wanted to test our connection before we needed to use it. I must tell you, this is a first for me."

"For me as well. A complete connection is rare, but ours is so...so..."

"Complete? I agree. We will make progress this sun-cycle."

"I hope so, for many reasons." He slowly withdrew and she felt the loss. She wanted to tell him their connection was very intimate, but she suspected he knew. The only risk to a complete mind-link was lowering one's guard and allowing the other person access to their thoughts. Some thoughts could be hidden, but it was difficult to maintain a safety wall, and not always reliable.

Dobie opened the door and went outside, she and Kane followed him into the cool, darkness of the early sun-cycle. Kane secured the door, then led the way to his transport vehicle. Dobie got in the back and she sat next to Kane in the front.

The air-ride back to the Capitol Building was short. Kane found the perfect location to leave his transport, which he backed in for a quick departure. It appeared she'd hired the best since he took every possible precaution.

When the hatch opened they all got out and Kane locked the transport. While they walked the short distance to the employees' entrance she pulled the proper identification from her pocket. When they reached the guard-cube, she checked in and received her assignments for the sun-cycle. Dobie had done a great job, since she was handed her temp-card for the duration of the meeting, and the man questioned nothing.

They entered the hall where several employees mulled around. Kane made small-talk with a few workers while he walked away with them. Dobie sided up to a very attractive woman and made her smile, then followed her toward Sector-Two's designated area.

It was a strange feeling to go to Sector-One's area when she belonged in Sector-Three. Of course, she had to steer clear of Sector-Three so she didn't run into herself.

Kane and Dobie were able to role play with ease, but she found it difficult, especially when all she wanted was to see her father and give him a hug—something an OA could never do.

****

Kane shook his head and leaned against the cool marbelous tiled wall in the hallway. So far he'd learned absolutely nothing. The staff was talkative enough, but he hadn't heard one single word that indicated a sinister plot against Alextor or Sector-Three. Dobie and Jorell reported the same, and it was well past mid-meal. Maybe he'd been wrong thinking this was the place to start.

Rand Arroray was the most suspicious person he'd seen. The fool flirted with every woman who crossed his path. How the man could find any woman more attractive than Jorell he'd never know. Jorell was naïve, and Rand knew it as well. She had no idea what she was in for if she life-mated Rand.

"Sir?"

Kane turned to face the man behind him. "Yes?"

"Should we serve the late sun-cycle refreshments?"

He checked his wrist-piece. "Is everything ready in the galley?"

"It is, sir."

"Then proceed." The man actually saluted him, turned and hurried back to the galley. He started toward the main conference room, but stopped when he spotted Rand in an adjoining hallway with yet another woman. Rand now held a pretty brunette that filled out her uniform in ways most women only dreamed about. He kept out of sight, but he was close enough to hear their conversation.

"Saina, I want you. Is there a place we can go?"

"I can't leave the building, they'll know, and I'll lose my pay for this sun-cycle."

"What if I make it up to you?"

Kane saw the woman lean into Rand, who put his arms around her, pulled her body against his, and explored her backside very intimately. He pressed his lips to hers and a very hot kiss erupted while their hands moved everywhere. It was a good thing Jorell was occupied, otherwise there could be a noisy scene.

The woman ended the kiss, took Rand's hand, and led him down the hall. They disappeared into an unoccupied room, slammed the door, and he heard the security device click into place. He had no reason to wait so he returned to the main debate floor.

The sight before him was amazing. Jorell sat behind her father as he spoke to the gathering. She was devoted to him and smiled broadly when the audience applauded. It seemed strange watching a Jorell he'd never met, and he laughed to himself every time he looked at the new Jorell, who was currently homely, fat, wrinkled and scarred. She had difficulty moving around with her newly acquired weight.

It sounded odd, but he enjoyed every version of her. They'd communicated several times and he'd experienced her distress. Jorell seemed close to the breaking point. Dealing with her father's condition, her position in the government, and maintaining the lie about her father put a lot of pressure on her. Everyone had a magical line they struggled not to cross, because if they did, all could be lost. It was his job to keep her from taking that fatal step.

"Kane. Are you there?"

Jorell's gentle probe hesitantly touched his mind. *"What is it?"*

"Nazar was talking to someone I don't recognize. I distinctly heard him say 'stop the Ruler', but I'm not sure what he meant."

"I'll check it out. Stay where you are and keep your ears open."

"Kane, be careful."

"Always." Jorell's emotions flowed through her thoughts into him. She'd paid him an exorbitant amount of credits and expected positive results. He desperately wanted to provide the outcome she demanded, and deserved.

Nazar bothered him, but they'd always rubbed each other the wrong way. From the day he'd met Nazar in the Academy he'd sensed dark energy around him. They never got along before, and he doubted anything had changed. Nazar seemed even more diabolical now than when he was younger. Was Nazar his number one suspect behind the psychic attacks on Alextor, or did he just want him to be? Either way, the man had no respect for anyone, or anything.

Kane cut through the food-prep section of the galley and entered the dark, lounge area like any typical employee. He walked behind the bar, poured three drinks and put them on a tray, all the while scanning the large, semi-dark room for Nazar. He picked up the tray and headed across the table-filled area, his gaze fixed on the back corner.

Nazar sat with a man he'd never seen before. He was an older man, but still good-looking, dressed elegantly, and he held himself with pride. On the surface he appeared to be an upstanding gentleman, yet he sensed a strong, dark aura around him. The stranger and Nazar had similarities, and he wondered if they were related. Whether they were or not, they were joined together in an intense conversation.

Kane walked to their table with the tray of drinks and stopped. "Gentlemen, a beautiful woman asked me to send these drinks over." He set one drink down in front of each man.

Nazar scanned the room. "I don't see any such woman."

"She left a moment ago, but insisted I serve three drinks to the two of you."

"That's a strange request."

Kane looked at the older-man who had made the statement. "She said to drink one for her. Just doing my job, sir." He set the third drink between them. "Will there be anything else?" As most of the elite did, Nazar indicated his wish for the lowly server to leave by a wave of his hand. He played his part, bowed slightly, then turned and walked away. Little did the mystery man know, he now had his digital profile image, prints, eye scan, and would soon learn his identity.

Back at the bar, he performed a few menial tasks a barkeep would do, with his ear tuned to the table in the back. They kept their voices low so he only caught a few words in passing. It seemed they were pleased with themselves for creating some unique situation that turned out exactly as they'd planned.

Could they possibly be celebrating Alextor Sutone's inevitable death? When the last original signer died, what would happen to the planet? Whatever resulted, life on Okeron would never be the same again.

The two men laughed loudly, and he wanted to physically wipe the conceited smiles from their faces. If they were behind the plot against Alextor, he doubted they'd be so obvious. Of course they weren't saying anything that would make sense to a lowly barkeep. To be honest, they were acting like any two men in a bar. His suspicious mind always worked overtime.

"Is everything all right, sir?"

Kane turned to find the assigned bar person standing behind him. "Fine. I just served the two men in the corner since you were gone. Please, be more attentive to your customers."

"Yes, sir. Sorry, sir. It won't happen again, sir."

"See that it doesn't." He left the apologetic man shaking in his shoes. It was amazing how much power some men were afforded, whether they deserved it or not. It was sad how this man, and many like him, cowered before any authority figure. He suspected that whoever poisoned Alextor did so out of fear for his life. For all he knew the man was already dead. Pakar Moran never left loose ends, and he trusted no one.

CHAPTER FIFTEEN

"Every time I got close they stopped talking. They're part of this, I know they are. Last I saw Rand, he was having a private party with a shapely server from Sector-One."

Dobie shook his head and groaned. "Wow. Poor Jorell. She's supposed to life-mate the jerk, isn't she?"

"That's the plan."

"What should we do about it, Chief?"

"Nothing. There's plenty of time for her to discover who Rand really is. And I have a suspicion that before this is over, she'll find out he's cheating in more than one area."

"Jorell deserves better than Rand Arroway, a man who deceives at love and politics."

"Did you learn anything else?"

"I've heard a lot of whispers about what happened to Marto Braxton, and Trom Carsun. It's not sitting well with either Sector. Sector-One is blaming Sector-Two, and two is blaming one, and they're both blaming three. What a mess."

"It's our job to save Alextor. And if he recovers, hopefully he'll expose the guilty parties and keep peace in the process."

"That's a tall order." Dobie scratched his head. "Ya know, Chief, I've been listening to Ruler Sutone speak on the floor and I really like the man. He's honest, and truly concerned about his people. He's not a typical, arrogant leader."

"True." There was nothing typical about his daughter either, but that was not for Dobie to hear. His partner already wanted to pair him with

Jorell. She was engaged to Rand, and he had no business getting in her way. He worked for her, nothing more, and he well knew he could not play with time for personal gain. "Alextor has an excellent ruling record. The people love him."

"And so does Jorell." Dobie slid off the stool. "I'd better get back."

Kane followed Dobie to the door which his friend opened.

Dobie rushed down the hall like a man being chased. He walked slowly since supervisors were rarely in a hurry; they simply moved about with a sense of purpose and dignity. He cut back through the lounge to check on Nazar, but found the table empty, as were all the other tables.

After a trip through the galley he entered the main floor in time to hear Alextor and Ramon Coster embroiled in a heated debate over how to best handle some water issues that had recently come to light. Alextor paused a moment while Jorell whispered in his ear.

The next words spoken were to the point. Alextor accused Ramon of pulling a scam to benefit Sector-One's treasury, and insinuated they wanted more control over water distribution. Then Nazar took the floor and defended Sector-One, which was directly in opposition of Sector-Three. Nazar claimed Sector-Two was entitled to a larger water supply than their current allotment, and his words drew mumblings from the entire gallery.

Nazar spoke with stern authority, demanding rights in direct opposition of the original treaty. He seemed overly aggressive for a newly appointed ruler. Then Ramon defended the claim Sector-Two was making, and threw in more demands for Sector-One. Something was very wrong with the entire picture.

Kane carefully watched Jorell and her father on the floor. They worked well together. Not all of Jorell's advice was spoken; they used barely perceptible hand signals most of the time.

The general meeting was nearly over, and they'd learned nothing definitive. He could only assume the poisoning would happen after adjournment.

The argument on the floor escalated. While everyone's attention was focused on Nazar, Rand slipped in behind the other members of Sector-Three. The double dealer had the audacity to act like he'd been there all along.

Rand's secret indiscretions were safe with him. Jorell had enough to worry about, she'd learn the truth by herself since Rand was too arrogant to be careful. He'd seen Rand's type many times, and he'd learned not to bother destroying them since they usually hung themselves.

He slipped out of the main assembly room to find Dobie. It didn't take long to spot his friend carrying a big stack of booklets, dropping a few as he walked down the hall. He followed behind and picked up after him.

"Hey, Chief. I know it's you behind me. Who else would do extra work?"

Kane glanced up and then down the empty hall. "It seems everyone is embroiled in the argument on the floor."

"It's kinda strange, don't ya think?"

"Very. Have you found anything helpful?"

Dobie shook his head. "Everyone's been closed mouthed. Way too quiet for my taste."

"Where's Jorell?"

"Time travel Jorell went to pick up more booklets. I ran into her when I was collecting mine. She seemed disappointed because she hadn't learned any more than we have. I'm afraid this trip is a bust."

"Don't judge it till it's over."

"Right. See ya."

Dobie headed away from him with his arms full of booklets and disappeared into the main conference area. He needed to check on Jorell himself. This was her first trip, and he'd forgotten to warn her about possible side-effects that set in after about twelve time-units.

****

Jorell desperately wanted to grab her stomach, but her arms were full of stupid booklets. When would the intense cramps stop? There hadn't been time to eat or drink anything so she had no idea why she was so sick. It didn't matter how sick she became, she was here to stop her father's poisoning, and that's exactly what she'd do.

She was glad the door to Sector-Two's area was open since she didn't have a free arm. The booklets got heavier with each step, but she finally made it to the back table and half dropped them on the shiny surface.

After she tidied up the stacks, she looked across the main floor and saw herself working with her father. It was past strange to see herself as First Advisor. It boggled the mind, and she was already confused.

Nazar's angry, authoritative voice carried throughout the meeting hall loud and clear. She'd heard his rant the first time she'd attended this meeting, but seeing him from Sector-Two's point of view put a different spin on his words.

She'd heard a lot of talk about creating a new water agreement, and if that happened, the entire planet could be under new rules, as well as rulers. Nothing she'd heard this sun-cycle boded well for Sector-Three.

A complex, well-hidden conspiracy theory was at work here, and it infused a new wave of dread and sadness.

"Ms. Ryele?"

It was Nazar's voice behind her, and she was shocked he would address her personally. "Yes, sir?" She hadn't realized he'd turned the podium over to his second in command, Rolland Morro. She knew Rolland from previous visits, but not well. Trom and his family had never been fond of Rolland or his political views.

"Get me a bottle of my personal wine that's being chilled in the galley."

"Right away, sir. Will you need glasses?"

"That's a stupid question, of course I do."

Nazar turned his back on her and returned to the podium, so she left to carry out his order. The moment she set foot in the hall she literally ran into Kane. "Sorry, sir."

"I need a word with you."

"Yes, sir." She followed Kane to a supply room a few doors down and stepped inside. Kane remained in the doorway, his muscular build filling the entire entryway. He glanced back over his shoulder and checked the hall up and down before he spoke.

"How are you doing?"

"Okay." Just then another stomach cramp seized her and she bent over, grasping her stomach. Kane rushed to her side, wrapped his arms around her and pulled her against his chest. She let go of her stomach and put her arms over his shoulders, clasping her hands behind his neck.

"I was afraid you'd have a physical reaction to the jump."

"Is that what's wrong with me?"

"It's perfectly normal. Dobie and I have both gone through it. You'll outgrow it if you travel enough."

"I look forward to that sun-cycle. In the meantime, I definitely feel sick. I'm glad I didn't eat or drink anything."

Kane's eyes were full of sympathy, but she heard a slight chuckle.

"Have you learned anything yet?"

"Nothing past the obvious. But Nazar just asked me to get him a bottle of his private wine. I don't know what he plans to do with it."

"Good. Follow up on that. I'm here if you need me. I'm watching you. I don't trust Nazar."

"That's good to know."

Kane gave her a nod and a smile then left her alone in the service room. She quickly made her way out, shutting the door behind her. She headed toward the galley, but stopped dead in her tracks when she saw Rand in the hall a short distance in front of her with his arm around a woman. They looked quite cozy together.

Rand casually pulled the blonde close to him and kissed her on the lips. To say this was a shocking sight would be an understatement. She'd suspected for some time that he had no feelings for her, but betrayal still hurt. When the kiss ended, Rand let go of the woman, turned his back to her and returned to the auditorium.

She continued toward the galley, passing Rand's new partner in the process. The woman was shapely, and well endowed. She looked down at herself and nearly laughed. She'd temporarily forgotten about her disguise. To be honest, she made an ugly old woman, perfect for spying on Rand. To see the real Rand was worth the makeup hours. What surprised her the most wasn't what she felt, it was what she didn't feel.

Seeing Rand with another woman should send anger and jealousy raging through her, but she had no emotions for what she'd just witnessed. It had taken her father's condition, meeting Kane, and seeing what Rand was up to behind her back to solidify the truth. She'd suspected Rand was no more drawn to her than she was to him.

She'd never once had an urge to make love with Rand, but she could barely control her need for Kane. A loveless life-mating is what Rand would provide, and she'd agreed to settle for less to please her father. This entire situation made her realize she deserved to be loved by a man, not used to gain position and credits.

She'd be a fool to think Kane would be interested in anything except a brief coupling, and for him, she'd gladly cooperate. There may never be another man who stirred her emotions and fueled her needs, so if Kane wanted her, so be it. Once in a lifetime was better than never experiencing real passion with an intriguing man, one so damned sexy she could barely keep her eyes off him.

She reached the end of the hall where one of the double doors of the galley entrance stood open. It was time to forget Kane and get back to the business at hand. She stepped inside and walked to the special cooler designated for the whims of the rulers and their delegations. Nazar's niche was labeled, and she removed a chilled bottle of wine. She set the bottle and six glasses on a tray, then hurried back to Sector-Two's area.

It didn't take long to locate Nazar down in front motioning for herewith a purpose to her step she hurried down the steps and over to Nazar. The moment she was close enough, he took the tray from her and immediately walked toward her father in the Sector-Three area.

This could be the moment they'd traveled here for. Her father's life could hinge on that one bottle of wine. The poison was either in the bottle, or Nazar would put it in the glass. Either way, she had to stop her father from taking that drink.

She all but ran to back of the room, into the hall and all the way around to Sector-Three's entrance. Since Sector-One had the floor, Nazar walked up to her father and set the tray on the table in front of him. Her father had a surprised look on his face. Nazar's gift caused everyone in the Sector-Three area to look skeptical while they stared at their nemesis.

"What do I owe you for this gift, Nazar?"

"Alextor, I want you to consider me a friend, not an adversary. We need to work together. Join forces for the good of our people."

She wondered how he could call himself a friend when they disagreed on every subject regarding Okeron. It was difficult to keep her mouth shut. Above all others, Nazar wanted Alextor Sutone dead. No way would she let her father drink the wine.

Her other self took the bottle and poured three glasses. She remembered the toast, then the three of them drinking the wine from the vid. She had to move now.

She grabbed a stack of booklets from the back and rushed to where the wine sat on the front table. She purposely stumbled and threw every booklet in her arms at the tray. She reveled in success when the bottle and all the glasses flew off the table, landed on the hard, marbelous floor and splintered into a thousand pieces. Had she just changed history?

She'd landed on her knees in the middle of a dark, red pool. Drips still fell, but when she looked up, the source was Nazar's custom tailored suit, currently dripping in splashed wine. The Sector-Two leader glared down at her, and if looks could kill, she'd be dead. She was afraid to get up so she remained kneeling on the glass and wine covered floor.

"You stupid bitch!" He bent down and brushed wine from the front of his pants.

She started to get up, but instead turned her head when Nazar raised his hand in an effort to strike her across the face. He pulled his arm back and she braced herself when the downward thrust began. She ducked and covered her face with her hands, but he never made contact. She glanced up and saw Kane's hand around Nazar's wrist which was a hair's-breath from her left cheek.

"I believe we can take care of this for you, sir. And please, accept a case of wine as compensation."

Nazar's face glowed red with suppressed rage. He jerked his arm out of Kane's grasp and stared at her with daggers in his eyes.

"I suppose that will have to suffice." Nazar turned to face the help. "I want *that* woman fired. She's useless!"

"Consider it done."

Kane walked over to her, grabbed her arm, pulled her to her feet, then escorted her to the back of the room. She'd expected his grasp to hurt, yet he was extremely gentle while looking angry and authoritative. When they reached the hallway he leaned down and put his mouth to her ear.

"Are you all right?"

"I'm fine. He never touched me." She looked into Kane's bright blue eyes and recognized deep concern. "Thanks to you."

"For the rest of this assignment I want you to stay out of Nazar's sight. He has it in for you. As far as anyone is concerned, I fired you."

"Got it."

"Stay invisible, and that is an order. Go find Dobie and see if he can use your help. Stay in Sector-One, but whatever you do, don't let Nazar see your face."

"Understood."

"Go. I'll catch up with you later."

She walked away from Kane and headed to Sector-One's area where she had no trouble locating Dobie. He looked up the moment she entered the service area and rushed over to her.

"Ms. Ryele, do you need something?"

"I need something from the supply closet in the hall. If you could please help me for a moment, I'd appreciate it."

"Certainly."

Dobie led the way into the hall and she followed. Once in the supply room she gave one last check of the walkway to be sure it was safe. "I got fired."

Dobie laughed. "This is good. What did you do, spill wine on Nazar?"

Her hand covered her mouth out of shock. "How did you know?"

"I doubt there's a person here who doesn't know. Good job, by the way."

"Nazar didn't find it amusing. He insisted Kane fire me, so here I am. Kane told me to help you and to stay invisible."

"Priceless!" Dobie chuckled. "I've been punched out, shoved down and beat-up, but never fired!" Dobie patted Jorell's back. "Imagine that, on your first jump you've accomplished what I haven't on hundreds of jumps." Dobie laughed. "Don't worry your pretty little self over this. Look on the bright side, you weren't getting paid anyway."

"With a little luck I saved my father's life. If I thought it would help, I'd break every bottle in the cooler." She looked into Dobie's brown eyes. "Why else would Nazar give my father a gift of fine wine? Nazar hates him, so it has to be the poison source."

"Maybe he wanted to make friends?"

"Who on Okeron wants to be Nazar's friend?" Dobie broke out in a loud laugh at her question and she couldn't suppress her own chuckle. "I believe he intended to eliminate an enemy."

CHAPTER SIXTEEN

Kane handed Jorell a glass of wine, then gave one to Dobie. "Let's make a toast." He picked up his glass and held it out toward Dobie and Jorell. "To a successful jump," he glanced at Jorell, "and to surviving this sun-cycle."

All three glasses chimed when they touched. After they each took a sip, he sat next to Jorell on the sofa. She looked tired and upset. The sad look on her face cut him to the core. He'd so wanted to solve everything this sun-cycle, but he'd failed miserably.

"I don't feel like celebrating." Jorell set her glass on the table and started to stand.

He put his hand on her arm and gently stayed her attempt to leave. "You must understand, these things take time. Answers can be hard to come by. Patience is a fine art that everyone loses when it comes to someone they love."

"So what's the answer?"

"We keep looking." Kane took her hand in his. We don't give up." She bowed her head and refused to look at him. He tipped her chin up with his index finger. When she turned her beautiful green eyes on him all he saw was sadness, and a woman who loved her father too deeply to be objective.

"I want to believe, Kane. I really do, but we just wasted an entire sun-cycle and learned nothing—absolutely nothing."

"Excuse me, but you two seem to be ignoring *me*." Dobie laughed. "Princess, I think you're under-estimating the information we collected."

"What exactly did we collect?"

She glared at him with inquisitive eyes, but he feared her desperation hindered her thinking. "Please, Jorell, lean back, drink your wine, and open your mind. This is where Dobie and I brainstorm. We talk about everything we saw, every conversation we heard, or took part in, plus anything and everything we encountered—important or not."

Dobie sat in the chair across from Kane and Jorell and crossed his legs. "As you both know, I was the insector-fly on the wall."

"The what?"

Kane laughed. "The ugly fly on the wall." She smiled and his emotional wall began to crumble. How the woman could do that to him he'd never understand, but she did, and he was beginning to like it far too much. She took a long drink of wine and he quickly refilled her glass.

Dobie cleared his throat. "Okay. I heard a conversation between Ramon Coster and his second in command, Senar Pollit. They were discussing the reservoir and what could happen to it if they let their guard down."

Kane poured more wine. "Everyone knows the potential dangers involved with the reservoir, which is why each Sector sends their best security teams to guard it."

"The problem has always been 'winner takes all'. I heard some buzz about making a move against Sector-Three, but there was no reference to Alextor."

"I eavesdropped on an interesting conversation in the hall behind the Sector-Two area." Dobie took a drink of wine. "A woman I didn't recognize, was talking to Rolland Morro. I heard him tell her to double the bribe to get the schematic. He said he wanted it at any cost. She asked how high he'd go, and he said to bring him a number and he'd decide. That's all I heard."

"That's quite a bit actually." Kane turned toward Jorell. "Did you hear anything like that?"

"I heard several questionable conversations. The realization that Nazar hates everyone was an obvious thread. The man is evil. I don't trust him, and I wouldn't turn my back on him—ever."

"Excellent observation. Dobie and I fully concur." Kane nodded. "Dobie, what did your research reveal about Nazar's family?"

Dobie stood. "That's the interesting part. It's like he came out of nowhere. I've tried to trace his place of birth and find where he spent his younger annual-cycles, but there's nothing. It's as if his life started fifteen annual-cycles ago when he entered the Academy with us.

"After graduation he became the 'chosen one' when he entered the political stage. He's one of the few who actually started toward the top and has done nothing but move up, and quickly."

"That's quite a story." Jorell looked down at her hands in her lap. "I have a bad feeling about Nazar. I can't put my finger on it. I mean, I don't know the reason, just the feeling."

Kane sighed. "I agree. The list of reasons are too long to recite, but I believe your premonitions are correct. I don't even trust him in my sight."

"You sound as if you've known him personally. How is that possible?"

"Dobie and I spent six miserable annual-cycles with him in the Academy. I wanted to kill him more times than I could count."

"What stopped you?"

Dobie cleared his throat. "I did. Most of the time. Actually there were a lot of guys that wanted to take him out, not just us. But none of us had weapons, and since Nazar is Kane's size, there were only a few guys who stood a chance against him. Nazar and Kane are quite physically matched, and not to take anything away from Kane, because he's the best fighter ever, but Nazar can hold his own, and he cheats. That's the part that scares me."

"I see your point, Dobie, but you're not making any points with…" Jorell nodded her head toward Kane. "Nazar is definitely a man to watch, and I think this entire plot revolves around him somehow. He's not working alone. I don't believe he's the mastermind, but he's definitely part of the scheme."

"I support that hypothesis. The mastermind is someone older, wiser, and more level-headed." Kane shook his head. "I sense this unknown person is completely evil."

"I don't have the same type of E.S.P. you two have, but I think you're both right." Dobie chuckled. "Don't look at me like that. I can have premonitions too, ya know."

"Of course you can, Dobie. I'd never assume Kane and I are the only two people who can have 'those feelings' as you call them." She turned her head from Dobie to Kane. "Have you teased poor Dobie about his psychic powers?"

"Daily."

"I keep telling him I'm talented and can do everything he can, but he never believes me." Dobie smiled. "And I told him anyone could see how psychic I am."

Jorell smiled at Kane. "I think you should apologize to Dobie. He's obviously hurt by your lack of appreciation."

"Dobie knows I appreciate him."

"Have you told him lately?"

Kane smiled. "Don't have to, he's psychic." He loved the sound of

Jorell's and Dobie's laughter. A sense of humor was a necessity, especially while facing dreary tasks. Life and death missions could stress anyone, but laughter was good for the soul—anytime.

"Kane, what did you learn?"

Jorell's tone had returned to the serious side and once again reeked of desperation. Back to the ugly realities of life. He wished he had something to reveal that would put her mind at ease, but the lack of information was painful for them both. "I saw Nazar in the bar with an older man. I got his digital eye image." Kane took a button off his shirt and handed it to Dobie. "See if you can learn who the mystery man is."

"Right away, Chief." Dobie rushed off to the communication room.

"They seemed to have a lot to say to each other. They kept their voices low. I heard nothing except occasional laughter."

"What did the man look like?"

"He was my height, a bit thinner, well dressed, grayish, well-styled hair, good looking for a man his age. He seemed physically fit, and appeared upper class. I don't know if he's involved in politics, but he was very friendly with Nazar. He resembles Nazar. I wouldn't be surprised if they were related."

"You have a strong resemblance to Nazar yourself. You both have dark-brown hair, pale-blue eyes, you're about the same height and build, and you share similar facial features. Maybe you're related to Nazar."

"Don't even joke about that."

Jorell smiled. "I said there's a physical resemblance, I didn't say your personalities were the same, not to mention your character."

Kane took a deep breath and sighed. "I'm glad to hear that." Jorell stared at him, her piercing green gaze full of emotion, pleading for answers he didn't have.

"If you were anything like Nazar I never would have hired you." Jorell stared at Kane. "Besides, you're much better looking than he is."

"I'm glad you noticed, but when you hired me you had no idea what I looked like, or who I was." She smiled slowly, and her serious gaze faded into a spark of mischief.

"You're right. At first I thought you were an ugly old man who wasn't capable of traveling across the lawn, let alone through time." Jorell put her hand on Kane's forearm and squeezed. "When you picked me up and carried me to the bench, I knew you weren't who you pretended to be."

"I thought that would make you mad." She scowled in a cute, feminine way, but he had no idea what she was thinking. He'd learned a long time ago that a woman's mind was a mysterious thing men never understood.

"Why would I be mad? You demonstrated you were careful. And being in politics, I appreciated your little charade."

"Little charade? That's what you thought?"

Jorell nodded. "You were afraid I'd arrest you, or detain you if I knew who you were."

"Dobie and I operate within the law, and we've never done anything to be arrested for, at least nothing we'd admit to."

"Cute. Now tell me, why you took take my case?"

"Credits."

"I still can't believe you had the audacity to charge me fifty-million credits."

Kane laughed. "I can't believe you paid it!" Her angry scowl was genuine so he abruptly stopped laughing. "Actually, I owe Doctor Willock a few favors, and he called one in."

"So, if I had contacted you myself, you would have refused me?"

"Dobie and I had just returned from a very dangerous and complicated jump. We were drained, and had plans for an extended vacation."

"Instead you got me?"

He reached out and placed his hands on her shoulders. "Jorell, I would have taken your case if you'd asked. I respect your father and the work he does, and I like the long-standing peace on Okeron. I'm willing to do whatever it takes to protect that peace and bring your father back. And as you know, Dobie and I are residents of Sector-Three."

"You're just making amends."

"Is it working?" She nodded at him, fighting a smile that pulled her lips to a perfect kissable expression. "I'm trying to tell you I choose jobs according to client's need, but I won't work for anyone who's only out for themselves, or out to make tons of credits at other's expense."

"Isn't everyone out for themselves?"

Kane gave her shoulders a comforting squeeze then released her. "You're very astute, Advisor Sutone."

"That only means I realize it's always about the credits."

Kane took her hands in his. He loved being close to her, and touching her was pure pleasure. "You're right. I work for credits, but so does everyone on this planet, and every other planet I've been to."

"Of course they do, yet you can call me selfish? I don't want to lose my father." She gazed into his eyes. "But there's so much more…"

He stilled her words by placing a finger on her lips. "No need to explain. I understand." A lone tear rolled down her cheek and he wiped it away. He'd always hated to see a woman cry, especially Jorell, who was the sweetest, most beautiful and caring woman he'd ever met. Her father meant the world to her, and so did the people he served.

"Kane, I worried about—"

He couldn't resist her any longer. This time he stilled her words with his lips, and they were even softer than he'd imagined. She opened her mouth to him and they dueled and searched. Her energy swelled and merged with his.

Jorell pressed her body against his, and her arms threaded around his neck. She tasted as sweet as the enchanting fragrance she wore. When her breasts pressed against his chest, all he could think of was kissing her bare skin and making her beg for more. He sensed she craved physical closeness as much as he did.

If circumstances were different, he'd take her to his bed this instant. Her mind tickled his and he heard her call his name in a sexy whisper. *"Jorell, my sweet, this is not the time or place."* She answered with a groan and deepened her kiss which sent his need into turbo-boost. *"Jorell, we need to stop while we still can."*

"Why do we want to stop? It feels so right."

"Are you testing me? If so, I'm about to fail."

"Your kiss is no failure, warrior."

"Why do you call me warrior?" She ran her hands across his shoulders then down the fabric of his long-sleeved shirt. She lingered on his biceps and squeezed his muscles several times.

"Need you ask?"

She kissed him with passion, and her mind screamed with need. He wanted to take her, wanted to make her his, yet he couldn't allow such a mistake. *"My sweet, there's a time and place for everything, and this is not the time, as much as I wish it were."*

Jorell moved back from him and ended the kiss. She looked as frustrated as he felt. He cradled her cheeks in the palms of his hands and looked deeply into her eyes. *"My sweet, you're a very special woman who deserves to be loved by a man who will love you back, unconditionally."*

"Oh Kane, I'm sorr..."

"No regrets, no excuses. Okay?" If she knew how badly he wanted her she'd run. He pictured her in his mind in his bed, naked, their bodies entwined.

"I like the way you think, Traveler."

"That's nice to say, but you don't know what I'm thinking." He thought he'd locked his last thoughts and images from her, especially that one more touch and he'd whisk her off to bed without hesitation.

"I believe I do, but we can't talk about it." Jorell looked Kane in the eye. *"Am I right?"*

"*Absolutely.*" Her cheeks turned bright red, which only served to increase his need. Jorell was not a woman to give her favors carelessly. At least he knew she had feelings for him.

"Maybe one day, somewhere in time, we can pick up where we left off."

She spoke her last statement, and she put her finger over his lips, so he sent his reply mentally. *"I hate the word 'maybe'."*

"Let me rephrase. We *will* meet again one day, somewhere in time, and nothing will stand between us--nothing will stop us."

"I want to believe that, my sweet, I really do."

"Believe it Time Warrior. I will find you."

"And I will be waiting."

CHAPTER SEVENTEEN

"Ready?"

Jorell nodded to Kane, but she wasn't ready at all. The side-effects were still in high-gear from the initial jump, and she was afraid the return trip could push her into the black abyss of time-everlasting.

"Jorell?"

"What?" Her voice sounded weak even to her. The look Kane gave her was nothing short of complete frustration mixed with sympathy.

"If you're not up to it we can postpone our return until you're feeling better."

"I feel fine. Let's do this."

"Chief, I think your instincts are correct. Jorell's in no shape to jump right now."

"Thanks for your concern, Dobie, but I'll be fine. I refuse to waste any more time here than necessary."

Kane took her hand and guided her over to the living area and seated her on the sofa. He sat next to her and placed his fingers on the inside of her wrist. It was obvious he was taking her pulse since he kept his gaze fixed on his wrist-piece.

"Your anxiety level is off the charts. Whether you want to or not, we're going to wait, at least until your reading is normal. And that's final."

She knew Kane well enough to know he was a man of his word and he'd hear no argument from her. It was reassuring to have him in charge. She was tired of making decisions and gladly passed the responsibility to him. Allowing Kane to take the lead was comforting, and a bit worrisome.

"The delay will help us all." Dobie sat in the chair across from the sofa. "Chief, we need a better plan."

Kane's gaze moved from Jorell to his friend. "What's on your mind?"

"Well, we thought our jump to the Tri-Sector meeting would show us who was responsible for the poisoning. We have a hunch, but nothing concrete. Granted, Jorell broke the wine bottle, and there's always a chance that was the culprit. However, if that wine wasn't the source, we're back where we started."

"What's your suggestion?"

Kane stared at his friend, but she couldn't take her eyes off 'The Traveler'. The calm way he handled everything was such a change from the world of politics, where everyone thought they were right, and would fight to the death to prove their point. But Kane and Dobie were the epitome of true collaboration.

"I have run every test, and hit every data bank, and that man Nazar was talking to in the bar never existed anywhere, and we both know that's not possible. Even if he were from another planet, or galaxy, he'd show up as an alien, but when I ran his scan I got nothing. Absolutely nothing."

"Maybe I didn't get a clean digital image." Kane shook his head. "It must be an equipment glitch."

"If that were the case I couldn't have run the other fourteen images you gave me, which yielded proper results."

"I know I'm not exactly a part of your team, but maybe your data base is too limited to find this mystery man?" Dobie and Kane both stared at her as if she were an alien from an unknown galaxy.

"Jorell, I wouldn't tell just anyone this, but Dobie's data base not only includes this entire planet, but many others as well."

Dobie smiled. "It was a very good question though."

"Sorry I interrupted you, Dobie. Please continue." He nodded at her and she sensed his true friendship, and the purity of his motivation. Dobie was one of the very rare people who did not conceal his personality, nor did he lie, or hide the truth. Kane had the perfect partner.

"Well, I was thinking we should attend the formal closing ball tonight. It would be a great chance to do some informal chatting with our suspects. But we have one problem."

"You're right." Kane scratched his head.

"What's the problem, Dobie?" Both men stared at her as if she should already know the answer.

Dobie smiled at Jorell. "The problem, Princess, is you."

"I'll behave myself, I promise."

"Which one of you will behave? There will probably be two of you there."

She glanced at Kane who leaned against the wall, his arms crossed against his massive chest, looking ruggedly handsome, but a bit too stoic." Can't I just wear a disguise like I did today?"

"First, tell us if you went."

"Rand insisted, or I probably wouldn't have. After the meeting I had a headache. There had been too much upsetting information and I was in no mood to party. However, Rand and my father wouldn't take no for an answer."

"Did you learn anything when you went?" Kane pushed off the wall and walked over to Jorell. "Do you remember anything significant?"

"I remember a parade of women around Nazar, and he enjoyed himself way too much. My father made his usual rounds greeting friends and associates. You know, the remaining original council members. But he retired early. He said the material of his new suit was scratchy and it made him itch. All he wanted to do was take a shower and go to bed. I stayed quite late, but I didn't talk to very many people."

"Did you dance?"

"Several times, with various partners, but only once with Rand. He seemed more interested in Nazar and his string of women."

Kane sat next to her on the sofa. "This is an important question, and I want you to think about it before you answer. Did anything happen that night that has played a part in the future?"

The serious look on Kane's face, and the soft, yet demanding tone of his voice scared her. Every nuance that happened that moon-cycle played through her mind and she tried to picture any ramifications that had surfaced since her last visit. "I understand what you're asking, but there were no conversations or actions resulting from any encounter I had with anyone."

"Princess, Kane is correct when he told you that the most minute word or deed can have a ripple effect going forward. And since you're in politics, I'm sure you've seen a little ripple turn into a tsunami."

"I think you're both giving too much importance to my words and deeds."

Dobie laughed. "I guarantee if I danced with you I'd remember, and I'd probably—"

"Dobie, we don't need to go there."

"Sorry, Chief."

The sound of Dobie's and Kane's laughter filled the room and made her smile. They didn't need to explain, she knew how a man's mind wandered. Rand's image came into her thoughts. Why couldn't Rand be more like Kane and Dobie? Had Rand ever been attracted to her? It was odd she picked this moment in time to question her fiancé.

"Princess? Hello?"

Dobie's voice drew her attention. Both men stood in front of her and stared at her as if she'd lost her mind. "Sorry, Dobie. What did you say?"

"I just wondered if you'd remembered anything. You looked lost in thought."

"Well, I was thinking about what Rand said while we were dancing." She tucked some hair behind her ear. "He asked if my father was wearing his new suit. I said he was, but that's the first time Rand ever referred to my father's attire. He then said how nice the suit fit, and how elegant it looked."

"Had Rand ever discussed any male fashion with you before? Anything about clothes? For him or others?"

"No." She looked up at Kane. "That was a strange question, don't you think? What part could clothing possibly play?"

"I'm not sure."

Dobie jumped to his feet and slapped Kane on the back. Why don't we just form a plan for this evening? We're all tired, and it seems getting a bit cranky?"

"I'm more than ready." Kane offered Jorell his hand, then helped her to her feet. "Come. I'd like to show you something." Kane started to walk down the hall and held her by his side. "It will make a much larger impression than any explaining I can do."

"I don't doubt what you've told me."

"Please, just watch a vid."

She allowed him to lead her to the viewer. The screen lit up and she watched two women casually talk about a man across the room. They were both interested until one of the women said she loved him, and the other conceded. The next view was four annual-cycles in the future, showing the woman who claimed to love the man, arguing with him in front of a building. Terrible words were exchanged, then the man walked away, both of them extremely unhappy.

Kane leaned toward Jorell. "It seemed the man wanted children, but the woman flatly refused."

"What are you trying to tell me with this vid?"

"What you just saw was one reality, in which a situation was not what it seemed. The woman never loved him, refused to give him the children he desperately wanted, plus, she'd managed to steal all his wealth, and you just witnessed the good-bye. Let me show you another reality."

This vid began the same, but the two women agreed to compete for the man, and he would choose the winner. Then she saw the future, where the opposite woman won him and they were walking through a garden hand in hand, each holding the hand of a child. They looked at each other with love, and she instantly understood.

"The reality of words and actions. Two people could live in heartache and deception, or sheer happiness. Plus two new lives depended on the outcome of that love."

She'd never thought about the simple things, only big political decisions and their ramifications. "How is it possible for you to have those vids?"

"Illegal activities were turned around. That's all I can say."

"I see." He obviously did that job, and she understood about client privacy issues. "Thanks for the demonstration."

"That was a small example of how different actions and words can, and do, influence the future. A simple word here and there can turn the tides of time negative, or positive." Kane picked up her hand. "Armed with this new perspective, you need to decide whether to attend the ball as yourself, or as someone else."

"Now I'm worried I don't know how to be myself." Every conversation she'd had that moon-cycle ran through her mind. She still couldn't believe anything she'd said or done had any significant effect on the future. She looked into Kane's blue eyes. "I believe there would be a problem if two Jorell Sutones went to the party."

"We'd have to incapacitate the original Jorell if you wish to go as yourself."

She absently nodded, trying to put everything in perspective. "I already know what I learned as myself, and since we don't want to draw attention, I think I should go as someone else." She watched Dobie walk toward them. "I'm sure you can disguise me again."

Kane stood in front of her with an anxious look on his face, yet he mentally sent understanding and caring vibrations, which she answered with gratitude. Her heart beat a little faster when he smiled, the way it always did when he was close.

"Aah, excuse me? I see that thing going on between you again. I'm only irritated because I'm not included."

She turned her gaze on Dobie who pretended to have hurt feelings, but he couldn't hide the smirk on his face. "I'd include you if I could, you know that."

"I wouldn't." Kane crossed his arms over his chest.

They all laughed and it felt good. Of all the times she spent with Rand she couldn't remember laughing—not even a chuckle, yet these two men made her happy under the worst of situations.

"Dobie, Jorell has decided to go as someone else to the ball. Any ideas?"

"You betcha, but I don't think she should be ugly this time, just different." Dobie clapped his hands several times. "She's gonna learn so much this way. She can dance with politicians from all three Sectors, and ask stuff like...'What do you think of Jorell and Alextor Sutone?' Most important, she can ask them about Nazar."

"I agree with Dobie, however you're the politician and client, so it's your call."

"After my blunder with the wine, I'm not sure I should even go with you." Dobie and Kane looked at her with their famous squinted eyes and half-smiles, the expression that verified she'd lost her mind.

"Jorell, there's no right or wrong, only time can prove the outcome. It's simply an intelligent guess, no more, no less."

She nodded while her mind replayed the entire ball she'd previously attended, along with all the questions she had no answers for. "I'll go as someone else, and I assume you'll make me look different?"

Dobie jumped to his feet. "You betcha, and I've got the perfect costume for you!"

It took willpower not to laugh out loud when Dobie scurried toward the warehouse and out of sight. "He does get excited about his work, doesn't he?"

"Dobie is very special. He's smart, loyal, and funny, all at the same time. I suppose that's why we get along so well." Kane turned his attention back to Jorell. "Do not second guess your decision. If you do, you won't be able to function, you'll be too worried about what you're doing."

"I'm glad you said that." She looked into his bright blue eyes. "How did you know what I was thinking?"

"Your guard was down and I heard you arguing with yourself."

"Oh." She hoped he hadn't picked up her thoughts about Rand. Those were private and needed to stay that way. One side benefit was she could keep a careful eye on Rand and his activities this moon-cycle since he wouldn't know who she was. That brought a smile to her face.

"I'm glad you're amused."

"You have no idea."

CHAPTER EIGHTEEN

Kane couldn't take his gaze off Jorell, or should he say Leyana, the beautiful blonde wearing a stunning long, black fitted gown that showed off her perfect curves. The garment revealed too much cleavage, and the slit up one side showed off too much leg. Her appearance invited every male to gawk, and he did not like it one bit.

What had Dobie been thinking? He reminded himself it was all for the cause, but it didn't work. Rand should be jealous, not him. Although a glance in Rand's direction found him groping the backside of a redhead that he held far too close. The man could not behave worse if he tried. He had no concept of fidelity.

The dance floor was crowded, yet Leyana stood out like a shining star. She'd danced with every good-looking man in attendance, except him. He'd stayed away so she could gather intelligence. She couldn't learn anything from him except that he wanted her more than any woman he'd ever met.

"Chief? Okeron calling Kane."

"What?" Dobie gave him his hurt look that indicated he had snapped his reply. He smiled at Dobie. "What, my friend?"

"Just wanted to tell you I heard Nazar talking to his friend. He said he wanted Jorell in his bed."

"Which one?"

"Both."

"Don't joke about this."

"I'm not joking. He said he wanted the original Jorell, but he knew she'd never accommodate him, so he said he'd take the new blonde over there."

His gaze moved to Leyana. "I can't fault his taste in women." When he looked at Dobie they shared the same reaction, the one that said, 'Touch her and you die'.

"I've been watching Rand as you requested, Chief."

"And?"

"Caught him kissing some brunette in the garden."

"About what I expected."

"He's a real slime-snaketor. I don't know how Jorell, or any woman, could have feelings for a man like that."

"They believe the lies. It's called trust."

"Maybe, but I don't understand how women fall for those pathetic excuses."

He looked at Dobie. "They don't realize they're excuses." Something caught his eye and he surveyed the left corner of the immense ballroom. There he was, the man Nazar had met with in the bar.

"What is it?"

Kane turned back toward Dobie. "See the tall, gray-haired man with the dark-blue suit standing in the far corner talking to the real Jorell?"

"Yeah, what about him?"

"He's the man who met with Nazar in the bar during the meeting. The man who doesn't exist."

"Ooh, that guy." Dobie stared at the man and shook his head.

"We need blond Jorell to have a chat with him to see who he is and what he's up to."

"I'll take care of it."

He didn't have to tell Dobie to be careful, he knew the rules of the game. After a glance around the room he spotted Rand dancing with a dark-haired beauty in a yellow gown. Rand's hands were so low they weren't on her back as the dance required.

Rand certainly enjoyed women, too bad it wasn't his future life-mate. He hated to see a woman like Jorell tied to a man who would never love her, or be faithful. He hoped the vid he'd shown her earlier helped make that point.

Dobie had made his way over to Leyana and asked her to dance. They walked to the dance floor and joined the crowd. As a blonde, Jorell looked good, but he adored her own silky, red hair and green eyes. Her appearance tonight was fantastic; however, her natural features were so perfect that any change made her less attractive to him.

Dobie had broadened her nose a bit, plumped up her lips, and fit her with blue eye-lenses. The package was beautiful, and looked nothing like the real Jorell.

Kane strolled the perimeter of the room without taking his attention off blonde Jorell who danced gracefully with his friend. Physical changes could not dim her appeal, or the energy that surrounded her. He wanted to mind-meld with her, to be close to her, but this was not the time.

Kane caught Nazar giving Leyana a come-on smile, and she returned the gesture, which made his stomach turn. He doubted he could hate anyone more than Nazar, but he had to keep his cool and maintain proper decorum.

Out the corner of his eye a pretty young woman gave him the look that begged for an invitation. He wanted to get closer to Leyana, so he walked over to the woman and asked her to dance. With a smile from ear to ear she offered him her hand.

He led her to the dance floor, and expertly paraded her around until they were next to Leyana and Nazar. Luckily his new partner just stared and remained silent. He smiled back and kept his gaze on her, but his ears were tuned to the conversation next to him.

"So tell me, Nazar, what plans do you have for Sector-Two now that you're the new ruler?"

"My plans depend on the other two Sectors."

Leyana looked Nazar in the eye. "Come now, you're much too smart to follow their lead. I've heard talk you'd like to see a one ruler planet, and I bet you have plans to fill that position." She giggled. "I love a powerful man."

Kane turned his partner's back to Jorell so he could see her face. He was thrilled she'd found such an innocent way to ask the burning question, but he did not care for the come-on look she saw. She was good at political games, he expected no less, but he hadn't expected such a convincing femme-fatal ruse. He was jealous, an entirely new feeling.

"I may have a few plans, but I'm not at liberty to discuss them. There's a long way to go before anything is settled."

"Of course. I hope I can be the first to congratulate you when the time comes."

"It would be my pleasure…aah…what's your name?"

"Leyana."

"Do you have a last name?"

"Do I need one?"

Nazar laughed. "Not really. Leyana is a beautiful name, for a beautiful woman." He reached out and stroked her hair. "I'll bet I can get you to tell me your last name." He moved his hand to her neck, then her shoulder.

Watching Nazar touch Jorell irritated him to the core, and he wanted to physically stop him by pounding him into the floor. However, Leyana was doing her job, and she delivered what would be expected. She was not portraying a professional-companion, simply a political groupie.

It had never bothered him in the past with other clients, but he knew from the moment they met that Jorell was different. He'd move mountains to make her happy. The woman in his arms cleared her throat, a subtle reminder he'd been ignoring her. "You dance very well."

"Thank you."

His partner did have good moves on the dance floor and seemed quite happy to dance with him. He should have worn his old man disguise, instead he'd worn his well-manicured moustache, small, partial beard with a longer than normal hair style. He'd always had good luck with the ladies while parading around in his rogue attire.

He looked down into the young woman's dark eyes. "I do apologize for being rude. My name is Liam Benak. And who is this lovely woman I'm dancing with?"

She chuckled. "I'm Mera Pollit. Senir is my father. He's—"

"The second in command to Ramon Coster, ruler of Sector-One."

"Correct. That isn't a problem is it?"

"Why would it be?" He watched the play of emotions on her young face. Without knowing, he'd picked the perfect dance partner.

"There are some who say my father and Ramon killed Marto Braxton just to take over Sector-One. My father would never do such a thing."

"I don't doubt your word, but you're right, many believe that."

"I'm not positive that Ramon...."Mera took a breath. "I'm sorry. I've said too much. I was instructed to dance and not talk."

"By your father?"

"And my mother. They think I'm too young to make any decisions for myself, and that I'm too young to understand politics. They're both wrong."

"I can see they are."

She laughed. "I knew I liked you for some reason."

Mera stared at him for the longest time, and he was afraid to know where her mind had wandered. She either said too much, or not enough. He wasn't sure which was better.

"I know I'm only nineteen annual-cycles, and you're older, but I don't see that as a problem, do you?"

It was his turn to remain quiet, at least long enough to think of the proper answer. "Mera, you're a very beautiful woman, and if I were younger I'd pursue you until you gave in. However, your father would never approve of me. Not tonight."

Mera sighed. "I knew you were going to say that, but I believe you.

After all, you did ask me to dance." She smiled. "So, tell me why you're here?"

"I'm an advisor for Sector-Three. But I haven't given much advice since they didn't allow me to attend the meeting. Were you there?"

"Of course. I never miss them. Is there something you need to know? I'd be happy to tell you. After all, nothing is a secret."

Little did she know the workings of politics. "Tell me what you think of all three rulers. It's always nice to hear someone else's opinion. Start with Sector-Three."

"Well, Alextor Sutone is getting up in years. Some say Rand Arroray actually runs the Sector. He's very handsome, don't you think?"

"You don't expect me to answer that, do you?"

"No." She giggled. "But I expect Rand will have to take over soon. Besides, Alextor is in very poor health."

"Who said that?"

"Over the last few days, about everyone I know. You're from Sector-Three, you tell me if it's true."

"You saw him for yourself today. He's fine. I haven't seen any problems with his health."

"Everyone can't be wrong."

"I suppose not." The music ended and he took Mera by the hand and escorted her back to where he found her. "Thank you for the dance, Mera."

Mera smiled. "Let's do it again?"

"It would be my honor." He half-bowed to her then turned and headed for blond-Jorell. An overpowering need to dance with her drove him through the crowd. When he couldn't find her panic surged through him. Someone might have seen through her disguise. He took a deep breath and kept walking, pushing aside negative thoughts. She was fine, she had to be.

Someone tapped him on the back and he turned so fast the person ran into him--the very blonde he was looking for. He sighed in relief. "I was worried about you. Where have you been?"

"And I thought you were too busy dancing with that lovely new friend of yours." Jorell smiled.

The music returned playing one of his favorite melodies. "May I have this dance, Ms. Leyana?"

"You may."

Kane offered her his arm and escorted her to the center of the floor. He slipped one arm around her waist and pulled her closer than he should, but he couldn't help himself. His other hand took hers and he tucked it between them, the warmth of her skin against his awakened the passion he so wanted to unleash on her.

"You seem different this moon-cycle."

"That's an understatement. If I'm not," he bent his mouth to her ear, "I've failed."

"I know what you mean." Jorell moved her lips to Kane's left ear. "I think you liked dancing with the little dark-haired flirt a bit too much."

He laughed. "You're jealous."

"Absolutely not. I'm engaged." She glanced around the ballroom. "To an invisible man."

"Invisible no, missing, yes."

Jorell nodded and rolled her eyes. For the first time he detected her feelings of distrust and displeasure for Rand. It was best he changed the subject. "What have you learned?"

"Nazar is full of himself. He intends to lead the entire planet if given the opportunity, and he's not one to leave anything to chance."

"And that applies to your family." The look on her face confirmed his statement, and he saw a flare of fight in her eyes. "We'll get whoever it is. I promise you."

"I believe you. I just hope we're on time."

"We'll be on time."

Jorell sighed. "Are you sure?"

Jorell laid her head against his chest. "Believe it." He kissed the top of her head and the sweet scent of exotic flowers tickled his senses. He inhaled her, every part of her, then tickled her mind and asked for entry to mind-meld.

"I hear you, Kane."

"Good. It's better to talk this way so no one can possibly hear us. But, my sweet, as much as I like your head on my chest you might want to pull back. People will talk about us, and we don't want that. The goal is to stay invisible."

"You should have thought of that before I danced with Nazar, the mmm...an with four hands?"

"That's an unusual number."

"Especially when they're wandering up and down your backside for an entire dance."

"Shall I try the same thing?" She pulled her head back and looked him in the eye with an expression that warned him not to try. *"I won't, but I'd certainly like to."*

"And I...I'd like you to."

He winked at her. "How much have you had to drink this moon-cycle?"

"Either not enough, or to...too much. I'm not sure which. Nazar gave me a drink of something, and it must have been really strong because I hav…haven't been the same since."

"I'll kill him."

"Not yet, we…we still need him."

"He is not what I need right now, my sweet." It would be so easy to seduce her in her present condition, but he'd never take advantage of her. If he ever made love to her, he wanted her fully awake and willing.

"I guess you might be rrr…right. I drank at Nazar's urging. He tried to make me ta…take care of him, if you kn…know what I mean."

"I will kill him."

"Don't b…be like that. He was only flirting and tr…treating me nnn…nice."

"Too nice." Her head fell against his chest again, so he danced her closer to one of the open doorways. *"Stay with me, Jorell."*

"My na…name is Leyanaaaa…."

So much for the mind-meld. She'd blurted her name quite loudly, but he whisked her outside so fast no one noticed. She scowled at him and he had difficulty restraining his anger. Jorell was unable to walk, or speak clearly at the moment. He'd always enjoyed all the silly faces she made, but not now under the influence of some sex drug.

Kane picked her up in his arms, stepped over the ground level balcony railing and briskly walked into the dark part of the surrounding gardens. He had to get her out of public view before she said the wrong thing to the wrong person. He took a deep breath and checked the area.

There was a bench under a tree a short distance from the walkways, yet sheltered in darkness. He carefully checked the area around him, then carried her to the bench.

"You seem to be making a ha…habit of carrying me around. I think you lii…like it."

"You have a habit of needing to be carried." He sat her in the center of the bench then took a seat next to her, careful to keep his distance. One never knew when someone might stroll by, and he didn't want to give surveillance vids a bigger show than necessary.

"I'm sorrrrry, Kane. I shouldn't have drrrrrank so much, but Nazar in…insisted. I was trr…rying to get information out of him. When he trrr…ied to kiss me, I turned my head and he got re…really mad. He didn't hit me, but he wan…ted to. He said no one de…denies Nazar anything!"

"Don't worry about it." He watched her eyes close and he knew the drugs had finally rendered her unconscious. This was a problem. He couldn't leave her alone so he used his special locator button on his wrist-com and activated it to summon Dobie.

Kane heard footsteps in the brush behind him, then a man cleared his throat.

"I thought as much!"

It was over. He'd been caught. When he turned he groaned. "I hate when you do that!" Dobie stood in the dark grinning like a catamoos, his white teeth gleaming in the moonlight.

"Sorry, Chief. I didn't mean to sneak up on you, but you did summon *me*." Dobie looked at the bench. "What happened?"

"Nazar drugged her and I have to get her out of here fast."

"You'd better let me take her home since there's a really cute girl in there that has a crush on you and she knew where you'd gone."

"Damn. I never should have promised her another dance."

"If you get back in there now she'll be thrilled and no one will notice." Dobie looked around. "That little girl is quite a handful.

"Fine. You take Jorell back to our place and I'll go finish the evening. But I want you to stay with Jorell and set the high security level." Kane shook his head. "Nazar gave her Keyotin."

"The rape drug? Why that…"

"Save it. I'll deal with him at an appropriate time."

Dobie groaned. "I'll help you."

"In the meantime you'd better get going."

"And you need to get back to your little sweetie."

Dobie chuckled while Kane turned and hurried back toward the open doors where the silhouette of a woman waved at him.

CHAPTER NINETEEN

The closer he got to the exterior patio, the faster Mera waved. He certainly hoped she had more information to reveal since being with her was no easy task. Young, excitable women could be quite troublesome. Especially when his heart had already left the party.

The smile Mera gave him would light an entire room. Too bad it was not for a man who had an eye for her. Using people would always be the downside of his business. There were times he hated his job. He smiled while he hurried up the side stairs.

"Didn't think I'd see you again, Liam."

"I'd never leave without that dance I promised you." His words lit her face. He offered his arm, which she willingly accepted, and hung on so tightly he doubted he'd ever get away from her again. He guided her onto the dance floor, where people twirled by, laughing and enjoying the evening.

Once in motion, Mera eagerly put her arms around his neck and pressed her body against his. The music was slow, and his young partner had consumed a substantial amount of intoxicants. Her eyes were glazed-over, and she floated in happiness. This was the perfect opportunity to dig deeper into her memory. "Tell me, Mera, what have you been up to this moon-cycle?"

"Wouldn't you like to know. You're such a big, bad boy." She giggled.

"You have no idea, my dear." Her cheeks turned red, a sure sign she talked the talk, but had never walked the walk. No way would he be her first. "So what gossip have you heard tonight? I love juicy stories."

"Let me think." Mera tilted her head back and rolled it from side to side. "I heard that Jorell Sutone has no idea who she's planning to life-mate. That Rand fellow is really a ladies' man." She winked. "If you know what I mean."

"I have a good idea."

"They say he'll make love to any woman, any time. I wasn't sure if I believed them until I saw him sneak off with some brown-haired woman. He must be pretty good because they were gone for a long time."

"Is that all you heard?"

"Hardly."

He watched Mera check to see who danced close to her. Whatever she'd heard must be important to send the young, intoxicated woman into paranoia. He whirled her in a few circles, and she giggled like the young girl she was before she leaned closer.

"You know, Nazar?" Mera stroked Kane's cheek with her hand. "Well, I heard he wants to be the single ruler of Okeron, and that he's willing to do anything to make it happen." She giggled. "Maybe I should be dancing with him?"

Mera lost her balance and he immediately caught her around the waist and pulled her tightly against him to keep her from falling to the floor. It seemed she could no longer control the movement of her legs, He doubted she could walk by herself. "Maybe you should. Who told you that?"

"Some woman who's been sleeping with him. Don't know her name." She shook her head. "I also heard my father talking to my mother, and he told her the same thing. So if you hear it twice, it must be a fact. Right?"

"Right. Did you hear how they plan to get rid of Ruler Sutone?"

"No."

"Where did your father first hear that?"

"He knows people. Why are you so inquisitive?"

"It's just the way I am."

"I like the way you are." Mera moved her hands over his shoulders and upper arms. "You're so...solid."

When her hands moved lower, he moved them back up to his shoulders. "Now who's being inquisitive?" Her legs wobbled so bad he held her tighter, and a bit higher to keep her feet off the floor and continued to dance. Good thing her gown was long so no one noticed.

He needed to distract her. "I've heard your original ruler, Marto Braxton was murdered. Most believe his air accident wasn't an accident." Her eyes closed and he wondered if she'd gone to sleep or passed out. Finally she opened them and blinked heavily several times.

"We think it was murder, but there's no proof, and…and…an…"

Out cold. He tried to wake her, but to no avail. He half-danced, half-carried her to the corner behind them. Luckily an upholstered chair with a high back and padded arms that half circled around was available. He set her on the chair, and positioned her so she wouldn't fall over. Everyone in the ballroom seemed occupied with their respective partners and friends. It was the perfect time to disappear.

****

Jorell tried to open her eyes, but her head pounded too hard. At the moment, she struggled to remember where she was and what she'd been doing. Or was everything a dream?

"Jorell?"

"What?" The voice sounded familiar yet she couldn't place who spoke to her. She concentrated hard and forced her eyes open. A long, slow glance around the room revealed she was alone. So, where was the voice coming from?

"Jorell. It's time to join the living."

"Who are you? Where are you?" It seemed as if someone was behind her, hitting the back of her head with a metal rod. She could barely focus let alone think who called her.

"It's Kane, and I'm in the galley fixing lunch. So get your pretty little self up and join us."

"Why do I want to do that?"

"You need to eat."

"Don't mention food again this sun-cycle."

"Sorry, but you have to eat."

She looked for the com speaker, but couldn't locate it. "No."

"If you're not out here before I count to fifty, I'm coming after you, and you might regret that."

"Fine!" The moment she yelled her answer she regretted it immensely since the sound reverberated in her head and sent shooting pains to her temples and forehead.

"I've started counting."

"Good for you." After a deep breath she managed to sit up and swing legs off the bed. She was dizzy, nauseous, and exhausted. Last moon-cycle's events slowly floated through her consciousness. She had a vague memory of Kane asking her to dance, but she didn't remember being on the dance floor, or anything else after his request.

When she stood she could not stop the ugly groan that escaped. It took complete concentration to put one foot in front of the other and not fall flat on her face. She grabbed a robe draped over the back of the chair by the door, slipped it on, and then opened the door.

Step by difficult step, she made her way down the hall and into the galley. The smell of cooking food overwhelmed her and she made a mad dash for the sink and waited. Nothing came up, but it wasn't for a lack of trying. Her stomach turned several more summersaults.

"A little under the weather this sun-cycle?"

She turned to look at Kane, which was a big mistake. Her hands gripped the edge of the sink while her stomach once again tried to empty itself, and the throbbing in her head escalated exponentially with every heave. The expression on his face was somewhere between 'should have known better', and genuine concern.

This was the worst hangover she'd ever had, even if it was only the second one she'd ever experienced. Surely *no* day-after could be worse than this current torture. Her legs wobbled and shook and she started to sink toward the floor. Before her knees hit ground, two strong, muscular arms wrapped around her.

Kane to the rescue. Again. With one arm under her back and one under her legs, he swept her against his chest and carried her to a chair at the table where he gently put her down. Once the room stopped spinning she looked at Kane's distressed expression, eyes squinted, jaw clamped tight. "What?" He didn't answer. "What are you looking at?"

"You. Nazar gave you more than wine. Would you allow me to test your blood?"

"Why not. It couldn't make me feel any worse." She kept her gaze on Kane while he briefly stood, pulled a small pouch from a drawer, then tossed it on the table before shutting the drawer. The tiny velvet bag hit the table and sounded like a small explosion.

"I know you've had this done before, and you know it won't hurt." Kane pulled a box from the cloth bag.

She placed her finger inside the round hole at the end of the small rectangular device. It was jokingly referred to as a 'lab-box' because it could detect nearly every chemical known, except the one given to her father. All it read when the doctor tested him was 'unknown substance'.

A needle inside made contact with her fingertip so fast it was over at the same time it began. Lights flashed on and off inside the top view-screen, and she held her breath while she waited for the little beep that indicated the test was complete. "What does it say?"

She watched Kane shake his head and grit his teeth, then slam his fist on the table. This was the angriest she'd ever seen him, and she wasn't sure how to calm him down. "What?"

"I swear I'll kill him." He stood and paced the small galley. "Someone needs to stop him, and I volunteer for the job."

"Who? For what?" He kept pacing and shaking his head.

Kane paused and looked directly into Jorell's eyes. "Nazar put a sexual stimulant in your drink. Commonly referred to on the street as the 'no-protest' pill."

"That's the rape drug, isn't it?" Kane nodded. "Damn him! But it didn't work, or at least I don't think it did."

"Exactly." He sat down and took Jorell's hand in his. "The drug works as an aphrodisiac, but if the dose is too high it can cause severe cramps, nausea, dizziness, and an extreme headache, which leads to unconsciousness, and the perpetrator takes his victim unconscious. Either way, it's a 'no-protest' situation."

"You rescued me so nothing happened." She looked into his eyes. "At least that's my last conscious memory."

Kane took a deep breath. "Luckily I was there, but his intentions were clear, and he's sadistically reprehensible!" He stood and walked across the galley. "I'll make him pay, Jorell. You can count on that."

The serious, calculated and controlled threat sent a shiver down her spine. He meant every word, and she knew him well enough to know how dangerous he could be. "Easy Kane. You can't make him pay without revealing yourself."

Jorell watched him pace the room, his hands fisted at his sides, his anger barely leashed. "You're a careful man. Don't exact revenge first, and think last." Dobie walked to the empty chair next to her and sat. He leaned his head close to her ear.

"He hasn't done anything stupid for quite some time, and he won't now. Trust me." He pointed at Kane. "Trust him."

"I trust you both. I'm just out of patience. I feel like I've been gone for weeks, and I have no idea if my father is dead or alive. And to top it off I just learned I was so close to being raped I think I need a shower." Jorell shook her head. "I hope breaking that wine bottle changed something."

Kane rubbed his chin and stared at Dobie. "We jump forward ninety sun-cycles from the date of origin. That should allow ample time for everything to be set."

Dobie scratched his head. "I agree."

"You'll make all the necessary adjustments upon our return."

"Timing is critical."

"What are the two of you trying to say?" She glanced at Kane who paced once again deep in thought. "Dobie?"

"If we go too far we'll run into too much change, and that confuses things. We've learned the hard way too many times."

"I'll be with you so--"

"He will not allow that."

"How do you know?"

"Think, Jorell." Dobie paused for a moment. "If you were to see something in the future that you did not expect, it might--"

Jorell held up her hand. "I get it. I'd know my father was dead and you two would not know what to do with me."

"Let's just say you could become emotionally paralyzed, which could put us all in jeopardy."

"I understand, and lucky for you, I'm too wiped out to argue. I'm going back to bed."

CHAPTER TWENTY

Kane paced the length of the living area floor for the thousandth time. Jorell was sleeping off the drug hangover Nazar provided for her, and Dobie was working on critical time calculations. He should get some sleep himself, but he could not quiet his contempt for Nazar that still surged through every vein in his body.

The Academy days were back to haunt him, only now the stakes were higher, and more personal. Why did fate throw Nazar in his face yet again? No matter. Any man who drugged a woman for sex deserved to be punished, and he'd take pleasure in making Nazar pay.

He still couldn't place the grey haired man who'd been in the bar with Nazar. Anyone who conferred with Nazar was suspect. The man had an air of controlled leadership, which meant experience had taught him well. Men who collaborated to overthrow a government did it for power, wealth, and control.

Okeron had enjoyed peace for over thirty-two annual-cycles. All three Sectors abided by the treaty until—what? Was the question "What?" or "Who?"

What was the underlying reason for the unrest? Was it one man's greedy ambition? Or was it a group of men who wanted riches? Whoever, or whatever force was behind the takeover had to be stopped. When Jorell first talked about saving her father, the thought of holding the peace of the entire planet in his hands had not been foremost in his mind.

At least Jorell and her father shared a close relationship. She knows what he stands for, what makes him tick. All he ever knew about his birth mother was that she died giving him life, and his father left the planet. If it hadn't been for Eunis *The Mage,* as she was called, he would have gone to an orphan-station.

Instead, Eunis raised him as her son. They may have been alone in the mountains, but Eunis gave him all the love and tutoring any child could want. He'd imagined her with him always, until she was brutally murdered before his eyes on his twelfth annual-cycle.

Never would he forget what the man looked like. He was very tall and muscular, but he was young then, so all adults towered over him. However, the one thing he'd never forget was a snake tattoo that wrapped around the man's right arm, with its mouth open, fangs showing, and venom dripping from long, sharp teeth.

He saw the tattoo when Eunis sliced his shirt with a knife during the fight. The bully ripped off the cut sleeve, and when he did, that horrible snake looked at him as if it were real, and he was dinner. That snake wrapped around the man's right upper arm, coiled down until its head ended the long body with a forked tongue on his forearm. When the man pointed at Eunis, he'd thought the ugly snake could fly off his arm and strike her.

Twelve had been an odd age for him. Almost a man, but still a vulnerable child who needed the love and care of at least one person. He knew exactly how devastated Jorell would be if she lost her father. Even now the emotional turmoil that had nearly destroyed him as a child remained fresh in his mind and heart.

Of course Jorell was an adult and he'd been a child, but she'd still fall into a pit of despair since the heart did not consider age, only the emotional loss.

He stopped pacing to study Jorell's sleeping form on the sofa. Long, beautiful, red hair lay provocatively on her shoulders and framed the fair complexion of her face. The hint of freckles on her cheeks brought out a natural beauty he found irresistible.

To say he was attracted to her would be an understatement of gigantic proportions. Even while she slept her energy pulled him closer and closer. If he wasn't careful, he'd make an utter fool of himself, unable to keep his hands off her. There had been plenty of women over the annual-cycles and tides of time, but never like this.

He took a seat in the large, upholstered chair across from the sofa where Jorell slept. When he'd carried her in his arms he'd wished he was taking her to his bed to make love all moon-cycle. Rand was a lucky man who didn't appreciate the real prize. Jorell was sexy, caring, sexy, smart, sexy, and loving. He had to get Jorell and sex off his mind.

He closed his eyes and willed his body to relax. Jorell remained in his thoughts. Maybe their complete mind-melding ability had a lasting effect that enabled him to see and feel her intimately on a level he never dreamed existed.

Jorell was a woman he admired in so many ways. He loved looking at her, touching her, but he also knew in his soul she was honest and loving, qualities not often found in such an adorable package. Even his very soul felt as if it had found its true mate.

He commanded his mind to be still, to forget about Jorell long enough to rest. If he didn't sleep he could end up jumping into the wrong century.

****

Jorell stretched and nearly fell off the sofa. Her back ached from whatever position she'd slept in. She sat up and found Kane asleep in the chair across from her. He looked so peaceful, so handsome, and so very dangerous. His physical features were intimidating. Even his clothes couldn't hide the contours of his muscles, or the power behind them.

From the moment she'd seen Kane she'd been attracted to him. No matter how she'd tried to deny the charismatic energy that danced between them, it was there. She wanted to run her hands over his rock-hard muscles, and feel the barely-leashed energy that flowed through him. She did not have to see him fight to know he could best any man.

It was painful to admit, but Rand had never set her senses on fire like Kane, nor did he make her so nervous at times she could barely function. She'd only been like that around one person; however, she was sixteen annual-cycles at the time, and that boy was a cadet from the military Academy. It had been a special formal dance planned between the girls' Academy and the boys' Academy.

The most handsome boy there had asked her to dance, and they spent the entire moon-cycle together, either entwined on the dance floor, or out in the garden. It was a magical moon-cycle, one she wished had never ended. But it did, like all good things, never to be experienced again. She'd thought about that boy many times, but never saw or heard from him again. He had affected her the same as Kane. She'd waited and waited to experience that feeling with Rand, but as of this moment, she was still waiting.

Rand was a safe pick, and her father had all but told her to take him as a life-mate. Why he'd pushed the union was still a mystery, but she'd honor her father's desire for the union.

She stood and took a few steps toward Kane. He slept like a baby, but he didn't look innocent. He needed his rest, and she was hungry so she headed for the galley. Just when she passed his chair his hand grabbed her wrist and his eyes opened.

Kane let go of her. "Sorry. It's an acquired reflex."

"I didn't mean to startle, or wake you. I'm feeling better and decided to get something to eat."

"That's a great idea. Mind if I join you?"

"Please. I hate eating alone." He smiled at her and her insides turned summersaults like they always did when she was around him. Why did he have such an overpowering effect on her? She followed him toward the galley.

Kane stepped into the room and the lights came on. "What are you in the mood for?"

"Whatever you're having, but I really need a cup of koffa."

"Coming right up."

By the time she seated herself on a tall stool at the eat-bar in the center of the room, Kane placed a steaming cup of koffa in front of her. She loved to inhale the rich aroma. After a couple of sips her body relaxed a bit.

"How's your headache?" Kane sat on the stool next to her.

"Better, thanks. I don't know what you gave me, but it certainly worked."

"I call it an old family recipe."

She smiled at the look on his face which was between 'I'll never tell' and 'you don't want to know'. "So, what have you and Dobie decided we do next?"

"First we take you home, then Dobie and I jump to the future. Whoever has taken charge will be the one we're after."

"You're sure of that?" She watched Kane nod. "You don't want me along?" Kane stared at her, his blue eyes filled with stubborn determination, and she knew better than to argue, but she had to know. "Why not?"

"You need to get back before your absence changes the present, which will change the future as well."

"I don't see how my presence makes much difference one way or the other. My father is the ruler, not me. I only assist him, and right now there's nothing for me to do."

"Right now excuses are being made as to why you're currently missing. If you go with us, you could learn, I mean you would see--"

"Kane, Dobie explained it to me. I get it."Kane reached across the marbelus counter and took her hand in his. Warmth immediately spread through her, and her body begged for his touch.

"Everything we do creates a ripple in time, like a stone tossed into a puddle. Ripples can vary from a tiny wave to a tsunami. However, even the tiniest ripple spreads and grows, like a boulder dropped in a lake."

She hung her head and tried to wrap her mind around the explanation. "I've never pondered how one thought, or action, contributes to, or changes the future." He squeezed her hand in reassurance. "I understand what you're saying, but I hate to be left behind."

Without letting go of her hand, Kane stood, put his arms around her and pulled her close to his chest. Her heart raced at the closeness and she could barely breathe. Then he dropped his head and kissed her like she'd never been kissed before. Seductive, tempting, strong, yet gentle.

A deep groan emanated from his chest, and he tightened his hold. His strength radiated through her clothes and flowed into her body. It was an experience like no other. She'd swear she was floating on air, and she'd never experienced such a sensation of protection. His tongue pressed, explored and teased while he promised more.

This time the groan came from her. She wanted him in the worst way; she wanted him in her bed, and in her. That thought was real, and she'd never burned for a man before, yet reality slammed into her. With regret so deep it hurt, she ended the kiss she so desperately wanted and took a step back.

"I shouldn't have done that." He returned to his seat. "But I won't apologize."

"Don't be sorry for something we both wanted." He stared at her for a moment then smiled. May the Gods forgive her. "I believe you should take me home so you can make your jump." She looked away before he noticed her sadness. She did not want him to leave her behind.

Kane stood, his eyes focused on her. Then the familiar, intimate tickle began in her mind. She smiled and he gave her the cutest little nod she'd ever seen, a nod that could only be described as a come-on.

"Jorell, my sweet, you need to relax. Trust me. I *will* save your father. I won't let you down. I promise."

"Your words are comforting, and so is the energy you're passing to me. I appreciate it, I really do." She dropped her gaze to the floor for a moment, then back up to Kane's handsome face. "It's just hard when all the odds are against us." He tipped his head, a move she'd learned he did to silently agree. How could she read him so well? "I'm sorry. I'm just tired."

Kane pulled her into his arms and guided her head to his chest. She loved the feel of his arms around her, and the strength he fed her so willingly. The steady beat of his heart soothed her jittery nerves, and the warmth of his body enveloped her like a safety blanket. "Thank you,

Kane."

"I'd do anything for you."

She lifted her head and looked into the depths of his soulful eyes. His words were sincere and meaningful, especially when they were sent from his thoughts to hers. "*I know. You're an honorable man.*" Talking with him through a mind-meld became easier each time, and the intensity of the words became so much greater, as if his thoughts and feelings were her own.

"I feel you, my sweet. All of you."

A smile tugged the sides of her mouth. "It's like we become one person instead of two."

"Exactly." He rubbed his hands up and down her back. "We could become even closer."

Jorell had to make sure he couldn't 'peek' into her thoughts any more than he had. "*What I'd like, and what I'll do are two different things.*" Kane released her and stepped back. She immediately suffered the loss.

"*Rand is a lucky man, and you are an honorable woman.*" Kane walked to the galley entrance, paused and turned slightly. "Get some rest. We'll jump early in the next sun-cycle."

Kane turned and left her alone in the galley, more alone than he'd ever know, and he'd just taken her heart with him leaving her soul crying for its mate.

****

Kane's wrists were burned badly, but he held on to Dobie. Jorell stood against him, her arms around his waist, her head on his chest. Taking two people with him strained the limits of his energy. He concentrated on the back garden, the only area not heavily covered by image collectors.

The heat was nearly unbearable. Sparks bounced off his Vambrace Cuffs, protecting them from the intense energy that attacked anyone who tore through the time curtain. The overwhelming sensation of falling through space at the speed of light made him dizzy. It was difficult to concentrate with Jorell's firm breasts pressed against his chest.

Even more than her tempting body he sensed her trepidation. She was afraid she'd find her father dead. He couldn't blame her for worrying about that possible scenario, nor could he tell her everything was fine. Before he could worry more, the landing was before them. He braced himself for the touchdown.

When he hit the ground he rolled, Jorell still in his arms. Dobie had rolled in the opposite direction, but one quick glance said they were both fine. He thanked the stars for a better than anticipated landing. He rose to his feet and pulled Jorell up with him. Dobie quickly walked over to him, and all three of them silently followed Jorell toward the ruling family's quarters.

It was a long walk, and it seemed longer since they maintained their distance and silence. They did not want to appear *together* on security vids.

"It sucks, I know." Dobie kept his gaze forward while he walked next to Kane. "Even if you could talk to her, what would you say? What could anyone say that would help right now?"

"You're right partner, it's total frustration."

"I've researched poison so much my brain is ready to explode."

"Can I watch?" He slapped Dobie on the back. "Sorry, I couldn't resist."

Dobie chuckled. "It's been a while since we've joked about anything. We're better when we do."

"I agree. It just doesn't seem appropriate around Jorell while she's mourning her father's situation." Dobie nodded his reply while they entered the building.

Dobie leaned closer to Kane. "You told her we'd save him, didn't you?"

"Of course, but would you believe us if you didn't understand how time travel works?"

"I suppose not. But I do, and I believe we can save him."

"We can, and we *will*." Kane watched Jorell enter Alextor's quarters, and after a quick check of the surrounding area, he and Dobie followed her inside, then down the hall into Alextor's bedchamber. He and Dobie stood behind her while she kissed him on the forehead and tucked a few hairs behind his ear. Alextor's skin had less color than when they left, but he was breathing.

"Jorell, we're so glad to see you, but we thought you'd be gone at least a couple of sun-cycles."

Kane watched the expressions on Jorell's, Alesa's and Ariel's faces. They all looked at each other with surprise, and unanswered questions.

"How long have I been gone? Seems I've lost track."

"Only four time-units. It's not even dark yet."

Jorell looked at the time display on the wall. "I thought I'd been gone longer."

Alesa walked up to Jorell. "We brought enough stuff for several sun-cycles. Are you sure you don't need us? We'll be happy to stay if you have other duties to perform."

"I appreciate your help more than you know. Right now I'll stay with him, but I'll call when I need you, if that's okay?"

"That's fine. We're available anytime."

Jorell hugged Alesa, then Ariel. "Thank you both. Go now. Have fun. I put a few extra credits in your accounts. I know you both love to shop."

"That certainly wasn't necessary, but we thank you." Alesa laughed. "We do love shopping."

"I know. Get going. You don't want the shops to close before you get there."

The two sisters left and Jorell all but fell into the chair beside her father's bed. She looked tired, mentally and physically. "You need rest."

"I can't believe it." Jorell shook her head. "How can that be?" She looked up at Kane. "Is it true?"

Kane nodded. "I told you time passed differently."

"I know, but the reality of being gone over two sun-cycles and being told it was four time-units leaves a person in shock."

He smiled. "It is hard to get used to, even for us."

"Yup." Dobie stepped closer to Jorell. "Are either of your friends available? Or are they life-mated?"

"Dobie, I'm surprised."

Kane shook his head. "I'm not."

Dobie slapped Kane on the back. "Just asking."

"About something you don't have time for." Kane turned toward Jorell. "We're going now. I don't know how long we'll be gone, but we'll be back as soon as possible. Hopefully we'll bring back good news."

"Just hurry. I don't know how much longer he has." She looked at her father then back at Kane. "Be careful."

Kane turned toward Dobie and gave him the look.

"I'll wait outside." Dobie quickly left.

He waited for the door to close, then bent down and kissed Jorell. She reached up and threaded her arms around his neck. He deepened the kiss, tasting her, and wishing he could explore every inch of her. He desperately wanted to experience what their rare and special level of bonding could bring.

Before he lost complete control and took her in the chair, he ended the kiss then straightened. "Duty calls, my sweet." He had to remind himself to respect Jorell's commitment to Rand since it still stood between them.

"Jorell, promise me, while I'm gone you'll stay close to people you trust, and don't put yourself in harm's way by wandering around alone.

It's more than possible whoever did this to your father might try something with you."

"I'm no threat to anyone."

"In your opinion."

"Okay. I'll be careful." Jorell stood. "Please hurry back. Time is running out."

CHAPTER TWENTY ONE

Dobie poured them both a second glass of wine and he watched the dark red liquid swirl, then turn calm in the stemmed glass. If only problems settled that easily. "I'm worried, Dob."

"So am I." Dobie held his glass up in front of him. "Toast. To a successful jump, and may it be productive, but uneventful."

"Here, here." He and Dobie clanged glasses, then took long drinks. "Something about this jump doesn't feel right. I can't explain it."

"I'm not as psychic, but I feel it too." Dobie took another drink. "It must be Nazar. That man gives me the creeps. As long as we've known him, he still makes me nervous, even when he doesn't know it's me."

"I know he teased you mercilessly at Academy."

"Every sun-cycle of every annual-cycle we were there!" Dobie groaned. "You beat him up pretty good many times. I still thank you for that. I loved seeing Nazar's eyes black, his lip bloody, and even a few crooked teeth. It did my heart good." He poured more wine.

Kane took another drink. "We had our differences. And believe it or not, it wasn't always about you."

"I'm crushed." Dobie stared at his friend. "What about now? Can we beat him up again for old time's sake?"

He laughed. "If it were only that simple. We need to find out who Nazar answers to."

"If anyone can, it's you. So, are we ready to jump?"

"Ready as I'm ever going to be. Besides if I stay here any longer I'll finish that bottle of wine." He took one last drink then stood. "Let's go."

"Should we take anything with us?"

"We're jumping from here and landing here. All we need to do is time jump."

"Convenient." Dobie stood, walked over to Kane and grasped his arms. "Let's do it."

Kane nodded and grasped Dobie's forearms. This was no time to lose a friend. He closed his eyes and concentrated on the date ninety suncycles in the future. It didn't take much to picture landing exactly where they were standing.

The air around him started to swirl, and the familiar crackling sound filled his senses. His wrist bands quickly warmed, and the pressure of moving through the energy walls that separated dimensions and time pressed down on him.

Sparks bounced off the metal cuffs, and the heat became nearly unbearable. He figured they should be about to land since their jump was short. Instead of the usual lightning of the atmosphere around them it became darker.

A sinister feeling of doom closed over him and he tightened the circle of protection he always held in place in case of intruding negativity. The 'dark side', as many called it, was always within easy reach should he choose that avenue, but evil never tempted him. Eunis had told him about the sweet song of malevolence and he recognized it instantly.

The falling sensation continued, and everything became black around him. He held Dobie tighter and concentrated on the destination. He visualized the date in huge numbers and held it foremost in his mind. His only reward was hitting one wall after another. It was as if someone had erected an impassable barrier between him and the future.

Never had this happened. Why now? He refused to be distracted. Dobie's skin was cold to his touch and he began to worry about his friend. "Dobie, can you hear me?" Nothing. "Dobie!"

Dobie's knees buckled and he slumped in his arms, then he began to fall from his grasp. In order to save Dobie he had to stop the jump. He focused on the moment they left until the pull of Okeron's energy grasped him and the familiar white energy pulled them back.

They returned faster than he'd planned and he held Dobie's lifeless body while they slammed into the unforgiving floor. He could no longer hold Dobie, and he rolled away from him. He scooted next to his friend and rolled him onto his back. "Dobie, open your eyes. Come on, open your eyes!" He waited, his patience exhausted. "Dobie!"

"You're yelling at me." Dobie opened his eyes. "What happened?"

Kane helped Dobie sit up, then squatted next to him on the floor. "Someone stopped our jump."

"That's never happened before. How is that even possible?"

"I'm not sure, but if I had to guess, I'd say there was someone out there waiting for us who has equal, or superior abilities to mine."

"That's scary, and amazing at the same time." Dobie shook his head. "Who? Certainly not Nazar."

"No, I've matched wits with him before, and he's not that strong."

"Do you know anyone stronger than you?"

"No, but I have a feeling I'm about to meet him."

****

Jorell took a deep breath, straightened in the chair and smoothed her gown. All she'd done since Kane and Dobie left was fight the need to cry her eyes out. It was all she felt like doing, even if it helped nothing.

Kane and Dobie were in the future right now learning who put her father in this near-state of death. That's what it was since she couldn't call it life. He had no idea she was here, nor could he function on any level.

The best she could hope for was that Kane would either find a cure, or erase her father's poisoning from ever happening. Even if he found a cure, she feared there could be permanent damage.

It seemed impossible to miss Kane already, but she did, and it was only one time-unit later. What was it about the man that made her want him with her all the time? She stood and walked into the lav and splashed water on her face. She looked in the mirror and faced a sad woman who would cheat on her fiancé if given the opportunity.

What did that say about her? How would Rand react if he knew? Would he care enough to be angry? She really did not know Rand. She'd worked side-by-side with him the past three annual-cycles, yet knew nothing about his private life, except what he did with her. Although now she knew what he did behind her back, which was a betrayal to her.

A tickle touched her mind and she wondered how Kane could reach her from the future. An overpowering sensation of evil washed over her so strongly it blurred her image in the mirror. Her legs became weak and wobbled. She grabbed the countertop to hold herself up and wondered how long this horrifying feeling would last.

Never had she experienced blackness or gloom while mind-melding with Kane. No, this had all the signs of a psychic attack. Then she heard a male voice in her mind, a wicked voice that shook her entire body. She strengthened the barrier around her thoughts so whoever begged entrance would be stopped.

"Submit Jorell Sutone. Listen to my words."

The wicked voice was clear and insistent. *"Who are you?"*

"That doesn't matter."

"I think it does." She put up another wall, and yet another to keep this villain away. She prayed for the strength to keep him out. This malevolent being could possess a person's mind, and render them insane.

"You think you're smart, but you will fail!"

She remembered Kane talking about the Energy-Lamia, and she searched every corner of her memory for exactly what he said that would ward off this demon before he could..."

"I heard that thought. You can't get rid of me!"

The best thing she could do was ignore the intruder. She would not give him more power than he already had. Who could possibly mind-meld with her from a distance like this? She ran into the other room to check the security vid screen. Nothing. Not even a maid or a messenger was about in the surrounding area.

"You can't escape me, Jorell. I'm too powerful. You'll soon see things my way. I could use someone with your talents when I'm the supreme ruler."

She was so angry she could explode. She had as many unanswered questions as she had things to say to this evil intruder, but she bit her tongue and maintained her silence.

"Those two men who are helping you are no challenge to me. You know that, don't you?"

The voice laughed loud and long, mocking her and everything she stood for. The laugh seemed to last forever before the sound of heinous mockery faded away and the darkness dissipated.

Dear stars. She sank to the floor. That nefarious presence had managed to suck every ounce of her energy, and if given the chance, would have taken her soul as well. This attack was so different from the first that there was no comparison.

"Kane. Where are you when I need you?" The evil had drained every ounce of her energy. She lay on her back and long-held tears rolled down the side of her face. Everyone had a breaking point, and she'd just met hers.

She'd tried to help her father, but so far she'd only met failure. Kane and Dobie pretended to be encouraged after their mutual jump, but she knew better. They couldn't very well tell her they'd failed after the exorbitant amount of credits she'd paid them.

The tears she couldn't stop managed to soak the hair on both sides of her head, yet she didn't have the strength to get up off the floor. Nothing mattered right now. How could she help her father when she couldn't even lift her little finger?

Her eyelids became heavy and she could no longer keep them open. How long would she have to lay here before someone found her? Doctor Willock was scheduled to arrive next sun-cycle.

Even worse, if she died, who would stop a global war?

CHAPTER TWENTY TWO

"Jorell!" Kane knelt on the floor next to Jorell's limp body, picked her up and pulled her into his arms. She was cold, unconscious and unresponsive. He carried her out of her father's room into the main living area and laid her on the sofa. He turned his gaze toward Dobie. "Check the quarters, then stay with Alextor."

"Right away, Chief."

Kane walked into the galley, found a cloth, ran it under the water-feed then returned to Jorell and wiped her face. She started to moan a bit and move her head from side to side. Thank the Gods she was alive. "Jorell. Wake up. Please, my sweet, open your eyes."

Her eyes opened and she looked straight at him. She raised one hand and touched his cheek. Slowly her fingers trailed down his neck then her arm fell and she lost contact.

"What did you call me?"

"My sweet." She gave him an approving smile. He picked up her hand and squeezed. "You're shaking."

"Kane, please, help me sit up."

He slipped his arm behind her back and pulled her to a sitting position then sat next to her. "Now, what happened?" She stared at him, but could not hide the fear in her eyes. "Did someone break in and hurt you?"

"Not exactly." She took a deep breath. "Remember the psychic attack we experienced before we left?" Kane nodded. "Well, the same dark energy returned, and he talked to me through a mind-meld. I don't know how he managed it, but he did. I fought him, I really did."

"I know." He rubbed her back with his hand. "What did he say?"

"He told me to submit." Jorell took a deep breath. "He said he was going to be the supreme ruler of Okeron."

Jorell's statement didn't shock him, but he was shocked a Lamia would admit it to Jorell. He'd assumed one man was behind the conspiracy, and this sounded like proof. "Anything else?"

"He said you and Dobie were no threat to him, and that we will all fail because he is more powerful." Jorell shook her head. "Kane, I'm scared. Whoever that was is evil, and he intends to create more evil."

Kane pulled her into his arms and held her shaking body against his. She began to cry, but after her experience she needed to release pent up emotions. He learned long ago that even strong women needed to shed tears once in a while. He enjoyed the feel of her against him, but her sobs pulled at his soul. He wanted to help her, to make everything right, yet this dark energy plagued all progress.

"Jorell, I *will* destroy this man, whoever he is." He tilted her chin up with one finger. "Never fear the unknown, and never give up. Save your despair, Princess. It will be he who is disappointed, not you."

"How can you say that? If you're wrong--"

"I'm right. Evil can only thrive where it is allowed. Evil can only take what is given, and fear is a giver. Therefore, never fear, just fight. Fight for what you believe in, and for those you love."

Jorell pulled away from Kane and stood. "Your advice is very noble. I only wonder how practical it is." She began to pace. "If it were that easy to stop evil it would have been eradicated long ago." She paused and looked Kane in the eye. "But evil is still here, isn't it? And you don't know how to stop it, do you?"

Kane stood and stepped in front of Jorell. "I may not know how to stop this man, but I know someone who might."

"Who?"

"Eunis, the woman who raised me."

"That's great. We'll have her brought here immediately."

"That's not possible. She's dead."

"What help could a dead woman give? You've lost your mind somewhere in time. You want me to believe a dead woman can destroy a man we don't know, and a man she never met when she was alive. Now, if that doesn't sound crazy, I don't know what does."

"It will require me to make a leap of faith."

"Should I ask what that is?"

Kane sighed. "You're better off not knowing."

"So, your leap of faith requires my blind trust?"

"In a manner of speaking."

"Can I go with you?"

"I need to go alone. Dobie will stay here with you." She stared at him like he was a hostile alien from an undiscovered planet.

"Why do I detect a deep seated fear in you when you talk about Eunis?"

"It's a long story and…"

"I have the time, Kane. Tell me."

Kane stepped away from Jorell. How could he possibly tell her when he didn't know himself? He walked over to the window and stared out over the city. "You have a great view here."

"You're avoiding the issue, Kane."

"It's complicated, and I…." He turned around and found Jorell standing in front of him, her beautiful green eyes pleading for answers. "I believe you're better off not knowing."

"My father's survival depends totally on you. I've paid you an unheard of amount of credits to work for me because I trust you, and that gives me the right to know."

"Sit down." He took her hand and led her back to the sofa where they both sat, side by side, facing each other. After a deep breath, he picked up her hand and held it tightly. "I'm a private person, and that's kept me alive. I've lived in secrecy, in ways you'll never understand."

"Let me try."

"What I'm about to tell you will seem strange, unbelievable, and you'll want to laugh."

"That's all the credit you give me? Why would I laugh?"

"Because I do. The story is capricious even to me."

"You can trust me, Kane. I promise I won't laugh--unless you do."

When she smiled at him his resolve melted, and an overwhelming urge to share his secrets pulled at what defenses he had left. Why this woman elicited such responses in him remained as big a mystery as his past. Her delicate scent tickled his desires, which did not bode well at the moment. If he thought about her much longer he'd embarrass himself.

"I've never told anyone what I'm about to tell you." She gave him a look that said she didn't believe him. "Before you ask; no, I haven't told Dobie. He knows some of it, but not every detail."

"I would have guessed you two shared everything."

"For the most part we do, but everyone has at least one dark secret they keep hidden deep within themselves." Jorell shrugged her shoulders and her expression said she understood. But could she understand his sordid past?

"Kane, we all think we have dark secrets, but they're never as bad as we think they are."

"I beg to differ." He brought her hand up to his lips and gently kissed her fingers. "I'm talking about the kind of secret that keeps you awake with worry every moon-cycle, and sad with reality every sun-cycle."

"You have a strange way of trying to make me feel better."

He loved the way she tilted her head back and looked at him skeptically. Her green eyes danced with questions and mischief. Her expressions were priceless, even when they bordered on anger. She made him think, and he liked that.

"I was going to say your last name, but I just realized I don't know it."

"You're right, I haven't told you. I never tell anyone, and they never ask, because they don't care, not as long as I give them what they pay me for. Jorell, we've all had experiences that put the person we love and trust in danger."

"You've been in my shoes? Really? You don't strike me as the type of man to allow that to happen to you."

"I lost the only person I cared about when I was twelve annual-cycles, and there was nothing I could do except watch the slaughter of my mother. She may not have given birth to me, but she was the best, and I loved her dearly. Her murder was horrific."

Jorell's hands moved to cover her mouth while she shook her head. "I'm so sorry."

"I'm not asking for your pity, I wanted you to know I share your heartache. I do know how you feel."

"Don't leave me, Kane. I need you." She reached out and cupped his cheek with her hand. "I need you more now than ever."

"My sweet Jorell, don't you know how badly I want you? If I could take you I would. Besides, your father needs you here, as well as your people." When she smiled he felt all his emotional walls melt away, and that new vulnerability scared him.

"I can't argue with your logic, but my heart doesn't understand."

She placed her hand on his cheek and pulled him toward her. He could not resist her invitation, so he lowered his head and pressed his lips to hers. She willingly opened to him and kissed him with such passion he wondered where her motivation had come from. The sad truth was, he didn't care why, he simply enjoyed the taste and feel of her. She was sweet, soft, and giving.

Her arms threaded around his neck. He eased her down on the sofa, her warm body pressed tightly against his. Her firm breasts pressed through the layers of fabric that separated them.

After a deep breath he tickled her mind and found her waiting for him. *Oh my sweet, how I've wanted to do this so many times before.*

And I've wanted your kiss so many times before.

That left him speechless. He'd purposely avoided serious relationships because of his work, since he could possibly travel through time and never find his way back. Due to that risk he knew it would not be fair to a mate. He wouldn't mind getting stuck in time if Jorell were with him.

Jorell, I.... Words escaped him so he kissed her deeply. It seemed as if they'd become one person in mind and body. He wanted to reassure her, to tell her he'd never leave her. Truth was, he had to leave her to save her father.

Her arms moved down his back and up again. She held him so tight he wondered if she'd ever let go. Her tongue danced with his, and she explored his mouth with a hungry need as great as his own. *Jorell, if only I could make this moment last, I would. I don't want to let go of you-- ever.*

Nor I you. Please Kane, don't leave. Don't go anywhere without me. I'll help you, you know I will.

I know. He slipped one arm under her back and pulled her against him, her breasts pressed against him and begged for attention. He moved one hand between them and let that hand find her right breast. The material of her gown slid down easily, and the front hooks of her undergarment were no obstacle.

In no time his fingers toyed with the taught tip of her nipple, and all he wanted was to see her in naked splendor, posing seductively for his enjoyment.

Kane, I feel you. I feel the real you. I know you feel it too. It's amazing. So personal, so special.

And inviting. Neither of them could relay any more mental talk because their senses were too full. His need for her grew uncomfortable. He had to have her. Now. His hands found the meticulous fastenings on the back of her gown and freed the bindings and eased the top of her gown down to her waist, leaving the strapless undergarment open behind her back.

He pulled his head back, unable to stop himself from staring at her bare breasts and perfect skin. His hands reached out, each encompassing a breast to fondle. Jorell was perfect, and he wanted her more now than a moment ago.

"What in Diabolous is going on here?"

By the planets! He'd let his guard down so much he hadn't heard the rude intruder. The door was locked, so who... a glance behind him revealed Rand standing ten feet away, arms crossed over his chest, a stern look on his face. *Jorell* hear me. It's Kane, in your mind. Listen carefully. Do not panic! That's exactly what he wants you to do. Just act normal. You'll be fine.

Kane, you must be a fool. That's my fiancé and I'm here, alone with you, in a very questionable position, half undressed, kissing you like the besotted fool I am!

Don't panic. Be calm. I'll stand first and you can use my body as a shield while you pull up your top.

Kane stood and sensed Jorell doing what he'd suggested behind him. He noted her undergarment had fallen to the floor when she stood so he pushed it with his foot safely into the darkness under the large sofa. Luckily the serving table hid his movement while Rand continued his condescending perusal with an arrogant attitude.

"What in the name of all that's holy, are you doing in this man's arms?"

Rand moved closer and stared at him with pure hatred in his eyes. He'd like nothing better than to take this fool down, but out of respect for Jorell, he'd play the game. She stepped out from behind him, safely dressed. She tipped her chin up a bit then walked toward Rand.

"What are you doing here, Rand?"

Kane crossed his arms over his chest and watched the play between the engaged couple. They both acted like they wanted to kill each other. Not a good start to a long life-mating. He suspected Rand was the type that could only be tough around women.

"I thought I'd check on your father, and see you. I had no idea you had *male* company, and that you were involved in illicit behavior. By the Gods woman! You're my fiancée, yet here you are acting like a common street whore!"

"I was…"

Rand held his hand up to silence Jorell. That move infuriated him past his peaceful limit. Kane's right hand fisted at his side, he then pulled his arm back and led his punch fly into Rand's left Jaw. The unmistakable sound of flesh against flesh sounded an instant before Rand fell to the floor in one big heap.

Kane stepped over to where Rand lay flat on the floor and grinned down at him. "Get up, coward."

Jorell's hand flew up to cover her mouth for a second before she spoke. "You'd better leave now, Kane."

"I will *not* leave you alone with this idiot." Kane kept his attention on Rand. "If you touch her, insult her, or treat her in an unkind manner, you *will* answer to me. Is that clear?"

Rand used the table next to him to pull himself to his feet. "Who in

Diabolous are you?"

"I'm helping First Advisor Sutone with a personal matter."

"I saw the personal matter." Rand took two steps back.

Kane's hands fisted at his sides. When he pulled one arm back he heard Jorell's voice screaming in his mind.

Kane! You're not helping. Rand won't hurt me. You need to leave…now!

Jorell, let me teach him how to treat a woman.

Please, stay out of this quarrel. It's not your fight.

I'll not leave you with this man.

Oh, but you will. And the sooner, the better. Trust me on this. That's an order.

Rand cleared his throat. "What's going on between you two? Jorell, I don't like the looks you're giving him, or me for that matter."

Kane smiled when Jorell turned the full force of her angry frustration on Rand, who blatantly took pleasure watching his fiancée squirm. One day Rand would pay the price, he'd see to it.

I'll be fine, Kane. Please, don't make me ask again.

As you wish. Call me if you need me.

Fair enough.

Rand combed his hair back with his fingers. "Get rid of your toy, we need to talk."

Kane pressed his index finger in the center of Rand's chest. "You need to be careful how you treat women."

"Let me guess, stranger, if I don't, you plan to teach me a lesson?"

"Count on it."

Rand laughed. "I'm scared."

Kane reached out, grabbed Rand's shirt and pulled the fool toward him. "You should be. I was going to teach you a lesson, but I fear you're a slow learner. I think I'll just kill you instead."

"Kane!"

He turned his head toward Jorell who had walked to the door and opened it for him.

"Please leave."

He shoved Rand backwards into the wall, then turned and walked to the door. He brushed by Jorell so closely the heat of her rage spurred his anger. Maybe she did love the loser. It didn't matter really. His job was to save her father, not bed the client. "Whisper my name in your mind and I'll be here."

The moment Kane stepped into the hall the door slammed closed behind him.

"Jorell!"

She turned her gaze toward Rand, and his hatred attacked her on more than one level. She missed Kane already.

"Get over here."

The tone of his voice said it all. She couldn't blame him for voicing his anger and betrayal, nor could she fix it. She'd violated Rand's trust and deserved punishment. She walked closer to Rand and stopped in front of him. When he looked at her, his eyes revealed a man she didn't know.

"I should call off this farce of an engagement, but I won't. Not yet anyway. However, you *will* act properly, and you *will* never see that man again. Is that clear?"

"Rand, I know what I did was wrong, but we are *not* life-mated yet, and you do *not* have the right to tell me what to do."

"Really?" Rand reached out and grabbed Jorell's shoulders.

His fingers dug into her skin and he purposely squeezed harder, and took pleasure when she winced in pain. She gritted her teeth and refused to give him the satisfaction of acting weak. Where had this Rand come from?

"You *will* be my life-mate, and you *will* behave yourself as befitting of your standing. Is that clear?"

She nodded. If she opened her mouth she was liable to say what she really thought, and this was not the time to stir more suspicion than already existed. Finally he released her and stepped away. He started to pace and she silently hoped he'd fall flat on his face. "I suppose if my father dies you'll have no reason to life-mate me."

Rand stopped pacing and stared at her, his expression blank. He'd always acted as if she were special to him, and that he cared for her. It was good to learn his true nature before she committed to him.

"I have a good reason." Rand shook his head. "I'll decide your fate at a later date."

He glared at her as if she had absolutely no say in the matter. It was a good thing he didn't know she'd actually just found herself. Until now, she'd faithfully done everything her father wanted. She'd worked hard to be a "good daughter," but she'd be damned if she'd spend the rest of her life trying to be a "good life-mate."

"You actually believe you have a choice?" Rand laughed. "You're a bigger fool than I thought. Your life is in *my* hands, and you *will* be attentive to me." Rand stepped closer to Jorell. "Even if you are used goods."

"That's so…nice of you." She wished she had a weapon that could make Rand disappear—permanently. From the look on his face he was past mad, crazed would be the word. The only thing he was right about was her being a fool. How could she have been so blind?

"No thanks are necessary. I'm glad you understand." Rand walked to the door, paused then turned. "Clean yourself up, you're a mess. I'll be back to escort you to the evening meal. And you'd better not let me down, or all of Sector-Three will learn they no longer have a ruler."

CHAPTER TWENTY THREE

"How could I have been such a fool, Dobie? I can't believe I acted like a smitten schoolboy."

Dobie chuckled. "Actually, I've witnessed you doing it a few times before, but you never got caught like *that!*" Dobie cleared his throat. "But, you deserve love and happiness, boss."

"Not at Jorell's expense. No." His friend stared and shook his head the way he always did when his point was not clear. "At least not until we've successfully completed this job."

"Such a web we weave, eah?"Dobie smiled.

"Web indeed." He knew Dobie was about to launch his lecture about women. This might be the right time to tell him something he wasn't ready to hear." I need to return to the past...alone."

"Alone? This must be serious."

"It is. You know about the energy attacks on Alextor?" Dobie nodded. "Well, I have to stop the Energy-Lamia."

"You've never done that before. Jupiters! We don't know anything about them, except they're dangerously evil, and have far-reaching power." Dobie cleared his throat. "What's the plan?"

"Jump back to my childhood and talk with the woman who raised me." He saw the skepticism on Dobie's face, or was it fear wrinkling his forehead?

"I thought the number one rule was never to visit your own childhood, or visit family, past, present, or future?"

"You're right, and that rule still stands, but this is the exception to the rule."

"Chief, as close as we've been, you've never talked about that woman, except to say she did a good job taking care of you when no one else would."

"Sit down." He and Dobie both took a seat at the table. Dobie put both elbows on the tabletop, tucked his hands under his chin and stared anxiously.

"Ready, Chief."

"Eunis is the name of the woman who raised me." He paused while Dobie absorbed the news. His friend was sharp and he knew he'd figured it out.

"Of course! You clever devil. Your last name, Sinue is Eunis backwards!"

"I had to provide a last name, and since I didn't know my parent's names, it was my way of paying tribute to Eunis."

"You loved her, didn't you?"

"Not because I had to, because she was an honorable caring woman. She protected me and saved my life. She raised me to be who I am, and she gave me the powers I have. Without her, I'd have nothing."

"That can't be true, Chief. You were born with your abilities."

"No. Eunis gave me *her* abilities, I had none of my own. Without Eunis, we would not be time traveling." Kane pushed up the sleeves of his shirt and held his arms out toward Dobie. "These Vambrace Cuffs belonged to Eunis. She was a member of the Mageous Sect, and they're very powerful wizards. Most people have heard something about them, but they're also very misunderstood.

"As Eunis hung close to death, she permanently affixed these cuffs, giving me the gift of time-travel, the ability to mind-meld, and the knowledge of how to help others. She taught me all the lessons necessary to survive, and she transferred as much of her magical powers of wizardry as I was able to absorb."

Kane took a deep breath to steel himself for the most difficult part. "On the day I turned twelve annual-cycles, Eunis sensed someone was coming. We lived in a huge, magnificent cave that Eunis turned into a modern, beautifully appointed home, but it was still a cave. Life for us was different than other people. Eunis was shunned by the majority of the local town's people who viewed her as a threat.

"They didn't comprehend her abilities, so they decided she must be evil and branded her a witch, so I became the devil's spawn. I've always wondered why people condemn what they don't understand." He paused, searching for the right words.

"Before anyone arrived, she hid me up high on a ledge behind some rocks, which was like a third floor balcony that overlooked the main living area. She told me no matter what I heard, or what I saw, I was to stay hidden. Then she put a spell on me that made it impossible for me to move. The moment she set foot back on the main floor, the strangers invaded our home."

"This is going to get bad, isn't it? Damnation, you're going to make me cry, right?"

He nodded, barely able to keep a dry eye himself, but Dobie had to know in order to help. "I heard voices, and Eunis' screams. I managed to move enough to see around the rock I was leaning against and saw six men tackle Eunis, tie her, and torture her for several time-units. Then a seventh man appeared, and when she looked at him she gasped. She knew him, and when she spoke to him her voice was filled with disgust."

Dobie sighed. "I'm surprised you didn't run down to help her and get yourself in trouble."

"Don't think I didn't try, but Eunis' paralyzing spell still held firm. I couldn't even watch all they did to her. I had to look away. I wanted to scream and tear them all limb from limb, but I couldn't move a muscle."

Dobie stared at Kane. "Well? Don't keep me waiting. Who is the evil bastard that came after you and Eunis?"

"Pakar Moran."

"By the Gods! You've got to be kidding. The most wicked, conniving criminal to ever walk Okeron? No way. Are you sure? You were very young at the time."

"I heard his name several times, and not just from Eunis, from his own lips. It was him, make no mistake. He kept telling Eunis she'd betrayed him. He swore he'd kill her if she didn't tell him the truth. The torture went on for what seemed forever. I covered my ears to muffle her screams. She suffered unbelievable torture with miraculous endurance.

"If she'd have known I could see her, she would have fixed it so I couldn't. She was very protective. Eunis and I had always been able to mind-meld, so while they tortured her, she used what strength she could muster to transfer information, powers, and to reassure me. She made me promise the gifts she gave were only to be used for good. She said I'd understand everything when I was older."

Dobie sighed. "It's difficult to hear, and I can only imagine what you went through as a child watching your mother-figure being hurt like that."

"Torture was bad enough, but I watched Pakar take her life's blood from her when he slit her throat with his cutter. He laughed while she bled to death. Even with her last breaths, she sent me the powers she had left. She even sent me memories of healings she'd done, time travels, and deeds I would never have dreamed she could do. Her last message to me was that one day I would be tested, and the results would have lasting effects for everyone on Okeron.

"At the very end of the transfer process, a huge bolt of energy flashed and entered my body. It was so hard and fast it rendered me unconscious. By the time I woke and managed to sit up, everyone had gone. When I climbed down and saw Eunis, still tied to a wooden beam, sitting in a pool of blood, her skin grey, void of all color. I knew she was gone, and my life as I knew it was over."

"I don't know what to say, Kane. Sorry is not enough, but I am truly sorry. Truly. I only wish you'd told me long ago, back in Academy so you'd have had someone to talk to, you know, to share your pain with. I would have been more than willing to help you."

"Back then I trusted no one. Even though we were friends, and grew closer each annual-cycle, I never wanted to burden you with this information. It's not something anyone wants to think about."

"I understand, but you know I've always had a need to help you. You're the brother I never had." Dobie sighed and stared at Kane. "What did Pakar mean when he told Eunis she betrayed him?"

"After all these annual-cycles, I still don't know."

"Chief, I usually know how to apply the stories you tell to explain the job at hand. You've shared enough of them over the annual-cycles, but they were nothing compared to this one." Dobie shook his head. "I don't understand how it all relates to Alextor Sutone's poisoning, or how to save him."

"Eunis was a poison expert. She was an accomplished herbalist and healer. Even those who called her a witch would come to her for cures. I'm hoping she knows of a possible antidote to save Alextor."

"How will she know what poison was used?"

"I'll take a blood sample with me and hope it survives the jump."

"I doubt blood samples have ever time traveled before." Dobie smiled. "But we've broken more rules than we can remember." He squinted at Kane. "There's something else, isn't there? Come on, I know you too well."

Kane took a deep breath. "She also knows how to destroy an Energy-Lamia. She may have passed powers to me before she died, but I don't know how to activate them. I realize I'm not a full Mageous, but she might be able to teach me enough to save Alextor."

"Do you really think this will work?"

"I wouldn't take the chance if I didn't."

"Alextor is very weak right now. What will happen if the Lamia attacks him while you're gone?"

"I have faith in Alesa, Ariel, and Jorell."

"Jorell's twin friends are very pretty. Will they need my protection while you're gone?"

Kane laughed. "You're sneaky and correct. I want you to hang close to all three of them. So yes, you shall be their protector. But *only* while I'm gone."

Dobie laughed. "Of course, Chief."

"I believe the poisoning and Lamia attacks are connected." Kane took a deep breath. "Make no mistake, they want Alextor dead, and they won't stop until they get what they want."

"I hate to think what will happen if he dies."

"I know." Kane sighed. "First Trom Carsun is found dead on a mountain while on vacation, then Marto Braxton has a fatal, air-trans accident. Now the only original ruler left, is near death. Alextor is no more an accident than Trom or Marto."

Dobie scratched his head. "We both know there's no such thing as an accident. Any more instructions?"

"Follow Jorell everywhere. Most of all, don't allow her to be alone with Rand. I don't trust him."

"That's a tall order." Dobie checked his wrist-piece. "Right now she's in a meeting."

"Good. She needs to act as normal as possible."

"What do you want me to tell Jorell?"

"I'll leave that up to you. You can tell her I jumped to the past, or just make excuses for me. Either way, she won't be happy."

"Have you forgotten lesson number one in time-travel basics? The one that says, 'if you play around with your own past, you can erase yourself'?" Dobie shook his head." I don't like it Chief. Not one bit."

"If we don't find an antidote for Alextor he will die. If he dies, we either go to war, or fall under a dictatorship. Be ready for anything."

Dobie rose to his feet." I don't have enough paper to list all the problems associated with this jump."

"That may be, but it's the only way to save Alextor."

"You're walking a tightrope over a gorge, without a safety net."

"You worry too much."

"Probably, but we're working in uncharted territory." Dobie walked to the galley computer.

Kane watched him order two drinks, then pick them up and bring them back to the table. He accepted the glass his friend pushed toward him. "You're going to miss me when I'm gone." He smiled, but Dobie was not amused. "I'll be fine, you'll see. It's the only way to get to the bottom of all this. And you know I'd take you if I didn't need you here."

"It's still risky. You could die, Kane. Then what? What will Jorell do if you don't exist? Have you thought about that?"

"What do you think?" Based on the look he received he shouldn't have asked. "I know it sounds crazy, but we've beat bigger odds before."

"Not exactly. We were never in danger of erasing ourselves! We're always in danger of erasing someone, but not us!" Dobie took another long drink. "I don't like it, boss. It doesn't feel right."

"Since when have you gone all psychic on me?" Dobie laughed and it was good to hear, but he quickly sobered.

"I wish I had, you could use a personal psychic right now, because I don't think you're doing very well for yourself."

"That may be, but I have to do this. You know how short the time window is. At best Alextor has sixteen sun-cycles left, and we're not even sure that's accurate. Every time-unit counts."

"Fine. I'll keep Jorell under surveillance at all times, and if Rand comes around I'll be the third man on their date. Just so you know, I can't stand the guy either." Dobie finished his drink. "By the way, did you get a lick in on Rand? I can't believe you just stood there and took his abuse."

"Jorell's esteemed fiancé forced me to punch him in the jaw. Then I may have slammed him against the wall and threatened him."

"Since he's still alive I'd say he's lucky."

"For the time being. I suspect he's involved with this plot against Alextor."

"Now that's an interesting theory. Any proof?"

"Not yet, but soon."

"Got it, Chief. When are you leaving?"

"Immediately."

CHAPTER TWENTY FOUR

Jorell wondered if the meeting would ever end. Since her father wasn't in attendance nothing seemed right or appropriate. Rand assumed she'd allow him to step into her father's shoes, and that she'd do her psychic thing for him as she did for her father. He couldn't be more wrong. Rand may be an adviser like she was, but he was second to her. Plus, he had no psychic abilities, and she was glad he didn't.

Right now her goal was to stand up for her people's rights and the good of Okeron, but she still wanted to do physical harm to Rand. Ever since he caught her with Kane he'd been argumentative and grouchy. She'd apologized profusely, which was all she could do.

She promised Rand she'd never be alone with Kane again. She made up a believable story about her family, and that Kane was looking for a long, lost relative. He seemed to believe her story, but she didn't really care if he believed her or not. Kane was working for her and she desperately needed him.

"If it pleases the council, I have an announcement." Rand leaned down and whispered into Jorell's ear. "Read their reactions closely, my dear."

"I will." What was he up to now? This entire meeting had been filled with hints that her father needed to be replaced, and no one except Rand knew the truth. It had *conspiracy* written all over it.

"Our respected leader, Alextor Sutone, has a delicate and pressing personal matter to attend to, and has asked me to fill in during his absence."

A silent hush fell over the room. It became so quiet she heard the beat of her own heart which sounded like a loud drum in her ears. Everyone in attendance wore a shocked look of disbelief. She took note of the facial expressions, whispers and innuendos of all the members, but it was the look of complete satisfaction on Rand's face that stood out above any of the others.

"Since he will be gone for an indeterminate amount of time, he wanted to be sure that I direct the council in all pressing business in his absence."

Mumblings could be heard all around the large, circular chamber. It was easy to see everyone's faces due to the tiered seating. Rand waited for the whispers to subside before he cleared his throat and continued.

"As we're all aware, the water situation has come under scrutiny once again. There are certain members of all three Sectors questioning the fair division of water rights, and arguing over who has the power over those rights."

The council and gallery became loud and appeared on the verge of physical violence. Water on Okeron was sacred, and everyone knew what could happen if the current control were to stop. She needed to speak with Rand because he had no authority to replace her father, or to broach the water subject. Anger roiled in the pit of her stomach.

Rand waited while the room quieted and the audience took their seats once again. "We are all aware of the past, and the ugliness of war. I suggest we do everything possible to avoid another conflict."

Jorell held her breath between each of Rand's sentences, hoping the next statement would be better than the last, but that was not to be. Who did he think he was?

A delegate across the room stood and the Director acknowledged him to speak. Was she ready to hear the opinions of the other delegates? Would they continue their loyalty to her father, or fall prey to Rand?

"Delegate Rand Arroray, this comes as a surprise to us all. We know you're close to Ruler Sutone, but you are not the next in line to rule this Sector."

She watched Rand's hands fist at his sides before he raised them to grip each side of the podium in front of him. Tiny beads of sweat broke out on his forehead, and she knew his temper was barely leashed.

"Esteemed representatives, of course I know the chain of command; however, Ruler Sutone thought the circumstances were unusual, and since I would only conduct the meetings for a short time, that the chain of command did not apply. It would only apply if he were not to return at all, which is not the case."

"My esteemed member, you must not understand the full extent of our law. I will excuse your announcement as ignorance, rather than a planned attempt to usurp Ruler Sutone."

If body language could talk, these two men would be shouting at the top of their lungs while they ripped each other apart. This was a Rand she always suspected existed, but had never seen. The new Rand could take a flying leap off a cliff as far as she was concerned. His deliberate attempt to gain control was abhorrent.

Rand could play all the games he liked, but she'd follow behind and stop him. He thought he was so much better than everyone, and that arrogance would be his downfall. Plus, she had Kane, and Rand did not know the real truth about what he was doing for her. She knew without asking that Kane would be happy to help bring Rand down.

"Distinguished members, I apologize for any insult. I was simply following the wishes of our leader, but I will defer to the proper chain of command. No hard feelings."

Her intuition said Rand's apology was a total lie. Not one word of truth had come his lips all sun-cycle. He was a conniver to be sure. All the nice things he'd ever said to her now rang hollow. But she'd play his stupid, back-stabbing game as long as necessary. It was always smart to keep your enemies close, and in the dark.

Rand still stood at the podium and lectured the congregation on the perils of war, and the loss of control. How and why would Rand turn against her? Power? Her father's position was critical to the peace of Okeron, and it appeared Rand had migrated to the dark side, which was where malicious intent always landed.

The three sector system had maintained peace and governed the people for over thirty annual-cycles, and she was not about to let it die along with her father. Her fiancé was busy trying to talk his way out of suspicion. Rand could talk until the end of the moon-cycle and she doubted there would be a shred of truth to his rant.

Rand had betrayed her and her father, and for that, she would destroy him.

CHAPTER TWENTY FIVE

Kane stood on the majestic mountain and surveyed the green valley below. He never appreciated the beauty of his surroundings when he was a child, so it seemed as if he viewed his home for the first time. He rolled down his sleeves so Eunis would not see the cuffs she'd yet to give him as of this sun-cycle.

The jump alone was strange. Without Dobie it seemed like a part of himself was missing. Jorell needed Dobie. Leaving her had been hard, for the simple reason he wanted to be with her. She was amazing in so many ways that he couldn't decide which of her talents he liked the most.

In the distance he saw Eunis picking her favorite flowers, the kind she always kept on her dining table. He walked up and stopped behind her.

"Kane, I didn't think you'd be home so soon." Eunis turned.

A flash of recognition crossed her face, but was quickly replaced with cautious skepticism. He knew she sensed his presence, but did not recognize his adult features.

"Who are you?"

He slowly smiled and gazed at Eunis, the only mother he knew. "I thought you might recognize me." She stared at him while she stepped closer, then shuffled in a circle around him. She always squinted when her mind worked, then she'd raise her eyebrows when something peaked her interest.

"Kane?"

"A much older Kane than you know now." He watched her cover her mouth with her hand. Tears formed in her eyes and she sank to the ground. He rushed to her and knelt beside her.

"I knew I *felt* you." Eunis reached out and cupped his cheek with her hand. "Kane...what can I say? You're a man, and yet I still have a young boy in my care."

"And I don't want you to change a thing you're doing."

"Then you have a lot of explaining to do. I don't understand why you're here, or why you decided it was worth the risk to find me. I'm sure I warned you."

"We both know what can happen when you play with your own destiny." She nodded, her loving, but concerned gaze followed him as he sat beside her. He stared into the depths of her dark eyes, and for the first time, saw the great wisdom of the woman who raised him.

"We do, which is why I'm concerned about this visit. But I must say, Kane, you've grown into a great man, and I'm so happy to know you're okay."

"Thank you." He bowed his head, picked her hand up, and kissed the back, then held on." I never told you how truly grateful I was as a child, and an adult, that you took me in out of the kindness of your heart. You are my mother in every way that counts, and I literally owe you my life." Eunis pulled her hand from his grasp, then cupped his cheek.

"Oh my dear Kane, you are the one who blessed me. Never forget that. Now, business. I know you well enough to realize you need my help. What can I do for you, my son?"

"I need to know how to destroy a very powerful Energy-Lamia."

Her hand dropped. "How powerful?"

"I've found no limits to his reach or effects. This entity is much stronger than I ever imagined possible."

"I've feared this moment my entire life, and now it's come to fruition."

"What do you mean?"

"Oh, Kane, it's such a long, painful story. Is the reason you're here critical?"

"The peace of Okeron depends on the outcome of my visit. The original rulers of Sector-One and Two are both dead and Alextor Sutone, ruler of Sector-Three, lies close to death. If I cannot find a way to save his life, well..." Kane paused and took a deep breath, "I fear the worst. There will be no one to stop the wrong people from taking over, and I hate to think of all the ramifications." Kane touched Eunis' hair and tucked it behind her ear." There is a conspiracy to take over the government, and I sense their leader is this unknown Energy-Lamia."

"You are wise, my son. Is it all right for me to still call you son? I've always thought of you as my own."

"I'm honored." Kane stood, then helped Eunis to her feet. "Let's go sit by the river. Remember how you always said water had spiritual powers, and made things easier to understand?" She smiled at him as he took her hand and walked with her to the water's edge just over the grassy mound.

They both sat on a large rock and listened to the trickle and splash of the water." I'm sorry to put you through this. You know I wouldn't if it were not a matter of life and death."

"You're a very excitable boy, but I believe you've outgrown that by now." Eunis shook her head. "I suppose I should start at the beginning, and," she laid her hand on Kane's forearm, "I hope you can forgive me for holding the truth from you. Just know I did it for your own good.

"Your mother gave birth to fraternal twins during the great war. Your father was angry. He wanted a son, but only one. And since you were born smaller than your brother, he ordered me to kill you, the weakling, as he called you.

"When he turned his attention back to your mother, I smeared animal blood on you, and made it look like I'd stabbed you in the heart with a cutter. The sleep spell I put on you was most effective, and I fooled your father into thinking you were dead. When I conjured real tears and sobbed, he was convinced.

"For a careful man, he wasn't careful that day. He just carried your brother off, satisfied you were dead and no longer a concern to him."

"What a great guy. How did you come to know him?"

"Your mother and I were friends, and I delivered you, and your brother. Besides, this area is not rich in population, so everyone knows everyone, and their personal business. It's impossible to have a secret here."

"Where is he now?"

Eunis rubbed her hands together. "I'll get to that." She threaded her fingers through Kane's hair and pushed it away from his face. "Bear with me, son. This is a complicated story, and since you took the risk to come here, you need to hear it all." She shook her head. "I thought I'd have more time before I had to explain the fight you were born to have."

"That sounds ominous, but as you can see I'm now thirty-three annual-cycles, so just tell me, I can handle it."

"To me you're almost twelve." She took his hand in hers. "I've raised you since birth, and you view what I do as normal. But you know some call me witch, a purveyor of the black arts, and other names indicating I'm a threat because I'm pure evil."

Eunis reached out, patted his shoulder, then trailed her hand down his arm. Love seeped into his body from her very soul. Seeing her was a joy, and leaving would be pure torture since he'd lose her all over again.

"I'm afraid you've had to pay a price for being alive, and for living with me. I keep you isolated up here on this mountain as much as I can, and insure the only people you come in contact with are friends and clients who accept me for who, and what I am."

"I heard the insults when I went to town. I didn't understand then, but as an adult, I've realized it's a judgment made from unfounded fear."

Eunis sighed. "You've become very wise. You're a good man, without a hint of evil in you. I worried about that, but I was wrong to do so. I see that now." She squeezed his hand. "I'd do the same thing again. You're worth every sacrifice and compromise I've made. I regret nothing. I love you, son. I hope you know that."

"I do, and I feel the same. I don't have enough words of thanks for what you've done for me." He hugged Eunis, his only mother. "How can I possibly thank you for saving my life?" He touched a finger to her lips to stop her response. "I know what you're thinking. I'm thrilled to have this chance to tell you how I feel, and to see you through mature eyes."

"Son, this moment will forever live in my memory." She wiped a tear from her cheek. "I'm just as grateful to see you as a man any mother would be proud to call son. However, you deserve," Eunis took a deep breath, "or should I say must hear the rest of your father's story."

Eunis bowed her head. "Your father took your brother and left. He had an important job in the government and was needed since we were involved in the war."

"What was his job?"

"Most people believe he was the main instigator of the war because he led a contingent of men who seized control of the water supply, and then overcharged everyone for their share. Hence, the war."

Kane took a deep breath. "We were all forced to study this in school. Based on what I already knew, and what you've just told me, I'm afraid to ask my father's name."

"You know it in your heart," she reached out and touched Kane's cheek, "but you need to hear it from my lips." Eunis squared her shoulders and looked Kane in the eye. "Pakar Moran."

Kane stood and stared out across the river. He'd hoped one sun-cycle he'd learn who fathered him, but this was the worst news he could have received. Pakar was the most hated and evil man in history, and that was hard to swallow. A lifetime of suspicions could not quell the shock of the actual words.

"I'm sorry Kane. I wanted to protect you, but you came to me for answers. Eunis stood. "You must know the truth before you face him in battle. My only regret is that I won't be there to help you."

Kane turned and faced Eunis. He put his hands on her shoulders. "I wish you could always stay close to me." Her smile always warmed him, and he so wanted to save her from her fate. "Tell me what you mean by *the battle I was born to fight?*"

Eunis sighed. "I always knew you were special. I experienced it the moment I first touched you coming out of your mother's womb. When I held you, an overwhelming feeling of peace enveloped me. And when that bright aura shone around you, I had no doubt."

"That tells me nothing."

"I see you're still a bit short in the patience department." Eunis smiled. "You already know the only thing that can erase evil is light. You, my son, are full of light. How that's possible, I don't know, especially considering who your father is. But your mother was a very special woman. She's the one who gave you light, so cherish it for the gift it is.

"You have the ability to stop Pakar's evil. The only advice I can give is to trust your heart, because that is where truth lives, and that is your strength."

"That sounds very esoteric."

"Kane, you know when you're dealing with metaphysics there are things no one can explain, only your heart knows if it's right or wrong."

"I'd hoped you could be more specific." Kane pulled her to him and gave her a long hug before he stepped back and shoved his hands in his pockets. "What about this brother I'm supposed to have? What did you feel about him?" He watched her gaze move to the ground, purposely avoiding his. "This is truth time. We may never have another opportunity."

"You're right, son, I'm sorry." Eunis laid a hand on Kane's cheek. "I'm still trying to adjust to you being a man." Eunis looked into Kane's eyes. "It's difficult to say what I felt about your brother. I sensed he could go either way, depending on who raised him. Since Pakar took him, I suspect he's been filled with anger and hatred."

Kane shook his head. "It depends on how much influence Pakar has had on him. Whether he took his role as father seriously, or simply ignored him."

"You're right, and we have no way of knowing. I don't even know the boy's name. When the war ended and Pakar was tried for his heinous crimes, then deported to Larent, he either arranged for someone else to raise him, or found a way to take his son with him." She sighed. "It would surprise me if Pakar gave him away, he never got rid of anything that belonged to him."

"I think you're right. Pakar would never give up his son. He would have a need to control his son, manipulate his thoughts and his schooling."

"You're right, Pakar is a manipulator, and always will be. His main concern is self. I doubt he can care about anyone." Eunis looked up at Kane.

"I believe Pakar is back on Okeron, and it's likely he brought his son with him, and they're behind everything that's happened recently."

Eunis cleared her throat. "If that's true, wouldn't someone have turned him in?"

He wanted to tell her he'd never forget the face of the man who murdered her, but she was alive and well before him. "I'm sure he's had his looks altered. He's probably had his DNA altered as well."

Eunis nodded. "I'd put credits on it. Fortunately DNA reconstruction has cured diseases and saved lives. The bad news is what that procedure has done for criminals."

"Altering one's looks isn't hard. Nearly everyone is into that these days, and not just to erase age. Pakar can change everything about himself, but he can't erase his evil. That you'll recognize." Eunis stood and stepped to the water's edge.

Kane walked to his mother and stood beside her. "You didn't say much about my birthmother. Did she love Pakar? Is that how I was conceived?"

"For your sake I wish I could say yes. Unfortunately, Pakar raped her, so she held nothing but hate and contempt for him."

"Why didn't she end the pregnancy?"

"Your mother thought every child had the right to be born. We talked a lot, and I still miss her dearly. She was a wonderful person, warm and loving. She told me all about the plans she had for her boys, but she…"

Eunis began to cry so he hugged her and waited for her to calm. "Better now?" She nodded and took a step back. "What is it you can't tell me? You already told me she died in childbirth."

"In these times women don't die from childbirth, we both know that. Your mother did have a difficult birth since you were a twin, but I could have saved her if I'd been allowed to. She was hemorrhaging, and I could have stopped it, but…he…" Eunis began to sob.

"Shall I guess?" She looked at him, her eyes full of emotion and tears he wished he could erase." The bastard that fathered me wouldn't allow you to help her. He had no use for her. She'd interfere with his plans, so he wanted her dead. He didn't trust anyone else with the job, plus he took pleasure in the act of killing. He slit her throat and watched her bleed out, and he didn't leave until he witnessed her last breath."

"How could you possibly know that?"

He couldn't tell her the truth and risk changing the future, he hated to deceive her, but it was necessary. "I've dealt with his type before. They're all the same. Some are more evil than others, and Pakar is the master."

"I am sorry, Son. I really am. I never wanted you to know the ugly details. I thought life would be better for you if you never knew your true parentage." Eunis shook her head and wiped tears from her cheeks." I hope this trip is worth your personal pain."

"As do I." The grief of learning Pakar fathered him was nothing next to the anguish of losing Eunis. She had no idea what would happen to her in the near future, and he wished he didn't know either. The personal pain she spoke of was all too fresh in his mind.

No matter how many annual-cycles passed, her death cut him to the core. It was time to change the subject before he said something he might regret. "Which brings me back to why I'm here." He reached in his pocket and removed a vial. "This is Alextor's blood. He's been poisoned and I thought you might be able to use it to find an antidote." She took the small, glass tube from his outstretched hand." I suspect Pakar poisoned Alextor, and has attacked him as the Energy-Lamia."

"Oh Kane." More tears fell. "I fear for your safety. I have faith in you, but I don't know if you're strong enough to fight Pakar. Even if I teach you everything I know, it may be impossible to stop him."

"We have no choice. If not me, then who?" He watched her search her mind for a name, but they both knew there was no one.

"As a mother I want to tell you to leave him alone, but I know what you must do."

Kane hugged his mother. She had more than earned the title. He desperately wanted to save her from her fate, yet to change the future that much would have monumental consequences. She'd taught him about 'the unwritten rules' which forbade such blatant changes.

"Promise me you won't do anything foolish." Eunis took a step back. "The rules are in place for a reason. You can't play with life and death outcomes. Tell me you're not thinking about…"

"As much as I want to alter the future, I will not."

Eunis tucked her hair behind her ears. "You've stretched the boundaries enough by coming here."

"I want to bring you back with me, and I could." His mother's face turned ashen, and her stunned look tore at his heart. "But I won't. I know I can't, and I know why."

"Of course you do. You might even erase yourself if you were to do something so foolish."

Kane put his hands on her shoulders. "Mother, relax. I'll obey all those unwritten rules you taught me. It's how I've survived so long, and why I'm able to do the work I do."

"Oh thank the stars. For a moment there I'd thought you'd lost your mind."

Kane laughed until Eunis joined him. "You're the only woman I know who can laugh and cry at the same time."

"I certainly hope so, otherwise you'd know a lot of crazy women!" Eunis gave him a hug then stepped back.

"I'm glad you still have your sense of humor. I suppose you had to have one to raise me."

"No truer words have been spoken. Right now you're a very inquisitive and stubborn son, who tests me every chance he gets, but I'll be your mother 'till the day I die."

Kane smiled. "You've done a fantastic job, can't you see?" He turned in a circle, then bowed to her. She took the bait and laughed at him, a sound he much preferred to her earlier tear filled voice. "By the way, where is the younger me right now?"

"You're on the other side of the mountain staying with a friend of ours who needed help building a fence for his livestock. Today, and in the future, you're a good man. I love you, no matter what age you are, and I don't want to see you hurt. Ever."

"I know, and I love you. My heart is heavy because I know your future, and I've never been able to put it behind me."

Eunis laid her fingers over Kane's lips. "This is where we tread on changing the past, and the future if we're not careful. You have all the knowledge, but I cannot." She took the hand Kane offered. "If I know, I might inadvertently change something, willingly or unwillingly. So, as much as I would love to heal your aching heart, I cannot. Just remember that what I did, and what I will do, is my free choice. And I suspect you would not be here if I hadn't made those choices."

"I may have changed things by just being here now." Eunis nodded at him, then smiled her all-knowing smile he remembered so well.

"I like to think we're both smart enough to use what we learn for the betterment of ourselves, as well as the planet. What happened to you in your youth has made you the man you are today. Even my passing shaped you in ways you may never consciously realize. Every moment of our lives molds who we are and what we'll become."

"You're even wiser than I remembered."

"Thank you, son. I so wish I could be a part of your adult life." Eunis looked Kane in the eye. "Relax, I know better than to ask how and when I crossed over. I have no desire to change the future, unless...."

"Unless what?" She stared at him, her silence told him more than words. He'd jumped long enough to know exactly how interlinked the past and the future are, and how a small change could multiply exponentially over future annual-cycles.

"Tell me, Kane, what vocation have you chosen?"

"I'm known as '*The Traveler*'. I choose my jobs carefully, depending on the client's needs."

"That's very tricky. If anyone could do it, it's you, but the risk is great."

"Believe me, I've learned what can be changed, and what cannot, and I never interfere in life and death matters."

"Isn't that what you're doing right now?"

CHAPTER TWENTY SIX

Jorell finished her second glass of wine and leaned back in the big upholstered chair next to her father's lifeless, sleeping form. She'd never been so frustrated, or helpless. Nothing about this situation had gone well. She missed Kane, and he'd only been gone a few time-units .Kane had not been in her life long, yet he'd ingrained himself in her mind, her plans, her hopes and dreams. Not a minor achievement.

What a fool she'd been with Rand. She should have stood up to her father and refused to become engaged to him when he first brought it up. Instead, he'd repeatedly pushed Rand on her, telling her what a wonderful political pairing they were. She never wanted a forced union, only a love match. But since her father shoved Rand down her throat, she'd tried to convince herself she loved him.

Rand loved himself too much to let anyone in. She refused to spend her life living a lie, pretending to be the faithful mate, always taking a back seat to her life-mate. Why hadn't her father seen the real Rand? Her father's insistence about Rand planted many doubts in her mind. Had it been his idea, or had he been forced somehow? He would have to recover for her to learn the true answer.

Kane clarified her feelings for Rand simply by showing up. He also had a pull on her that went far above the normal, a pull that made her want to be with him every moment of every sun-cycle. She had nothing in common with Rand. Lately when Rand entered a room, she had the need to leave. She'd never thought a man could make her physically sick when he touched her, but Rand now filled that emotion.

With Kane there had been that immediate spark everyone talked about, but couldn't explain. How could Kane be the polar opposite of Rand? It made no sense. She'd never believed any man could ignite an instant connection that could make her body tremble in anticipation, and yearn for completion; the most important ingredient to a long term relationship. She was wrong—dead wrong. Kane did exactly that.

The problem was, no one believed in romantic unions any more, they tended to mate only for convenience, social standing, politics, or credits. To make matters worse, she'd failed her father. Why hadn't she 'felt' someone wanted him dead? She'd never forgive herself. She picked up her reader from the table next to the chair. If she got into a good romantic mystery she might forget her circumstances for a while. She began to read, forcing all other thoughts from her mind.

Several time-units passed peacefully, and her novel delivered a temporary reprieve from reality, but she caught herself dozing. She needed sleep. She reached out to put her reader on the table, and when she did, something tickled her mind.

It had to be Kane trying to contact her. She focused on the tickle, and let the wall down so he could enter. When she did, pain seared through the left side of her head. She put a hand over each temple as if she could stop the searing ache by holding her head, but it had no effect.

The sensation of evil overtook all thoughts, and everything went black. She closed her eyes and concentrated on light, love, and every possible good deed that could be done in life. Instead of pushing back the sinister quagmire of malevolence, it began to possess her, inch by inch. The wall that kept her safe was forever damaged, even though she tried every trick she knew to rebuild her line of defense.

"He'll die, and there's nothing you can do!"

She couldn't believe she'd heard the deep, male voice so clearly. The Energy-Lamia had just made direct contact, and she had to fight him.

The pervasive wickedness rapidly consumed her entire body. She concentrated on mending her mental wall. The Lamia filled the space she'd opened for Kane. By the stars, why had she thought only Kane could gain entrance? Now she had to pay the price for her negligence. Her head throbbed so hard she feared it would split in two. She pressed her hands tighter against her temples as if it would help. She mentally pictured blocks being added in the opening of her protective wall, but it seemed the Lamia knocked them away as fast as she set them into place. He was in and not about to leave.

"You can't stop me! You're not strong enough!"

Depraved laughter reverberated in her mind, which made the intense, stabbing pain worse. She tried to block his effort to widen the attack zone, but she could not ignore his taunts and threats. If she lost this battle it could be fatal for her and her father.

"It won't be long now before your father is dead, so enjoy the breathing corpse before you bury him!"

Malicious laughter rang in her ears, louder than if the man were physically standing right in front of her. She had some choice words for him, but chose not to provoke him further. Dear stars, what would Kane do?

After a few deep breaths, she was able to push him back some, and his hold lessened slightly. The pressure on her lungs lessened, and the grip on her heart dissipated. She'd actually made progress against this creature from Diabolus.

Dark energy still pressed against every part of her mental wall, but each time she sent healing energy he backed away a bit further.

"You have not won, Jorell, I've decided not to destroy you this moon-cycle. I much prefer to watch you suffer in fear! Sleep well. I'll be back. You can count on it."

The Lamia pulled back, laughing as loudly as he could. The further back he moved the easier it became to inhale clean air. She knew when he was gone because there was an immediate and complete freedom surrounding her. She sighed deeply. The next time she might not be as fortunate...maybe next time Kane would be beside her to help her fight. They made a good team, and they *were* stronger together than separately.

****

Kane stood in the center of the main area of his childhood cavern home. Most things a child remembered turned out to be a big distortion of the truth when they revisited the place. However, everything here was the same in reality as it had been in his mind. The high ceiling with stalactites reaching down in their perfect display of rainbow colors, enhanced by selective lighting, was truly a sight to behold.

His home may have been a cave, but it was magnificent in its natural glory, enhanced by fine leather furniture, and accented by beautiful décor, like the silveron statue of the Elterost Eagle with its wings spread while perched on a tree limb.

Eunis had turned nature's finest work into a complete masterpiece, a true testament to her loving personality. It also highlighted her keen eye for the stunning, and the way her unique creativity pulled it all together. He hadn't been able to see Eunis as an amazing, brilliant and talented woman due to his young age. He only remembered the good mother she'd been, not the beautiful and amazing woman that opened her heart to him.

Eunis walked into the room and set a tray on the table in front of the long, curved sofa. They both sat and picked up a cool glass of popola juice. "You remembered."

"Of course I know it's your favorite." She shook her head. "Kane, you're the one who's been gone. I still have the younger version of you living here." Eunis smiled." I love both of you."

He picked up his glass, brought it to his lips and took a drink. "Both versions of me love you." He took another drink. "The young version of me saw you only as a mother, now I appreciate you for all your talents and beauty."

"I'm not beautiful, but you're sweet to say so."

"There are many kinds of beauty, and you absolutely possess more inner beauty than anyone I've ever met, but you're also beautiful on the outside." He thought he saw her blush in the subdued light. She'd always been overly modest.

"I'm happy to have this chance to see you as an adult." Eunis set her glass on the table. "Say no more about us. Let's attack your problem."

"I need to identify the poison."

"What are the symptoms?"

"It's slow-acting, but all consuming. The patient is in a comma, and has been since shortly after ingestion. The doctor has never seen a poison like this, and he says the patient will die within twenty sun-cycles of ingestion, and we have less than that now."

"Do you know how it was given?"

"At first we thought it was through food or drink, but so far there's no proof."

"Were there any immediate symptoms?"

"A couple of time-units after dinner he returned to his room, fell unconscious, and has been in a coma ever since."

"Have you made contact with him?"

"Not really. I probed and found him to be an honest man with good intentions. He didn't know I'd entered, nor did he sense my presence. To me it seemed like he was already dead."

"Are the doctor and his staff trying to decipher the genetic code to learn the source and possible antidotes?"

"All they've learned is that the source is a living organism."

"I have a pretty good idea of the poison's source."

"Don't keep me in suspense."

"It's from the venom of a female Crodola snake. They're very rare, and even more difficult to find. But, if a person wants something rare and impossible to identify, then that's the poison to use. The reason it's seldom used is because it's so slow acting, taking between twenty and thirty sun-cycles. Most murderers are in a hurry for their victim to die."

"I think whoever did this wanted it to look like an illness rather than a murder. Remember, the other two rulers' deaths were accidents, and many believe they were not accidents. Time works for the murderer here." Kane took another drink. "How is the poison commonly used?"

"The usual way is putting it into food, or drink, but that can be risky since it has a bitter taste, and often the victim will refuse the food, or drink. It can be injected, but that can be too obvious. The sneakiest, most effective way is to refine the poison to a dust, then dust the inside of clothing that will have direct contact with the victim's skin. Since skin is porous, it absorbs the poison, and in about eight to ten time-units, the victim is rendered unconscious. The length of time it takes for a victim to die depends on the size and weight of the victim, and how much was actually absorbed."

"That explains a lot. So, what's the antidote? And do you have any? Or do I have to chase down those snakes and milk them?"

Eunis laughed and he joined her. Then she turned serious. "I don't have any antidote on hand." She shook her head. "The good news is you don't have to milk them, you just have to steal their eggs."

"I'd ask if you're kidding, but your expression says you're not."

"You know me too well. It will not be easy to obtain Crodola eggs. The female stays coiled around her egg-clutch, and the male does not leave her, so you have to get past both parents."

"Where do I find these strange snakes?"

"High in the mountains, they live in crevasses and boulder overhangs. They also like caves. Basically, anywhere that's difficult for other animals, or people to reach them. Be sure to take the proper equipment with you, or you'll never be able to harvest the eggs."

"It doesn't sound promising."

"It's your only hope. Now for the bad news, they only lay eggs once a year, and you're a bit too early."

Kane shook his head. "If I didn't have bad luck, I wouldn't have any luck at all!" He laughed in an effort to put Eunis at ease. She looked bothered by what she'd just told him. "Can we find any eggs right now?"

"Possibly."

"Let's say I'm successful, then what?"

"You'll need to insta-freeze the eggs to transport them. You'll have to take them with you and give them to a doctor in your time, because once he makes the serum, it must immediately be injected. I'll write the formula down so he'll know exactly how to prepare and dispense it. The cure must work as slowly as the poison. If the wrong amount is given, or the mixture is wrong, the patient could die."

"Nothing is ever simple, is it?"

"So many variables make it very difficult, but not impossible."

"Does it matter how big, or how old the male snake is?" His mother gave him a look he was very familiar with, the one that asks, "What do you think?"

Kane shook his head. All this new information, and the task before him had created a headache he had no time to nurse. "Let me guess. The bigger and younger the snake, the more potent the poison. The older the snake, the less potent."

"Nice try son, but wrong. That may be true for most varieties, but not the Crodola. The skinny, old ones are the most potent, and the hardest to catch."

"Does it really matter that much? I assume they all have enough poison to kill someone."

"You're correct. However, when giving the antidote you need to know the intensity you're dealing with so you don't kill the person you're trying to save."

"Great." Kane took a deep breath and tried to put everything in perspective. It was difficult since nothing made perfect sense, or fell into any type of clean category. Every case he'd ever taken on, even the most complex seemed like child's play next to saving Alextor and the entire planet from war.

"What is it, son? I see those mental wheels turning." Eunis put her hand on Kane's shoulder. "You'll do it. All will turn out as it should."

"How do you know? So many things can go wrong. I'm dealing in life and death—so many lives. I don't know, it's just too…"

"You've never been a quitter, and I don't think you'll begin now. You must never forget that light always transcends darkness. You are light, but you fight darkness, which means you have the ability to emerge victorious if you believe in yourself and the light you carry."

"That's one tall order." He looked into Eunis' loving eyes. "You have too much faith in me."

"Promise me to have as much faith in yourself as I have in you."

"I suppose I don't have much of a choice, do I?"

"One always has free will, which means you have choices to make, but I trust you will make the right ones. I know you, Kane. Better than you know yourself. You've always trusted me, and in this, I ask you to have that same blind trust in yourself." Eunis placed her hand on top of Kane's. "I sense there's something else you need my help with."

"Aah yes, how to destroy an Energy-Lamia."

"I don't know if it's ever successfully been done, but I can tell you how to fight one." Eunis took a drink. "It will take a bit of time."

"I'm assuming this is the battle I was born to fight?"

"My premonition showed that fighting the Energy-Lamia leads you to your ultimate battle. It's all connected. Does that make sense to you?"

Kane smiled. "Actually, it fits my theory."

Eunis nodded, then reached out and put her hand on Kane's wrist. She immediately pulled back. "What's under your shirt?"

Reluctantly he rolled up his sleeves and revealed Eunis' Vambrace cuffs. She covered her mouth with her hand to stifle her shocked gasp.

"How did you get those?"

His mother ran her left hand over his right wrist-cuff while she shook her head slowly. He wanted to tell her the truth, but he could not reveal her future. It was a well-known fact in the Mageous Sect that any information about someone's future, good or bad, must never be revealed. It was for that person's peace of mind, and to keep them from trying to change the outcome. *No one* wanted to know the day they would die.

"How is this possible?"

"You gave them to me." Kane wanted to tell her everything. He hated keeping secrets, especially from those he loved. It seemed like betrayal, yet he knew what the knowledge of actual events would do to her. Eunis took a deep breath. He knew she understood why he couldn't tell her, but it still tore at his heart.

"Many annual-cycles in the future, I hope." Eunis took several more deep breaths. "Back to the subject. To fight a Lamia you must concentrate on light. You have to expand that light until it encompasses the dark energy and swallows it. Light is the key to destroying evil. Remember, darkness is only an absence of light. With enough light, darkness is destroyed."

"That sounds easy."

"It's not, and you already know that. I also think you've already fought this evil with light energy."

"I have, but I did not destroy him, he pulled away."

"If it makes you feel any better, I don't know of anyone who has succeeded in destroying one." Eunis shook her head. "I won't lie to you, Kane. I don't know if you can destroy him. You can thwart an attack, although that's not much consolation."

"You've been a great help." Kane refilled both their glasses from the pitcher on the table in front of the sofa. "Tell me more about my father. The more I know about him the better I'll be able to stop him." At that Eunis just stared, her lips slightly parted, fear in her green eyes.

"You think the Lamia is your father?" A tear ran down her cheek.

Kane nodded and watched the tear run down his mother's face while they both sat in silence. He did not have to ask why, he knew the risks were higher because of their connection. "Why don't you tell me about my birth-mother."

"We were very close. She had an exuberant kindness with a gentle soul. She never hurt a living thing. Then there was your father," she took a deep breath, "and there are no words to describe his malevolent, depraved wickedness, or the way he raped your mother."

"I understand why you said they both died in a tragic accident."

"I wanted to protect you from the stigma of your birth, and having *him* as your father."

"I understand."

"She never chose to go near him."

Kane watched more tears run down her cheeks. "I can well imagine." He shook his head. "I know this is difficult. I appreciate your honesty."

"You need to know." Eunis wiped her cheeks with her hand." I pictured telling you so many times, but I never imagined you'd take it so calmly." She laughed. "Of course, I never expected to tell you this at your current age."

"I've had a lot of time to wonder, think, dream, and assume." Kane pushed his hair back from his forehead. "What you've told me is the worst scenario I imagined, but it's not a surprise."

"I'm sorry, Kane. A part of me always believed you'd be better off if you never learned the truth." Eunis hung her head. "Ignorance is bliss, and I wanted you to have a good life, blessed with all good things. I never wanted you to struggle just to survive."

Kane put his finger under her chin and tilted her head up to look into her eyes. "I know how much you love me, and you've done well. I have no complaints. Without *you* I wouldn't be here, or currently living with you. I wouldn't be alive, would I?" He saw her confirmation. "Never sell yourself short, and never regret anything you've ever done."

"When did you get so smart?" She chuckled. "If that's true, why do I feel like such a failure?"

"Human nature. You're not a failure, and you must promise to quit thinking like that." She looked away so he gently turned her head back. "Promise?"

"I'll try, but it's not easy."

"I know, but it's time to stop beating yourself up." She reached her arms out and pulled him to her. Her tight hug said, *never leave me again*, and he wished the same, but wishes were exactly that.

When she released him he immediately missed her, the burden of her future a hard reality. He picked up her hands in his. "Remember, I appreciate you, and love you beyond words. I thank you for your loving care, and for all the special things you taught me. You made me the man I am, and there is no way to thank you properly."

Eunis smiled and nodded. "My only regret is that I apparently don't live long enough to see you as I do at this moment. But you've turned into a very special man, and I'm proud to call you son."

Her tears, and her words pulled at his heart, and if she didn't stop soon he'd join her. She was exactly as he remembered, and more. So much more.

"Now, my son, let's go find some snake eggs."

CHAPTER TWENTY SEVEN

"Dobie, where is he?" Jorell paced the floor behind the breakfast bar in her father's private quarters.

"I told you, he's in the past trying to find another piece of this rather complicated puzzle. That's all I know, honestly."

"He's been gone over two sun-cycles, and that makes me nervous."

"Jorell, I assure you, if he's away, there's a good reason, and it pertains to your father."

She sat on the stool next to Dobie at the kitchen bar." Thanks for getting me away from Rand. He was being a jerk. That man is driving me insane!

"I'd love to go hurt him for you, but I promised Kane I'd keep an eye on you."

Dobie smiled at her, which told her he really would like to put a hurt on her fiancé. "I can't let you enjoy yourself that much."

Dobie laughed. "Guess I don't hide my feelings very well. Sorry."

Jorell took a deep breath and smiled. "You do have a way about you."

"So I've been told. Kane says I come in handy at times."

"Seriously Dobie, when will Kane be back? I need to talk to him."

"Me too." Dobie patted her hand. "I'd tell you if I knew. You jumped with us once, so you know how uncertain things can be. And you know Kane will do anything to help you and your father."

"How long have you two been together?"

"We met on our first day of Academy, we were both twelve annual-cycles. We haven't been apart since that day."

"You're more like brothers than friends."

"He's the brother fate gave me, and that's an even better kind. We stay together because we have a bond, and we truly respect each other."

"I've always wished I had a sister, someone to talk to, confide in, play with, to be close to like you and Kane."

Dobie looked into Jorell's eyes. "When Kane and I met we instantly bonded because we had so much in common. Unfortunately, we also shared emotional scars."

"I'm sorry."

"Don't be. It made us stronger. It made us who we are, and I think we're pretty good people, even if I do say so myself."

The door chime sounded and Dobie hopped off his stool and took a couple of steps. She stood and started to follow, but he put his arm out and stopped her in her tracks.

"Are you expecting anyone?"

She shook her head. The chime sounded once again and her stomach did a flip. She reached for the counter to steady herself, but her hand was shaking so bad she doubted it would do any good.

"You wait here. I'll take care of it."

Dobie hurried out of the kitchen to answer the door. She leaned against the counter and took solace in the cool relief the polished marbelus provided. The unmistakable sound of the opening door made her wonder if Dobie knew what he was doing. She had no choice but to trust him. She laid her head on her hands and took a deep breath.

"Jorell?"

Her head jerked up so fast she nearly fell over. That voice. She turned to see Kane's commanding, sexy form in the kitchen doorway. How she wanted to throw herself at him and kiss him senseless, but she collected herself instead. "It's good to see you, Kane."

"I certainly hope so." He stepped into the room.

Dobie walked in behind Kane and slapped him on the back. "Bout time. What took ya so long?"

"Travel is bad this time of annual-cycle."

"Never can trust those nether-realms, can ya?"

She laughed at Dobie's joke along with Kane. It was nice to laugh, even for a moment, but it was even better seeing Kane...knowing he was back. He shook Dobie's hand and they shared a couple more back slaps.

"Jorell, is there any change?"

"Father's the same, but there was another Lamia attack. I was alone with him at the time." She stepped closer to Kane. "He called me by name. How did he know?"

"The Energy-Lamia's visits are by astral travel, which means his spirit is there, but his body is not. So, he can see you, but you don't see him. Everyone on the planet knows your name, either from pictures, vids, or events."

"But he said my father will die, and there's nothing I can do to stop it." She lowered her head and stared at the floor. Large warm hands cupped her shoulders and she looked up into Kane's hypnotic, blue eyes.

"Jorell, this is what he wants. He's a master at implanting doubt and fear. We will *not* let him win."

Kane pulled her into his arms and held her tight against his chest. She listened to the steady beat of his heart and inhaled the fresh outdoor scent on his shirt. She'd missed him--too much.

He stroked her hair, and gently rubbed her back. His touch was magic, and she never wanted him to stop. The safe feeling he provided was like an aphrodisiac, and she wanted more. He eased her back so she could see his face.

"When did this attack happen?"

"Last moon-cycle."

Kane rubbed his chin and glanced at Dobie. "Where were you?"

"I was monitoring the quarters to be sure no one entered."

She watched Kane shake his head, then he began to pace in front of the bar. What was going on in that mind of his? Back and forth he walked in silence. She took her cue from Dobie not to interrupt him, so they waited...and waited until she thought she'd scream.

Kane stopped in front of Jorell and took a deep breath. He still did not speak. Thank the stars the door chime went off, at least it broke the silence.

"That should be the doctor." Kane left the galley and walked toward the entry door."

Dobie stared at her with an uncomfortable look on his face. "What's wrong with him?"

"I'm not sure I've ever seen him like this."

"In all the annual-cycles you've spent together? I find that hard to believe."

"You'd be surprised, Princess."

Before she could say another word, Kane returned with Dr. Willock who rushed to her and gave her a hug."

"I'm so happy to see you, my dear. I have good news." He pulled a vile from his pants' pocket and held it up. "The antidote, I have the antidote for your father."

"You found it!" Jorell hugged the doctor. "I can't believe you found it."

"It wasn't me. Kane brought it. I only refined it to make it injectable."

She walked toward Kane and stopped in front of him. "Why didn't you tell me?" Her heart raced and her breathing became rough.

"I had to be sure Dr. Willock could process it properly."

Dr. Willock cleared his throat. "If we're lucky, this will save your father's life." He shook his head. "There is no guarantee, I want you to understand that."

She turned toward Kane. "Where did you get this antidote?"

"That's a long story. Just trust that the person who gave this to me is completely trustworthy, has good intent, and is *not* political."

She turned back toward the doctor. "By all means, give it to him. Now." Jorell stepped closer and placed her hand on his arm. "How quickly does it work?"

"You'll need patience. It will take many doses. The antidote must work as slowly as the poison. If the antidote works too fast, it could kill him. Slow is better."

"I'm out of patience."

"You'd better find more because I cannot hurry this process. At least not if you want your father to live."

"Sorry." She sighed loudly, and it felt good to let out some of her frustration. She'd never been a complainer, or a negative thinker, but this situation had her second-guessing herself and everyone around her. Right now she wanted to scream at the top of her lungs. Instead, she looked the doctor in the eye. "Let's give him his first dose." She gestured toward the living area. "Shall we?"

Kane walked up to her, slipped his arm around her waist and escorted her to her father's chamber. She admired the way he carried himself with confidence, and right now she needed his strength.

Kane leaned his head down to Jorell's ear. "It's okay you know."

"What?"

"Being frustrated."

Kane always seemed to know how she felt. "Are all your clients like me?"

"None of them are like you."

"How can that be? Aren't clients all the same?"

"Truthfully, I've never had a client with as much at stake as you." Kane shook his head. "No other client of mine ever held the peace of the entire planet in their hands, then put that responsibility on me."

"No wonder I have a headache that won't quit." She watched while the doctor gave her father his first injection. "This has to work, I want my father back, and Sector-Three needs their ruler—desperately." She looked into the doctor's eyes. "If you have the antidote, have you figured out how he was poisoned?"

"The poison was most likely put on his clothes and absorbed into the skin. He did not eat or drink it."

"By the stars!" Jorell ran to the closet, grabbed the suit her father had worn to the dinner, the headed for the bedroom door.

Kane reached out and grabbed Jorell's arm. "Hold it. Where are you going?"

"I need to burn this!" She held up the suit on the hanger that was wrapped in clear plastica.

"That is evidence." He took the hanger from her hand and gave it to the doctor. "Please have this garment examined so we'll know for sure."

The doctor examined the suit. "It appears to have been cleaned, but there could still be trace evidence available. Our lab is good. If it's there, they'll find."

"Good. It could be of the utmost importance in the near future." Kane looked at Jorell. "You can burn it when this is all over."

"Fine. I'll wait, but I will burn it."

"And we will all watch. Now, Dobie will escort you into the living area so you can rest." Jorell started to speak so he placed a finger on her lips. "Please, go with him. I'll be right there."

She took the arm Dobie offered and allowed him to take her back to the couch where she sat willingly. She was tired, very tired. Dobie stared at her for a moment, then sat in the chair next to the sofa. He looked nearly as confused as she felt. "Dobie, where did Kane travel to?" He stared at her with a look that said he knew, but wasn't about to tell her. It didn't matter--only results counted.

"Princess, Kane needs to tell you that. But the good news is he knows what he's doing. He's the best, and I'm not just saying that because I work with him. He really is the best."

"You're a good friend to him, Dobie, and I understand what you're trying to tell me without actually saying anything."

"I'm glad you understand, because I'm not so sure I do."

Dobie laughed and she joined him. When she was exhausted everything became funny. Laughing was also the self-defense mechanism she used when she didn't want to think. Dobie leaned forward, took her hand in his and gave a quick, friendly, squeeze.

"Kane will fix everything, you'll see."

She looked into Dobie's eyes and he leaned away. "I pray you're right because I don't want to contemplate the outcome if you're wrong."

CHAPTER TWENTY EIGHT

"What's going on here?"

The sound of Kane's voice caused Dobie to jump to his feet. She glanced up at Kane who met her with a teasing smile. Dobie looked nervous, as if he'd done something wrong, which he hadn't.

"Chief, I think Jorell is tired. How about if I stay here with Ruler Sutone, and you take her to her own quarters."

"Good idea."

She opened her mouth to protest, but Kane shook his head and gave her a look that explicitly said not to argue. Before she knew it, Kane offered her his hand and she took it, letting him pull her to her feet.

"Kane, I really think I should stay here and…"

"And what? Watch your father breathe? Protect him from something Dobie can handle?"

She nodded then looked down at the floor. He was right, of course, but she hated to leave her father's side. Common sense said she couldn't help him, but her heart wanted to be there to try.

"Dobie promises to keep a close eye on your father, and he'll contact us if there's any change at all. Right, Dobie?" Kane looked at Dobie, then back at Jorell.

"Absolutely." Dobie stepped closer to Jorell. "Go, Princess. You need your rest. If the Energy-Lamia visits, I'll call both of you immediately. I can sense him, so go on now. Your father is safe with me."

Both men stared at her as if they could move her with their eyes. It worked. She walked to the door, Kane right behind. Her quarters were only the next door down the hall and they arrived before she even had a chance to worry.

She looked into the scanner and the door slid open. Kane entered first so he could check the premises. He seemed to think someone might be after her as well as her father. Kane was a cautions man, a trait she appreciated. She waited in the main living area while he checked the other rooms.

"Everything seems to be in order."

"Really?" She laughed and Kane smiled.

"Actually, your quarters are very nice. I like your decorating taste."

"Thanks. I'm very fond of blues and greens. I suppose because I don't get outside as much as I'd like to, so I bring nature's colors in. It relaxes me."

Kane walked to the window while she watched his casual, unintentional swagger. An overwhelming feeling of dizziness overcame her. She grabbed the back of the nearest chair to regain her balance. She closed her eyes and willed herself steady.

Two strong hands grasped her waist. Before she could take another breath she was in his arms. He carried her to the sofa and gently laid her down. He knelt on the floor beside her, took her hand in his, then looked into her eyes in his sexy, masculine way.

"What's wrong?"

"I felt dizzy."

"And I know why."

Kane released her hand, nodded, then walked into the galley. The clang of glasses and the sound of the food fabricator brought a smile to her face. Kane returned with two goblets, a bottle of wine, a tray of various cheeses, meats, and petite-bread. She sat up and he made himself comfortable next to her, then proceeded to make a sandwich. He handed the creation to her, then filled two glasses and offered her one. She took the wine and immediately took several sips.

"Eat. You'll feel better. Besides," Kane took a drink, "I won't let you up until you do."

"I suppose I did pay you enough to take care of me, along with solving the mystery, saving my father—not to mention the entire planet."

"Of course you did. It's all in a sun-cycle's work." Kane held up his glass. "This wine is excellent."

"You're changing the subject."

"You're right. Now, about the wine?"

"It's a private brand from a little known vineyard. My father knows the owner, and together they came up with our private, royal label." She watched Kane pour more wine. "Kane, do you really believe the antidote will work?"

"I do."

She shook her head. "I wish I had your faith."

"It's because I trust the person who gave it to me, and I've sensed the fight in your father. He may be lying still and unresponsive, but his life force is strong, and his commitment to his people is foremost in his mind. For you, and for them, I believe he will recover."

Jorell took a long drink. "I want to believe that."

"Visualize him alive and well. The power of visualization is strong. Hold on to it tightly."

She looked deeply into Kane's eyes to measure his sincerity. The eyes were always a glimpse into a person's soul, and in Kane she found a mixture of anger and compassion, logic and recklessness, love and hate. But above all, his honesty stood steadfast and true.

"What do you see, Jorell?"

"Forgive me for staring."

"It's what you do, isn't it?"

"You know it is."

"Then tell me."

"I see a lot of inner conflict that pulls at your heartstrings. You're fighting many internal battles, and you're constantly searching for answers." It seemed to be his turn to stare, but she didn't mind. In fact, she craved his attention.

"You're either very astute, or the best reader I've ever encountered." Kane shook his head. "I've never met anyone who could read me." He sighed. "Even a little."

She reached out and touched his cheek with the palm of her hand. His warm skin had a bit of beard stubble, a feature she found sexy. Touching him stirred emotions inside her that never existed until Kane entered her life. Her stomach did summersaults that tickled and tantalized.

Her hand inched down the side of his face and she heard a moan from deep inside him. He reached out, pulled her to him and pressed his lips against hers. The kiss began slow, then his tongue found hers and instant fire erupted between them.

She welcomed his every move and dueled back with taunts of her own. His hands inched their way up and down her backside. Desire surfaced so strong she could barely breathe. Kane slowly laid her down and pulled her legs onto the sofa, then he lay against her, his obvious hard desire pressed tightly against her.

This was a moment she'd imagined more than once, but the reality was far better. Judging by Kane's kiss, he was well experienced, yet he made her feel as if she were the only woman on the planet.

How could she be so willing to give herself to Kane when she was engaged to another man? Because she never loved Rand, nor did he arouse her sexual desires. Even Rand's kisses were shallow, which hit home for the first time. Rand was only fulfilling a political decision, even though he claimed differently.

What she felt for Kane was love, unlike the pretend version she'd claimed for Rand. Kane was exactly the man she'd dreamed about. His qualifications were endless, but most important was his ability to set her body on fire, to make her feel desirable, wanted, and loved.

Kane's hands moved to her shoulders, then slowly inched toward her breasts, which sent tingles through her. She'd waited for this moment, his touch, his need, but never thought it would happen. She wanted him, needed him. Rand entered her mind, and the thought scared her. She pushed him back and broke the kiss.

"Something wrong, Princess?"

"Everything is right. Very right. But not here. Remember the last time we were on the sofa? I think we should move to my bedchamber."

"Say no more." Kane stood, then helped Jorell to her feet. "Are you sure? I don't want regrets, or guilt to consume you for betraying your fiancé."

"First, I'm positive I want you. Second, as far as I'm concerned, I have no fiancé." Jorell kicked off her heels and they landed half-way across the room. "And if my father recovers, sorry, *when* he recovers, I'll tell him so."

"You're sure?"

"Absolutely." She put her arms around Kane's neck and hugged him tightly. "I sense you're ready to make love to me."

Kane smiled. "You don't have to read me to know that."

"You're right, warrior."

"You see me as a warrior?"

"Warriors are sexy. I love warriors."

"Then I shall be *your warrior*."

He lifted her off her feet and carried her down the hall to her bedchamber and stepped inside." Stop right here." The door slid closed and she looked into the high-security lock. When the mechanism engaged she smiled at Kane. "We cannot be disturbed under any circumstances."

"That's all I need to know." Kane let Jorell's legs down and she stood on the floor in front of him. "Have I ever told you how sexy you are?"

She shook her head. "Please, feel free."

"I love the way you look in your clothes, but I think you'll look even better without them."

His hands roamed her back until he found the fasten-tab on her gown. When he pressed the tab the dress opened, and he stepped back to watch it slide down her body and pool on the floor. His gaze became so intense and hot she could feel it move about her body.

"Better, but not quite there."

She reached behind her back, unfastened her one-piece undergarment, then inched it down her body until it lay on top of her gown. When she straightened she was naked, and the urge to cover herself was too strong to resist. Her arms wrapped over her breasts.

"My sweet, you're the most beautiful woman I've ever seen. You're absolutely perfect."

Kane took her hands and moved them away from her body. An instant shiver ran down her spine. Never had she thought of being a naked statue before a man, but Kane made it an act of love.

"Never feel embarrassed by your nakedness, I adore every inch of you. Looking at you pleases me more than I can say."

Kane scooped her into his arms and carried her to the large, circular bed in the center of the room and laid her down. The lights were dim, yet bright enough for her to see the admiration in his eyes. She would know if he lied, it was her gift, and she'd already used it on him. Before another thought crossed her mind, He bent over her and kissed her again, not leaving any part of her mouth unattended.

She ended the kiss and pushed her hands against his chest. "Okay warrior, it's your turn." With a big smile on his face he rolled off the bed, stood in front of her and pulled the front fastenings of his shirt loose and dropped the garment to the floor. His bare chest sported a couple of small scars, but to her it looked absolutely perfect in every way, his abdomen tight and muscled. She doubted there was any part of him that didn't bulge with toned muscles. He was a fantastic combination of warrior and athlete, the kind of man any woman would lust after.

If there were such a thing, Kane would be the perfect man. He then unfastened his belt, undid the fastener on the front of his pants, and the garment fell to the floor next to hers. He then made fast work of his undergarment, and stood in front of her naked as the day he was born, except for the two gold wristbands that made him look like the mysterious warrior he was.

The smile on her face showed, even though she'd tried to hide her adoring approval. Kane was magnificent and she wanted him. He returned her smile. With one finger she summoned him to join her on the bed. He knelt on the edge then slithered up next to her. She reached out and caressed his chest, his smooth skin warm beneath her touch. It was difficult to believe this incredible man wanted her, that he lay on her bed, visually ready, willing, and very able.

"You seem surprised, my sweet." He pulled Jorell tight against him and she wrapped her arms around him. "Do I please you?"

The best she could offer was a nod since his magnificent form took her breath away. Her hand found his abdomen, then worked its way around to the curve of his backside. Magnificent was the only word that came to mind while she traced his every bulge and curve of his toned physique. She'd seen naked men before, but Kane was the finest specimen on this, or any planet.

When his arousal pressed against her she unwillingly gasped. "You please me, warrior, but I feel the best is yet to come."

"Indeed it is."

Kane's hard, muscled body fit against hers in a way that defied logic. She was in awe of the strength he possessed, and when his lips found hers, his sensuous kiss melted any lingering resolve to stay true to Rand. She wasn't being weak by giving in to her desires for Kane, she was following her heart, a rare act for her.

It didn't matter they'd only known each other a short time, the dynamic pull between them sparkled. She'd been aware of his strong, masculine appeal from the moment they'd met. Even when Kane was an old man in the garden, she'd felt his strong, sexual energy. With that thought, a familiar tickle touched her mind.

Jorell, my sweet. I'll stop only if you ask me to. Kane groaned. I want far more than a kiss.

"*As do I.*" His body set hers on fire, and she never wanted him to stop.

Kane ended the kiss and pulled his head back. I do not want you to feel pressured to do anything you'll regret.

"*How could I regret...*" She caught herself. Of course, he was referring to Rand. "*No one owns me.*"

He released his hold on her, then leaned back. "*I don't want to cause you heartache.*"

Jorell tickled Kane's consciousness to tease him. There were so many things she wanted to say, but words were hard to find. She didn't want Kane to think she was pressuring him into anything, or that she expected anything. "*Whatever heartache I may suffer, will not be from you*"

"*I want to take away your heartache. I want to show you....*"

She concentrated on Kane, the one man who made her happy. "*Show me?*"

"I'm not sure you're ready."

She took a deep breath and began to explore with her hands what she'd only admired. *"You're wrong, warrior. I've waited my entire life for you. I'm more than ready."* She moved her hands across his chest then down his arms to the wristbands that covered half of his forearm. The intricately carved, dark gold bands were a part of him. Kane was amazing from the top of his dark brown hair down to his toes, and every inch in between.

"You're absolutely sure?"

"I've never been more sure of anything."

Kane sighed. *"I'd be a fool not to believe you."*

"You're no fool, traveler." He answered her with a kiss that set her world upside down. She didn't know it was possible to convey so much emotion and sex appeal in one kiss, but Kane knew how to deliver. She doubted a kiss could be any deeper, or intimate than his.

Kane's energy encircled her, and she mentally reached out and pulled it inside. As their energies melded, a knowing as old as the ages floated through her consciousness. Somehow, she sensed she'd known Kane forever, like they'd been together before, and would remain connected forever.

The sensation was disorienting, yet comforting. It was so right and soothing that she wanted to linger with him in this surreal world that held only loving vibrations, and nothing negative. She'd heard about soul-mates her entire life. Was this what it was like?

Her fingers explored the rigid, contoured muscles of his chest and down his stomach. His body was finer than the best warrior in Sector-Three. Kane could never be called average. She savored his strength, and tucked it away in her memory. Never would she forget this experience with the one man who could read her, as well as make love to her.

Ever so gently he kissed his way from her lips, down her neck to the swell of her breasts where he lingered, licking and exploring. She tilted her head back and enjoyed each new sensation his mouth created.

His hands were busy as well, and she enjoyed his sensuous investigations. Then he sucked in her nipple and she gasped at the sweet, loving feeling that spread through her entire body. She never would have imagined such a large, muscular man could be so delicate. She'd briefly seen the hungry look in his eyes when he meandered down.

With precision, he situated himself over her on the bed, and moved his attention to her other breast. His tongue teased, and moved in small circles while sweet pleasure rippled up and down her body, building anticipation.

Kane expertly kissed his way down her stomach until he reached the part of her that was so ready for him she thought she'd burst. A moan escaped her when his tongue found her most sensitive place and lingered. He knew exactly how to pleasure her, and she never wanted him to stop, but she needed him inside her so she could feel him, savor him--love him.

Just when she thought she could no longer hold back, he moved his mouth up to hers and entered her with one, swift movement. He was everywhere. He filled her, he excited her, he completed her. He moved in and out, her desire increasing with each calculated thrust. His movements pushed her ever closer to being one with him.

In her mind sparks of energy burst outward from both of their bodies. She opened her eyes, shocked to see the reality of her imagination. It wasn't her imagination, she and Kane were actually producing energy that sparkled all around them. With each new surge a faint popping sound touched her ears, while glimmering points of light spun and created a rainbow of colors all around them.

She took a deep breath when Kane stepped up the pace. The harder and faster he thrust, the more her mind filled with thousands of thoughts and emotions, all about Kane. She was so near completion she could no longer hold back. She found total consummation with the man of her dreams. She gazed into his eyes and knew he too had found his complete satisfaction. She wanted him in her arms—forever

Kane groaned low in his throat, then laid down beside her, breathing heavily. He put his arm around her waist and pulled her to her side until she rested against him. She reached out and wiped beads of sweat from his forehead. After several deep breaths her breathing returned to normal. Kane was still breathing heavily. "I think you worked too hard."

"I would not call that work, my sweet. If it is work, then I shall never stop working for you."

She smiled. "Nor would I want you to."

He scooted his arm up so she could rest her head on it and cuddle even closer. It was difficult to return to reality from something so all-consuming and beautiful. It was difficult to deal with all the lingering feelings.

While her head rested in the crook of his arm, her ear against his chest, she took pleasure in the steady beat of his heart. She loved the feel of skin on skin, especially his.

"Jorell, I'm not like other men." He tilted Jorell's head up to look into her eyes. "I don't take what I want, I receive what is freely given." He tucked a few loose hairs behind her left ear.

"I freely gave myself to you."

"That may be true at this moment, but what will you tell your father when he wakes up? What will you tell Rand when he looks you in the eye?" Kane pulled his arm out from under Jorell, stood and walked to the window." I fear a part of you belongs to your father, and the other part to Rand." He walked back to the bed and sat. "I'm selfish, my sweet. I want all of you."

"Are you like this with all the women you bed?"

"You're the first."

"Don't tell me you're a…"

"Of course not, but you're the first woman who really matters to me. I'm not sure what that means, but that's how I feel. Damn, you have a strange effect on me."

She laughed which made Kane squint his eyes and wrinkle his forehead while he tried not to frown. "I'm not laughing at you, Kane." She scooted across the bed, stood, then walked up behind him. She put her hands on his shoulders, her breasts against his back. "I'm trying to tell you I feel exactly the same."

Kane turned so fast she nearly fell backward, instead he caught her and pulled her tight against him. He looked at her with a surprised expression, a first for the warrior who was always so sure of himself. "I don't know why that should shock you." Jorell put her arms around him "Our mind-meld is so complete we created new energy. Didn't you see it?"

"I've never done that with anyone." Kane took her hands in his and raised her right hand to his lips and kissed her fingers. "You're a remarkable woman, Jorell Sutone."

"But?"

"But I'm working for you, and I never mix business with pleasure."

"I think you just broke your own rule."

"I've broken many rules in my life, but none that felt that good." He bent down and kissed her.

Kane's kiss could only be labeled exotic and erotic. His tongue danced with hers, and explored in such an alluring way she probably would have fainted if he hadn't been holding her. His hot body fueling her, giving her courage, and a need for more. Breathing became difficult for both of them. All too soon he ended the kiss and pulled back. "Why do I sense what you're thinking even when we're not mind-melded?"

"Then you should be ready for what I'm about to do."

CHAPTER TWENTY NINE

Pakar Moran stared at Rand. He didn't trust the man, but he didn't trust his own son either. When it came to politics, credits, and women, he never trusted anyone. "Well, are you going to life-mate the tramp, or do I have to change my plans?" Rand cowered in front of him, not a good sign. "What?"

"I...I..."

"I'll take that as an admittance of failure." Rand had no courage, and he'd never find any. No wonder the slut didn't want him. It wouldn't take her much to do better than this pathetic excuse of a man. However, he still needed him since he was a political insider. "We'll have to resort to other options."

"I didn't realize we had any."

"Of course you didn't." He paced in front of Rand then looked him in the eye. Luckily he did not pay the fool to think. His only job was to occupy Jorell." Kill Jorell Sutone."

"Aah...aah..couldn't we just finish off Alextor? I'll make sure Jorell doesn't talk. That's the simplest plan, isn't it?"

"Sector-Three is more complex than the other two. Alextor has more loyal council members and friends. If they knew what's happened to him they'd come knocking on our door."

"Why? We've been careful. We've laid all the right diversions, put all our people in crucial places. What could possibly go wrong? Nazar is running Sector-Two, and Ramon Coster is in charge of Sector-One."

"But to complete the takeover we need total control of Sector-Three, which isn't possible with Jorell in the picture. The life-mate plan is no longer an option." Pakar shook his head while he stared at Rand. "So far you're a total failure. The only recourse is to eliminate the bitch."

"You can't do that!"

"You failed to control her. Remember your promise? 'I'll control Jorell, she will not be a problem." He watched the stupid man nod. "So, you will be responsible for her death, not me."

"Give me one more chance to prove she's not a problem."

"No!" Anger boiled in his veins. He wanted to reach out and strangle the stupid man. He only included this idiot due to his position, but Rand should not part of his genius plan. "Never question my judgment, or authority!"

Rand wiped his forehead with his sleeve. "I'm sorry. What do you want me to do?"

"Kill her!"

"I ahaa...aah." Rand raked hair off his forehead with his fingers. "I...I...could make it look like suicide? She's mourning her father's condition already, so we'll just say she was weak and couldn't deal with it anymore."

"I'm sure you're proud of that suggestion, but once again, you show your stupidity since no one knows about Alextor's condition yet. Maybe you should be in the accident with her?"

"Sorry, sir. Slip of the tongue."

"I have a cure for loose tongues, but I'm not in the mood for that much blood right now. Jorell must keep her mouth shut, and that can only happen if she'd dead. If I can't trust you to..."

"I can do it, I won't let you down. I'll..."

Pakar held his hand up and Rand immediately stopped speaking. A wise move. He was fed up waiting for all the underlings to pull things together before he could claim power." See that it's done before next sun-cycle is over."

"Of course. But won't that conflict with her father's passing? How will we explain to the public at large that Alextor will not attend his only daughter's funeral?"

"We'll say he's too distraught for a public affair and will keep her funeral private—family and close friends only. Then Alextor becomes sick and dies."

"That's perfect, sir."

"Of course it is. Your part will be simple. Just make sure Jorell is with you at all times, and keep me informed of your every move. I'll arrange the hit." He could not trust Rand to do the job himself, and he had to trust it would be done. He was glad the fool didn't know his real name. If he did he'd probably squeal like a stuffed pigor.

"I understand, sir."

Pakar waved his hand, then turned his back. "Dismissed." He listened to Rand's retreating footsteps, and sighed in relief when the door slid closed. He'd call his best exterminator, who was as bad as they came, and *always* delivered.

No man could stop his takeover. He'd successfully replaced two Sector leaders with his own men. The only remaining obstacle was the Sutones. It would all be his soon, and the Sutones would be removed— *permanently*. Soon it would all be his.

****

Kane paced back and forth, the early sun beating into his living area through the skylight. The memory of making love to Jorell played over and over in his mind, each thought pure joy. He had learned one thing, she had no feelings for Rand, but that was the least of his problems.

How could he tell Jorell she couldn't jump with him? He wanted her to, but she had to remain viewable to the public. Her father might wake and need her, and of course, there was Rand. He viewed the man as useless, but Rand would surely notice if Jorell was missing.

Dobie was busy working on research in the other room while Kane waited for Jorell. A fuzzy feeling invaded his mind and he knew she'd arrived.

He opened the door just in time to see one shapely leg leave the vehicle and one high-heeled foot hit the ground, followed by the second. Before he blinked again she stood, her long gown slid down and covered his entertainment. She walked up to him in with a purposeful stride, looking far too sexy. Damn, he wanted to kiss her so badly, to throw his arms around her, and feel her firm breasts against his chest. Instead he'd have to settle for gawking at her enticing cleavage while he suppressed his desires and acted like a professional.

Every muscle in his body screamed for her. She had an uncanny ability to make him feel fulfilled, happy, and at peace with himself. Her presence caused him to be more aware of his senses, which could explain their deep connection. From the moment of their first kiss, he hadn't been able to get her out of his mind.

"Kane? Is something wrong?"

"On the contrary, something is right."

Jorell smiled. "And, that would be?"

"I'm planning a jump to the future."

"Why?"

"To learn the identity of who wants your father dead. If he wakes up, this person will try again, and they won't use a slow kill twice."

"When do we leave?"

"*We* don't, Dobie and I do." Kane took her hand and guided her to the sofa where they sat next to each other. "You need to stay here and make everything appear normal. If you're missing, it will be noticed. We can't afford the future to change."

"I don't see how my absence would make a difference."

"If you change your regular routine, those people you would have seen make adjustments to their schedules, which in turn changes what transpires in any given time period. You do something different, they do something different, and the future is altered. What we see in the future depends on your actions this sun-cycle, and the ones that follow."

"How can I stay here when all I'll do is worry about you? Everyone that sees me will know something is wrong. I'm not a good actress, Kane."

"You'll do fine."

"I really want to go with you."

"Trust me, Jorell. Promise you'll trust me."

"Princess," Dobie called while he walked into the room, "you know Kane's right. And take it from one who knows, you can trust him with your life."

He had to change the subject before the tears in her eyes spilled down her cheeks. "Jorell, what's on your schedule this sun-cycle?"

"I have three meetings, followed by a meeting of the assembly."

"Good. Go to your meetings, act normal, do your job, and we'll do ours."

"That sounds too easy."

"It is, Princess. Don't you worry, I'll keep an eye on Kane. A real close eye."

Kane laughed with Dobie and Jorell. Tension ran high, and he worried about her more than he cared to admit. He had a bad feeling about leaving her alone, but he couldn't risk taking her. With luck he'd be back before the sun-cycle ended.

If Alextor's condition became known, the entire Sector could fall into a panic. Their only chance to thwart the takeover rested on Alextor's recovery; no easy task, and that had to happen fast, before a new leader took control.

"I know you're right, Kane. I just…" Jorell took a deep breath. "I'll miss you."

When she looked down toward the floor, he suspected her admission embarrassed her. He tilted her chin up with his free hand." I'll miss you too." Out the corner of his eye he saw Dobie scurry from the room, thankful they were now alone.

"Then please, let me go with you."

"Jorell, do I really need to tell you what you might learn if you venture into the future? I don't want to put you through that."

"If the future can't be changed, I'll learn about it anyway, right?"

"That's why you hired me, to change the worst scenario. Let me do it. You need to protect your father. Remember, you're covering for him, you're trying to convince the assembly, and everyone in the government, that your father is away on a personal matter. You can't do that if you're not here."

Jorell squeezed Kane's hand and nodded. "How far are you going?"

"Dobie is doing research to pinpoint a time. He's also compiling a suspect list of who might be involved, and where we can find them. Boring stuff."

"That still didn't tell me how far you're going."

"Ninety sun-cycles, unless Dobie thinks we need to go further." She looked worried, but he couldn't sugar-coat the problems ahead, she was too intelligent. She understood the risks now, and in the future.

"I know what you're thinking, Kane, and you're right. I'm worried."

"And how do you know what I'm thinking?" Like he needed an answer to that question. She smiled with a devilish twinkle in her green eyes. The sun from the skylight danced on her red hair and all he wanted to do was run his fingers through the silky strands. Her smile turned from playful to seductive.

If he stayed next to her any longer he'd lay her down and make mad, passionate love, but that would not help the pending decision. He let go of her hand, stood and walked toward the galley. "Can I get you anything? Koffa maybe?"

Jorell stood. "I wish I had time. I love my koffa, but I'm about to be late for my first meeting." She turned toward the door.

Before she took another step he rushed to her, pulled her close, then kissed her. The good-by gesture instantly turned passionate. She deepened the kiss, which drove him crazy, especially when her breasts pressed against him the way they were.

May the stars forgive him, he'd fallen for this woman, and he was helpless to stop his runaway passion. Her arms threaded around his neck and she hung on as if her life depended on it. By the galaxy, he wanted her—all of her.

Her mind tickled his, and as much as he wanted her, he had a job to do. He slowly withdrew and ended the kiss. She looked as if he'd taken away her favorite toy.

"Be careful Kane. I want you to come back to me safe and sound."

"I *will* be back."

CHAPTER THIRTY

Rand had talked more during this assembly meeting than he had his entire political career. At least it seemed that way. He forgot to tell her about all the proposals he'd submitted for consideration. She disagreed with all of them, but she did not dare to draw attention, and Rand knew that fact.

He rambled on and on about water distribution changes. Most were feasible, but a few were way out in space somewhere. The only good his grandstanding served was delaying questions about her father.

The excuse she'd chosen was flimsy at best. As far as everyone knew, he was with his only living relative, his great-aunt Corrine and he'd probably be gone for about thirty sun-cycles. It wasn't unheard of for a ruler to take an extended vacation, especially for a family crisis.

Their only problem was they really had no family to speak of. Everyone knew her father hadn't taken time off in over five annual-cycles. He wasn't known for taking time off, only for his devotion to duty and his genuine love for the people.

In a conversation with her father shortly before his poisoning, he voiced serious concern about his people, and ever since Marto and Trom died, he'd feared he'd be next. He also thought the conspirators would harm her as well.

Rand finally finished his never-ending speech, votes were taken, and the dismissal process went swiftly. Everyone was busy picking up their satchels and belongings, leaving as fast as they could. It was late, and every assembly member and their staff were exhausted.

One of her father's closest friends walked toward her with visible concern on his face. She smiled. "Greetings, Bacone. How are you?"

"Oh, my dear Jorell, I'm fine, it's your aunt Corrine I'm worried about. I know how much your father adores her."

"That he does. I'm not sure she's going to survive this illness, which is why father went so quickly."

"He's spoken to me about her many times over the annual-cycles, which means he cares deeply since he normally keeps his private life private."

"Thank you for asking."

"I am sorry, my dear. I've tried getting in touch with Alextor, but he's not responding. Did he forget his com device?"

"He did, but I'm sure he'll get to you as soon as he's able. Corrine is in the extreme-care med-quarters, so it's really hard to get in touch with him. I did speak with him last moon-cycle, and he's tired, but doing fine."

"Please, tell him to call me. I'd really like to talk with him."

"I will." Jorell picked up her bag, put the strap over her shoulder, and began to walk up the aisle. "Have a good evening, Representative Bacone."

He waved. "You too."

She sighed deeply, extremely relieved that Bacone hadn't dug any deeper. All she wanted to do was get back to her father's quarters and check on him. Just as she picked up her pace toward the door, a hand grasped her arm, the touch familiar.

"What's the rush? If I didn't know better, I'd think you were trying to get away from me."

"Oh Rand, don't be paranoid. I'd never do that." It sounded good, even if she didn't mean a word of it. Rand would never know her true feelings because he didn't care enough. Her father's life depended on her silence, and she remembered Kane's advice; trust no one.

"Come with me. I'm taking you to dinner at the best restaurant in any Sector."

"And you've tried every restaurant in every Sector?" Rand looked at her as if he wanted to growl. He did resemble a zoo animal. She laughed to herself. The man had no sense of humor, an aspect of him that stood out more since she'd met Kane and Dobie. He ignored her question, took her free hand and walked her down the hall and out of the building.

An attendant brought his transport to the bottom of the stairs. She took one step toward the vehicle, but was instantly stopped by a piercing burn in her upper chest. Everything around her went fuzzy. She fell and hit the marbelus steps and pain ripped through her. Step by step she rolled before coming to rest at the bottom walkway.

Loud voices became muted, and she could no longer focus enough to distinguish the identity of the people who stared down at her. Where had they all come from?

Her dress was wet against her skin, so she reached up to touch it, only to find a large amount of a warm, sticky substance. She held her hand up and saw blood drip from her fingers. It was strange, but she felt nothing. No more burning, no heat, no cold, no voices—nothing.

Was this what it was like to die?

****

"Who is he?" They were high in the gallery, sitting among thousands of Sector-Three citizens who had come to the open assembly meeting to listen in person to the first speech of the new Sector-Three leader. Curiosity ran high, but not as high as his. The man at the podium held responsibility for Alextor's fall from power. Or should he say death?

"Chief, he's not in the system. I've searched all three Sectors for the name Loran Narom, and I've run face recognition. Nothing. I'm going to have to get close enough to run eye recognition."

"Then that's what we'll do." Dobie followed him out of the third floor galley, up the walkway, then onto the lift that took them to the ground floor where their target was speaking.

Kane visually searched the officials seated behind the new Okeron dictator. He found Rand, but Jorell was not there. She'd never miss an important meeting like this even if her father were out of the picture. Everyone who wanted to attend was allowed in, space permitting, with government officials and employees accommodated first. There must be a logical explanation.

When he focused on the speaker his skin began to crawl, and every alert system in his body screamed enemy! "Dobie, that's the man from the pub during our first jump. The same eye scan you couldn't identify before."

"By the galaxy! No wonder he isn't in the system." Dobie leaned closer to Kane's ear. "Who in Diabolus is he?"

"If I told you, you wouldn't believe me."

"Try me, Chief."

"I have no proof, but I believe it's Pakar Moran." He watched Dobie's eyes grow large and his expression turned to total disbelief.

"By all that's holy!" Dobie shook his head.

"I know. He should have been executed, not deported. There's one way we could know for sure, but we'd have to see him without his shirt on."

"Are you serious?"

Kane nodded and Dobie's eyes grew large. He'd shocked his partner for sure. "There's a snake tattoo that winds around Pakar's right arm with its head in the center of his forearm. If it's there, then there's no mistake. He may have altered his looks, but Pakar is too vain to remove that intimidating tattoo."

"How do you know that?"

"I have a strong hunch, based on what I was told long ago."

"I see." Dobie shoved his hands in his pockets. "What now?"

"We listen to his speech then return." His friend nodded and leaned against the back wall. He settled in next to Dobie, but he couldn't concentrate on the speaker's words because his chest burned so badly he wanted to double over. The pain wasn't connected with the evil at the podium. He tried to ignore what his body was telling him—something was dreadfully wrong with Jorell.

They hadn't searched for her since she wasn't the reason for their journey. Dobie's calculations were exact since they'd jumped forty-nine sun-cycles into the future and landed exactly at their target time and place to see the take-over of Sector-Three.

The assembly meeting needed to end. Now. His insides screamed something was dreadfully wrong with Jorell. In fact, his stomach was so sick he nearly lost what little was in it, and there was a sharp pain in his is left chest area. He'd been shot once while working, and this was the exact same pain. There was no explanation for how or why, but he knew what was in his heart. He shifted on his feet and tried to will away the pain, but it did no good. He held his breath while another excruciating wave coursed through him.

The speech continued with the same old promises all politicians spewed. He took a deep breath. Pakar was certainly a dynamic speaker who knew how to excite his audience. Then he addressed specific issues that were expected. After he'd completed an important list, he paused and surveyed the audience. The quiet was far more deafening than any applause.

"I have spoken to Sector-One Leader, Ramon Coster, and Sector-Two Leader, Nazar Ferris. They, and their staff, have all agreed it is time for Okeron to embrace one leader and a one government program. We're no longer fighting children, we can live peacefully under one leader, and *I am* that leader!"

Sparse applause began, and slowly more joined in until everyone clapped and the noise grew loud. The people in Sector-Three stood first, then the other two Sectors joined them until everyone in the assembly were on their feet, applauding vigorously.

The applause became deafening. He tapped Dobie's shoulder and they snuck out before anyone noticed. They'd learned firsthand what they'd come for, and it was not good.

They left the main auditorium and walked briskly toward the empty offices. There was one very important source of information they needed to collect before they left, and now was the perfect time with everyone otherwise occupied.

Dobie had created a special device that recorded conversations in all pertinent offices, as well as tapping into encrypted files, confidential materials, and top secret documents. Somehow through Dobie's programming magic it always worked. Dobie didn't let on to others how capable he was, but the word genius belonged to him.

They navigated several different halls, took the lift to the personal offices of the government leaders, including Alextor and Jorell. They arrived at Jorell's office and Dobie used the special 'entry device', as he called it. The door finally slid open and they both hurried inside. "Chief, whose office is this?"

"You know it's Jorell's; she holds the position on the door plaque, 'First Advisor'."

"That's Jorell's position all right, but look at this place—what in creation happened here? I see nothing that's Jorell's." Dobie scratched his head. "I don't like it."

"Neither do I, and I have a really bad feeling about this." Dobie looked at him in complete agreement. The bad feeling he'd had earlier returned. Another wave of nausea rolled through him and he had no apparent explanation.

"Boss? What's wrong? You started looking sick back at the assembly, and you're looking even worse now."

"Hurry Dobie, we need to get back to Jorell in real time. Something is wrong with her." His friend nodded, walked over to the large view-screen and pulled a tiny device from the back, left bottom corner.

"Luckily I planted this on our first jump." He tucked the little box in his pocket.

"Do we need to check any other systems?"

"No, this little baby holds everyone's secrets."

Kane nodded. "Before we jump back, I want to see Jorell and Rand. I think there's little hope Alextor is alive. If he were, that conceited bag of wind would not be at the podium."

"Unfortunately, it's what we expected." Dobie shoved the device into his pocket.

Kane glanced around the room. The only item in the large office space that remained the same was the huge built-in vid-screen. The color scheme had gone from a beautiful light-blue to a dull grey. Judging from the sparse placement of masculine décor, a man had become First Advisor. Even the window treatment had been changed to dull and boring. It looked like Rand.

"Where do you want to look for Jorell?"

"I don't know." He walked to the door, Dobie on his heels. "Any suggestions?"

"Chief, I just felt a chill, and that's not good."

"I know." Some things were changeable, and if anything happened to Jorell, he'd move mountains to keep her safe. "Let's go back to our place, that little device in your pocket contains exactly what we need to know."

"I agree." Dobie stepped closer to Kane and patted his back. "Bad vibes are everywhere."

"Right." He followed Dobie out of the office and down the hall, but he felt like one of the living-dead characters in a horror vid he'd seen as a child. Everything seemed surreal, as if a part of him had just been ripped out. He'd never experienced such an empty sensation, nor had he ever been so hollow and devoid of emotion. Actually one emotion gripped him--deep depression triggered by grief.

Dobie walked so fast he struggled to keep pace with him, which was unusual since his friend always walked slower since he was shorter by nearly a foot.

They arrived at the special secret exit Jorell had told them about. He missed her...he really missed her. Their transport was in sight, and he tried to walk faster, but dizziness gripped him and he started to fall.

Dobie rushed to Kane's side and grabbed him. "What's wrong, chief?"

"Feel weak...help me."

With one arm over Dobie's shoulders and Dobie's arm around his waist, he managed to hobble to the vehicle. Dobie steered him to the passenger's side, and helped him into the seat. Before he could protest, Dobie jumped in the pilot's seat and took off vertically. His friend scared him whenever he flew. "Don't hit anything."

"You worry too much. Besides, I've gotten better since my last crash."

He had to chuckle at Dobie. His friend had saved him so many times over the annual-cycles he'd lost count, and this added one more incident to the list. "Get me home fast. I don't know if..."

"Chief? Are you okay? Say something!"

****

Bright lights kept her from opening her eyes. She heard several people calling her name, but Rand's voice was the only one she could identify. Pain shot through her left side. She tried to get comfortable, but whatever she was lying on was hard and cold. Where on Okeron was she? "Rand? Where are you, I mean…where am I? Rand? I know you're here. Talk to me!"

"Sir, she's whispering your name. You'd better hurry, she's fading fast."

Why was that man talking about her like that? "Rand? Where are you?"

"I'm right here, Jorell." Rand picked up Jorell's hand. "I'm so sorry, sweetheart."

Sweetheart? He'd never called her that before, why now? He sounded nervous. "What's going on?" She blinked several times and managed to open her eyes a tiny bit, just enough to see through a small slit. Why was Rand holding her hand with one of his hands and rubbing her arm with his other hand?

She closed her eyes and concentrated on Kane. Where was he? She needed *him*, not Rand. If she were going to die, she wanted Kane's face to be her last memory. Her pain had subsided. She'd once heard that if pain became intense enough the patient would either pass out, or become numb to everything. She was numb.

The only thing still alive was her love for Kane. She wanted him here…now…forever. It was clear now, she was dying. She felt every cell in her body shut down. Then she tried to take a deep breath, but her lungs could not pull in any air. She was not strong enough to lift her own hand. She'd lost all control of her body. She concentrated on moving one finger, yet even her brain let her down.

In her mind she screamed for Kane. She must be completely delusional because she swore she heard his voice in her head telling her to hold on, that he was coming. But she couldn't. All her strength had drained from her body, and her lungs screamed for air. It would all be gone in another moment.

"Bring me up to date, doctor."

That voice, she knew it. She couldn't forget her lifetime friend. Doctor Willock was present at her birth, so it was fitting he should also witness her death. She wanted to talk with him, but her lips wouldn't move. It no longer mattered. Nothing mattered.

"Jorell, listen to me. You must stay. You cannot leave now. Your father needs you. Don't go, my dear. You're needed. Please stay."

Doctor Willock's voice was so soft she barely heard his words. She wanted to answer him. In fact she needed an update on her father, but she could not respond since she was no longer in her body. She floated above herself, looking down at her blood covered body. Standing beside her was Rand and the doctor. The doctor gave her an injection, a last try he said.

"I'm afraid she's gone. The laser tore through too much heart tissue. The damage was extensive." Doctor Willock picked up a clean sheet and covered Jorell's body. "I know this is difficult for you." He looked into Rand's face. "I'm sorry."

Rand cleared his throat then walked to the door. "Thank you doctor."

Doctor Willock nodded then turned and stared at her lifeless body with tears in his eyes. Rand had barely blinked when the doctor said she was gone. So much for tears and mourning. There was nothing she could do. Her life was over and all that was left now was remorse for leaving those she loved. She'd so wanted to see Kane again, and she longed to see her father recover. It wasn't meant to be.

Fate was a funny thing. It had a way of sneaking in when you least expected it. She hadn't done much with her life, and she regretted that. There would be no children, no life-mate, no future—nothing.

She saw a bright light and floated toward the inviting brightness. Whatever awaited meant her time on Okeron had expired. She was finished. Game over.

CHAPTER THIRTY ONE

Why was Dobie hovering over him? He was more nervous than a new-mother. He found himself lying on the sofa, and judging by the sun, he'd been out for about three time-units. It took effort, but he managed to sit up. "Well, are you going to talk, or not?"

"Not." Dobie glared at him, and he watched his eyes grow large, then he furrowed his brow and squinted. "You look ridiculous when you do that."

"I'm not doing anything. You scared the Diabolus out of me! Care to explain? I've never seen you like that."

Kane smiled. "Have I ever told you how glad I am to have a friend like you?"

"No, and you'll never have another one. I doubt you could find anyone who would put up with you. Whether you know it or not, I worry about you, especially when you do what you did this sun-cycle."

"You mean passing out?" Dobie nodded at him." I apologize for that. I'm afraid I can't explain it. Right now I feel okay, but for a while there…well…you saw me."

"I did, and I don't want to see that again."

"I agree." Kane stood and walked into the galley. He ordered a glass of fruit juice. Dobie walked in and sat on a bar stool so he took the seat next to him. After a couple of swallows he looked at his friend and recognized the expression on his face, and it wasn't good. "Something you want to tell me?"

Dobie shook his head. "I'm not sure how…I mean…it's bad, really bad, and I'm not sure you want to know."

"Of course I do. What have you learned that's so bad?" Dobie hung his head and stared at the counter. Kane sat up straight and put his feet on the floor. "Come on, give…"

"Fine. At least your sitting down."

"It can't be that bad."

"It is, so brace yourself. Jorell Sutone was hit by a laser sniper while leaving the capitol building. She was taken to the hospital where she succumbed to her injury. The next sun-cycle it was announced that Alextor Sutone took his own life because he was too distraught over his daughter's death." Dobie looked up at Kane. "And everyone believed the story, hence Loran Narom, new world leader."

Kane's heart ripped in two, which hurt even worse than the pain he'd had before, but in a different way. A strange tingle shot through him and it felt as if all his blood just drained out of his body. He was numb. The news slowly sank into his consciousness which triggered one thought after another. "When?"

"The same sun-cycle we made our jump. From the time stated in the vid-report," Dobie looked at his wrist-piece and shook his head, "she was hit about the same time you started having pains." He turned his gaze on Kane. "How is that possible? I mean, it seems you two are connected somehow. You were feeling what she was feeling in real time, as it happened, and you were in two different times and places."

All he could do was shake his head. It was too unbelievable, yet considering the mind-meld they'd shared while making love, it seemed plausible. He'd never been able to completely mind-meld with anyone before, yet with Jorell, it came so naturally, and completely that Dobie's theory confirmed what he already knew.

"Is there something you want to tell me, Chief?"

"I was with Jorell." He looked his friend in the eye. "You know—with her."

Dobie sighed loudly. "That isn't exactly a secret. I know you too well to not see what was going on between you two. I'm glad you found happiness with her." Dobie looked Kane in the eye. "I'm sorry she's…"

"I will *not* let her die!" Kane slipped off the stool and stepped over to the tall window. He looked out, as if there were answers written in the sky. He had to bring Jorell and her father back to life. "We need a plan, and a damned good one."

"What kind of plan?"

Dobie joined him and patted him on the back. "We must prevent what just happened."

"So you now want to violate the number one unwritten law we vowed to uphold. Never interfere with life and death." Dobie pulled his hand back and rubbed his eyes. "I know this is different on many levels, but...."

"You're right. This decision effects all of Okeron. It's about our planet's entire future. Which means, Alextor and Jorell must remain alive."

"That's not the most important thing."

"What is?"

"You're in love with her."

"I'm..." He started to deny Dobie's observation, but he couldn't. How had he let himself become so involved? It went against his first rule of business, never mix friends with credits. When he moved his gaze to Dobie he noted the smile on his face. At least his friend supported him.

"I did some calculations while you were out cold, and there were no big surprises. I was able to tap Rand's palm-com, and he's been a busy boy. Seems he's quite friendly with a wide range of people, some of which are from the low-lands, if you know what I mean."

"How low are they?"

"Exterminators, mechanics, thieves, and identity-cons. Other than those characters, he hasn't communicated with anyone recently."

Kane ran his fingers through his hair. "Did you learn anything from tapping Jorell's vid-screen?"

"It's interesting actually. Rand comes in, looks around and leaves. A couple of time-units later, he comes back and checks out her desk, then leaves. And he does that about four more times. Either the guy's crazy, or he's desperate to find something in her office."

"I suspected as much." Kane returned to his seat and took a drink of juice. He tilted it up and finished it in a few swallows then slammed the glass down on the countertop. "Did he take anything?"

"Not that I could see."

"Rand is an inside plant. He's always been my number one suspect."

"I don't like slime-snakes either, but are you sure you're not making a jealous accusation?"

"I'm sure. Get that spy-thing from the computer." Kane slapped Dobie on the back. "Come on, partner, we have a jump to make." Without so much as a blink, Dobie popped a small device out of the computer then walked over to him, and placed his arms on his shoulders. "Concentrate, my friend."

Kane concentrated on their intended landing time and location while sending Dobie calming messages, which his friend gratefully absorbed. He sensed a nervousness in Dobie he wasn't used to. His companion rarely let anything bother him, but this was different for both of them, and so were the risks. The Vambrace Cuffs around his wrists grew hot, the winds blew hard, and darkness streaked with light carried them through the portal of time.

So much rested on this jump that it was easy to ignore the burning in his arms. Freedom. Something most people never gave a thought to, yet if Pakar got his way, no one would ever be truly free again. The man had no heart, and cared about no one but himself.

Jorell's life depended on this jump. If Jorell and Alextor died, there would be nothing in Pakar's way, and Okeron would become a dictatorship with the worst excuse of a man in control. But the most devastating consequence if he failed would be the loss of the woman he loved. He'd been with many women, but he'd never loved any of them. It was always for a good time, never a relationship. Everything rested on this jump.

When his feet hit ground he fell. Dobie lost his grip, and rolled out of the way. Kane sat up, took a deep breath and looked around to get his bearings. It appeared he and Dobie had landed right where they'd aimed, in the back corner of the capitol garden.

The memory of seeing Jorell here for the first time remained fresh in his mind. He'd been stunned by her beauty, but those thoughts had to wait. He glanced over at Dobie who kept patting his pockets as if he'd lost something. "Everything still there?"

"I think so. Ya know, Chief, we might want to consider retiring after this job. These jumps are hard on my body."

"Mine too. Retirement sounds good, my friend, but first we need to make sure we have a peaceful planet to retire on, governed by rulers who care about the population. So, let's find Jorell, and verify we hit our target date." He and Dobie exchanged the look they always did when they weren't sure if they'd hit the right time. Nothing was ever for sure in the time travel business.

They both quickly walked the meandering path that led to the personal quarters wing of the capitol building. His heart raced. She had to be alive, and he had to save her from her future fate. It was never as simple as glimpsing the future then traveling back to avoid the incident. If a professional assassin were after Jorell, he'd simply find a different time and place to take her out.

One thing was a given, he'd have to keep her close to him at all times, no matter what. However, she might not be as cooperative as he wanted her to be. How would she react when he implicated Rand as part of the conspiracy? She probably still harbored feelings for Rand, which might make her think he was jealous and consider him the enemy.

They reached the building and walked inside through the unlocked employees' entrance. The security at this entrance was lax, a flaw he needed to rectify. Right now he was in a hurry to see the woman who'd captured his heart.

Two hallways later, they stood in front of Alextor's quarters. He rang the announcement buzzer and waited. It seemed like forever before the door slid open and Jorell stood in the entrance to greet him, a smile on her radiant, beautiful, alive face.

"Welcome gentlemen. I'm glad you stopped by. Anything new?"

Kane grabbed her around the waist, pressed his lips to hers, lifted her off the floor and turned in circles while he kissed her. He could kiss her like this all sun-cycle, but he knew Dobie was watching. "It's *sooooo* good to see you."

"Kane, you're scaring me. You make it sound as if I just rose from the dead."

Dobie chuckled and Kane stared him down until he stepped away and walked to the far window. "You don't know how accurate that statement is."

"You'd better explain."

"First, tell me how your father's doing?" He wanted to know Alextor's condition, plus whether their jump was successful.

"I believe the antidote is working. He moved one finger not long ago. That's more than he's moved since this happened."

"I'm glad to hear that. Now, what are your plans this sun-cycle?"

"You only caught me here because of mid-cycle break. I have to return shortly."

"Is someone staying with your father?"

"Ariel will be right back, she just went home for a bit."

"Good. You need to announce you're meeting your father and will be away for a few sun-cycles."

"Kane, what's going on?"

Dobie walked back toward the door. "Jorell, may I use your office to do some research?"

"Of course, Dobie. There's no one there, help yourself."

"Thanks Princess."

Kane waited until the door slid shut behind Dobie. "Jorell, I'll explain everything to you when we're away from here. I'm taking you with me, so make your contacts now."

"You're not making sense. First you tell me you're leaving, you're jumping to the future, then you show up here with a new plan after being gone for only four time-units. I don't understand."

He reached out and pulled her to him. "Do you trust me?" She nodded. "Good. For now, do as I say, and I'll fill you in later. I promise."

He bent his head and pressed his lips to hers. The sweet kiss soon turned into desperate need. He would keep her safe no matter the cost.

****

The last of the vids played on Kane's view-screen and it wasn't a pretty sight. She tried to assimilate what she'd just seen and heard. In fact, it made her distrust everyone she called a friend. Of course that wasn't fair since there was probably only a small slice of greedy, hungry and controlling people trying to gain power illegally. However, she now understood why he whisked her away to stay with him.

"I can't believe Rand is involved. All the vid showed was him talking with people I don't know, but that in itself doesn't mean he's guilty of anything."

"Really? And how often does he, or you for that matter, come in contact with people you don't know inside the walls of the capitol building?"

"Security is tight. Strangers can't just stroll in and cause trouble, if that's what you mean."

"How did you end up walking down the front steps with Rand when you'd normally use a different exit?"

Jorell wondered if Kane would believe anything she said about Rand. Right now he seemed mad enough to break things. Of course, she had just seen herself shot by an unknown assailant with a laser, and Kane had become so angry she thought he'd explode. "He offered to take me to dinner at the best restaurant in all three Sectors."

"Don't you usually use a back entrance?"

"Usually, but he said he was having his transport brought to the front."

"It was just too convenient for you to be on the front steps, in a perfect location for the sniper to take his shot." Kane shook his head. "I know he's your fiancé, and he's supposed to be a loyal member of your government, but none of that excuses him."

"I'm sorry. I need more proof."

"Let me guess, you're prepared to believe every one of his convenient lies?"

"I'm sorry Kane, but you sound jealous." She took a deep breath. "Like you're trying to erase Rand completely." Jorell raised her hands in front of her in exasperation. "Just because you make Rand the villain, do not assume I'll throw myself at you."

"Is that what you think of me?" Kane stood and walked into the galley. She heard him rattling around in a drawer. He wasn't after anything, he was letting off steam. For Kane to react like this she must have stepped on his feelings by hitting too heavy with the truth.

It all seemed surreal. She'd just witnessed her own death at the hands of a stranger, with Rand by her side. Kane, whom she hired for an exorbitant amount of credits, blames her fiancé, which clears the way for her to get back in Kane's bed without one ounce of guilt.

Of course she'd been fighting guilt ever since she'd made love with Kane. If he were correct, she could free herself of those feelings. If her father recovered she could explain to him that she had no feelings for the man and did not want to life-mate him. She doubted whether she, or her father knew the real Rand.

This situation made her wonder if Kane had lovers in every place and time. What would happen if they all merged into one time and place? She could just imagine a long line of beautiful women, waiting for their one time-unit with Kane. Or was she trying to make Kane the villain so she wouldn't be tempted to make love to him again?

Love? Did love play a part in this? She hadn't known him long enough to love him. Her grandmother's words flooded into her mind. Before she died she'd given lots of advice, but what she said about relationships stuck in a strange way. She'd said true love knew no boundaries, nor did it depend on time, but when it hit, she'd know it as the truest emotion she'd ever had. She couldn't argue with grandma.

If she were anyone other than the ruler's daughter, Rand would not be an issue. But why was she also a target? She didn't run the government, she only aided her father in some of his decisions by supplying him with a bit more insight. She provided nothing worth dying for. So why would this so-called conspiracy need her eliminated? Kane asked her to trust him. At the moment she didn't know who to trust. Her entire world had turned upside-down, which left her wondering about everything.

Kane paced back and forth in the galley like a caged Tigra-cat. What was going through his mind right now? There was one way to find out, that's if she dared to mind-meld with him. When they were connected, it was easy to see the truth. She concentrated hard on him and asked permission to enter.

His hesitation held strong, but she sensed how much he cared about her, which was why he relented and allowed her entrance. *"Kane, I'm sorry if I upset you. I do trust you. Please come back to me so we can talk."*

His athletic frame moved toward her, but his stride seemed to give away his reluctance. All she really wanted to do was let him love her. As strange a thought as that may be, it was her heart's desire. When he held her in his loving way she was protected and safe, a feeling she hadn't had in a very long time. Her grandma may be gone, but the truth of her words could not be contested.

Kane walked to the couch. "You called?"

"I did. Please, sit down." She waited while he made himself comfortable next to her. "I'm sorry for doubting you, and for assuming you were jealous. I know you well enough to know that's not true."

"You're half right. I might be a bit jealous, but I don't like that man. I've bad feelings about him even before I met him." Kane held up one hand. "I admit, I don't know him like you do, but I can't ignore my gut anymore than you can."

"Point taken. Can we agree to disagree about Rand?" He nodded and relief spread through her. Kane was an intelligent man, and a careful one. When she smiled at him his facial features relaxed, and he became even more appealing. The correct word was sexy—damned sexy.

She took his hand in hers and looked into eyes that were bluer than the sky, and deeper than all the water on Okeron. Slowly he moved toward her until their lips met. His arm circled around her shoulders and he pulled her against him, exactly the way she wanted.

This man was addictive. The more he gave, the more she wanted. His kiss deepened and they teased each other, their tongues meeting sweetly. He tasted good, felt good, and looked even better. He was everything Rand was not.

She heard herself moan, and he did the same. It was the sound of lovers wanting more, and taking all they could. She memorized his every touch, every move, because their time together could end any moment.

Then he was in her mind asking to meld. His request differed from hers. She knew exactly what he was asking, because she also wanted the connection. She wasn't about to break the kiss to speak, so she gladly gave him permission. *"Kane, don't leave me. I need you in so many ways."*

"My sweet Jorell, I'll never leave you."

No more words were necessary. His hands found her breasts and he nearly made her scream with need. *"Make love to me."* He heard her plea, ended the kiss then stood. He took her hands in his and pulled her to her feet.

He scooped her into his arms and carried her down the long hall. She wrapped her arms around his neck and he turned the kiss into a passionate assault. He carried her with ease and didn't stop until they were at the door to his bedchamber.

The door whooshed open, but it was the closing sound that gave her a chill. They were alone, at last. He walked to his bed, laid her down, then snuggled next to her. He stroked her hair while his hands caressed. She shivered from excitement, her anticipation building. Being with Kane was so very right.

Then their energy began to meld and dance around them. His feelings flooded into her, and she was helpless to stop hers from doing the same to him. Every thought they'd ever had transferred at the same moment, which made everything muddled. It seemed impossible to separate one thought from another.

His hands worked to free her from her garments, and she attacked his clothes like a woman possessed. She didn't care. Fabric ripped, and she worked even faster. The urgent need ignited the energy around them which further fueled their frenzy.

Kane managed to free her last garment, then he helped her remove his pants. She ripped open his shirt and shoved it down his arms until he shrugged it off. Then he lowered himself against her, the feel of his naked body against hers made the energy swirls to rise higher and sparkle brightly. *"Now Kane, please. Hurry."*

"As you wish."

CHAPTER THIRTY TWO

"You're a complete idiot!" Pakar walked closer to Rand and the sniper. "What do you mean 'the little bitch' left?"

"She wanted to check on her father during the mid-sun-cycle break. I assumed she'd return right after."

"All you did was make a fool of yourself and me! I should have known you were not capable!"

"I promise to do better next time."

"Next time?" Pakar tilted his head back and laughed. How he could be so stupid was anyone's guess. The next time he should put the hit on Rand. "Jorell's public story is that Alextor is staying with a sick relative outside of the city." He watched Rand nod. "Now my sources tell me she announced she was going to meet him and would be gone for several sun-cycles."

Rand shook his head. "She never told me."

"How in Diabolous would she go anywhere when Alextor is in his own bed at the capitol?" Pakar took a deep breath in an effort to control his temper. He'd like nothing better than to exterminate the stupid man, right here, right now. Unfortunately, his services were still required to complete the plan. "Where has she gone?"

"I don't know. The last time I saw her was in the meeting before the break, and she didn't say anything."

"It's your job to know! How in Diabolous can my sniper make a kill if he can't find his target! You have one assignment right now; get Jorell Sutone in the snipers view! Can you do that?"

"I'll convince her to go to dinner with me and I'll bring her out the front entrance so the sniper can get a good shot. I'm sure he can find a place to hide."

Pakar watched the sniper nod his agreement. "You two bumbling idiots had better have your plans set, because I want to hear the announcement this moon-cycle that Jorell Sutone is dead. Is that clear?"

The two men gave their 'yes sir' answer in unison, which was probably the only thing they could do right together. He was glad they didn't know his real name or they'd screw that up as well. With his luck they'd announce it to the media, proud they knew something others did not. They'd better not fail him. If they did, they'd pay the price. "Now, get out of my sight and do your job before I lose what little patience I have left."

****

Kane sat across the table from Jorell and Dobie. They were having their early sun-cycle koffa, the news-vid playing in the background while they tried to find a workable plan. It seemed an impossible task considering they knew the future, the past and the present. All three presented a negative case scenario.

Jorell's green eyes danced in the early light, her gaze pinned on him, and he loved every moment of her attention. But he had the task of keeping her safe--and alive. He'd give his life to save hers if necessary.

"Chief? You're doing it again." Dobie set his cup on the table and ran his finger up and down the handle.

"Doing what?" His friend had that 'you know what I'm talking about' look on his face.

"Shutting us out and not telling us what you're thinking. We're all in this together, like it, or not."

"I'm aware of that, my friend. I count on you. So, do either of you have any suggestions?"

"To keep me alive, or to save my father?" Jorell took a sip of koffa.

"Both, my sweet." Dobie blushed at his endearment. His friend was always shy around the ladies. He didn't mean to make him uncomfortable, but he didn't see a reason to keep his feelings for Jorell from Dobie. After the moon-cycle they'd just spent, he doubted he and Jorell had any secrets left between them. If they weren't making love, they were talking.

It was good to share thoughts and feelings with someone. Of course, he and Dobie had shared everything their entire life, but this was different. It was the kind of sharing only lovers could do.

"Chief, you're scaring me. You haven't said much of anything, and you always have a plan smoldering in that head of yours somewhere. So, what gives?"

"The doctor told Jorell her father's vitals are improving. If Alextor wakes up, his life is in serious jeopardy."

"I think I know where you're going, Kane, but the public, and every government employee, believes he's away."

Dobie scratched his head. "Isn't that a good thing?"

"Yes and no. We need to get him out of here."

"And do what?" Jorell shook her head. "What do I tell his doctor?"

"Tell him you've moved your father to keep him safe, and that you're counting on him for his continued silence."

"Okay, but where will we take him?"

Dobie and Jorell both stared at him, anxiously waiting for an answer. "That's why we're having this meeting."

"You're thinking about bringing him here, aren't you?" Dobie took a long drink.

"We have the best security anywhere, so it's the most secure location." Kane noticed tears forming in Jorell's eyes. "He'll be safe here, Jorell."

"You can count on us, Princess. We can kick some...well, you know what I mean."

"What Dobie means is that we'll protect you and your father with our lives." One tear rolled down her cheek and he wanted to kiss it away. It was impossible to shield her from the reality of this situation.

"Okay, Chief, we keep him alive, that's great, but how will he ever be able to return to his position? We know what the future holds so it's going to take some doing to undo what is slated to happen."

Jorell sighed. "You both know I have no idea where to start since this is my first experience tampering with the time continuum, but my father must be restored to his seat of power."

Kane stood, walked over to the counter, grabbed the Koffa carafe, returned to the table and refilled all three cups. "That's exactly what I want. But here's the problem. The other two Sectors have been taken over by Loran Narom's men. The only obstacle he has is Alextor Sutone, and his daughter. He has to eliminate you both in order to claim power for himself."

Dobie cleared his throat. "Okay, we know Marto and Trom's death were *not* accidents, which means Nazar Ferris and Ramon Coster belong to Loran Narom. The question is, how do we get rid of them?"

Jorell coughed, then leaned against the back of her chair. "We don't. They're in power, and they'll stay in power. There's only three of us. There's no way *we* can take over an entire planet."

Kane returned to his chair. "I'll bet your father knows how to get rid of them and pull off a takeover."

Dobie stood and began to pace. "Are you crazy? You know what condition he's in, and there's no guarantee he'll wake up. And how long do we wait? And what if he never does? There's more questions than answers."

"Kane," Jorell cleared her throat, "Dobie's right. What if he doesn't come back?" She shook her head. "I'll tell you what happens, exactly what's happening now. This power-hungry villain will take the reins while we're here dreaming up ridiculous schemes." Jorell stood. "I'm sorry, I can't do this."

Kane watched her leave the galley and walk down the long hallway to his bedchamber. He should have allowed her to get some sleep last moon-cycle, but he couldn't get enough of her. This moon-cycle he'd leave her alone. She needed rest.

"Chief?...Chief?...Okeron calling Kane!"

"Why are you yelling? I'm not deaf. What?"

"I think you and Jorell should sleep more, and play less."

He couldn't stop the smile that pulled up the corners of his mouth. Dobie knew him too well. His friend may pretend to be the imbecile, but he couldn't put anything over on him. "Playing is more fun."

"Don't get me wrong, I'm thrilled you two are happy together. You, above anyone, deserves to be happy. With that said, Jorell is at her wits end. Stress is all over her face."

"I agree, my friend. We need to get Alextor and Jorell out of the capitol building and settled here. To preserve their lives, and to get Jorell to relax."

"What's the plan, Chief?"

"This place is engineered to lock people in as well as out, we'll finally make use of that feature."

"Jorell won't take it well."

"She'll have to. If she has to attend meetings, I'll escort her. She does not get a choice in the matter."

"I hope you know what you're doing."

"So do I." Kane stood and stared at Dobie. "Come on. We have a pick-up to make."

CHAPTER THIRTY THREE

Jorell blinked several times in an effort to focus. Where was she? She sat up in the center of the bed built into the far corner and looked around the room at the sleek black furniture with gold hardware. Kane had good taste. Everything he owned was the latest trend, and very expensive. Did he charge all his clients as much as her? Doubtful, but he'd obviously been well paid.

Memories of Kane rushed into her mind. What they did here last moon-cycle warmed her heart, and her entire body. He'd kissed and loved every inch of her, from top to bottom and back again. He left no place unexplored, proving once again, he was an intense, careful, skilled lover, aware of her needs--and a lot more.

She glanced at the timepiece on the wall. How long had she slept? If the blasted thing was right, she'd been out for over eight time-units. It was past time to get up, shower, and dress.

When she slipped out of the bed she commanded the lights to brighten from the muted level they were on. Kane's converted warehouse, if you could call it that, had more luxuries and updated features than the capitol building. It didn't surprise her that his place reflected masculinity, nearly everything was black or white, with accents in varied shades of gray.

Kane was a complex man, with many talents, most of which he was all too aware. He definitely had one fantastic talent she didn't dare talk about, one she planned to always enjoy. He'd shown her a new realm of reality when they mind-melded, one that was theirs alone. They were connected in every way, and she'd never been closer to anyone.

She hurried into the private lav and commanded the shower on. The water adjusted to the perfect temperature, but she hated to take off Kane's shirt since it had his masculine scent all over it. She hung the shirt over the back of the ornate chair by the dressing table, then stepped into the steamy warmth of the pulsating water spray.

Unfortunately, the water massage did little to help her problems. Would her father recover, or die? Would there be war? If she lost her position as First Advisor, she'd also lose the only place she knew as home. There was nothing like losing life as she knew it.

It didn't take long to shampoo her hair and finish her shower. She stepped into the auto-dry chamber, and tried to relax in the warm flowing air, but all she pictured was the treaty over water rights that ended a bloody war drying up as quickly as her body just had, and that scared her to the bone.

She quickly dressed in the same clothes she'd arrived in since it was all she had. When Kane brought her here she didn't have time to pack a bag. Ariel messaged her last moon-cycle that her father was doing well. Her friends were reliable, and she was fortunate they'd agreed to work with her.

It was time to find Kane and ask him what he planned to do. She opened the door and stepped into the long, empty hall. While she walked toward the galley she followed the aroma of fresh brewed koffa. Light from an open guest bedchamber stopped her, and she peeked inside. She gasped and her hand moved to cover her mouth.

"Are all the lines hooked up?"

"Yeah, Chief. All is well."

Both men turned and stared at her while shock ripped through her at the sight of her father lying on Kane's guest bed.

"Jorell? Are you all right? You look pale." Kane walked over to her side and put his arm around her waist. "Come look. He's doing well."

"You're not just saying that, are you?"

"My sweet. I only lie when it's necessary, and in this case, it's not."

She allowed Kane to escort her to her father's bedside. He actually looked better than the last time she'd seen him. His color was better, even his breathing appeared normal. She reached out and touched his hand. "He's warm!" She looked up at Kane's deep blue eyes. "I became so used to feeling his cold skin. You're not exaggerating. He really has improved."

"One of these sun-cycles you'll learn to believe me."

She smiled and he returned it, but he did not hide the desire in his eyes, or the satisfaction in his voice. "You're beginning to convince me. Keep up the good work."

"I have some even better news. He moved his arm all by himself."

Dobie rushed over to Jorell and Kane. "And I heard him moan!"

"Really? That's great news. But how did you two get him here without being stopped? I thought our security was top notch, or so I've been told."

"Whoever told you that doesn't know Dobie."

"Or you, Chief. Oh, you should have seen Kane, he was great as a frustrated delivery man for the wine company. He had the entire staff of the main galley running around like chickatous with their heads cut off!"

All three of them laughed loudly, letting off anxiety and stress. Then her father moaned and they immediately silenced their laughter. "Father! I'm here. Talk to me."

Alextor's head moved from one side to the other then stopped and she saw eye movement behind closed lids. "That's it. Open your eyes. Please, open your eyes." She knew he was trying, but his efforts must have worn him out because he fell still again. Her heart sank. She sighed deeply and turned toward Kane.

"The antidote is working." Kane grasped Jorell's shoulders. "It wasn't your imagination. He's beginning to wake. It won't be long. Just remember what I told you—it takes time and works slow, so be patient."

"I'm trying. Do you know how hard it is?"

"He's so close. I know he'll recover. Listen to Kane, princess. Be patient."

"Thanks, Dobie. Thanks to both of you for bringing him here. I can only imagine what might happen if the people who want him dead learn he's on the road to recovery."

"Jorell," Kane took Jorell's hand in his, "don't forget the Energy-Lamia."

"But we're not in the capitol building anymore. He won't be able to find us."

"I wish that were true. If the Lamia searches for Alextor's energy he'll find it."

"I was hoping he couldn't." Jorell brushed stray tears off her cheeks with her hands. She hated when emotions got in the way, but frustration and anger were hard to hide.

"Just remember, he can find him if he wants to."

She put her arms around Kane's waist and laid her head against his chest. It was good to lean on someone, especially when they were handsome, smart, not to mention capable, and dangerously sexy.

Kane moved his hands and placed them on her cheeks. "I'll keep him safe. You have my word."

"I believe you." His magic touch made everything seem brighter.

"Come on. I know what you need."

Dobie walked out of the room and turned toward the galley. They followed and took a seat at the table while Dobie grabbed the koffa pot and cups.

Kane took the seat next to her while Dobie filled three cups, then slid one in front of her. She took a few sips and immediately felt better. She held her cup up in front of her. "I'm addicted to this."

"We all are." Dobie sat across from Kane. "Now, what's the plan?"

Kane took a drink then stared at Jorell. "You're not going to like it."

"How do you know? I haven't even heard it yet."

"You need to tell Rand you're breaking your engagement, and you no longer want him working for the government. Can you do that?"

By the look on Kane's face he anticipated her arguments and anger, but he was in for a shock. "Without blinking twice. What else?"

"Princess, are you feeling all right?"

"Dobie, how can you ask her that?"

Kane shook his head. "Jorell, are you sure you understood?"

"I'm fine, thank you very much. And yes, I understand completely. You want me to give Rand the official black-card and tell him to kiss-off, as in, don't come back. Right?"

"I thought you'd be upset. I also thought you'd put up a fight."

"You thought wrong, and you don't know me as well as you think you do." She smiled. For some reason it gratified her to have one-upmanship for a change.

"Rand is supplying information to whomever is behind the plot to control Okeron."

"I believe you're right." Jorell looked at Dobie who nodded at her, but she nearly laughed at Kane's shocked expression.

"After you tell Rand, Dobie and I will follow him. He's bound to meet with the man he reports to. Even if it's not the number one man, it will put us closer than we are now."

"You hope."

"Princess, that's all we can do right now. Kane and I have been at this a long time, and we're usually right." Dobie smiled. "And we're hoping this will be one of those times."

"Well said." Jorell turned her gaze to Kane. "Is that your sentiment as well?"

Kane nodded. "Is there a problem?"

"I suppose not." Jorell concentrated on Dobie. "Do you have something beautiful I could borrow? I want to look great when I meet with Rand."

"I have just the thing for such an occasion."

Dobie nearly fell over his own feet while he made a hasty retreat from the galley. She smiled. "Is he always in such a hurry?"

"Only when he's doing a favor for you."

"He's a good man. You're lucky to have such a friend. I used to have a friend like that, but she…. That was a long time ago."

"Jorell, forgive me, but I have to ask, what are your feelings for Rand?"

"Kane," Jorell turned on her stool to face him, "I thought that question has already been answered."

"No, it hasn't."

He looked truly worried, but was he asking because he cared for her from his heart, or simply to solve the mystery? "For a smart man you certainly ask foolish questions."

"It's not a foolish question. He *is* your fiancé, the man you're supposed to love and pledge your troth to."

"Please, tell me you only asked me that question out of jealousy."

"You've accused me of being jealous more than once, and I've given your accusation a lot of thought, and the answer to your question is *yes*."

"Thank you." She leaned toward Kane and lightly kissed his lips. "I was worried you might still deny it, and if you did, well, I…aah…."

"Be hurt?"

"I'm glad to see it matters to you. I'd be hurt if it didn't." She blinked several times to keep the welling tears from rolling down her face. Jorell leaned closer and threaded her arms around his neck.

"I don't want you hurt."

Jorell kissed him with all the passion in her, and he adamantly returned her kiss. It felt too good and she never wanted to let him go, but she pulled back in case Dobie returned.

"If you'd have kept that up you wouldn't need the dress Dobie is looking for, and you'd never get to the capitol."

"That is a tempting idea." She moved her hands to his chest.

He grabbed both of her hands with his. "Dobie will be here shortly, and he'd be happy to embarrass us if we acted out our thoughts."

"You're bad, very bad. I know what you're thinking because I'm thinking the same thing." Kane slid off his stool, picked her up off of hers and began to walk down the hall toward his bedchamber.

"What about Dobie? He's no fool. He'll know what we're doing."

"Is that a problem?"

She shook her head. "But what about my meeting with Rand?

Kane laughed. "He's waited this long, what's a little longer?"

She leaned her head against his shoulder and held on to him. He was the most perfect man she'd ever seen. His baby-blue eyes showed his love, and she couldn't wait to run her fingers through the length of his gorgeous dark-brown hair that rested lightly on his shoulders.

The door opened and he carried her inside and laid her on the bed. He leaned over her and unfastened her blouse before the door was completely shut. Her breathing grew faster along with his, and she loved every moment of it. A burning need consumed her. He opened his mind to her and she grabbed the invitation. Immediately his fiery lust pushed him into high gear.

Kane ripped open her blouse. I love that undergarment, and the way it makes your breasts even more tempting.

"Some things should not be rushed, warrior." Heat rose in her cheeks and she was glad he was so busy kissing her so he couldn't see her blush. She never thought she'd want a man so badly it hurt. He stirred a need that surpassed the physical--a need she did not fully understand. Soon she'd be free of Rand, then she would be all his.

He continued to undress her until she lay naked. He broke the kiss, pulled back and looked her up and down. She smiled at the cocky grin that pulled the corners of his mouth. They were still mind-linked so she heard him groan then mentally clear his throat.

"My sweet, you're beautiful in so many ways I don't have the words to tell you. But I don't need words, I only need you."

"I never want to disappoint you."

"You never could." For such a muscled warrior, Kane was soft when it came to her, and she loved that side of him. If she were lucky, he'd never look at another woman, only her. Kane was the only man she wanted. Ever.

CHAPTER THIRTY FOUR

Jorell stood in the center of her own living area and waited impatiently for Rand to arrive. She'd almost been late due to Kane and his 'exploration' as he called it.

She smoothed the skirt of her pale lavender gown, then tried to pull the top up a bit higher so her cleavage did not show as much. She'd always been self-conscious about low necklines, but Kane assured her she looked perfect. He had looked at her with such hungry, loving eyes that she nearly melted inside. Making love to him came so naturally it scared her. What would she do when he left? Without a doubt, anyone named '*The Traveler*' would leave. It was his job.

How could she say good-by to a man she'd fallen in love with? Oh, she'd tried to deny Kane's spell but when they mind-melded, she felt complete, and so very loved. What woman wouldn't want that feeling? Especially when it came in such a virile body, built to fulfill a woman's needs in every way.

The arrival chime abruptly ended her pleasant yearnings. Rand. He tried to get in with the pass she'd given him long ago, but luckily she took Kane's advice and reprogrammed the system to reject him permanently. She let him stew a bit, then touched the button that allowed the door to slide open.

Rand charged inside like he owned the place. His blatant, arrogant attitude showed, and so did his disgruntled frown. For once she liked the fact he was angry. This little game could be fun. If he got angry enough he might let the truth slip, a truth she'd never hear if they life-mated.

"Well, are you going to tell me why you dragged me over here?"

He crossed his arms over his chest and stared at her as if she were some kind of off-world alien with horns. She drew her shoulders back, stepped closer to the window, then turned the full force of her gaze on Rand, who now looked more like a wheezelice than a man. "What kind of an attitude is that? We're supposed to be in love, soon to life-mate."

"I apologize. What do you want, Jorell?"

"You know, Rand, my father wanted me to marry immediately if anything ever happened to him so I'd have a man to protect me."

"Your father is a wise man." Rand wiped his brow with the back of his hand.

It felt good to watch the man sweat, a reaction she had not anticipated. So far so good. "I think we should life-mate before my father passes."

"You don't know when that will happen. Besides, how will you explain his absence at the ceremony?"

"I thought we'd have a private ceremony in Sector-Two. Wouldn't that be nice? You know Nazar quite well, don't you?" Rand's face suddenly lost all its color, and his hand shook while he wiped his forehead again. "Maybe he'd be free to officiate for us. Do you think he'd mind?"

"He's very busy right now. There's much to do since he recently took power. You might make other plans."

"What do you suggest?" She kept her gaze on him but he refused to look at her. Instead, he stared at the floor shaking his head. "Well, Rand. Speak now, it's your last chance." At that statement he finally turned his gaze on her, still pale, and looking scared. Why hadn't she taken the lead in this relationship long ago?

Long ago she needed to do what her father wanted. Now, she was on her own, and without a doubt, Rand was not the man for her. She'd wanted to drag this out, but she'd become bored with him and decided to end this useless conversation. "Fine, since you have nothing to say, I'll tell you what I think. First, I would not life-mate you if you were the last man on Okeron. Or any planet for that matter."

"What are you saying? You love me, you know you do."

"I do *not* love you. I never did." He covered his face with his hands and bent forward until his elbows were on his knees. Again, afraid to make eye contact, and he held his tongue as well. "Have you nothing to say?" She shook her head in disgust,

One word summed him up nicely. Pathetic. "I only agreed to our engagement because of my father. But since he's out of the picture, it no longer matters." Rand did not move a muscle. For all she knew he'd fallen asleep. "By the Gods man. Say something!"

Rand dropped his hands from his face. "You're a real bitch! You always have been. I'm relieved. I couldn't stand to be stuck with you for life. I can't think of a worse fate."

Rand rushed toward her. He grabbed her arms and pain shot through her. Then he shook her hard and fast, jerking her neck harder with each shove. "Let me go! Stop this right now!" He shook her a few more times then stopped and stared. She saw evil like she'd never seen before.

"You think you're so smart, don't you? You bated me into this conversation, and it gave you pleasure. You love the power, don't you?" Rand pushed her backward. "I'm not done with you *bitch*! You can put credits on it. I *will* be back?"

"How could I ever have thought you were life-mate material? This 'real you' is even worse than I imagined."

He lunged toward her, and there was no time to run, and nowhere to go. He grabbed her arms, his foot planted firmly on the hem of her gown. When he shoved her away, the material ripped away from his foot, and she fell backward to the floor.

Cool air on her exposed legs made her shiver. He violently charged toward her with his arm raised, his hand fisted. She turned her head to avert a blow to her face, but there was no contact. Instead the unmistakable sound of flesh hitting flesh caused her to turn in time to see Kane's second blow to Rand's jaw. Kane struck him with unleashed anger and Rand stumbled back several steps until the wall brought him to an immediate stop. Rand's head struck so hard he slumped to the floor.

Blood trickled down and left side of his mouth, and she noted two of his teeth on the floor beside his unconscious body. Kane rushed to her and knelt. He gently brushed hair from her face with his fingers, his blue eyes full of concern.

"Are you hurt?"

"I don't think so." He placed his hands on her shoulders then slowly moved them down her arms until his hands clasped over hers. What woman wouldn't feel better with Kane's intimate touch, and concern? Her hands trembled, but so did his. She reached up and traced his right eyebrow. "Don't worry. There's nothing wrong with me you can't fix."

Kane glanced around the room, then bent his head down to her ear. "And fix I will. But first, I need to get you out of here to a safe location. We'll talk in private. We're being watched." Kane stood, then took her hands and pulled her to her feet.

"You need to change. We don't want to draw attention."

She looked at her torn gown. "This is a serious wardrobe infraction. Rather indecent I suppose." She'd tried to make him laugh, but he only gave her a half-smile. Kane helped her stand, but it was his troubled gaze that held her hostage.

"Are you sure you're all right?"

"Quite sure. I'll go change." She looked over at Rand. "What about him?"

"I'll take care of him."

"Looks to me like you already have." She shook her head. "Are you going to...kill him?"

"I'd like to, but I won't."

Kane walked toward Rand's unconscious body. She watched him pull Rand to his feet and hoist him over his left shoulder, then he started toward the door. "Where are you taking him?"

"I'll dump him at his door. That way he'll be home when he wakes up. Kane turned to look at Jorell. "Don't worry. He won't bother you again. I'll see to it."

Rand's arms swung back and forth while Kane walked to the door. A helpless Rand was a strange sight to see, but one she rather liked.

"Lock the door behind me."

"Yes." She hurried to secure the entrance so no one could enter, then turned and walked into the bedchamber. When she entered the closet she searched for something that completely covered her. For some reason Rand left her feeling violated. She opted for pants and a tunic, which was unlike her, but at the moment she did not feel like herself.

The political games had taken a dramatic turn for the worse, and she was sick--physically sick of the power grab. Her father did seem to be improving, yet the threat to him, and to her remained real. Possibly worse. It was hard to remember the last time she did something fun that she wanted to do.

She was tired. Tired of it all.

CHAPTER THIRTY FIVE

"Chief, sit down. You're making me nervous." Dobie took a drink of his wine. "Jorell and Alextor are safe here. What we need now is a plan."

"A plan for Alextor to return to his position? A plan to keep him alive? A plan to keep Jorell alive? A plan to stop a complete government takeover?"

"All of those situations need a plan, and right now, we don't have one."

"That's correct." This job's problems seemed to exponentially multiply. Countless lives were at stake, including the life of the woman he loved. Love? Was he really in love with Jorell? He stared down at the table, shocked he acknowledged the fact, but yes, he was in love. It may not be the best time or place to finally find the woman he wanted to share a lifetime with, but love never had good timing.

"Boss? Hello?"

He looked up at Dobie. "Sorry, what were you saying?"

"Plan, we need a plan."

"We've never been this far over our heads before." Dobie stared at him as if he were a stranger. "What's that look for?"

"I've never seen you give up before. This is not the time to quit. A wise man, you, once told me to take one sun-cycle and one situation at a time. And *I* will add that we do not have to do this alone. The new leader of Okeron cannot take complete control without help. We just need to separate our friends from enemies and solicit some help."

Kane clapped his hands. "Very good, my friend. Very good." He laughed. "It's about time you remembered what I've taught you. Thanks for reminding me." He stood, looked around, then walked to the com-center and took a seat. Dobie followed and sat next to him with a big smile on his face. "So, where do we start?"

"Depends if you want to start at the end and work backwards, or at the beginning and work forward."

"Good question."

Jorell's voice made him and Dobie turn on their stools. "I didn't hear you come in."

"Sorry to disturb your brainstorming."

Dobie jumped from his stool and brought another and set it next to Kane. "Please Princess, have a seat. We can certainly use your help."

Kane took her hand and helped her settle on the stool. "I've been waiting for you."

"Really? Why?"

"Because you, above all others, know who your father's true friends and enemies are. As Dobie brought to my attention, we can't do this alone. So, with your advice, we can decide who will help us."

"And here I thought you could do anything you put your mind to, *Traveler*."

"I can, and will, but I need your help." Jorell nodded and her gorgeous red hair bobbed about her lavender covered shoulders. He wanted to run his fingers through those silky strands. They had work to accomplish, but that did not suppress the urge that throbbed in his loins every time he looked at her.

"Okay, Chief. I've divided the vids into three sections and we can all take one to speed things up."

He turned toward Dobie. "Good. But don't hurry, we can't afford to miss anything." He looked into Jorell's sexy eyes, swallowed hard, then took a deep breath. "Jorell, make a list of your father's friends and enemies in all three Sectors. On the friend list, only include those who you and your father trust with your lives. If you're in doubt about anyone, don't list them."

"I can do that, but I don't understand why you need such a list."

"When Dobie and I traveled to the future, we witnessed a man named Loran Narom claim total rule over Okeron. During a tri-Sector council meeting he told the audience there would now be only one Sector with him in charge." Kane watched Jorell's hands cover her mouth while she grasped his words. "I didn't mean to bring bad news, or to scare you."

"Dear stars." Jorell turned away from Kane, slid off her stool, and walked to the window in the main living area.

"Chief?"

He kept his eye on her, afraid she'd fall into a deep depression. She was a strong woman, but how much could she take before she fell apart?

"Chief!"

"What?"

"You need to go to her. Support her. She needs you."

Kane looked at his friend and nodded. "Go ahead and begin checking your Sector. We'll join you in a bit."

"Just don't play too long." Dobie smiled.

"Remind me to teach you a lesson."

"You always say that when I'm right."

He slapped Dobie on the back while they both slid off their stools. Dobie headed for the com-center and he walked over to Jorell. She was on the verge of tears and did not turn when he stopped behind her. He put his arms around her waist and pressed his chest against her back.

"Was I at the meeting?"

"No."

"My father?"

"No."

"What do we do, Kane?"

"We stop him. Knowledge is power. Loran Narom has been planning this take-over for a long time, and his people infiltrated all three Sectors quite some time ago."

"Why didn't I see this? Or at least sense it?" Jorell shook her head. "That's my job and I've failed!"

She began to cry harder so he moved his hands to her shoulders and turned her to face him. She didn't want to, but he had to stop her from falling into an emotional abyss. "Jorell," he wiped tears from her cheeks with his fingers, "listen to me carefully. There's no way you could have known. I'm not even sure those he put in place know the whole truth."

"One of those is Rand...right?"

Kane nodded.

"I've failed! By the stars, I failed!"

He pulled her to him and guided her head to his shoulder. He gently rubbed her back for a few moments to calm her. Her rapid breathing slowly returned to normal. "You have not failed. Loran Narom is evil incarnate, and very resourceful. He's the most effective person on the planet at disguising his feelings. He's an accomplished liar and manipulator."

He tilted her chin up with his finger. "You have not failed. You hired *me*, didn't you?" At that she actually smiled at him, and he'd never been happier to see those lovely lips curve upward.

"I did hire *you*, and that's probably the smartest thing I've ever done."

It was his turn to smile. "Probably? That's the best you can do?" She laughed and playfully hit him in the arm. "If we didn't have so much work to do I'd take you down the hall..." She pulled his head down to hers and kissed him. If she only knew what her kisses did to him, she might not be so willing.

He wanted to make mad passionate love to her all sun-cycle, but time was the enemy, so he reluctantly ended the kiss and set her back from him. "We have much to do."

"You're right. I'll go check on my father." She kissed Kane on the cheek. "I'll be right back." He kissed her on the forehead.

"Good." She walked away and he couldn't take his eyes off that cute little sway of hers which was accentuated by those tight pants. It was a good thing she only wore pants once in a while or he'd never be able to concentrate on anything. At least Dobie was busy at work with his back to him so he hadn't seen him drool after Jorell.

He walked back over to Dobie and stood behind his chair. Several vids played and Dobie paused one of them. "Any luck?"

"I've been following the newest government hires to see who they are and where they came from."

"How far back have you gone?"

"Eight annual-cycles."

"Good." Dobie was a wizard with technology, always finding a way to make it work for them efficiently and accurately. He had neglected to tell him lately how much he did appreciate him. Everyone needed to hear praise once in a while. "You are brilliant, my friend."

"What do you want?"

Kane laughed. "Nothing. Take the compliment."

"How about adding how inventive, resourceful, accur..."

"Don't push it."

"There's the old Kane I know and love!"

He laughed and so did Dobie. "Have you found anything interesting yet?"

"The earliest plant appears to be Nazar. It's hard because all of their backgrounds appear normal, but the program I ran says there have been changes to the data records. Changes are illegal, but these were done well."

Kane shook his head. "Evil knows no bounds."

****

Jorell sat on her father's bed. She'd held his hand so long hers had begun to sweat. If he knew she was here he might respond, but he lay unconscious and still. When would the antidote finally work? She had little patience left.

She stood and walked to the foot of the bed. It was past time she helped Kane and Dobie. On the dressing chest lay a notepad and writing implement, so she picked it up and headed for the chair next to the bed. She could at least start the list Kane requested.

Twelve names later she laid the pad and implement on the bed-table. She hated to leave her father, but Kane and Dobie needed her input. She stood, walked to the door and waited while it slid open. Just when her foot stepped into the hall she heard a moan behind her. She spun around so fast she nearly fell.

She rushed back to the bedside and grabbed her father's hand. "Father? Wake up, please wake up." His fingers moved, then he squeezed her hand. "That's it. Squeeze my hand if you hear me."

This time he squeezed harder than before, and she heard him groan out loud. "Wake up father. Wake up!" She gasped when his eyes opened and he blinked several times before closing them again. "Father? It's Jorell. Please wake up for me, I need you. Okeron needs you!"

"Jo…Jo…rell?"

Tears burned her eyes at the sound of her father's voice, weak as it may be, it was still his. "By the Gods, it's good to hear your voice. Open your eyes, I need to see you." She held her breath while he blinked several times before his eyes opened and he actually looked at her. He squeezed her hand again and her heart raced.

"Daughter, good to…to…see…you."

His voice, a mere whisper, was music to her ears. "How are you?"

"Wha…what in Diabolous hap…pened?"

"You were poisoned and you nearly died. But you're back now, and I couldn't be happier. Oh father, I was so worried."

"How long?"

"How long have you been in bed?" He nodded at her. "It's been, aah…"

"Too long." Alextor rolled his eyes. "Help…me."

Jorell let go of her father's hand, took a deep breath and ran to the open door. "Kane, Dobie, come quickly!" A moment later both men nearly ran into her.

Kane stopped in front of Jorell and grabbed her shoulders. "What's wrong? Talk to me."

"My father." She pointed to the bed. "He's awake!" She rushed back to her father's bedside and looked down. His eyes had closed again and she silently prayed this wasn't a dream. Kane and Dobie stood at her side. It was now or never. "Father, open your eyes."

Alextor opened his eyes. "Who a...are you?"

"I'm Kane, and this is Dobie."

"Wha...." Alextor looked around the room. "Where am I?"

"You're in my facility, not far from the capitol building. I brought both you and Jorell here for safe keeping."

"Jorell?"

"It seems the same people who want you dead now want Jorell dead as well." Kane stepped closer to Jorell. "Would you like us to leave so you can explain all this to him?"

She looked into Kane's deep blue eyes and saw complete understanding. "It might be better. If you don't mind."

"Of course. I'll see you later."

Kane and Dobie quickly left them alone. Her father was still awake, but he looked confused.

"St...start at the be...ginning."

"I hope you're awake enough to understand, because I've lived it, and I don't get it." Her father tried to laugh, but coughed instead.

"That's normal, isn't it?"

"There's nothing normal about this story." Explaining to her father all that had transpired might take awhile. She took a deep breath in preparation, but stopped when a tickle touched her mind. It had to be Kane, yet it didn't 'feel' like him.

By the Gods, evil swirled then surrounded her. She recognized the Energy-Lamia immediately. This could be a disaster. She leaned down and put her lips to her father's ear. "There is a presence in this room that wants to destroy you. Close your eyes, clear your mind. Think of nothing but pure white light, and I mean nothing. Can you do that?"

He nodded slightly. "Good. I'll protect you." She straightened and looked around the room. Nothing was out of place, and no one was visible, but there was definitely a pressing, malevolent presence that turned the room dark, even though it was early in the sun-cycle.

She needed Kane. The Energy-Lamia was calling her name repeatedly. She concentrated on calling Kane to come help her, but she knew she couldn't get through to him. Every time she thought his name the Lamia laughed in a deep, mocking tone.

Jorell Sutone. Still sitting by your father's side I see. You can't help him.

Maybe not, but I can help him die in peace.

I can help him die this very moment. Want to see?

What do you want from me?

Wouldn't you like to know.

He laughed again to mock her. There was no entity as evil as this. She envisioned pure white light surrounding her and her *father*.

Do you really think you can stop me? He laughed. You'll both be dead soon, and there's nothing you can do to stop it. You have no idea who you're dealing with. Your father already has one foot in the grave, or should I say two?

The Lamia's sardonic cackle echoed in her head so loudly she thought it would split in two. She put a hand over both her temples, as if she could physically hold her head together. It only took a moment to realize she was bowing to the Lamia, exactly as he planned.

After a fortifying breath, she dropped her hands, tilted her head back and pictured the most blinding white light she could conjure. She held that vision in place without wavering. Her and her father's life depended on this battle. Kane had told her to concentrate on light and positive energy. That's exactly what she was doing.

The Lamia pushed on her defenses, blew fire at her white energy circle. Then she distinctly heard Kane yelling at her to hold on. Thank the stars her father lay still with his eyes closed, but she had no way of knowing if the Lamia had attacked him in any way.

Kane ran in and didn't stop until he was at her side. He sent the brightest glowing light she'd ever encountered. The Lamia groaned loudly, and it sounded as if he had a physical body and was thrashing in pain about the room, trying to extinguish the light before it destroyed him.

This is not over! I've just begun, and I will win!

His extremely loud voice sounded very determined. When she took her next breath, she knew the evil entity was gone. It was difficult to explain how such a malevolence could move in and out of nowhere, and take whatever he wanted.

"Kane?" He faced her, concern written all over his face.

"I'm sorry." Kane pulled Jorell to him and hugged her. "I'm sorry I didn't get here sooner. For some reason your communication didn't reach me." He rubbed her back. "He's strong, whoever he is."

"I'm just glad you got here when you did." She reluctantly pulled back from his firm chest and turned her attention to her father. She leaned down, afraid of what happened to him during the attack. "Father? Are you all right?" He didn't answer and she began to panic.

"Father, talk to me, now!" He moaned and she looked at Kane. "I think he's coming back around. "Father, wake up!" He moved his head and finally opened his eyes.

"Jorell? What's wrong?"

"I thought you'd left us again."

"You told me to lay still, so I did."

"Good job." Kane moved closer. "I'm happy to finally meet you, sir."

"And who exactly are you?" Alextor looked at Jorell. "Well?"

"Father, I'd like you to meet the man who saved your life, Kane, or as he's commonly called, *The Traveler*."

"Help me..."

Her father tried to rise, so she helped him sit up in bed, then propped pillows behind his back, which was supported by the headboard. He whispered in her ear, asking her who hired him. "I hired him father, because I didn't know what else to do, nor did I have anyone I could trust."

"You have Rand, he's a capable man. I know you're reluctant to trust him, but he's very reliable, and loyal."

Jorell straightened and stepped back from the bed. "Father, I know how you feel about Rand, however, he is working closely with your enemy."

CHAPTER THIRTY SIX

"He'd never do that!"

"He would and he did! I would never make something like that up. Plus, we have proof if you need it." She glanced up at Kane who nodded his approval. She took what strength she could from him and leveled her gaze back on her father. "Rand is out for himself. He's never wanted what was best for either one of us, and I don't care what you think, or what you've been told. Rand is as much your enemy as the man who poisoned you." Her father stared at her, then at Kane.

"How do you know you can trust this man you've just met? Plus you're paying him. Loyalty can be bought."

"You're wrong, father. You thought you bought Rand's, but someone else paid him more

"I will not have you...."

"Ruler Sutone," Kane held up his hand, "I would never presume to tell you how to rule your Sector, but I would ask that you listen to what Jorell and I have to say before you make up your mind."

Alextor rubbed his chin with his finger. "What you ask is reasonable." He scooted closer to the edge of the bed. "I need to get up."

"I don't think that's a good idea, father."

"I think it's a great idea. How long have I been lying in a bed?"

"Twenty sun-cycles, if I've counted properly."

"No wonder I'm stiff. I want to get dressed, I want a cup of koffa, and then you may explain more."

Jorell turned toward the door just as Dobie rushed in and stopped. "Dobie, I'd like you to meet my father, and father, this is Dobie, Kane's

233

partner."

"How do you do, sir. It's a pleasure." Dobie bowed at the waist then stood back up straight. "We've waited a long time to see you awake.

Kane held out a hand to Alextor and so did Dobie. They helped him to his feet, but he fell back to a sitting position on the bed. "I suppose I've been lying here too long, I've gotten weak."

"I'll be happy to help you sir."

"Fine, fine." He looked up. "Kane, why don't you take Jorell out. Dobie and I will manage just fine."

"Father, are you sure?"

"Very. I don't need an audience, just a bit of help."

Dobie nodded. "I'm your man, sir."

Kane took Jorell's hand and led her out. The moment they stepped into the hall, the door whooshed closed behind them. "Do you think they'll be okay together?"

"Dobie is a great helper. They'll be fine." Kane took Jorell's hand. "I can't believe your father is speaking and sitting up. I couldn't be happier for you. Plus, he can help us."

"How? He's not fully recovered yet."

"We only need him to advise. I also want to hear his assessment of those involved in this power play. Once I know how they think, I can create a plan."

"When you put it like that, it sounds simple." Kane smiled at her, then walked up to the galley-serve and ordered four cups of koffa.

"I'm glad to know your father drinks koffa, because I don't trust anyone who doesn't."

"Now, that's a strong statement. Are you trying to say everyone who doesn't drink koffa is your enemy?"

Kane laughed. "Pretty much." He picked up two cups and set them down on the bar in front of where Jorell sat on the stool. "I think it would be best if you were the one who explained the series of events to your father. He trusts you, and he doesn't know me, or Dobie."

"You're right, but I want you with me."

"My sweet, this should be between you and your father. He'll feel more comfortable. If you need me, I'll be in the other room. Once he's up to speed, we can work together."

"You make it sound so simple. I pray you're right, but I have my doubts."

"Jorell, don't think negative. Stay positive and project only the outcome you desire, not the outcome you fear. You actually have more control over events than you think."

"I don't understand." She sighed. "I know you're *The Traveler*, and you've had lots of experience, but I haven't. I'm afraid I'll hold you back—that I'll ruin whatever plan you put into motion."

"Whoa, my sweet. That's neither positive, or desirable." He tucked some loose hairs on her cheek behind her ear. "It's actually simple. Tomorrow is only your future yesterday."

"Aren't you the cute one." He gave her a funny grin and nodded. "You like playing games, *Traveler*?"

Kane nodded. "There are many games I'd love to teach you, but for now, let's play the faith game. Such a simple word for a difficult task."

"I shall endeavor to play with you."

"That's all I ask."

"Then let's start." She leaned forward and pressed her lips to Kane's. He didn't hesitate to claim her and kiss her senseless, and he was excellent. Along with the rapid beat of her heart came the hungry need for his hot, naked body against hers. To be alone with him in his bed.

Kane ended the kiss, leaned back and looked into Jorell's eyes. "I hear you thinking, my sweet."

"Really? What am I thinking?" He was teasing her since he couldn't hear her thoughts unless she wanted him to, and she'd blocked him so she wasn't worried.

"You want me in your bed, naked against you. Am I warm?"

"Very warm. Hot actually."

"I meant my guess about your thoughts, not my body temp."

"Aren't you the sneaky one. You're fishing, you don't really know."

"I wasn't guessing, Jorell."

Warmth flooded her cheeks, then slowly encompassed her entire body. Kane's abilities were even greater than she'd thought if he could read her thoughts that well. It really didn't matter. She'd read his mind enough to know he wanted her, and had deep feelings for her. Whether she wanted to admit it or not, she had fallen in love with Kane.

The Traveler was kind, considerate, caring, tough, smart, and to top it all off, he was gorgeous from the top of his dark brown hair down to the tips of his leather boots, and she loved every inch. But she loved what was inside his heart even more.

"I didn't know you felt that way about me, my sweet."

"What do you mean?" Her face grew hot and she knew her cheeks were red from embarrassment. "You can't possibly know what I was thinking!"

"What about kind, considerate, caring, tough, smart? Shall I continue?"

"No!" She turned away from him and wished she could slither down the stool and disappear into the floor. The urge to run was strong, but there was nowhere she wanted to go, except with Kane.

"Jorell, don't turn away from me. I'm honored you feel the way you do." He put his hands on her waist and turned her around to face him. "I feel the same about you. Don't you know that?"

She shook her head. "How would I know? I'm supposed to be the mind reader here, yet I can't read you in the same way you read me. It's humiliating, to say the least."

Kane pulled her against his chest. "I never meant any harm, or to embarrass you. I only wanted you to know that I find you kind, understanding, thoughtful, smart, and you're the most beautiful woman I've ever met, and I mean in all directions of time." He reached out and ran his fingers through her hair. "From the top of your shiny, fire-red hair, to the tips of your sexy heels, you're perfect."

Kane had heard her every thought and said he shared the same feelings. If she hadn't just had her own words spoken back to her she wouldn't have believed him. She opened her mouth to speak, but he stopped her by placing his index over her lips.

"I have to work hard to read you, and I promise not to do so again without your permission. When I gained access, it was so beautiful I could not help myself." He tilted her chin up with his finger. "I promise not to do it again unless you invite me, the way we usually do."

She smiled, completely taken by the worry etched across his handsome face. "I should make you squirm for a while, but I won't. I think Dobie and my father are coming. I accept your apology, *'Traveler'*, and I believe you're sincere about asking permission so we won't have future problems."

Kane sighed. "Thank you. Trust is important in a relationship, and I..."

"Chief, look who's walking!"

Jorell eased back from Kane and he did the same. She looked down the hall and smiled. Her father was actually walking. Dobie may be helping some, but he was walking, when only a few time-units ago he was unconscious and on the verge of death. She glanced at Kane and it was obvious he shared her joy. "Thank you isn't enough for what I feel. Without you, my father would be dead right now. You saved him, and I'll forever be in your debt."

"Just earning the credits you paid me, my sweet." He leaned close to her ear. "I'd do anything for you."

Kane pulled his head back and stood nonchalantly waiting for Dobie and her father to reach them. He had a bit of scoundrel in him, which only made him more attractive. What woman didn't love a bad boy? She smiled as much for Kane as for her father's progress.

Dobie walked Alextor to a chair in the main entertainment area. Once Alextor was seated Dobie bowed then straightened. "May I present, Sector-Three Ruler, Alextor Sutone."

"Thank you Dobie, you've honored me with your help." He held his hand out toward Jorell. "Daughter, please, come closer."

Jorell hurried to her father and knelt on the floor by his feet. "I can't tell you how happy I am to see you up, and speaking. I thought...." She bowed her head and blinked back tears. Everyone knew what she almost said. She raised her head and looked him in the eye. "Welcome back, Father."

"I'm glad to be back, although, I have no memory of being in a coma, so I feel like I just went to sleep after the Tri-Sector meeting, and this is the next sun-cycle."

"I hate to tell you this, but..."

Alextor held up his hand. "I made Dobie answer questions while he helped me clean-up and dress. I have a pretty good idea of what's going on, and I'm sure you'll correct me if I'm wrong."

Jorell glanced at Kane who stood next to her with a professional, emotionless expression on his face. "I'm sure we will."

"Ruler Sutone, since Dobie filled you in, you realize we need your help to stop the takeover."

"Explain what is behind this takeover. I need more details, please."

"Power, and credits. That's what it's always about. I'm sure you know that. However, in this case I believe there is one more motive—revenge."

"Revenge on who?" Alextor shook his head. "That's not possible. There's no one that angry at all three leaders."

"One man is that angry--Pakar Moran."

"It can't be. A reliable source reported Pakar died fifteen annual-cycles ago. How could this be?"

Jorell saw the honest disbelief written all over her father's pale face. He was too weak for this, but she knew if she interfered he'd insist on having it his way, he always did.

Kane looked directly at Alextor. "I have a theory, and at this moment, that's all it is, but once I meet with him, I'll know for sure."

"That sounds like doubletalk. Why should I believe you?"

"I've seen the tattoo on his right forearm, and that's the only way to tell his identity. I believe he's had multiple face surgeries to dramatically alter his appearance. He's power hungry, and out for revenge, but he's not stupid. He's taken time to plan all this, and he's had the patience to wait for the right time. He most likely planted the rumor of his own death."

"How in creation is this the *right time*?"

"Father, stay calm. You're too weak to get excited."

"Stop fussing over me, Jorell. There's work to do, and we've already lost too much time from what I understand. Isn't that correct, Kane?"

"Correct, sir."

"Do you have a plan?"

"I'm working on one, and I'm pleased to have your input."

"If we're just fighting one man, that shouldn't be too difficult."

"I'm afraid there's more. Ramon Coster, Nazar Ferris, and Rand Arroray, to name three of the most prominent. We are not sure how deep it goes. Currently this man has control of Sectors One and Two, and believes Sector-Three will be his in a few sun-cycles. He does not need an army to take over. He plans to announce himself as supreme ruler, and everyone will agree with no argument."

"Over my dead body!"

"Father! Don't say that. You nearly paid that price."

"True." Alextor glanced up at Jorell. "How close was I?"

"Closer than you know. You scared the Diabolus out of me."

"That was their plan, sir, and they nearly succeeded."

"Kane, you mentioned Rand. Are you sure?"

Kane nodded.

"How do you know?"

"We have vids of him talking to your enemies. If he weren't involved, he would not be talking to them." Kane took a deep breath. "You can ask Jorell about his behavior, although she's too nice to tell you he treated her worse than the dirt under his feet. And if that's not enough proof, he aided in her assassination."

"That's not possible; she's fine."

"I traveled and changed a few circumstances." Kane looked into Jorell's eyes. "Jorell can explain it to you in detail later, but I broke my own rule. I could *not* let her die." Kane took Jorell's hand. "She means too much to me," he returned his gaze to Alextor, "and to you."

"You're right. I owe you my sincere thanks for her life, and my own." Alextor leaned back in his chair and crossed his legs. "Now, there is much to do, and I have very little strength. I believe you have a better grip on this situation than I do, so tell me what you need?"

"First get some rest, then I need a list of the people in your Sector, and the other two Sectors that you'd trust with your life, and I mean that literally. If you have an ounce of doubt, do not list them."

"I can do that. What else?"

"Jorell will work with you, and I'll let you know once we have a solid plan." Kane stepped closer to Alextor. "Talk to no one. We don't want anyone knowing about your condition. Your citizens and your government believe you're visiting relatives, your enemies are waiting for word you finally succumbed to the poison. Therefore, you must stay inside here and contact no one."

"I thought I was the one who was supposed to give the orders."

Jorell knew by her father's tone he was joking, but Kane didn't and a worried expression marred his handsome face. "It's fine Kane, he's kidding."

Kane smiled. "Forgive me, sir, I seemed to have lost my sense of humor lately."

"A word of advice, son. Never lose your sense of humor. Sometimes that's the only thing that gets you through the tough times." Alextor uncrossed his legs and scooted to the edge of the chair. "Dobie, please help me back to my room. I'm afraid I need to rest. It seems that twenty sun-cycles in bed wasn't enough for me."

Kane laughed. "It appears not."

Jorell watched Dobie help her father stand, then walked with him down the hall at his pace. "Dobie is a treasure. You're fortunate to have someone so loyal and talented." She watched Kane nod. "How long have you been with him?"

"Twenty-one annual cycles."

"That's a long time considering your age."

"Maybe I'm older than I look?" Kane laughed. "Remember how I looked when you met me? Well that's the real me, this," Kane pointed to his face, "is the disguise."

"Then I'll have to check it out to be sure." She walked over to Kane and put her hands on his cheeks and gave them a little pinch. "Seems real." She stood on tiptoe and kissed his cheek and gave it an extra lick. "Tastes real."

Kane pulled her to him and pressed his lips to hers and gave her the most passionate kiss she'd ever had. It was the kind of kiss she never wanted to end, and hoped he'd give her more. Instead he pulled away and left her lips throbbing, as if they missed his mouth and were begging for more.

"What's the verdict now?"

"Not too bad, for an old man." She laughed at the strange look on his face. "I wonder what you kissed like in your prime?" This time he laughed with her. They certainly needed to lighten the mood, considering the problems at hand, not to mention the entire planet's future.

"Maybe I need to demonstrate a few things for you." Kane put his arms behind Jorell and swept her off her feet and into his arms.

Jorell giggled while Kane walked her down the hall toward his bedroom. "Are your walls soundproof?"

"Let's find out."

CHAPTER THIRTY SEVEN

Dobie pointed at the display screen." Look Kane, there's Nazar talking to Loran."

"I just found Loran, Nazar, Senar Pollit, Ramon Coster, and Rolland Morro in a meeting of their own before The Tri-Sector meeting began. Unfortunately there's no sound, but they're obviously making plans together."

"Be sure you play this vid for Alextor. He needs to see it for himself and not just take our word for it." Kane pushed the hair on his forehead back with his fingers. "It's hard to tell how deep this goes."

"Does it matter?"

"I'm not sure. If there's an entire army standing in our way it might, but if it's just Loran and a few of his men, then it shouldn't be too hard. As soon as we get Alextor's list we'll set up a meeting so we can bring them up to date as to what's coming, and who plans to deliver it. Once they understand, I'm sure they'll help us."

Kane pushed back from the com-board, stood and walked around the room. He'd sat on that stool so long he was stiff. "When we started this, Alextor wasn't physically in the picture. Now we have to consider how to keep him safe, and how to effectively use him."

Dobie scratched his head. "Is that good or bad?"

"Good, I hope. I know Alextor will help us, I just don't know how hard it will be to protect him and Jorell."

"Well, we have exactly nine sun-cycles until that fateful Tri-Sector meeting where Loran Narom takes power." Dobie scratched his head. "Chief, do you think it's just coincidence that this guy's name is Loran when Pakar was exiled to Larent, a planet outside of our solar system?"

"Need you ask? We put it together, but I'm sure no one else will. If there's one thing about Pakar, or Loran, is that he's too arrogant for his own good. And that my friend, will be his downfall."

"Gotcha. Our best weapon is his weakness, but how do we use it against him?"

Kane shrugged. He hadn't worked that detail out yet, but something would come to him, it always did. Divine intervention? Possibly. Whatever the source, it was always good.

"I read you, Chief. You'll know it when you see it?"

"Something like that. Right now we need to worry about Jorell."

"Yeah. She's gonna be really pissed when she learns Loran is Pakar, who's your father."

"Okay genius, what am I supposed to do about it?"

"You could start by telling her?"

"And how will that help anything?"

"You can be so dense at times. I realize I'm the one who has problems with women, but this could turn out to be the biggest woman problem you've ever had. I see what's between you two, and I know a commitment when I see one."

"Commitment?"

"Yes, oh stubborn boss of mine. Commitment. It's time, and you know it. And Jorell is the one, and you know that as well as anyone who sees you two together. You share more than attraction, you share an energy that defies explanation."

"That's one way to put it." Damn, Dobie was spot on this time. From the look on his friend's face he knew denial no longer applied. Diabolus, he couldn't explain it, so how was he supposed to verbalize it to his friend?

"Chief, I know what's floating around in that over-calculating brain of yours. All I'm asking you to do is acknowledge how you feel about Jorell to me. Not the world, just me."

"Okay, for just you, I'll admit that I...I..."

"Love her?"

"Don't put words in my mouth."

"Why not? You can't seem to put them in yourself."

Kane laughed. "You're doing it again you know."

"What? Little old me, doing something to the big, bad 'traveler'?"

"Yeah, little old you is making me admit I love Jorell Sutone, and that she's the one woman I could settle down with. Okay, nosey? Happy now?"

"Okay, I'm happy now, but you didn't tell me anything I didn't know, you just told yourself."

"Don't make me hurt you."

"I think you need to save your fighting energy for Nazar and Pakar."

"I think you're right."

****

"What in Diabolous is wrong with you?" Pakar reared back and punched Rand's jaw as hard as he could. The blow was more effective than he planned since the stupid man hit the floor with one punch. Inflicting pain usually helped him get his way, plus it had a fringe benefit—he enjoyed it.

"Loran, sir, aah, I'm...aah...so sorry."

He watched the pathetic man pull himself up off the floor and straighten his clothes. He could tidy all he wanted, but he was still a royal screw-up, inept and ignorant. He never would have recruited Rand, but he was already in place and very willing to help, or should he say easily bought?

Greed made the planet go-round. Everyone he employed had a huge greed-streak, but none had his degree of need. Then again, he was the brains behind the operation, therefore he deserved greater payment. "Jorell must die immediately. You need to set her up so my sniper can take her out."

"Aah, sir...that will be difficult. You see...I...aah..."

"Just say it and quit stuttering like a handicapped idiot!"

"She cut me out of her life. We're no longer a couple, nor do I have a job at the capitol."

"What?" This simpleton tested his patience. "That had better not be true!"

"I'm afraid it is."

"You'd better grovel for her to take you back."

"She won't. She's sweet on this man she hired to help her."

"Help her with what?"

"Aah...well..."

"Spit it out, it can't be that hard."

"I'm not sure exactly."

"Not sure? How could you possibly be so incompetent?"

"Sorry, sir. It won't happen again."

"You're damned right it won't!" He turned his back on Rand before he beat him to a pulp. He took a deep breath. He still had jobs for Rand to complete and he couldn't very well look like he'd been mugged in the 'black alleyway'.

"I'll make it up to you. I'll work for free. Please, give me another chance."

"Exactly why should I?" He turned around to look in Rand's eyes. The eyes always revealed if a man was lying.

"You won't regret it. I promise."

"I'm supposed to believe your promise to succeed when you've done nothing but fail?" Pakar laughed at the fool standing before him. Rand looked pathetic and small. "Give me one reason to trust you."

"I may have screwed up, but I never betrayed you. I've kept your secrets, your plans. I've told no one, nor will I."

The man was shaking in his boots. Good. He deserved to suffer for his mistakes. "You'd be dead right now if you'd opened your mouth."

"I understand, sir."

"You *will* set Jorell up for the sniper. I don't care how you do it, just do it!"

"I will. Send me the details and I'll take care of the rest."

"Get out of my sight!"

****

Jorell couldn't believe Rand was at her door, making so much racket. She should have him arrested, but Kane had told her to 'play along', so they could set their traps and learn what the other side was up to. For that reason alone, she opened the door and let Rand inside her quarters.

He dropped to his knees in front of her, head bowed. What had she ever seen in him? A better question was what had her father seen in him that made him want Rand in the family? She had to admit, she'd believed Rand was on her father's side. His betrayal had come as a total surprise to both her and her father. "What are you doing, Rand?"

"I'm begging you to take me back, Jorell."

"Why would I?"

"For the people? For you? For your father?"

"What is it you can do for all of us?"

"I can serve you well, as I always have."

"And I'm to believe that after the way you acted?"

Rand rose to his feet. "You're the one who was with another man. I never cheated on you."

"Not that I know of, but you don't respect me. Knowing that, I don't understand why you want me back?" She knew he either wanted to kill her, or use her in some political way. This game could prove interesting.

"I love you, Jorell. I always have. And if you give me the chance,

244

I'll prove it to you."

Rand never loved anyone except himself. Kane said to play along, so she'd have to give in to him, but it rubbed her the wrong way to be with the man who participated in her death. She would be dead if Kane hadn't traveled back to stop it.

"Let me take you to dinner. We'll go to the best establishment in three Sectors." Rand picked up Jorell's hand, brought it to his mouth and kissed the back. "Please? Say yes. Give me that chance."

The feel of his lips on the back of her hand made her skin crawl, and her stomach turn. It was time to pacify him, even though she hated the thought of being with him. "I'll go to dinner with you."

"Fantastic!"

"I'll be ready in about one time-unit. Come back and pick me up."

"Perfect. Can't wait."

Rand put his arms around her and pulled her tight against him. He was about to kiss her and she began to gag. She had to act normal or he'd know something was up, but this was the most difficult assignment she'd ever had. He pressed his lips to hers and she gathered her courage to kiss him back.

He tasted of liquor, something she wasn't used to. Rand drank, yes, but never during the sun-cycle, unless it was a luncheon and everyone had drinks. She wanted him gone. Instead she had to play the dueling tongue game with a man she despised. She should win an award for her performance.

Finally he ended the dispassionate kiss, pulled back and smiled at her. He looked as pathetic as his kiss had been, which sent her mind to Kane, and how his kiss enveloped her in a special world, and lit her body on fire. Rand kissed like an inexperienced school boy who did not know what to do next. Rand did not respect her, and there was not an ounce of love in his body. She walked to the door and opened it for him. "See you in one time-unit."

"Can't wait, my dear."

He nodded, gave her a forced smile, then walked out at a fast pace and quickly disappeared down the hall. "Thank the powers that be," she mumbled while the door whooshed closed.

This was where she was supposed to take a deep breath and relax, but she couldn't since she had to spend the evening with Rand. Kane expected too much. That familiar tickle touched her mind and she opened to Kane.

"You did great, my sweet. I'm very proud of you."

"*Thank you, I think.*" She looked toward her bedroom and watched Kane strut toward her. He showed a bit of arrogance in the smile on his face, but next to Rand, it was nothing. Kane earned his, Rand stole his. No two men could be as far apart in every aspect of their lives as Rand and Kane. Her choice was a simple one, no thought required. Her heart had always known.

Kane entered her living quarters, then turned straight into the galley, returned with two glasses of wine, handed her a glass, and then took a seat next to her on the sofa. For once she really needed a drink. "It could take an entire bottle to get me to go with Rand." She turned her gaze on Kane. "Are you sure about this?"

"Positive. It might be a bit different than the first version, but we'll get the same result, without losing you this time."

"I'll only be dead to the entire world."

"But not to me." Kane smiled. "I need you with me, Jorell."

"I can't be with you if I'm…" He placed a finger over her lips so she couldn't continue.

"I have literally changed time itself. I've violated my own rule, as well as every rule, written and unwritten, regarding time travel and the future."

"I don't know what to say, Kane."

"Just say you trust me, because there's no turning back."

"That I understand." She took his hand and looked into the depths of his blue eyes. She found only truth and compassion. "My life is in your hands. There's no greater trust than that."

"True." Kane pressed a button on his com-unit.

Dobie rushed in through the living area with an armful of stuff. He dropped it on the floor, looked up and smiled. "It's all here. Everything we need. I've checked it personally. It will not fail."

"Good. Explain it to Jorell. You're better at technical stuff."

"Okay." Dobie picked up a shiny black garment and held it up in front of him. "This, Princess, will be part of your new evening attire." He shook the object several times and the bottom bounced and jumped.

"That's a beautiful evening gown, Dobie, but how's that going to…."

"Save your life? Well, feel it." He held it toward Jorell. "See how it feels like the finest silk?" He waited while Jorell ran her hand over the fabric. "It is a bit heavier, I admit, but it will do the job."

"What job?" Dobie looked surprised at her question, then shook his head and smiled.

"Sorry, I got carried away. This garment is made from a light, complex, rare metal called volcor, and it resists any kind of ammunition, including lasers of all types. Plus, there's a hidden lining that will release blood out of any area that has been hit. The fabric, as you can see, has tiny holes in it." Dobie held it up to the light.

"The weave is loose because it makes it more effective. I know, Princess, I thought that was strange too, but it's true. It's effectiveness is unequaled.

"A sniper will aim for one of three places; the front of your head, the back of your head, your heart. Those three areas guarantee death, and that's what a professional is looking for. This," Dobie held out another piece of fabric, "will protect your head. It's made to look like an accent piece to your gown. Drape it like this."

Jorell watched Dobie carefully put the piece on his head, then wrap it in a precise way that draped gracefully under his chin, protecting the neck area, then he tossed the long end over his left shoulder. She smiled at him while he pretended to be a woman primping for a date. "Nice job, Dobie."

"Yes, well," Dobie removed the head wrap, "this outfit will protect you quite well. And if the sniper does the same thing as last time, he'll go for your heart." He shook his head, then looked directly into Jorell's eyes. "I wish I could tell you it won't hurt, but I'd be lying. It's going to hurt like Diabolus! You won't have to worry about faking pain. It always stings to the bone when you're hit, but you won't die, and that's the plan. However, you can expect a nice bruise."

"Jorell," Kane took her hand in his, "you don't have to do this if you don't want to. We can devise another plan."

"I'll be fine. This is the only way to tie everything up in a timely manner." She glanced first at Dobie, then Kane. "I appreciate you both trying to spare me pain, but I assure you, if I fail, the pain will be far worse, and not just for me, for the entire planet."

"You're a brave one, Jorell Sutone." Kane reached out and tucked stray hairs behind her ear. "Your sacrifice will pay off. I'll make sure of that."

"Really? Can you honestly say you and Dobie can stop an entire conspiracy that has already taken multiple lives and gained control of two Sectors?"

"Don't underestimate us, Princess." Dobie thumped his chest. "We're mighty warriors. We'll save you!"

She laughed at Dobie's comical victory dance. All three of them laughed hard, but when the moment passed she looked at Kane. "I need to know exactly what to do when I'm shot."

"Just fall, which will be easy because the impact of the shot will take you down. Then just do what comes naturally." Kane sighed. "Have you talked to the doctor?"

"He knows what to do."

"Then all *you* have to do is die."

CHAPTER THIRTY EIGHT

Kane glanced at his wrist-piece for the twentieth time since he'd parked the med-vehicle. Doctor Willock had arranged for him and Dobie to be the med-tecs sent to attend the shooting victim. He absolutely hated this plan, but *he* was in control this time.

"What's wrong Chief?"

"You know good and well what's wrong. Jorell's life is on the line, and I don't like it."

"All the safeguards are in place. I checked everything myself. Even the listening device is working fine. She's waiting for Rand to pick her up."

"I know. That's what bothers me."

"He's a sleaze-star, that's for sure."

"He's a murderer, and that's far worse."

****

"Jorell, my dear. You look...lovely."

Rand's voice echoed in the cab of the med vehicle, and Kane wanted to punch something. Just hearing the traitor's voice sent his temper off the charts. If he could, he'd kill the saboteur himself.

"Thank you."

"Let's go. Our reservation awaits."

Kane's hands fisted and he took a deep breath in an effort to control his anger." I'll bet it does." He couldn't let jealously blow the charade. Besides, he knew Jorell's feelings for the man, and that was all that mattered.

"It seems weird, Chief, to listen to two people on a date, especially when it's Jorell. I feel like I'm eavesdropping on a friend."

"We're saving her life, remember?"

"Yeah."

"Rand, why are we walking to the front of the building?"

"I had my transport brought to the front. I thought it would be quicker."

Dobie slapped his head with his hand. "Yeah, he knows the security is tighter in the back where the officials park."

Kane took a deep breath before he spoke. "It doesn't matter, we have her protected, and they'll believe they succeeded."

"Rand, you're very quiet. Is something wrong?"

"No…no…I just…" Rand paused and looked at Jorell, "want to make this moon-cycle perfect."

"Good."

Kane watched the security vid that followed Rand and Jorell on their walk through the Capitol Building. The moment they exited through the front entrance, his heart began to race. When they began their descent down the front steps he silently prayed their plan went perfect because he knew the original outcome. One glitch could end it all.

A flash flew across the screen and he heard gasps, then screams. He helplessly watched Jorell's knees buckle and her body fall, her head hitting the hard, marbelus steps. Before anyone could reach her, her body rolled down the dozen or so steps until she landed on the docking pad below.

His need to rush to her immediately nearly overwhelmed his better sense, but he had to wait for the call. What caught his eye was Rand, who looked in the direction of the shooter instead of his fiancée. He was truly despicable.

"Chief, tell me what you're thinking."

"Look at Rand, searching the crowd for something, or someone."

"Yeah, you'd think his life was in danger."

Kane looked at Dobie. "If I had my way—"

"He'd be a dead man." Dobie stared at the vid-screen.

"I *will* make him pay."

"Med-unit twenty-four, emergency at the main platform of the Capitol Building. Respond immediately."

Dobie tapped the com device. "Unit nine responding."

Kane started the med-van, and moments later they were at their destination. Dobie sounded the siren several times before the assembled crowd moved enough to allow them access to Jorell's lifeless body. It never took long for the curious to gather.

Once on the ground, med-case in hand, he ran to Jorell's side. She lay face down so he placed two fingers on her carotid artery, relieved to find a pulse. He gently rolled her over to reveal a blood-stained gown. The entire bodice was soaked in red. Thank the stars the shooter had replayed his previous shot. He looked up at Dobie who waited for a command. "Start an MMR23-drip."

"Right away." Dobie opened his case and took out the necessary supplies.

"Will she be okay?"

Kane looked up into Rand's eyes and wondered how he could ask such a question when he already knew the answer. "You'll have to speak to the doctor after he examines her."

"Is she alive?"

"Barely. She's lost a lot of blood." He inserted the IV under the skin on top of her hand and taped it securely. In the line he injected a painkiller. When he looked up, Dobie had arrived with the transport-bed. Together they carefully picked her up and laid her on the narrow, white mattress, raised the side rails along with the bed itself. Once he secured the straps over her, he pushed the bed to the back of the med-van. He was ready to jump up and ride in the back, but Rand grabbed his arm.

"Have we met before?"

Confident in his disguise he shook his head. "No, sir. Now, if you don't mind, we must get this patient to the main med-unit."

"That is Alextor Sutone's daughter, Jorell!"

"We'll do our best, sir." Kane closed the hatch door in Rand's face, then turned toward his patient lying still on the transport gurney. The vehicle jerked at the abrupt upward move, then quickly took off, sirens screaming while traffic yielded.

"Jorell? Can you hear me?" He checked her pulse and blood pressure. She was fine. "Jorell, it's okay, we're alone. Talk to me." Fear surged through him when she didn't respond. He had to remind himself of the intensity of the hit she took. "Jorell, please, talk to me."

"It hurts really bad. Make it go away."

Kane pulled the specially prepared syringe from the box the doctor provided. He sterilized her arm, then gave her the injection. Doctor Willock insisted I give you this to stop your pain and bring you to a suspended state that will render you deeply unconscious." Two beautiful green eyes blinked at him and he'd never been so relieved in his life. Reality had been changed, and he prayed his interference did not change anything else.

"Thank you, Kane. My brave warrior."

"I like the sound of that." The sweetness of her voice lit up the emerald depths of her eyes. He doubted she had a mean bone in her body, which was good since he had enough for the both of them.

"Where's Rand? My date from Diabolus."

"He'll meet you at the med-unit." He brushed hair from her forehead with his fingers. "Jorell, you know the plan, right?" She nodded. "Not a word to anyone. For everyone's purposes, you're dead. Try not to breathe too deeply, don't open your eyes, and don't speak."

"Got it." She smiled. "You look too serious for a man with short, dark blond hair, and a funny moustache. I need to kiss you to see if it tickles." She laughed. "You seem a bit fuzzy right now. I think you're...aah...handsome when you act tough. I...I...like it."

The meds he'd given her finally rendered her unconscious. He started a MMR23-drip line exactly as Willock had taught him. It had to look like a valiant effort to save her life had been performed. He probed her mind, but found nothing. She was under *the sleep of the dead* as it was called. Not many knew about the drug, which should make this charade more convincing, and it had to succeed. There was *no* other choice.

The transport stopped in front of the priority entrance of med-unit, and he waited for Dobie to open the back hatch. He pushed Jorell's gurney toward his friend, who grabbed the bottom and eased it out of the transport. Together they moved her into the building where the doctor waited with Rand beside him. He heard the door open behind them, and when he turned he saw Rand.

He wanted to knock Rand from here to the farthest planet where he could stay for the rest of his miserable life! The only man he hated more right now was his biological father. Rand was bad, but far from the most evil man on any planet.

"How is she, doctor?"

Doctor Willock moved the scanner up and down Jorell's body, shaking his head. The doctor was a good actor after all, and it didn't hurt that he hated Rand also, a little information he confided in him during his training.

"Well, how is she?" Rand reached for Jorell's hand, but the doctor stopped him.

"I'm afraid she didn't make it." He pulled the thin med-cover over her face. "I'm sorry. I really am."

"Men, take her body to the morgue." He turned back toward Rand. "Please, accept my condolences."

Dobie started pushing Jorell down the hall, and he took his place on the opposite end. Rand began his act of a man who had just lost the love of his life. He even began to sob, but he was far from convincing. Even the doctor shook his head and walked away. If he ever got the opportunity to put his hands on Rand, he'd do so much damage the phony would never be able to pick himself up again.

"I know what you're thinking, Chief, and I suggest you don't go there. He'll get what's coming to him, you'll see."

"I might believe you if I hadn't seen slime like him get away with their crimes far too many times."

"Think positive."

The lift door opened and Dobie backed in while he steered in his end of the gurney. When the door closed and the downward motion began, Kane took a deep breath. So far, so good, but the worst was yet to come.

****

"Are you sure, father?"

"For the last time, yes!"

"You have to forgive her, she's not used to being dead." Kane laughed.

"That's not funny!" Jorell stared at Kane who seemed to find this amusing. "I'm sorry, but I don't find anything funny right now."

"You and your father just sounded like Dobie and me. That's all."

"Sorry. Dying left me with a headache. It's probably from the drugs you neglected to tell me about."

"Sorry, but I had to knock you out."

"Dobie explained it." Heat rushed into her cheeks so she quickly turned her head away. Surprisingly, all she wanted was to be alone with Kane, but she might never have the chance again. Her father had no clue what was going on between her and Kane, not yet anyway. He was still trying to deal with his feelings toward Rand. It was confusing. "Father, have all the key men been confirmed?"

"They have. The meeting is set to begin immediately following your funeral service. We're using the guise of a private mourning service, as is custom, especially for well-known people. And you, my dear daughter, are very well-known."

"Just so Rand isn't there."

Kane cleared his throat. "I'll be happy to take care of him for you."

"Kane, I see you've become attached to my daughter, and I approve of such a pairing. However, murdering her past fiancé would not suit our purpose at this juncture. If you know what I mean?"

"Unfortunately, I do. But I reserve the right to put the traitor in his place anytime you deem necessary."

Alextor laughed long and hard. "You have my word, I'll only call you to do the dirty work. Will that suit your needs?"

"For now."

"Back to business." Jorell wanted to laugh at the devilish grin on Kane's face. "How many will attend?"

"Twelve. Four from each Sector. Once we convince them, they'll return and engage those they trust. It will work." Alextor walked over to Kane and put a hand on his shoulder. "I'm grateful for your plan, and the opportunity to participate."

"Thank your daughter, sir. She's the one who hired me to save your life."

"I'm glad she did."

"You may not say that when you see the dent in the treasury account."

"If we fail, the new leader will have less credits at his disposal. If we succeed, well, I'll deal with that later." Alextor chuckled. "At least I'm here to see what you spent on me, daughter, but, I'm sure I'm worth it."

Alextor's comment made everyone laugh. Her father was right, he was worth every credit she'd paid. But the real battle was about to begin, and there could only be one loser, and it would *not* be her father.

"Alextor, tell me about the men you invited. A bit of background would be helpful. It's always good to know who I'm speaking to."

"Careful. I like that. I respect anyone who thinks before they allow the wrong words to escape their lips."

Alextor made himself comfortable on the elegant, cushioned chair in the main living area. He looked like a king, the way one expected a leader to be. "You could say that's how I stay alive."

"I'm sure." Alextor held his hand out toward Jorell. She walked to his side and took his hand. "Jorell knows these men as well as I do." He smiled. "Maybe better."

"Father, don't...."

"Sorry, dear. Bad habit of mine, I know." He waved at Dobie. "I'll take that footstool now, son."

"Right away." Dobie left the room.

"I have the most knowledge of the four men from Sector-Three, of course, they're all close friends of mine. In fact, we often spoke about how the other leaders' deaths were suspicious. Our unanimous conclusion was murder, plain and simple. You'll have no trouble convincing them of a plot to kill me. They expected it."

"Who do you, and your colleagues, suspect the mastermind is

behind the murders, and possible takeover?"

"We had no idea then, or now. I've been aah...out of commission, but last I spoke with them, we had no suspect in mind."

Dobie entered the room and placed the footstool under Alextor's legs, then left again. She'd seen Kane give his friend 'the look' that said leave. Kane realized that most people were comfortable confiding in one stranger, but not two. "Father, do your friends in the other two Sectors suspect a takeover?"

"I doubt it since they already have a new ruler, or so they believe. Both new rulers entered the picture, in lower positions, about five annual-cycles ago." Alextor rubbed his chin. "In fact, that's about the time Rand arrived." He looked up at Kane. "Why didn't I see it?" He shook his head. "How could I have been so stupid, and trusting?"

"Father, don't do that to yourself."

"She's right sir. Berating yourself is foolish."

"I certainly feel foolish. I blindly trusted Rand, and look what happened." He stared at Jorell. "I almost made you life-mate the fool! I'll never forgive myself for that."

"I forgive you, father. But now there's no chance of a union, and I couldn't be happier."

"You've always been wise, daughter, which is why you're First Advisor, always by my side."

"Thank you, but I wasn't wise enough to see any of this coming either. I pretended to like Rand to please you, but I suspected his only intent for life-mating me was for position, never for treason."

"And that, my sweet, was your mistake. Not listening to your inner voice." Kane stepped closer to Jorell who stood beside her father in the chair. "Have you learned to trust yourself now?"

Alextor raised his arm. "Okay, you two. I think you both need to work out the details. Jorell can tell you everything you need to know. And Kane, it's obvious you'd rather talk to her than a sick, old man."

"Sir, I never..."

Alextor laughed. He took his legs off the footstool, pushed it aside, then stood. "I need to rest before the meeting, so I'll leave you two alone now."

"Thank you, father." Jorell watched him disappear down the hall with Dobie at his side, then she turned toward Kane who had the biggest smile on his face. "What?"

"I like your father."

"I'm glad."

"No, I mean I *really* like him." Kane shook his head. "I've worked for a lot of people I didn't like." Kane took Jorell's hand in his. "You, my sweet, and your father are different."

"I bet you say that to all your women clients." Kane raised her hand to his lips and kissed the backs of each finger. A shiver raced up and down her spine. The man made her react to him in ways she never thought possible. He was not only physically attractive, his mental skills and strength fascinated her.

"I believe you're thinking about me."

"What gives you that idea?" Of course he knew, he could read her thoughts, especially since she'd learned to open to him so easily. "You don't know everything I'm thinking."

"I'm not sure I want to know *everything*."

"Maybe I should just show you what I was thinking."

"That sounds appealing."

Kane gave her his now familiar come-on look, and she certainly didn't want to disappoint him. She pulled her hand from his, threaded both her arms around his neck and pressed her lips to his. His tongue found hers and they fought for control, a battle that was better enjoyed than won. He deepened the kiss and wrapped his arms around her back and pulled her tight against his chest.

She heard a moan escape from deep in his chest while his hands roamed her back, settling on her derrière. He was the most amazing man she'd ever met, and he had the capacity to stir her emotions. Thoughts of forever love, children, and sharing a home, all came bursting to the surface. Most women had nesting thoughts at one time or another, but she'd pushed those ideas so far back they had no meaning—until now. Kane changed everything.

His kiss turned demanding, then his strong arms lifted her off the floor. An excited tickle began in her stomach and she shivered while he carried her to his bed chamber.

In her mind she sensed a familiar tickle that was his alone. It was a pleasure to communicate with him mind to mind because everything held more emotion and meaning. *"Where are you taking me?"*

"I think you know."

"What about the meeting?"

"It's two time-units away, we have plenty of time."

His lips worked on hers while he waited for the door to open. When it did, he rushed straight to the bed and laid her down. He was so gentle and caring, no pretense, no ulterior motives, and she cherished every moment.

He leaned over her and tried to unfasten her gown. She began to unfasten his shirt, which set off a sense of urgency between them stronger than ever before. He pulled on the fabric of her gown and she felt the pull seconds before the ripping sound filled the room.

In her mind she heard him giggle and say he was sorry, but right now she didn't care what he did to her clothes as long as he hurried. She needed him inside her, now.

"Did I hear you say you needed me?"

She smiled. "You did. And I said to hurry if you know what's good for you."

"You'll never have to ask twice."

CHAPTER THIRTY NINE

All the men and women on Alextor's list sat quietly in the small chapel. The pretense was for Jorell's private funeral, but the attendees knew she was still alive. The media was abuzz with ideas on who killed the ruler's daughter, but they were happy to report Alextor's return to Sector-Three. Only Alextor's assassins would be surprised by his presence.

Everyone was ready and Alextor stepped up to the raised podium for the introduction. He was an amazing man to return from the dead, learn the fate of his Sector, then agree to his plan.

"Greetings my friends." Alextor looked over the room. "Please don't panic, but there are guards at the doors. No one gets in, and no one gets out, unless I say so." He smiled. "Consider yourselves my command audience. It may be the last request I ever make."

Kane heard mumblings throughout the room at Alextor's words. He wasn't sure if they agreed or disagreed. Alextor had assured him that those here this sun-cycle were loyal to their Sectors, and to him.

"I'll start at the beginning. I have not been away attending to my sick relative. I've been in bed, in a coma, on the verge of death. I was poisoned. I'm supposed to be dead."

Alextor was forced to pause while the audience mumbled their shock at the news. Kane carefully analyzed each man, looking for any signs of duplicity. So far, everyone appeared legitimate, honestly shocked by what they'd just heard.

"As for my daughter, she became collateral damage in the scheme to take over Sector-Three. Luckily, this man," Alextor held his arm out toward Kane, "not only saved my life, but also my daughter's. I am forever in his debt.

"But I asked you here to discuss an even larger issue, one that involves the entire planet. We have all discussed the possibility that Marto Braxton and Trom Carsun were murdered. I know this because I've personally had conversations with each and every one of you. I believe the attempt on my life confirms the conclusion we'd all come to previously.

"Unfortunately, this proof came too late to save Marto and Trom, our dear friends that should still be with us, but were abruptly taken before their time. This leaves us with only one question; what do we do now? I'm going to turn this over to Kane Sinue, who will fill in some of what I'm sure I left out—especially since I've been 'missing' for nearly twenty sun-cycles!"

Laughter erupted and Kane was happy for the diversion from the seriousness of what he had to say. Alextor waved him over so he climbed the four steps and stopped at the leader's side. They shook hands then Alextor turned toward the audience.

"Please welcome a man I have hired, who has special skills we need to succeed, and as I said, skills that saved my life. Let's give this talented man a quiet round of applause, because we're having a funeral here, so please welcome, Citizen Kane Sinue."

The audience stood, held up their hands, and in a mock clap to let him know they welcomed him. He hoped they'd feel the same when he was finished. "Please, take your seats."

Kane waited while they settled down. "Thank you for your warm welcome, and for being here. I believe you know that all three Sectors are in danger. Sector-One and Two are under new leadership, and if the takeover had gone as planned, Sector-Three would be under a new Ruler as well. I may not have a position in government, but I live here, like the rest of you, and I do *not* want to see a one dictator world. Do you?"

He created a lot of chatter with that question and they needed a moment to assimilate. He couldn't hear any of the conversations, but he knew what they were thinking. This was more difficult than he'd anticipated. Bad news was never pleasant, especially when it immeasurably impacted every citizen's life.

"You're here because you're trusted, and loyal to Alextor Sutone, and he shares your concerns. One man plans to claim power of the entire planet. You may, or may not know him, Loran Narom. My plan is to stop his takeover without a planet-wide war.

"Loran's plan consists of putting new rulers in all three Sectors, rulers hand-picked by him. Once they're in place, he claims total control. He already put Ramon Coster in Sector-One, Nazar Ferris in Sector-Two, and he was about to have Rand Arroray in Sector-Three. I must add, it was no easy task keeping Rand from Jorell's *private ceremony* since they were engaged. All I'm going to say is that Rand over-slept, and my thanks to Doctor Willock."

The audience snickered and laughed softly at his disclosure, once again chattering, and he used the short reprieve to catch his breath. He'd decided not to tell them that Loran Narom was Pakar Moran. Would it make any difference? Loran would be tried for treason, and put to death, exactly what they should have done to Pakar originally. How credible would he be if they suspected he was Pakar's son?

The chatter died and Kane took a deep breath. "We can prevent this. Are you with us?" Every pair of hands in the audience raised into the air for a subdued clap of approval. Their approving reaction sent relief coursing through him, and his nervous, racing heart finally beat a bit slower.

"After conferring with Alextor, we need to make our move at the next Tri-Sector meeting when Loran Narom declares total control. Loran will not expect opposition, but we'll be prepared and waiting. Instead of becoming the planet's new leader, he will become the planet's most notorious prisoner."

Another round of muffled applause confirmed their full support. He hoped it would be as simple as it sounded, but with Pakar, nothing was simple. "Thank you for your loyalty. Now, I'd like to bring Alextor back so we can move forward with our plan."

Alextor joined him at the podium, gave him a slap on the back and a hand shake that said the man was back where he belonged. He leaned close to his ear. "I want you to spearhead the plans, use me any way you like."

"Thank you, Kane. I'm indebted to you."

Kane stepped back and allowed Alextor to play to the crowd and absorb the support of his comrades. He was a beloved leader, and a good one. He thanked the Universe for Alextor's recovery, and for a man who really cared about the people he served.

"Thank you, thank you, my dear friends. First, we need to…" Alextor grabbed his throat and sank to the floor.

Kane reached out and caught Alextor before his head hit the marbelus tile floor. The instant he touched the man malignant energy oozed into him. The Energy-Lamia literally held Alextor's life force in his hands.

Jorell rushed to where her father lay on the floor and knelt down next to Kane. She put a hand on her father's forehead, then looked at Kane. "How do we save him?"

"Bond with me. Send me your energy. I'll fight him. The Lamia can't know you're alive." Jorell nodded at him and he immediately found her in his mind, and he created a special place to hide her identity before he directed his attention on Alextor. The evil had taken over Alextor's mind and body. He heard a sadistic laugh from the entity, as if he said he'd won the battle. *"You've won nothing!"* His mental scream stirred a type of growl from the man, and he wished he could face him in person so he could physically put him in his place.

"Isn't that 'sweet', trying to save one useless soul. It won't happen! You're not strong enough to stop me. I'll have what I want, and I want this man dead!"

"Over my dead body!" A hard and fast backlash of fiery, dark energy shoved Kane two steps back. It engulfed him totally, and it took every ounce of energy he had to push back. Jorell sent all she had and he pulled it into himself, then assailed the Lamia. The darkness inched back, but the pervasive malevolence hung like an encompassing cloud that refused to leave.

"It will be my pleasure to kill you. You're an unwanted complication, right along with Alextor, who should have been dead by now!"

Kane listened carefully to the seditious laugh that followed. *"Too bad you're such a coward."*

"You dare call me a coward?"

"Just stating a fact. You're the true definition of coward." This time Kane sent the Lamia a long, mocking laugh which had the effect he'd hoped for. The Lamia's hold slipped, which enabled him to push an infusion of energy against the dark force, this time making substantial progress.

"Think you're smarter than me?" He chuckled. "Think again, fool. You'll never beat me, do you hear me? Never!"

Kane used the Lamia's new surge of anger against him and was able to completely take over Alextor's mind, which was the main target. He suspected he was the first person to ever fight him during an attack. Entities like this Lamia always got their way with their prey, but not this time.

"You're a dead man!"

With that last threat the Lamia left as swiftly as he'd entered. He looked at Jorell, and of course she knew he was gone. "I'll calm the audience. Call for his transport to the med-unit so Doctor Willock can check him over. But remember, you're in disguise because you're actually dead to everyone else."

"I remember."

Kane watched her leave then turned to face the audience, who were asking what happened, and if Alextor survived. "Ladies and gentlemen, to answer your questions, Alextor will recover from this attack by an Energy-Lamia."

There was more audience mumblings now than earlier. Kane held his hand up to silence them. "I understand your confusion, and I know some of you may not believe in Energy-Lamias. But you cannot deny what just happened.

"This is not the first attempt by this evil Energy-Lamia to take Alextor's life. He's getting quite bold to strike in front of an audience. He will only stop when the Ruler is dead. I was able to stop him, with Jorell's help.

"What we're about to do is no easy task. I won't lie to you. There are possible risks for each and every one of you should we fail. However, we will prevail, because I won't stop until we do." Hands raised in quiet applause.

"I want each of you to compile a list of those you trust. My partner has installed a secure program on your computers. Only use that secure program to send your lists, and you will be contacted via that program with more details. There are twelve sun-cycles before the Tri-Sector meeting, which give us eleven to solidify our plans."

Kane was pleased to see all the understanding nods. "When you're contacted you'll be asked how many are on your list, should we need backup forces. When you listen to the media you'll hear that Ruler Sutone was overcome with grief and taken to the med-unit for observation. However, you know what actually happened. The media will be fed what we want them to know, so do not rely on them for correct information.

"Our enemies will be watching those reports, exactly as we want them to. Believe only what is sent to you, and follow those directions to the letter. It will be the only way we can win and return Okeron to the peaceful three Sector system.

"For now I'll end this service. Speaking for myself, and the Sutones, I thank you for attending and offering your help." This time everyone stood and applauded vigorously. Relief spread through him knowing he and Jorell weren't alone in their effort to save the planet.

He buzzed the guards to open the doors, and the audience began to file out of the room. Before all the attendees were out the door Dobie pushed through with two med-tecs and a transport- stretcher. Doctor Willock was with them and led the way to the front where he knelt beside Alextor. He removed the scanner from his bag and ran it up and down Alextor's body.

"Men, take him to the private wing on the top floor of the med-ward. I'll attend him there." The doctor stepped closer to Kane. "He should be fine." He glanced around before speaking again. "The attack he sustained here today robbed him of nearly all his energy. He's been through a lot even before exerting himself here. I'll do my best under the circumstances."

"I understand. Do not leave him alone, and be sure I'm called if you even think he's being attacked again."

"I'll stay in touch, you can count on that. Alextor is my main concern. He'll be well taken care of."

"Use only the new program to communicate." The doctor nodded his understanding, then turned and followed the tecs out of the chapel. Willock was a good man, and he was happy to have him assist.

"Chief?" Dobie walked up and slapped Kane's back. "You did it. You stopped him. You and Jorell should be proud of yourselves."

"I'm not proud, just grateful we succeeded."

"I can't believe Alextor finally made it this far, then wham! Struck down by the Energy-Lamia. What's next?"

"You don't want to know."

CHAPTER FORTY

"Answer me, Nazar. Who is this Kane person?"

"I met him my first year in the Academy. We weren't friends."

"Explain."

"I hated him. He was my competition in everything. We were too evenly matched to claim victory over each other. He'd win one day, I'd win the next. You know how school kids are, always wanting to be the best. Father, you know…"

"Do *not* call me father, or Pakar, the same as I cannot call you son. You must stick with Loran Narom. Do not forget, even when we're alone, or you'll slip at a critical time."

"Understood."

"Go on."

"Kane and I fought most of the time. I tried to learn where he came from, but no one seemed to know, or care. He roomed with that Dobie Platon, whom everyone called an idiot."

"Is he?"

"Far from it. If he is, he's the smartest idiot I've ever known. That said, he's a genius in technology, but in other areas he's completely stupid."

"I've done my research on both of them, but I wanted your take." Pakar rubbed his chin. "They're loners, but have earned a substantial amount of credits time traveling. I even contacted a few of his clients, they all praised him, except one man, who felt he was arrogant and charged too much. But they all said they knew nothing about him personally."

"Do you know anything about him you haven't told me?"

"I never found him 'nice', only competitive. We were paired against each other more times than I can count, mainly because we were evenly matched physically, but it usually ended in a tie. He's a good fighter, and he won't quit."

He walked closer to his son. "What's his weakness?" Nazar shrugged his shoulders and shook his head at him. "Every man has a weakness. Think!"

"We heard rumors he was fond of Jorell, but she's out of the picture now. The only other person he cares about is Dobie."

"You believe he'll do what we ask if we have the fool?"

"Absolutely. It's his only friend on the planet. They're partners and constant companions." Nazar nodded. "He'll cooperate."

Loran smiled at his obedient son. He'd never cared for another person, but Nazar was different. How could he not love a piece of himself? Besides, Nazar was loyal, what more could he ask? "Sit, we have plans to make."

****

Jorell stepped into Kane's bedchamber to find him stretched out on the bed, clothed only in loose fitting, thin pajama pants. His contoured chest and stomach, was a work of art, but so were his biceps and triceps, a sight she never tired of, a sight that excited her down to her toes. He took her breath away, and she still wondered what she'd done to deserve such a man.

"Hello, my sweet." Kane patted the bed next to him. "Come. Sit. Talk to me. I've missed you."

She smiled and walked to the bed, then sat where he'd indicated. "I'm sorry, but I had to stay with my father until I knew he was all right. I still can't believe you rendered Doctor Willock unconscious to bring him here. Was that necessary? Really?"

"It was for our protection as well as his. This way he can honestly say he doesn't know where to find me."

"Do you really have that many enemies?"

"No, but I do have the worst enemy ever known to this planet. Plus, there are some who'd like to find me for their own reasons."

She reached out and ran her fingers through his hair until she reached the back of his head. She cupped the back of his head in her hand and pulled him to her. "You'd better not be talking about a bevy of women chasing after you, *Traveler*." She pulled back and looked deeply into his gorgeous, seductive blue eyes.

"Would you be jealous, *First Advisor?*"

"Let's just say I'd have to hurt them." She bowed her head to conceal her smile, but it was to no avail. He tipped her head up with his finger so he could see her face. His eyes danced and revealed his devilish intent. Her heart raced and felt warmer than normal. He'd dropped all the protective walls in his mind and allowed her to read his true feelings.

"I love it when you're possessive."

"Really?" She grinned. "You haven't seen anything yet." She opened her mind to him which revealed her deepest feelings for the first time. It was dangerous territory to be in, but she had to know his true feelings.

"Thank you for trusting me. I'm humbled by the honor you've bestowed upon me."

She trailed her hand down his cheek. *"Do you see what you've done to me?"* He looked at her with that dangerous little twinkle in his eye that said he wanted her, all of her.

"You've turned into a little vixen." He smiled. "I love it."

"Really?" He nodded, and opened his mind to dark places she'd never seen before. Then her mind's eye saw a door open and inside was bright with loving light, and warm with good feelings.

"You're the first. I've never allowed anyone access before."

"I'm honored. I love what I see." He'd just shown her his hidden feelings, a true show of trust. He may not say the word '*love*' but without a doubt, she'd seen the love he held for her, and she couldn't be happier.

Kane definitely had that come-on look in his eyes, and she knew he'd do anything she wanted him to do, so this was her chance to manipulate him for a change. She took his hand in hers and scooted off the bed. *"Come on."* He willingly let her lead him.

She walked him into the lav and shut the door. "Take off my clothes." Her command lit up his face like a child looking at candy. He stepped closer to her and put his hands on her shoulders and turned her around. He freed the back closer of her gown and slowly opened it, easing it lower and lower, so slowly she had the impulse to help. He tenderly whispered his pleasure.

"I know you're in a hurry, but that's exactly when we need to take our time, and saver every movement, every touch, every emotion."

She sighed. "That's very romantic. I like it. No, I love it. Is this really coming from The Traveler? The tough warrior man in charge?"

"Absolutely. And it's the first time I've ever said that to anyone, because it's the first time I've ever felt this way."

The back closer reached the end, and her gown slipped lower on her shoulders. She did nothing to help it, or stop it, she was enjoying the moment. Then his hands grabbed the loose fabric and eased it down, over her hips, then the fabric pooled around her ankles.

"You looked gorgeous in black, but you're far more beautiful without it." She closed her eyes, and shivered while tingles trickled down her back. The lav was cool, and her two, small undergarments provided no warmth, but it wasn't the temperature, it was Kane. His large hands slowly explored the exposed flesh of her back, from top to bottom before he unfastened her support garment, and it joined the pile on the floor.

Kane moved his exploration to her newly exposed breasts before he kissed his way down over her waist, over her hips, and when he went further, her last undergarment hit the floor.

Slowly she opened her eyes and focused on Kane. His gaze darkened while he looked her up and down. He didn't have to say a word for her to know he liked what he saw.

"Fair is fair." She put a hand on each side of his hips and pushed down his pajama bottoms, not surprised to find him naked underneath. Her breathing quickened. Kane was every bit the man he appeared to be, and as usual, he was well prepared and very ready.

When he tried to pull her to his chest she laughed, and pushed back. "Not so fast, Traveler. First we need a shower. A real water shower, not the fast, sanitizing kind. I want to wash every inch of you."

"Do I get the same pleasure?"

"Only if you're good."

"I'm always good." Kane stepped to the shower enclosure. "Water on, level four."

She stepped in front of him and entered the enclosure, then pulled him in behind her. His level four setting was a gentle hot water flow that was perfect on her skin. Kane's shower was the largest, most enticingly elaborate shower she'd ever used. and she'd traveled a lot. Whenever the water sprayed, soft music filled the marbelus enclosure, keeping time to the water running down the clear glass wall that sealed them inside. The beautiful enclosure consumed the entire back wall of the immense lav.

Kane's arms slipped around her waist, and his mouth covered hers. His magic kiss promised sweet love. Kane disproved the rumor that warrior types were fast, cold, and uncaring. His tongue teased and taunted, and she'd never enjoyed the battle more.

Water bounced off her face, back, and every part of her from the numerous spray-heads that surrounded them, and she'd never felt better. But the real reason for her euphoria was the man she'd come to love. Yes, she admitted it. She loved Kane. He made any feelings she might have had for Rand seem like a young, school girl's crush. Kane was the real thing.

The thought of being vulnerable still scared her, but it was past time she took the plunge and put her heart on the line. Kane was worth the gamble. Although, with his hands roaming her breasts while he kissed her passionately, it was difficult to think. He was exactly where she wanted him to be, and doing exactly what she wanted him to do.

He tickled her mind, sending her picture after picture of them together in various places, making love, and holding each other. All she managed to send him was an unqualified, *yes*. Pure happiness wasn't a feeling she was used to, but Kane was busy giving her a long, healthy dose she'd remember for all time.

Kane reached over her shoulder and applied a smooth substance on her back, and the most pleasant fragrance tickled her senses. His hands worked the soft, creamy bubbles into her skin. He ended the kiss, filled the palm of his hand with more of the soapy cleanser. This time he eased her backward and put the lather at the base of her neck, then worked his way down, over, and under her breasts.

For a large man with big hands, his touch was velvet and enticing. Chills coursed up and down her spine while he caressed every swell, nook and cranny between her neck and bellybutton. He took more of the luscious liquid and slid it down her abdomen, paying special attention to the triangular area between her legs.

A moan came from deep within his chest. He made her forget her responsibilities and problems. She tilted her head back and enjoyed the sensual touch of his hands, lips and body. Jorell filled both hands from the dispenser with creamy bubbles, then began at his shoulders and worked her way down his chest to where the chest hairs grew only in the center. She loved men's chest hair, especially when it was like Kane's, very sexy and not too much.

Kane tipped his head back and closed his eyes while she carefully lathered his nipples, then lower over his abdomen. She didn't take her gaze off his face until she ran into the object of this little adventure. He was more than ready for her, all man, with a throbbing need.

"My sweet, I don't think I can wait much longer."

He eased her under the water spray to remove the soap, and made sure it rinsed off her bubbles as well. Then he quickly guided her to the corner, her back against the tile. He lifted her up and set her back down on his manhood. When he entered she felt complete. His mouth covered hers and he kissed her with burning desire and began to move, slowly at first, then harder and faster.

She closed her eyes and surrendered to him, from his all encompassing kiss to his extraordinary manhood that filled her with a deep love she'd never thought she'd find. Then lights flashed in her mind, so brightly it was difficult to focus, but impossible to look away.

"Stay with me."

Kane's hands held her derrière firmly against him, guiding her to accentuate his movements. He was amazing. The need he created had grown to the point she thought she'd explode any moment. A sweet tickle crawled through her abdomen, building and building. *"Oh, Kane, hurry, my love."*

His movements increased along with his breathing. She gasped for air, not realizing she'd been holding her breath. An overpowering infusion of love overwhelmed her. It was the kind of love that was complete, simple, and forever. Was that her feelings, or his? How could she tell the difference when they were so joined and melded?

It seemed she could read all his thoughts at once, and she allowed him to read hers as well. She didn't want secrets between them, only pure, honest love that evaded most couples, but the kind she'd dreamed of her entire life.

Kane groaned out loud, revealing his pleasure, and she joined him. He coaxed her to welcome the approaching light that grew brighter, warmer, and closer. Kane found his completion and she let go, joining him in the most precious fulfillment anyone could hope for. It was a physical high, with an emotional euphoria that remained.

She relaxed along with Kane, the feel of the shower once again registering in her consciousness. He'd made her forget everything but him. They'd melded so completely it was as if neither of them existed separately, only together.

Kane cupped the side of her face with his hand. "My sweet, sweet Jorell. I've never experienced anything like that before. We...aah..."

"I know. I feel the same. It defies explanation." She reached up and pushed hair off his forehead with her fingers. "It was perfect in so many ways, and on more than one level." She had to laugh. "Not bad for a dead girl, huh?"

He hugged her so tightly she thought her ribs might break, but she loved it. She laid her head low on his shoulder, his heartbeat thumping in her ear. He was real, and he was exactly who she wanted to be with— forever.

"I think we need to get out of the shower. I'm feeling a bit waterlogged."

She nodded and listened to his command of, "water off". "Your lav, and especially this shower is amazing." Kane reached outside the enclosure, took two towels off a recessed rack, then handed her one.

"I'd dry you off, but I'm afraid if I did we'd never get out of here." He grinned. "That was too good not to want it again—and again."

Jorell sighed. "You're right. But behave yourself." She watched him dry his hair with the towel. "At least for now." He smiled, kissed her on the forehead, then stepped out of the shower. He offered her his hand to steady her step out. Before she knew it he'd wrapped her in his towel and his hands were moving it around, drying her off.

It only took one glance down to realize this may not be a good idea. "Kane, we can't stay in here. Dobie is waiting for us, and we have to--" His mouth covered hers in a fast, but passionate kiss before he pulled his head back.

"You're right. I almost forgot." Kane smiled broadly. "Or should I say, I wanted to forget?"

"Be a good boy. We don't always get what we want." She walked toward the closet on the opposite side of the room. She had to laugh when he gave her several pats on the rear while he followed her. She looked around the massive closet, which was as large as the bedchamber.

Kane's clothes hung neatly, color coded and perfect. Everything on the numerous shelves was folded neatly, stacked flawlessly, with like colors together. "You know, I never would have guessed, especially when I first met you, that you were a neat-fanatic."

"Blame Dobie. That's how he is, and over the years it rubbed off on me. Plus, I got tired of listening to him complain about the way I put things away."

"With all these clothes, how can you even decide what to wear?"

When she turned to look at Kane and he'd already donned his underwear and was securing his pants. He then pulled socks out of a drawer and sat on the dressing bench to put them on. A perusal of the countertop in the center of the room revealed the bag she'd brought on an earlier trip. She pulled out a pair of pants, a matching tunic, and clean undergarments. She quickly began to dress.

After she slipped the top over her head and settled it in place she turned to find Kane's gaze fixed on her. She wished she knew what was going through his mind, but the look on his face revealed no emotion. "Why are you staring at me?"

"I was watching you dress because I've never had a woman get dressed in my closet before."

"Should I leave?"

Kane stood and walked over to Jorell. "Absolutely not. I love having you here."

"Really?"

"I say what I mean, you should know that."

"I do." Jorell picked up a brush from the dressing table in the center cabinet area and ran it through her hair. In the mirror she watched Kane put on his shirt, and then added a belt. He'd never looked more handsome or appealing.

"I'll meet you at the control center. I'm sure Dobie is impatiently waiting."

"Be right there. I need to dry my hair."

CHAPTER FORTY ONE

"Chief, it says Nazar's records are sealed." Dobie turned and looked at Kane. "I've only run into this problem once before, but that was about a priest and a church issue, and the government sealed the records for the priest's safety as well as to protect the church."

"I remember the incident well, and it was the wise thing to do under the circumstances. But Nazar? That's insane! What could he possibly be hiding?"

"His parentage?"

"Possibly. Or illegal activities, something in his past that would prevent him from being a Sector ruler?"

"I just don't understand why my special program doesn't work on Nazar's records. It always kicks galaxies, getting into forbidden places. But not this time. All I get is a message that says, "sealed".

"That sets off alarms."

"We don't want that. Not now. I'll keep digging, with caution. Everyone who attended the service has received my special program that cannot be hacked, intercepted, or decoded. I've told them if they receive any communication outside of that program not to reply, and to let me know immediately.

"Good. Your programs *are* pure genius. The good news is Loran is not expecting any resistance, so our takeover should be peaceful and unexpected, and we need the surprise factor."

"Did I hear the word surprise?"

Kane turned at the sound of Jorell's voice behind him. He stood, helped her to the seat next to his, then sat back down on his chair. Dobie was busy moving stuff around the giant screen. "The surprise isn't for you, my sweet, it's for Loran."

"I see. I was hoping for some expensive gems."

"That's not realistic."

"You forget, I know how much is in your credit account, *Traveler*."

She feigned a frown that made him laugh. He didn't know how she managed to look so beautiful and tempting while pretending to cry, but she certainly did. "At best you might get flowers."

"Maybe I should have a word with Dobie." She turned her gaze to Kane's partner. "What do you think?"

"I think never to get in the middle of a lover's spat."

Kane cleared his throat. "A what?"

"You heard me, Chief." Dobie laughed. "And I'd like to add, it's about time."

Dobie gave him the look that said, "Don't argue, you know I'm right." He couldn't hide the obvious, especially in front of Dobie, the one person on the planet who knew him inside and out. However, it was Jorell's expression that stopped him cold. Her red cheeks screamed embarrassment, and she also had a quizzical look that begged him to affirm his feelings for her.

He smiled at Jorell then winked. He had no words, at least none he wanted to say in front of Dobie. His feelings were private. This deep caring feeling for Jorell was totally foreign. He'd never cared about a woman enough to be around her for more than a couple sun-cycles of vacation fun.

Jorell offered something deeper, longer lasting, and what he wasn't ready for—permanent. Could he offer her what she was looking for? He wanted to, he really did, but he feared he still carried too much hatred in his heart to make room for love. "How's your father?"

"Much better. He's awake and moving. The doctor is still with him."

"Good. He shouldn't be alone."

"What if the Lamia attacks again?"

"I'll stop him."

"What if you're not here?"

Kane sighed. She was right, he couldn't be with Alextor every time-unit, sun-cycle and moon-cycle. "I'll be close, most of the time."

"I know, but he found him here, in your secret hideaway!"

"Jorell, the next time we leave we're all going to the Tri-Sector meeting to stop the takeover. And if I'm correct, the Lamia will be quite busy, along with us."

"How could you possibly know that?"

"I believe the Energy-Lamia and Loran Narom are one and the same. I'm more convinced now than ever."

"Chief? Did you hear me?"

"Sorry. What did you say?"

"Only that Nazar entered the Academy as an orphan, the same as we did. After graduation he went straight to Sector-Two as an Apprentice Advisor, then moved up to Advisor. He managed to be appointed First Advisor last annual-cycle, then took over as ruler when Trom Carsun died."

"When he was murdered, you mean." Jorell shook her head.

"There's no proof yet, but soon." Kane took her hand in his. "I know how you feel, but be patient."

Jorell pulled her hand out of Kane's. "You know how I feel?" She stood. "You don't know how I feel, so don't pretend you do." She walked away toward the galley.

"Where did I go wrong, Dob?"

"I'm not an expert, but I don't think women like to be told how they feel."

"You're probably right, but I haven't been around the same woman for more than a couple of sun-cycles, so I didn't have to worry about making mistakes like that."

"We're both *inexperienced* when it comes to committed relationships. But Chief, there's always a first time, and this is yours." Dobie smiled at Kane. "I wish I'd found mine."

"I'll ask Jorell if she has a friend for you."

"I'd rather find my own, thanks."

"I heard my name." Jorell stared at the two men who turned in their chairs. "Ask me what?"

"Aaaah, I was going to ask you—"

"You both have guilty expressions on your faces and I'm wondering why?"

"We're not guilty of anything, Princess. I was trying to nudge Kane into asking you if you had any lady friends that might like to go out with me." Dobie tilted his head down and stared at the floor.

"Let me think on that and I'll see what I can do." Jorell patted Dobie on the back. "Of course, I can't contact anyone while I'm dead, but as soon as I return to the living, I'll be happy to find someone for you." She looked at Kane. "Let's make a plan. I'm tired of being dead."

****

"Nazar, you must be sure. There can be no mistakes."

"Father, it..."

Pakar held up his hand. "You called me what?" He couldn't believe his stupid son had made such a repetitive mistake.

"Sorry, sir. It will be done before the Tri-Sector meeting. You have my word."

"I won't be able to claim power if Alextor is still alive! The meeting is only nine sun-cycles from now." Pakar walked around the table to stand next to his son. "He should already be dead! Why? I want to know how he evaded death when he was infected with the rare, and most deadly poison on Okeron. The antidote is nearly impossible to find, even if you know what it is."

"I'm aware of that, but I don't have an answer for you." Nazar took a sip of wine from the stemmed glass in front of him.

"I can't totally blame you. We both discussed the best way to get to Alextor. It was a perfect plan."

"I agree. No one had to actually give it to him. Who would have dreamed it could be powdered and put on his clothing and absorbed through his skin. I bought the best people to dust Alextor's clothes, and keep the secret. They got enough to retire for life. The man should be dead now."

"Someone figured it out. I want to know who." He stared at his son who was, for the most part, loyal to him. He'd educated him well, and secured his place in the Sector-Two government, and he was ready for the tasks at hand, but it didn't excuse mistakes. "I want you to bring me a name." He grinned. "Better yet, his head."

"I'll be happy to kill the man responsible."

"Or the woman?" He waited until Nazar nodded. "I see you never considered that possibility. I hadn't thought about it either since there's only one woman who would know what the poison was and how to stop it."

"Give me her name and I'll go to her."

"She's dead. Killed her myself many annual-cycles ago." Pakar rubbed his chin. "You might try going to where she lived, talk to the people there. She may have confided in someone before she died. It's a long-shot, but worth a try. Which brings us back to Alextor. No matter what happened with the poison, Alextor must be out of the picture before the Tri-Sector meeting. That's a must. I cannot seize control with him alive."

"We could use the same sniper we did for Jorell."

"That would draw too much attention. I want you to set it up as a suicide. The headlines will be, "Alextor Sutone, overtaken by grief, takes own life." Pakar crossed his arms over his chest. "Yes, that's it. Grieving father ends it all."

"I like it. Once again, you've outdone yourself."

"I believe I have. I don't care if you do it, or one of our men, and I don't care if he's shot, or takes an overdose, just make sure it's done, and don't leave until you confirm he's gone!"

"I won't let you down, sir. I promise."

Pakar slapped Nazar on the back. "You'd better not." He started to walk away, then stopped and turned back to face his only son. "Failure is *not* an option."

CHAPTER FORTY TWO

"I can't believe they're still talking about my funeral. They even said I looked beautiful, even in death!" Kane smiled at her and she instantly calmed down. He caused the strangest emotions in her, but they were all good.

"Dobic's proud of his work, as he should be. No one makes a life-mask as well as he does."

"He certainly fooled everyone. It was creepy seeing myself lying in state like that." Kane smiled at her in a way that said everything would be okay, and she loved him for it. He made life easier by just being with her.

Kane walked over to Jorell and put his arm around her. "It would only be creepy if it were true. At least now you know what you'll look like crammed into that little box."

She slapped his arm teasingly. "Little for you. I fit in it just fine, thank you." He pulled her to him and kissed her lips softly. His tongue teased, then he deepened the kiss. Familiar tickles danced in her stomach, and each sensation he created made her want more.

More. She'd never get enough of Kane's tender attentions and loving touches. Anticipation grew and she wanted him. All of him. They'd made love so many times over the past few sun and moon-cycles that making love was all she could think of. The way he held her, the way he told her she was precious to him, and the thoughts they'd shared were indescribable. He was perfect.

His hands roamed her back and his heartbeat quickened against her chest, along with hers. Then the familiar feeling in her mind appeared, like a feather brushing lightly against the protective circle she kept around her thoughts. He wanted a deeper intimacy, and she opened her every thought to him. He groaned from deep within his chest.

"Chief! Chief! Oops, sorry to interrupt, but this is extremely important. Sorry Jorell, I really am, but this can't wait."

"This had better be good, partner."

Kane gave Dobie a disgruntled look, and she couldn't stop the smile that pulled at the corners of her mouth. Dobie looked terribly uncomfortable so his news must be crucial. Kane released her and took a few steps toward Dobie.

"Jorell, this is for you as well, and I think you'd better sit down. You won't like this news."

Jorell nodded and all three of them walked into the main living area and took a seat, Dobie on the chair, she and Kane on the sofa.

"As you know, I bugged several places, and installed programs on every com device in the Capitol Building, and areas outside, depending on the various lists. One of them paid off." Dobie took a deep breath. "Nazar contacted the top *Utility Man* on the planet."

Kane shook his head. "Who's the hit on?"

Dobie looked at Jorell. "I'm sorry, Princess, it's on your father."

"By the stars! Why can't they leave him alone?"

"Remember," Kane picked up Jorell's hand in his. "The takeover can't happen if your father is alive, so this should not come as a surprise."

Jorell hung her head and stared at the floor. "You're right, but...."

"Look at me, Jorell." Kane tilted her head toward his with his finger. "We'll protect him, and we'll stop the takeover."

"Chief, I know we're good, but are you sure we can do that?"

Kane stood and began to pace. She knew that's what he did when he was deep in thought, and he did not like to be interrupted while concentrating. There were so many questions on the tip of her tongue. Would this ever end?

"Dobie, what's the press currently reporting about Alextor?"

"Right now Media-One is saying Alextor is in the hospital, under guard because he's suicidal."

"What about the other stations?"

"Only one so far."

"They want it to look like a suicide to avoid questions. And if Jorell were actually dead, he'd be in the perfect place emotionally. That one reporter could be tied to the scheme. All it takes is one to report it and they all believe it. And the public will buy the story because they know how close Alextor and his daughter were."

"Gotta admit, Chief, that's perfect."

"There's no way you'll be able to stop them." Tears welled in her eyes and she couldn't stop them from running down her cheeks. She was tired of being strong, tired of worrying, tired of it all. "What if my father and I go hide out somewhere."

"You're hiding right now. You're both safe here at my warehouse. No one knows we live here. To the public it's just another warehouse in the old, industrial district. Have you ever noticed traffic outside?"

"No, but they'll find out he's not in the hospital and come looking for him, then what?" Kane smiled and she wanted to hit him. How could he be happy at a time like this? Or was he being egotistical?

"Don't underestimate us, my sweet." Kane nodded at Dobie, then turned his attention back to Jorell. "Dobie will put the finishing touches on the Alextor CC-D, then put it the hospital for the Utility Man to kill."

Jorell let out the breath she'd been holding and smiled. "I did underestimate you and Dobie." She stood and walked to where Kane stood, leaning against the large, stone fireplace. "I might have to admit you're worth your fee. However, I'll wait until this is over and completely successful."

"You don't want much, do you?" Kane turned toward Dobie. "Partner, I believe you're right about women."

Dobie chuckled. "You shouldn't believe me, a guy who hasn't been right about women since the day I was born."

Jorell shook her head then focused on Kane. "What can I do?"

"Dobie, what can a dead woman do?"

"Stay dead!"

Jorell waited while both men had a good laugh. It was nice to see them relax a bit. The tension they'd all been living under had taken a toll. She'd had trouble sleeping, of course that could be due to Kane's attentions. He was a fantastic lover, and she made sure he proved it over and over.

It seemed more than strange to listen to Kane and Dobie talk about killing her father. Rather how to make a dummy of her father respond to the hit. At least she now had complete trust in Kane and Dobie.

Kane turned to face Jorell. "We know the utility-man will make his move on your father well before the Tri-Sector meeting, since that's when Loran Narom plans to claim sole leadership of Okeron. Your father's carbon-copy-droid will be in place soon, and it is anatomically correct. It looks and feels exactly like him. It even has a heartbeat that will stop when it is appropriate to do so."

"What do you mean, appropriate?"

"Depending on the method of death, the simulated heartbeat is programmed to cease in the amount of time it would take a real person to succumb. For instance, a different amount of time is required to die from a chemical as opposed to suffocation."

"I didn't know that was possible."

"My sweet, anything is possible these sun-cycles."

"I never thought much about dummies until you two showed up." Kane laughed, but Dobie laughed so hard he doubled over.

Dobie grabbed his stomach. "Good one, Princess!"

They laughed so hard it became contagious. She grabbed her stomach the same as Dobie, and it was good to be silly. Unfortunately they all slowly regained their better senses.

Kane took Jorell's hand. "You asked me what you could do." He waited for her to nod. "I'd like to put you in a nurse's disguise this moon-cycle. That way you can observe who comes and goes. Dobie and I will be with you, and Doctor Willock will be there as well."

"Now I know you're kidding. Me? A nurse?" She had to chuckle at that idea.

"You don't need to do any nursing functions, just pretend you're the supervising nurse because a real nurse would spot a CC-D. The doctor will be there to cover you."

Jorell shook her head. "Kane, I know nothing about nursing. I'll screw up, I know I will."

"You trust Dr. Willock, right?" She nodded at him. "He'll guide you. Besides, you'll be in a private suite-room. You'll wear an earpiece and we'll tell you everything you need to do and say."

"Okay."

"Good, because we can't afford to involve anyone else. The less anyone knows, the better."

"I get it." Jorell sighed.

"Once your father's proxy is dead, he'll be safe, and all Willock has to do is show up at the meeting, where we'll put the rest of our plan into motion."

"That sounds neat and simple. Why do I have my doubts this will work?"

Kane cleared his throat. "As with all of life, nothing is simple, and there are never guarantees. This isn't our first deception, but it is yours. Dobie and I had doubts the first time we did this, but it actually works better than you think. The killer doesn't have time to waste, so he's only concerned the deed is done. He's in and out in a flash because he doesn't want to get caught."

She looked deeply into Kane's blue eyes, which were filled with frustration and concern, but she also saw confidence and determination.

"I trust you and Dobie, you know I do."

"I'm waiting." Kane stared at Jorell. "For the *but*. I trust you, but?"

"I'm worried about you, my father, Dobie, and myself. We haven't had much go our way recently. Look at me, I'm dead!" Kane and Dobie burst out laughing, and she had to admit it sounded pretty silly.

"First, I have to say, you're the most beautiful dead woman I've ever seen. Second, this plan will work. Your father *will* be safe."

"I'm sure of that, but what about the final outcome?" Kane looked at her quizzically. "The Tri-Sector meeting?"

"Princess, I've contacted everyone on our list, and all have answered. The plan progresses nicely. Everyone on that list has a lot to lose if we're not successful, so think positive."

"Dobie, that's next to impossible." She immediately regretted her words when disappointment covered Dobie's face. "I'll try."

"Try? That's not very positive." Kane smiled at Jorell. "Positive is; we *will* succeeded. Try means no conclusion because you're always trying and not completing anything."

"Thanks for the inspiration." She smiled at Kane and Dobie. "I think I'll go check on my father. You two have plans to make." She stood and walked toward the hallway, but she hadn't expected Kane to follow her. When she was far enough to be out of Dobie's site, Kane reached out and grabbed her hand.

"I didn't upset you, did I?"

"Of course not. I just want to check on my father."

"I'd never do anything to hurt you, you know that don't you?"

Genuine concern filled his words and his gaze. She reached up and cupped his cheek in her hand. All she could think about was what a perfectly gorgeous man stood in front of her. "I know."

"I worry about you."

"I hope so." She smiled and slowly trailed her hand down his chest and arm until her fingers entwined with his. "You say that as if it were the first time you ever worried about a woman."

"It is."

"Oh Kane, come on. A handsome, sexy, intelligent man like you? That's hard to believe."

"Believe it." Kane kissed her on the forehead. "And when this is over, I'll tell you why." He smiled. "If you're still interested."

Of course she'd be interested, but for now she'd keep him wondering. She'd been too honest, forthcoming, and accessible to Rand, and this was no time to repeat that mistake. She turned away from him and opened the door to her father's room. After a brief glance back to be sure he was watching, she entered with a smile on her face.

Kane, *The Traveler* was worried about *her*. It was still a mystery why a man like him had such feelings for her. Now she recognized Rand's feelings as forced. Rand had pretended, and that was hard to swallow when she thought he loved and admired her. She hadn't had much luck with men, not even during her carefree days in the Academy.

However, Kane's devotion and attention made her wonder if she could be the woman he needed. It couldn't be credits, she'd already paid him a fortune. He didn't hang around for sex, because a man like Kane could easily have any woman.

All her other suitors wanted everything but her. Connections, credits, advancement, power, and the list went on. Could Kane really be that different? She'd learned the hard way what men wanted, and the bottom line was never her, only what she offered. Was she playing the part of a fool once again?

She stepped inside and saw her father chatting with the doctor. "Hello, you two. Feeling better I see."

"My dear, come, sit with us."

Jorell walked around the bed and sat on the bottom corner so she could see both men. "Doctor, how is he, really? He won't tell me the truth."

"Actually, he's doing very well. Every function is back to normal. He may be a bit weak, and he still needs extra rest, but otherwise, no problems."

"I hear you'll have another CC-D to nurse in your hospital." The doctor smiled at her, but it did little to ease her anxiety

"Between my lab and Dobie, it's nearly completed. Dobie's facial masks are better than any craftsmen I know."

"I see." She turned her attention to the doorway when Dobie entered the room. "Dobie, where did you learn the art of CC-D's? You did a wonderful job on me."

"Necessity is always the best teacher, and I've had a lot of practice. Kane and I have to be different people consistently, so all of our work is creative."

"At least I know you're earning your fee." Her father gave her *the look* and panic settled in the pit of her stomach.

"How much is their fee, daughter?"

He only called her daughter when he was angry, and her answer would not sit well.

The doctor stood and walked to the door. "I'll give you two some time alone. You obviously have things to discuss. I'll be back later."

Dobie walked toward the door. "I'll go with you so we can finish our project."

She watched the door slide closed behind Doctor Willock and Dobie. After a deep sigh, and thoughts of lying, she looked into her father's eyes. He could be intimidating, but he no longer looked mad, in fact he was smiling. "I paid him fifty-million credits." She watched a myriad of emotions play across his face and wondered which one he'd settle on. There it was, the angry, thoughtful look. "I'm sorry father, I aah—"

Alextor chuckled. "Don't defend yourself. You did what you had to do." He smiled. "I should be honored you find me that valuable."

"You're not angry?" He shook his head and she sighed. "I thought you'd…"

Alextor took his daughter's hand and squeezed. "My dear, I'm honored you cared enough to save my life." He smiled at her. "I already knew all about it, the good doctor told me. He's been working closely with Kane and Dobie, and he agrees with you, they're honorable men, and I'm thankful you found them."

"I can't believe he told you."

"I forced him to tell me. You should thank Doctor Willock. He recommended *The Traveler.*"

"I've seen the way he looks at you."

What could she say to that? It was embarrassing to explain to her father her relationship with Kane. "We're friends."

"Friends?" Alextor laughed. "My dear daughter, you act like I've never been in love, or desired a woman before."

"Father!" Jorell stood and walked to the other side of the bed.

"He cares about you. I see it in his eyes. And you have a glow about you I've never seen before. I know what it means." Alextor scooted a bit higher up in the bed. "Is this the real thing?"

She met her father's scrutinizing gaze. What could she say to him that would make him stop asking questions she couldn't answer? She'd always told him everything, but couldn't very well share her intimate relationship. "I don't know. I mean, I'm not sure." She took a deep breath. "I've had too much on my mind to think about my feelings."

"I see." Alextor shook his head. "Will you tell me when you know?" He sighed. "I thought I'd picked your mate. Obviously, I was sorely mistaken."

Jorell opened the door, but her father's hot glare bore into her back. How could she admit she'd fallen in love with a man who would be gone when this job was over? They had never talked about the future, only the present.

She glanced back over her shoulder. "I only pray Kane's able to keep us both alive."

****

"Dobie, look." Kane pointed at the monitor to his left on the security desk. He straightened the buttons on his Security Master's uniform. Rulers always received the best of everything, and as Security Master, it was his sole responsibility to keep the ruler safe.

"It's going down, Chief." Dobie looked at Kane. "Jorell and I just left that room. He certainly didn't wait long to do the deed."

"I'd like to get that guy, but we have to let it play out." Kane tapped the table with his fingers. "If this wasn't such a serious situation we might get a good laugh out of watching a Utility-Man kill a CC-D."

"It's still funny because he doesn't get it. Look at that, every movement precise and swift."

"That's why he won't notice it isn't really Alextor."

"Chief, look, he's going to use a laser to the head." Dobie looked at Kane. "Don't worry, the doc and I planned for every eventuality, and the CC-D will bleed. Guaranteed."

"By the galaxy! There's blood everywhere!"

Kane watched Dobie zoom the camera closer. "He's put the Laser weapon in Alextor's hand and perfectly positioned it for a suicide shot."

"Listen, the alarms are going off, and the Utility-Man is already out of the room and he's entering the men's facility."

"There's doc, Jorell and several other staff members rushing into Alextor's room. Looks like chaos to me. They're all doing their part." Kane released the breath he'd been holding. "Jorell actually looks like she knows what she's doing."

"Were you worried?"

"Kind of. She was nervous and thought she'd screw things up, but she's doing fine." Kane turned toward Dobie. "What can I say, partner? You did a fantastic job."

"Thanks. It wasn't easy, but it's worth the sacrifice. I need to retrieve my tool bag from the supply closet, but I'll have to wait for an empty hallway. Why don't you go get the transport and meet me in front of the building in the loading zone."

"I'll wait for you out front. I told Jorell to get out at the first opportunity. She'll take our city-jumper back to the warehouse." Kane stood and walked to the door. "See ya soon." Kane left Dobie in the control room and headed down the main hall.

His partner was more than capable, so he hurried toward the private entrance the doctors used. In his ear he heard Jorell calling out orders and acting her position perfectly. He'd believe she was a nurse, and a damned good one.

The door in front of him opened as he approached, the special eye reading his fake doctor's pass and he rushed out into the staff parking lot. Their transport set straight ahead in the surgeon's area. It paid to be privileged, or should he say it paid to have a partner who could fake anything from people to parking permits.

He opened the lock on the side door and entered the transport. Dobie was probably finished by now, so he powered up and then drove the craft out of the parking area. He maneuvered around the barrier and secured a place in line in front of the hospital. He cut the engine when he didn't see Dobie. Must have taken a bit longer than he'd planned.

Kane listened while the doctor proclaimed Alextor officially dead, and Jorell made arrangements for his body in the background. So far, so good. He wasn't worried about her since her main job was now complete. All she had to do was slip away and drive back to the warehouse.

Dealing with life and death issues took a toll, especially when the peace of the entire planet was at risk. That was more stress than any lifetime deserved. Where was Dobie? He looked up and down the exit stations and walkways. There were a lot of people, but not his partner. He'd give him a bit longer before he went looking for him. He leaned his head back against the high seatback, closed his eyes and tried to relax.

Dobie knew how to take care of himself, yet he couldn't stop that sick, nagging feeling in the pit of his stomach that grew worse the longer he waited. Something was wrong.

CHAPTER FORTY THREE

The palm-com in Kane's pocket sounded its alarm and Kane nearly jumped out of his seat. He checked his timepiece and gasped. He'd dosed off for nearly a full time-unit, and still no Dobie. He opened the door and bolted out of the transport, and ran to the hospital entry, reaching it before the auto-hatch had secured itself.

Once inside the building he took the lift to the fourteenth floor. The moment the door opened he forced himself to walk instead of run, to the main desk. Kane pulled his palm-com out of his pocket, then brought a picture of Dobie he'd taken this sun-cycle to the screen. He held it for the middle-aged woman behind the desk to study. "Excuse me. Have any of you seen this man?"

"I did see him. He left with four other men. I can't tell you where they went, but those men escorted him off this floor. They were rough with the man in that picture. They acted like he'd done something wrong."

"When was that?"

"About one time-unit ago."

"Thank you."

"I'm sorry I can't tell you more."

Kane nodded at the woman. "I appreciate your help." He walked back to open the lift, and when the door closed he punched the back metal wall with his right fist. Where could four men have taken Dobie? Who were they and why did they want him? Where should he start? Too many questions.

The door opened and the reception lobby of the hospital lay before him. There was only one place he could go, home. All the equipment he required would be there, and so would Jorell. He needed to see her, make sure she was all right, and he wanted to feel her in his arms.

He briskly walked to his transport in the pod loading zone, trying not to draw attention. After he settled into the seat, he carefully maneuvered out of the docking and parking areas, then up into the prescribed low flying zone.

It didn't take long to reach the warehouse and secure his transport. When he entered the living area he found Jorell fast asleep on the sofa. She was beautiful, and the soft recessed lights illuminated the shiny red hair that covered her shoulders in a cascade of loose curls. Her perfect features begged to be kissed. He wanted her.

When he realized Dobie had been taken, his first thought was to tell Jorell, proof he wanted, no needed her in his life...always. Did he dare tell her? Could they endure through time? He had more questions than answers, but right now, Dobie took precedence.

Jorell needed her sleep, and he had work to do so he moved over to Dobie's tec-center. Now if he could remember everything his partner had told him he might be able to find what he needed. When the system powered up he asked for the hospital's surveillance vids from the moment the Utility-Man arrived.

After watching Alextor's proxy die, he ordered the vids to follow the killer. Once in the hallway he ducked into the men's facility where he changed attire and appearance. He and Dobie were more than familiar with that procedure. Then three other men entered. Not one word was spoken by any of them, only a few nods. Together they moved to the waiting area directly across from Alextor's room.

Hospital staff didn't pay attention to who came and went from the waiting area, they only entered it when they needed to speak to a family member. Time dragged on, but he didn't dare fast forward. Several more moments passed, then it happened.

Dobie exited Alextor's room and walked to the lift. The four men meandered up behind his partner and pretended to patiently wait for the lift to arrive. When the door opened they shoved Dobie to the back wall. When the door slid shut Dobie's fate was sealed.

Sure enough, when the lift arrived in the lobby the Utility Man exited first, then Dobie with the two largest men on each side, each with a tight grasp on his arm, plus one man behind him. What an escort.

The group left through the doctor's exit so he located the corresponding camera and accessed the vid. It was no surprise they all boarded one large transport and sped off. When the vehicle turned and the next camera caught it, he hit the freeze-frame and recorded the

Okeron identification number.

When he ran the number through the system, he found it belonged to the Sector-Two government transport pool. That meant one thing, Nazar Ferris was behind Dobie's abduction. He should have known. Nazar had plagued him every sun-cycle in the Academy, and now he'd returned to curse him once again.

What had he done to make Nazar hate him? Nothing. Absolutely nothing. Nazar wanted to hurt him, and he'd certainly found his one weak spot—Dobie. He didn't have much in his life that was a constant, except Dobie, and he could always count on his friend to have his back, no matter what.

Nazar was about to have a rude awakening. They'd had their problems in Academy, but he was no longer the inexperienced boy he'd once been. He did not know what Nazar had been up to since graduation, but when they'd been in classes together, Nazar struggled with his studies, and he doubted the man had become any smarter. Nazar was a follower, not a leader, which confirmed his suspicions that Pakar, or Loran Narom, or whatever he called himself these sun-cycles, was the mastermind behind everything.

He'd save Dobie, no matter the risk, which provided more motivation than ever to uncover Pakar, and unseat Nazar. As long as he was still breathing, Pakar would not take control of Okeron. Eunis confirmed the murdering bastard was his father, but that unfortunate twist of fate had nothing to do with his plan to stop the conniving, power-hungry man permanently.

Another strong memory sprang into his mind. Eunis said he had a fraternal twin who had been under Pakar's supervision since birth. Had the malicious man killed his son during the process of raising him? Or had he simply turned the unsuspecting offspring into a smaller version of himself? Whoever his brother may be, he had his full sympathy for having to suffer as a young man. No child deserved Pakar for a father.

Brother? The word sounded totally foreign. He'd never even considered the thought before. Many times he'd wished for a brother, someone he could confide in, someone who would be there for him, no matter what. But he had Dobie, who was more of a brother than a stranger with shared genetics could ever be. Had Pakar told his son the truth of his birth? Including the fact *he* had a twin brother? Highly unlikely. Pakar believed he was dead, so why would he ever mention him to his brother? Or anyone.

The truth never passed Pakar's lying lips. In fact, if his lips were moving, he was lying. The only exceptions were his threats, which were actually promises since he meant every word. When the evil man executed revenge, it was like a holiday to him, especially if it involved unspeakable torture and death. There were so many reports of Pakar's antics that it would take a lifetime to read them all.

This was the opportunity he'd waited for; to exact revenge for all of Pakar's innocent victims, including Eunis, the sweetest woman on the planet. It would be his pleasure to permanently eradicate Pakar's evil presence. He never wanted to be like the man who fathered him, and he would take pleasure ridding Okeron of its worst criminal. That thought had been foremost in his mind from the moment he witnessed Eunis' murder, a deed he'd never forget, or forgive.

Every action created a reaction, and in Pakar's case, neither of those were good. Pakar deserved a taste of his own medicine—torture, because death was too easy and swift. *The Traveler* had never inflicted torture, but the evil man needed to suffer and feel real pain, the same as his countless victims.

There were only a handful of truly heartless men on the planet, but Pakar could serve as mentor to the evil cult. He could teach them things they'd never think of themselves. Just his luck to have a father that was so selfish he did not think anything he'd done in his life was wrong. Pakar was the perfect example of a man without a conscience. It was still a mystery how any man could live a loveless life, devoid of emotion, with no sense of right and wrong.

Somehow he had always known the sun-cycle would come when he would face the man who fathered him, and would only be resolved by the sword. Pakar was the only man who could push him over the line he'd sworn never to cross. This time he would make sure Pakar knew what he'd done, and how others suffered from his heinous deeds.

Before he could deliver punishment, he had to find Dobie. It had to be about credits, it was always about credits. Either Pakar or Nazar had Dobie, either way they had better not harm one hair on Dobie's head. He was worried, but hated to admit it, even to himself. Someone knew his one weakness, Dobie. This was the one reason he'd never gotten close to a woman, because she would become a target, and his greatest weakness. At least no one knew about his relationship with Jorell, and at the moment, she was believed dead.

It was dangerous to be his friend. He'd always been extremely careful not to let his true identity be known, nor did he tell anyone what he did. Whenever he met a client he wore a disguise. To the best of his knowledge, the only people who knew were Dobie, Jorell, Alextor, and the good doctor, and as far as he knew, they'd keep his secret.

Patience. He had to stay calm, and be ready for the unexpected, if that were possible. He turned to check on Jorell. She slept peacefully, and he could only describe her as gorgeous. The woman could not look bad even if she tried, her natural beauty glowed from within to light her perfect skin. He didn't deserve her.

He stood, walked across the room and headed for the hallway, but paused to have one last look at his sleeping princess. Dobie was right, she was far more woman than any real life princess could ever be, and he'd met a few. No woman compared to Jorell, not in looks, brains, or courage. His loins burned with desire, and he wanted to kiss her so bad he could almost taste her sweetness. He shook his head and started to walk before he gave in to carnal needs.

He tried to remember how many credits were currently in his safe. There was no way to know what the actual demand would be, but at least he had some emergency credits as Dobie called it. This was an emergency he could not put a credit amount on. He'd give every credit he owned to keep his friend safe.

The amount of credits at his disposal was far greater than he'd charged Jorell, and with that amount added to the hefty balance, he and Dobie were very wealthy men. Time travel to the future provided invaluable information as to where to invest. Some might call it stealing, or insider trading, but it was just smart investing. Even with advance knowledge of certain business' income, it could prove risky since the future could change based on events that may, or may not happen depending upon the free will of the people. Each leap only foretold what would happen based on the current trends in business and the most likely path of growth. However, he knew well that many events could change, and the future could be altered by those changes.

He entered his bedchamber and walked straight into the lav. The sick feeling in his gut would not stop until he brought Dobie home. He stepped into the shower and stopped a little off-center facing the back wall. First he touched a tile on the left, then on the bottom, a few select ones along the side wall. Then he pressed his hand against the center panel and the entire wall rotated which allowed him access to his large, walk-in safe.

How much should he take? That hadn't been negotiated yet, but he stuffed a large, eleacrin leather bag full then secured the lock-clasp. He selected a weapon belt that held several of his favorite toys, as Dobie called them. Damn, he missed his partner. He also missed Jorell and she was only in the other room.

The thought of separating from her when the job was completed stopped him in his tracks. How could he let her go? He loved her. Truly, he loved her. Never before had he experienced such deep feelings for a woman. She brought out the best in him, and he liked how it made him feel.

If he survived this ordeal, he'd open his heart and put it firmly in her hands. Kane Sinue loves Jorell Sutone. That would certainly make an interesting headline, one the media would have fun with for a long time.

However, plans for a future with Jorell had to wait until Dobie was safe at his side once again. His numerous trips through time taught him that most expectations and worries never materialized the way he imagined. Most of the time things went better, but occasionally, when he least expected it, a situation turned ugly and the outcome was a total surprise. He hated surprises.

He grabbed the bag and started toward the door, but it slid open and there stood Jorell, red hair curled around her shoulders and cascading down her back, the overhead lighting kissed the golden highlights, making his fingers itch to touch the silky strands. She still had that sleepy look in her green eyes, and a smile tugged at the corners of her mouth. "You look amazing."

Jorell shook her head. "I don't feel very amazing." She ran her fingers through her hair pushing it back from her face. "You look worried. Was there a problem at the hospital?"

"They killed your father and the entire charade went according to plan, but...."

"Where's Dobie? I didn't see or hear him."

"That's what I'm trying to tell you. They took him."

CHAPTER FORTY FOUR

"Hang him by his wrists from that beam." His men jerked the man's arms over his head so hard and fast that he heard one of his captive's bones snap, but unfortunately the man feigned bravery and stifled a scream. He smiled. Torture was such a fun game.

"What's the matter boy? Something break?" He took pleasure in the little man's groans and squirming. "You *will* tell me what I want to know, or you'll hear more bones snap."

"I'll tell you nothing!"

"I can, and I will make you tell me everything I want to know." Pakar stood, walked closer to Dobie and stared him in the eye before he walked several circles around him. "What's your name?"

"It doesn't matter."

"You're right. I can kill you whether I know your name, or not. Right, Dobie?" He stopped in front of the man and stared him straight in the eyes. "Do you know who I am?"

"I don't care."

"You're lying! You know exactly who I am, and you care enough to hate me."

"You're Loran Narom, and you're right, I don't like you."

Pakar laughed and picked up his favorite knife from the table. He raised it up to Dobie's neck and pressed hard enough for blood to ooze. "Do you want to die?" Dobie's body shook, which made the blade against his skin to move, so he pressed harder and drew more blood. He was always fascinated by the way blood trickled from a wound.

"That's a stupid question."

He pressed the blade tighter and slid it around to the other side. The cutter was not deep enough to kill, just enough to loosen his lips. Blood dripped and oozed down his neck, but his ridiculous looking shirt sucked it up. "Never use that word where I'm concerned again." His prisoner nodded with a confused expression on his face, one that indicated he'd developed respect for his captor. As he should.

Even in the subdued lighting Dobie's skin appeared pale and clammy. He didn't want the fool to die yet, he needed *The Traveler's* name. "I'm enjoying our little conversation, but you'd better pick up the pace. I'm getting bored, and when I'm bored, I tend to play with my knife."

"I noticed."

He laughed at the man's raspy reply. "Knife wounds tend to settle people down." The idiot was still too sarcastic for his own good, but he didn't want to cripple him until he got what he wanted. "If you want to stay alive, give me his name!"

"Sorry. Can't do that."

"That's admirable. It's nice to see loyalty like yours, but it won't help you protect him, or yourself."

"Be serious. You're going to kill me no matter what I tell you, and I bet you're going to kill *The Traveler* when you figure out who he is."

"You're a smart one, but you're wrong. I'm not going to kill you, I'm going to use you." His captive appeared dumbfounded and he laughed at the fool. "Don't be so surprised. You should have figured that out already. Even if you don't tell me his name, having you here will bring him to me." He shook his head. "Surely you've considered that."

"I have, but you'll kill me first. Your temper will get the better of you. I can be quite irritating when I want to be."

"I've noticed. In fact, you don't have to do anything. Just the sight of you irritates me."

"Good!"

Pakar pulled his fist back and punched him in the gut with all the strength he had. The idiot asked for it, and he could cough all he wanted, but there would be no mercy for anyone who talked to him that way."

"Is that..." Dobie coughed several times, "all you've... got?"

"I said you were smart earlier, but I take that back now." He made a fist, drew back his arm and unleashed a blow to the side of his head. He turned around. "Nazar! Get the meds. I'm tired of waiting. It's time for this fool to talk." He'd learn everything in detail, that's how the truth drug worked. It had taken a long time and lots of medical researchers to perfect the formula, but now it worked perfectly, every time.

Nazar went to the supply bag and pulled out a syringe. He walked back to Pakar and held it out to him. "Do you want the pleasure?"

"The pleasure is all yours." He watched his son move closer with the needle in the air in front of him, as if he were teasing the man.

"Well, well, if it isn't my old friend, Nazar. Still a looser I see."

"You're pretty mouthy for being tied up. Ready to be injected?" Nazar waved the syringe back and forth.

Dobie shook his head. "You're a bit quieter these sun-cycles. And you've gotten better with authority figures, I see."

"It appears you're better at nothing. Still the ultimate loser. By the way, whatever happened to your friend, Kane? You know, the guy you can't live without." Nazar laughed. "I'm surprised you've lived this long since your head was so far up Kane's ass you couldn't breathe."

"Well, I'm doing better than you. You're supposed to be ruler of Sector-Two, yet you're here in this stupid cave playing games with that arrogant bastard. You must be related since you both have the same attitude problem."

"Enough! Do your job!" Pakar watched Nazar push up the man's sleeve then literally jab the needle in. When he withdrew the needle he jerked it up on purpose to hurt the fool and make him bleed. Of course he enjoyed inflicting pain, after all, he'd personally trained him since birth. Unfortunately, Nazar didn't have the stomach for the really ugly stuff, but he would, soon.

"It won't be long before it takes maximum effect."

"Can't wait to hear this story." He watched his son nod. He turned at the sound of footsteps, but it was only Rand coming to join them. "Nice of you to show up."

"Sorry, sir."

Rand walked over to him. This should be good. He needed Rand since he was a part of the upper echelon of Sector-Three, but he did not like him. The man was far too arrogant, and thought he should be in charge.

"Let me question him, sir. It would be my pleasure."

"We're not here for your pleasure, now are we, Rand?" He liked the man less and less every time he saw him. There was something about Rand that irritated him even more than Dobie, and he hadn't thought that was possible. Yet Rand was quite full of himself, and there was nothing more dangerous than the help thinking they were important, and that they should have special privileges. He needed to learn his place.

"Nazar will question our guest." Rand opened his mouth to speak, but Pakar held his hand up to stop him. "You dare argue with me?"

"No, sir."

He walked over to his son, put his arm around his shoulder and took him a distance away so they couldn't be heard. "I want to know everything. You know what to ask." He leaned closer to his ear. "This is important. This fool and his partner could stop our plan, and that is not acceptable."

"I understand."

"We've come too far to let anything get in our way." He turned and walked back to where Rand impatiently waited. One glance at Dobie rolling his head back and forth told him the man was ready to spill his guts, and he was ready to hear it all. Every last detail. Then he could kill Dobie and his partner. Nothing would stop him. Nothing!

****

"Dear stars! That's my father." Jorell ran down the hall to the room where her father was staying and tried to pry it open since it moved too slow at the moment. The instant there was enough space she rushed to her father's side. He lay on the bed writhing in pain, screaming at the top of his lungs, and his hands held his head as if it were about to explode. "Father? Can you hear me?"

He moved his head from side to side as fast as he could. "Kane? What's happening?" There was a commotion behind her and she turned, relieved to see Kane. "The Lamia?"

Kane nodded. "Meld and work with me like before."

She took Kane's outstretched hands and closed her eyes and concentrated on melding with him. She touched his mind with hers and they bonded, and it was far more intimate than before.

"Send me every ounce of energy you can so I can save your father. This attack is worse than the others. Now, give me all you have."

She did as he asked willing her very soul if it would help. It seemed strange, but it seemed she could see things through Kane's eyes. He pictured a man she knew to be Pakar Moran, and shock surged through her when he spoke. All she could do was send her positive light energy to Kane and listen to the two men converse.

"I have your little friend, Kane. He told me everything."

"And I care about this, why?"

"You're as big a fool as he is. I can kill him right now, along with Alextor. You see how well he's doing. Plus I know that whoring bitch he calls daughter is alive and I could attack her as well."

She cringed at Pakar's words, but it was his demented laughter that gave her chills since it sounded as evil as the man himself. Kane's anger welled, but she let out the breath she was holding when he relaxed for a moment, then inhaled deeply and sent a huge bolt of bright light at Pakar.

The result was better than she'd anticipated since it made him cough, and temporarily robbed him of his voice.

"Jorell, every time he hesitates, laughs, or falters, immediately send me more light."

"I will."

"I might let him live if you bring me one-hundred million credits."

Kane laughed long and hard, and Pakar's anger grew exponentially. The man had no control over his temper, which was a weakness she hoped Kane could utilize.

"Do you think for one moment I'd trust you?"

"You have no choice if you want your partner back." Pakar chuckled. "I must say, that was a good trick using a CC-D. The man I hired to kill Alextor in the hospital will never make that mistake again!"

"Shall I assume he's dead?" Kane squeezed Jorell's hands.

She looked into Kane's eyes, and when she heard Pakar laugh again she sent a surge of energy to Kane, who passed it along to the enemy. If she could see Pakar right now she was sure he'd stumble backward. At least since they occupied the evil man's attention her father was doing better. Obviously he couldn't attack two entities at a time.

Then it came, a hot, hostile gust of evil the likes of which she never knew existed. She stumbled backwards as if she'd been pushed, and it jerked her from Kane's grasp.

"Jorell!" Kane pulled her to him. "Put your arms around me and don't let go, no matter what."

"I know that little whore is there with you. Somehow you raised her from the dead. I could use a man like you to manipulate time and space for me. But, I assume that's out of the question? Although, by the time you buy back your friend's life, you might need the credits. I pay very well."

"So I've heard, but your employees don't usually live long enough to collect their pay."

Pakar laughed. "You're a fast learner, I like that. Now, if you don't hurry, your friend won't live long enough for you to collect him."

Jorell dug deep into herself and sent more light and energy than she knew she had. Kane mixed his brightness with hers and kneaded it like dough, bounced it around her mind and his, then sent the bolt to Pakar. She sensed his fight against the onslaught, and the light died quicker than the other attacks.

"Your partner is running out of time, and you're wasting mine. Bring the credits before I change my mind."

"Where?"

"To the cave of many myths."

Jorell gasped when the evil suddenly withdrew and she saw a large void in Kane's mind, as if the man took something from him. "Are you all right?" She spoke out loud, but barely heard her own voice.

"Just a bit tired. How about you, my sweet?"

"I'm fine." She turned her attention to her father, who lay still on the bed, his eyes closed. "I'm worried about him." His breathing is shallow, but for the most part normal. Kane reached past her and took his pulse. She waited patiently while he stared at his wristpiece.

"He seems fine. I think the encounter drained his strength as much as ours. I expect he'll sleep for a while."

"As he should." Kane stared at her with a concerned look on his face. "Is there something you're not telling me?"

"About your father? No. But I must leave. You need to call Ariel and Leyana. Have them meet you here."

"Won't that be a bit odd since I'm dead?"

"I forgot. Okay, I'll personally go get the twins, and I'll explain everything to them on the way here. But promise me, the three of you will stay together until I return. And if I don't come back, Doctor Willock will help you."

"Why wouldn't you come back?" She held out her hand to him, but it was shaking so bad she lowered it to her side.

"Don't make me say it. You know what I'm facing." Kane pulled Jorell to him and held her against his chest. "I plan to come back to you." He rubbed her back. "I *will* be back."

Tears welled in her eyes and some spilled onto his shirt, but he did not react. She knew he was worried about her, and her father. If the Lamia attacked while he was gone, he could possibly kill them both, but he had no choice if he wanted to save Dobie.

"Jorell, look at me." He tilted her chin up with his finger. "I love you. I *really* love you."

"I love you too." More tears escaped and rolled down her cheeks, but she didn't care what he thought right now. He said he loved her and that was all she needed to know. "Just come back to me, Kane. I couldn't go on without you."

She waited for his answer, but he only nodded. His eyes told her what she needed to know. Sincerity was a quality very few people could convincingly fake, and she knew him well enough to know he meant every word he said. She had to put her faith in him.

"Pack up what you and your father will need and I'll make arrangements to get you safely back. I'm sure Doctor Willock will help in any way he can. Hurry. Dobie is waiting."

She prayed that love would keep him safe, that fate would be on their side, and that *The Traveler* would be in time.

CHAPTER FORTY FIVE

Kane pushed the throttle forward, but it was no use, the transport was already maxed. He glanced at the bag that occupied Dobie's usual seat next to him. It wouldn't be long before he faced his childhood home.

Pakar had drastically changed his life in that cave, and he had the feeling more changes were on the way. His and Dobie's life lay in the evil man's hands, as well as Jorell's and her father's. But it went deeper than that, Pakar also held the future of the entire planet.

Of course the monster would choose a location where no one knew him, and no one would interrupt his plans. Pakar was more than familiar with the cave, he'd murdered there before. To the best of his knowledge, Pakar did not know he was his son, and he'd keep that bit of information as his trump card should he need one.

To Pakar this was about credits, to him it was personal. He'd waited a lifetime to take revenge for Eunis' death. Pakar just invited him to the finale.

Some things never got better with time, and Pakar was proof positive of that theory. Evil knew no bounds, and destroyed all it touched. How the man had lived this long he'd never know. Surely someone wanted him dead, but his survival proved he was crafty, diabolical, and more calculating than his opponents.

In the distance he glimpsed the mountain that housed his childhood home, but without Eunis it was no longer home. He needed to steel himself against all emotion, and that would be difficult because so many memories were connected to the cave. Pakar viewed love as a weakness and would use his love for Eunis, Dobie, and Jorell against him in an instant if he knew how he felt.

To beat the man's evil attacks and save Dobie, he'd have to control his temper, and he was not always the best at patience, or stopping himself when he heard lies that angered him. But if he gave in, he'd be handing Pakar the kill shot.

He cut power and used the silent landing mode, a feature well worth the cost. Once down, he grabbed the credit bag and exited the craft. When he secured the hatch he hoped he'd see his transport again for his return trip.

While he climbed down the embankment toward the secret, third-level entrance, he thought about the Energy Lamia's attack on Alextor. Pakar had to be the Lamia since he made his ransom demand during the attack. The real question was, how did he know Alextor was alive to attack? Obviously it didn't matter, he was here, and about to make a grand entrance.

No one knew about the entrance he'd discovered as a child. He'd used it to sneak out at night and gaze at the stars, but the most fun had been spying on the pretty neighbor girl who lived over the hill.

Fond memories were just that, and he had to cut them off—all of them. The only one that worked to his advantage was Eunis' murder, which motivated revenge and the need to punish. That memory activated anger and hatred, the perfect emotions for this mission.

He pushed back long branches from a large bush that concealed the small opening. Over the years nature had obscured his secret entrance, but he was almost there. When the opening was clear he realized his memory failed him again. The hole was far smaller than he remembered, and he'd really have to squeeze to get through.

After considerable effort and exhaling, he managed to slide through and land on the soft dirt. The concealed room had a ceiling so low he had had to stay bent over. Funny how adult memories and children's memories were so different.

He set the bag on the ground behind a tall, flat rock. At twelve he'd had to stoop to walk, now he had to crawl, but he didn't have far to go. Even though the voices below filtered up and echoed off the cavern's rock walls every word was audible. He hadn't planned on how agitating it would be to listen to the deep voice of the one and only Pakar Moran.

He laid on his stomach and looked down from between two rocks, shocked to see a tall, muscular, older man, who could be called handsome--the same man he'd seen in the lounge with Nazar.

His stomach tensed when he spotted Dobie tied to a beam between two tall pillars. His friend was alive, but he'd been through some rough interrogation. A trickle of blood ran from his scalp down his right forehead, over one of two black eyes, down his cheek and over badly swollen lips. It appeared his throat had been cut as well since his neck and shirt were covered in blood. Thank the universe the man was tougher and braver than he looked.

One of the men yelled at his companion who had his back to him. When the man turned Kane's mouth opened in surprise at the sight of Rand. Just as he'd suspected. No wonder he never liked the guy.

"You lied to me, and you failed! I should slit your throat." Pakar pressed his cutter against Rand's neck. "You told me she was dead! How is it possible for you to be so stupid?"

"Pakar, I'm sorry, I...I...was badly informed."

"And whose fault is that, you idiot! They worked for *you*. *You* hand picked them. *You* trusted them." He pushed the knife harder and smiled when blood dripped on the collar of Rand's shirt. "You'd never get up the aisle with Jorell. In fact, I'm not even sure why she accepted your proposal." He held up his hand. "Oh, that's right, her father told her to, and she's a good daughter." He laughed. "And speaking of her father, he was also supposed to be dead. But as usual you failed!"

Kane took several deep breaths while the realization that the unknown man he'd seen before was definitely Pakar. He'd had hunches and feelings, but no proof until now. The man obviously had his face completely redone so no one could recognize him. How else could he have managed to stay out of the hands of the law, yet continue to operate all these years?

"Tell me, Rand, why did I have to learn for myself that Alextor and Jorell are alive and well?" He reached his right arm back and then thrust his fist into Rand's face.

Rand coughed and spit blood onto the rock floor beside his feet. "I did everything you asked. It wasn't my fault she didn't die."

"Really? Tell me how she survived the perfect laser shot? And how did she know to be prepared?" Pakar pulled the knife back. "Did you open your mouth to the wrong people?"

"I didn't tell anyone. You have my word!"

"That's priceless!" Pakar shook his head. "Your *word* has cost me dearly." He raised his hand, but before he could thrust the cutter into Rand, a hand grabbed his wrist. He turned his head. "Nazar, what in Diabolus are you doing?"

"You need to calm down. *The Traveler* will be here soon and we need to be ready. Do you know what you're going to do with him?"

Kane held his breath and waited for the evil man to answer. This should be good. Pakar's normal mode of operation was to kill everyone when he was done with them, or at times, before. He seemed to think murder and torture solved everything. The thought of killing Pakar made him smile and he reached for his laser, but stopped. Killing Pakar would be too easy, especially without making him suffer for his crimes.

He turned to leave, but the sound of voices stopped him. He looked back down to the scene below and saw two other men appear. Pakar nodded at them and they just walked over to Dobie and sat on a rock close to where he was tied. They must be guards, and capable ones judging by their size and the amount of weapons they carried.

It was time to make himself known, but he wasn't about to take the valise with him. He'd enter through the only entrance anyone knew about to face Pakar, which left his secret escape route safe.

While he crawled out the same way he entered, he wondered how Jorell and Alextor were doing back at the capitol. They should be safe since he had his eye on Pakar, and there remained no doubt he was the Lamia, who could not attack as long as he remained occupied.

The exit seemed smaller now as he worked his way back up through the opening toward the dark of night. Finally free, he brushed off his clothes and steeled himself for the confrontation that awaited. He checked to be sure he had all his weapons. He had many visible, and even more stashed in various pockets. He was ready.

For Jorell, Dobie, himself, and the entire planet, he'd walk through fire. Since nothing was burning yet, he made his way down the steep slope toward the entrance. He was anxious and apprehensive. This confrontation was the culmination of his lifetime, and that of countless others.

After all he was human, but he'd always told Dobie, that was his only downfall. He really missed his friend. They'd spent time apart before, but not for a long time. Whenever they'd been separated he'd always known Dobie was safe, unlike now. The last thing he wanted was for Dobie to pay with his life for being his friend.

What made a man so evil? The reasons were endless, but he'd always wondered what motivated people to do the things they did, and why greed always played a part. He and Dobie had become rich men, paid by clients who would offer them anything they wanted to make things right, or to communicate with those they loved. Those clients had hearts, and their motives were pure, unlike Pakar, whose bloodthirsty greed erased all other emotions.

The main entrance lay ahead, but he saw no guard, no security device, nothing. Just the way he remembered when he'd shared the simple life with Eunis, who taught him about true love and concern. All he could do now was avenge her passing, and try to right the wrongs. Killing Pakar would not solve all evil, but it would be a giant leap forward.

He stepped into the light of the entryway and walked forward, his shoulders back, his hand itching to grab the laser fastened on the side of his belt. The moment he stepped into the main, open area, five men's heads turned toward him, their gazes fixed.

"I brought the ransom." Pakar stepped forward with the same malevolent glare he'd seen in his nightmares. It didn't matter how the man had altered his facial features, the eyes reflected the soul, and there was nothing left of Pakar's.

"You're *The Traveler*?" Pakar scratched his head, then crossed his arms over his chest. "I expected someone special, and *you* don't look special to me."

"Special or not, I came for my partner, and I intend to leave with him."

Pakar laughed. "So you say. This is *my* meeting, and *I'm* in charge here."

Nazar stepped forward. "As I live and breathe, my old Academy nemesis. Never thought I'd see you again."

"I'd hoped not to see you." Kane sighed deeply. "Pakar, you're not a king, or ruler of anything, and I'm bored with this small talk."

"If you want your friend to stay alive, it might serve you better to show some respect."

"You mean *nothing* to me." Kane held up his right hand. "That's not true. I hate you more than I thought possible to hate anyone."

"And what is it I've *supposedly* done to you?"

"Nothing you haven't done to thousands of others to gain credits and control."

Pakar dropped his arms and walked in a slow circle around Kane. "So you're one of the little people I've inadvertently damaged while carrying out one of my plans?"

Kane chuckled. "You might say that. By the way, what do I call you, Loran Narom? Pakar Moran? Or just Energy Lamia?"

"You think you know who I am?" Pakar spit on the floor. "You know *nothing*!"

"I watched you torture a woman before you slit her throat. Did that make you feel manly? Powerful? Do you get high by attacking those weaker than you?"

"I do enjoy a good kill, but you're right, it's usually about power and credits."

"Absolutely, and you destroy anyone who gets in your way."

"That's the price of progress. I *will* lead this planet. I'm the only one who can."

Kane laughed. "Of course. No one was in charge while you were on Larent, paying for your crimes, or since you've been back."

"Larent is a miserable place, and I don't intend to return." Pakar stepped closer to Kane. "I wasn't there long." He laughed. "If you want your friend alive, you're not doing a very good job of getting on my good side."

"You don't have a good side, and I suspect you plan to kill me, and my friend the moment the credits are in your hands, so why should I bother?" Pakar appeared to be growling at him. Why did he continue to fight with Pakar when he should be working to beat him at his own game?

When would Rand and Nazar say something instead of looking like mannequins behind their leader? With luck he could win them over enough to let him and Dobie go. "I see you have loyal followers. Did they do all your dirty work?" Kane noticed a flash of anger hit Pakar's otherwise stoic expression, even Rand and Nazar exchanged looks.

Kane heard someone behind him. He knew the cave well, every sound, echo, and drip of water. Distance could be deceiving, and the slightest sound magnified. If Pakar had another man with him, he would have seen him already. It could be one of the numerous creatures that inhabited the cavern that he'd made friends with as a child. In any case, the three men in front of him hadn't noticed what was second nature to him.

Ransom negotiations usually ended badly, but this one had to be different because he had no intention of dying, or leaving Dobie behind. He normally thought everything through and considered all his options before acting on a plan, but if he didn't save Dobie immediately, no one would, and he knew Pakar would not keep him around long. The man had no patience.

Nazar and Rand joined Pakar, each taking a place beside him. "Think you can take all three of us?" Pakar lifted his hand and snapped his fingers so his two goons would move closer, and they did. "Not to mention these two."

"I may not get you all, but I will take *you* with me."

Rand took a step forward. "This is wasting time. Where's the ransom?"

Pakar grabbed Rand's arm and jerked him backwards so hard he fell. "Learn your place, and keep your mouth shut."

Rand looked up at Pakar from the rock floor. "Listen, old man, it's you who needs to learn his place." He scrambled to his feet. "It's time for you to step aside and let a younger man take your place."

"And you're that younger man?"

"I am."

Pakar pulled his laser, and aimed it straight at Rand's head. "Wrong answer." He pulled the trigger.

CHAPTER FORTY SIX

Stunned, Kane watched Rand slump to the floor. It only took a moment for a pool of blood to surround his head and stain his hair. He may not have liked Rand, but would never have taken his life. Without a blink, Pakar then turned back around to stare at him.

"Rand's challenge didn't work well for him. Either of you two want to be next?"

Kane noted Nazar's angry reaction, but he shook his head. Behind him he heard Dobie let out a painful moan. He had to be uncomfortable hanging only by his wrists which were chained above his head, blood dripping from where the metal dug into his skin. His ankles were also chained, his feet pulled far apart, and blood oozed from a cut on his forehead that ran down his cheek before it dripped to the floor. Seeing his friend in this condition only created more anger and resentment. Before he could end his partner's torture, he had to end this useless battle. He stared at Nazar and Pakar.

Dobie was semi-conscious, which was good since it gave him the opportunity to play Pakar without being interrupted. He was about to appeal to the evil man's wicked side, and that would give Dobie a breakdown if he were lucid.

Nazar looked into Pakar's eyes. "I realize Rand wasn't the most likeable, or trustworthy man, but why kill him?"

"I kill anyone in my way."

"Including me?" Nazar took a deep breath.

Kane let out a groan. "Look, you two can argue later. I came for my partner, nothing more, and I'd like to get this over with and leave."

Pakar chuckled. "Then show me the credits and I'll free him."

"I can trust you?"

Pakar glanced toward Dobie. "Guards, go search the outside area, I heard something." Once the two men were gone, Pakar looked back at Kane. "Oh yes, trust. I should trust a man who slept with the ruler's daughter to get what he wanted?" He shrugged his shoulders. "I suppose that's admirable."

"We all make sacrifices to get what we want, don't we?"

"I never sacrifice. I take. Only the end result matters." Pakar tilted his head. "Did that little bitch really pay you fifty-million credits?"

"Why wouldn't she? She was too emotional about her father to think straight. Of course I used her grief to get what I wanted. I knew she'd pay me what I asked. I've been stringing her along because I have a plan in place for far more than credits." Kane's hands fisted at his sides. He hated talking about Jorell like that, but he had to convince Pakar he too was just selfish, uncaring and greedy.

Thank the Gods, the stars and everything else Jorell wasn't here to hear him disgrace her. Of course he didn't mean a word of it, but judging by the half-smile on Pakar's face, his words had the desired effect.

"Saving her father really pissed me off, but I have to give you credit, your plan was genius. It fooled a professional."

"I'm good at what I do." He opened his fisted hands, his gaze still on Pakar. "Right now I have Alextor and Jorell in my front pocket. They'll do anything I want since I saved their miserable lives. I suppose that makes me just like you."

"You think you know me? You don't!" Pakar slapped Nazar on the back. "My son knows me, but don't even pretend you do. Just because you convinced the whore you're interested in her, and you managed to save her father, does nothing for your case before me."

"Of course I started with the easy part. I had to convince Jorell I loved her to get her to give me her damned virginity, which was no gift, believe me. She was too scared to do anything. For an adviser she's very naïve, or should I say stupid?" Kane laughed as sarcastically as he could conjure. "I've made her believe I love her, and that idea really is stupid. She has nothing to offer a man."

"Rand took her virginity. Or so he claimed." Pakar glanced at Rand's body. "All women are stupid. Tell me something I don't know!"

Kane laughed, then Pakar joined him, which caused his blood to boil. "I knew we had a connection." He noted that Pakar instantly sobered which meant he'd just made a mistake.

"Are you calling that mind-meld with me a connection? That's an insult, especially since you had that little slut helping you. You just gave me one more reason to kill you." Pakar aimed the laser at Kane's head. "I don't convince as easily as that whore, so give me one reason not to pull this trigger."

"You only care about power and credits. And I brought you credits—lots of credits. If you kill me, you'll never get what you want."

"If you brought credits, I'll find them." Pakar moved the weapon in his hand and aimed it at Kane's head. "I believe it's time to rid the planet of you, and your partner over there, if he isn't already dead by now. Unless you have that reason ready?" He stepped closer and pressed the laser to Kane's forehead.

"I have a reason, Pakar. You can't kill your own son!"

Pakar looked up. "*You*! How in Diabolus can you be here? I killed you with my own hands!"

Kane turned so fast he nearly lost his balance. That feminine voice belonged to Eunis, he'd know it anywhere. He looked up toward the ledge where she stood. Her natural beauty was enhanced by the light of the cavern, her dark hair lying in stark contrast on her shoulders over the pale blue gown she wore. She appeared regal, strong, and determined. How was this possible?

"*I* am not your concern, Pakar. I came to stop you from killing your own flesh and blood."

"My son Nazar, stands here," Pakar put his arm around Nazar's shoulders and pulled him closer, "beside me. So you're still the foolish old witch you've always been."

"Not as foolish as you think. I fooled you and protected Nazar's twin brother. You believed I killed that innocent newborn, when instead I raised him." Eunis pointed to Kane, "If you remember correctly, you said one son was more than enough, and decided the bigger one would be best." Eunis laughed. "I'm still shocked you took either child."

"You back-stabbing bitch!"

"Call me what you like for speaking the truth, but I wanted you to know this *fine* man is your son. Can you really kill your own flesh and blood? Have you finally stooped that low?"

Pakar laughed. "You know I'm capable."

"Pakar, I know well what you're capable of, after all, you murdered me didn't you? If I remember correctly, it was a slow death, your usual torture, with slapping, punching, hitting, cutting, burning. And when you were bored with that, you cut my throat so I could bleed to death in front of my son. You do like bloody outcomes. It's too bad you've never done anything worthwhile in your entire, miserable life."

"According to you, I fathered a fine man. But I should cut your tongue out for claiming to be his mother. I did not rape *you*! I find *you* too disgusting!

Eunis laughed long and hard. "I'm glad you found a reason not to torture me further by violating my body. But, let me make one thing perfectly clear, you are *not* a father. A brutal rapist can only be called an *unwanted sperm donor*."

"That's it!" Pakar removed his arm from Nazar's shoulders, aimed at Eunis and fired.

The laser beam left the barrel before Kane could do anything, and his heart nearly stopped when he looked up at Eunis. She lifted her arms in defense and the beam bounced off her Vambrace Cuffs. He let out the breath he'd been holding, then threw himself at Pakar and knocked him to the cavern floor.

They rolled over and over. For a man his age, Pakar was strong, but he finally managed to knock the weapon from Pakar's hand and it flew through the air, hit a rock, then slid a safe distance away.

Pakar struggled violently, and Kane took a blow to the chin and one to the gut before he shoved Pakar off him. He jumped to his feet, only to find Nazar holding a laser to his head. The words between Eunis and Pakar played over in his mind. He was still in shock to learn Nazar was his brother. Somehow all those years of competition between them finally made sense.

Pakar knelt, then pulled himself to his feet. "Glad to see you have things under control, Nazar. A bit late aren't you?"

"Late? I'd say it was you who were late, *father*, in telling me I had a brother."

"I told you not to call me *father!*"

"At least now I understand why. You never wanted a son, a fact you've made quite clear to me over the years. And of course, you never mentioned my brother since you ordered his murder."

"Nazar...." Pakar held out his hand, but Nazar shoved it away. "It's not what you think...son."

Kane recognized the deep-seated resentment in his brother's eyes, along with a long-suffering pain he could only imagine. Nazar had obviously paid a high price for the incomprehensible, emotional torture Pakar used on him every sun-cycle of his life. He sent Nazar a mental wave of sympathy. It surprised him when Nazar looked his way with an expression of thanks and understanding, as if he heard his every thought.

"Kill him, Nazar—now!"

"Why, *father*?" Nazar held up his free hand. "Never mind, I know the answer. He's a complication." He shook his head. "You ordered my brother killed to eliminate a complication. What I don't understand is, why you didn't have us both killed?"

"The way you're acting right now proves I made a mistake!"

Nazar refocused his aim from Kane to Pakar. "Really?"

"You've always been a disappointment. You never excelled at anything. Second at this, third at that. You wasted your academy years, and since then as well. I thought I could depend on you when you started working for me, but no, I had to hire professionals to do my bidding."

"You mean your murders?"

The hatred in Pakar's eyes nearly glowed red. He actually felt evil energy build inside the man, and sensed he wanted to unleash every bit of it on Nazar, the only son he claimed. There truly was no limit to his cold, calculating ways, and it revealed the man absolutely had *no* remorse, *no* conscience, and *no* heart.

"I put faith in you, and all you did was let me down time after time. I thought there was hope when the Academy punished you for fighting— that made me proud. But you would just disappoint me at something else. I never should have put you in charge of Sector-Two, you'll fail there as well!"

Nazar shook his head. "That's what I've always liked about you, your mind is always made up, and you're never wrong, are you?"

"Of course not. Now, point that laser at Kane. Kill him and get it over with!"

"You miserable old man!" Nazar stepped forward and pressed the weapon against his father's forehead. "I should take you out right now!"

"Do it! Prove you have the guts!" Pakar pushed the laser aside with his hand. "I knew you couldn't. It's not in you. It's never been in you. You've failed me too many times already. This time I think you failed yourself."

Nazar reared back and unleashed a punch to Pakar's face and hit him in the nose. Blood flew everywhere and a gush opened up down the front of his face. Kane watched him wipe the blood with his right sleeve, then the old fool smiled at Nazar with blood stained teeth. Nazar pointed his weapon once again at Pakar with a steady hand and a determined look on his face. "Nazar, don't do anything you can't live with."

Just then Pakar's two hired goons returned and charged at him and Nazar in order to protect their boss. For them it was simply credit. "Nazar, look out!" One guard attacked Nazar and the other one was his. They were big men, strong and determined. He got in a couple of face punches, but that did little to dissuade his opponent who landed a gut punch that took all his air.

He rushed against the man and shoved him backwards and did not stop until the rock wall intruded. With a hand on each side of the man's head he slammed it backward, relieved when the man crumpled to the floor unconscious.

Nazar was embroiled with his assailant, fists flying. Kane picked up a smooth, palm-sized rock and waited. When the opportunity presented itself he hit the man in the back of the head and he slumped to the floor.

"Thanks, brother."

"Don't mention it." Kane laughed. "I like fighting with you instead of against you."

"I never thought I'd see this sun-cycle."

Kane nodded. "I never thought I'd have a brother."

"Nor did I." Nazar brushed off his shirt. "What now?"

"Do you mean the three unconscious men? Or our future?"

"Both, but one at a time. Let's deal with these three first."

"Good plan." Kane picked up the weapon his attacker dropped. Out the corner of his eye he saw Nazar do the same thing. He looked over at Dobie, who still hung unconscious. A loud moan made him turn. Pakar had begun to wake up, and Nazar was ready for him. Too ready actually, since he now aimed Pakar's own weapon on him. "Nazar! Don't do it."

"What are you saying, *brother*, that you don't want me to kill your newfound *father*?"

Kane walked closer to Nazar and stopped at his side. "This has nothing to do with *our father*, and everything to do with you. Personally, I believe the man needs to die a thousand deaths for every wrong he's committed, but we both know that's far too easy for him." Kane took the laser out of Nazar's hand. "Besides, there are many victims that want, and need to see justice done on their behalf. Plus, if you kill him, it will haunt you, and you don't want that on your conscience."

Kane sensed Eunis moving toward him, but he wasn't worried, Nazar had no reason to hurt her. Pakar struggled to open his eyes, which was difficult since his eyes were coated in blood from his profusely bleeding, broken nose. Somehow it satisfied him to see the man suffer a bit, no matter how petty it might seem. He put his hand on Nazar's shoulder. "Shall I call you, brother?"

"I would be honored. We have much to discuss, but not until *our father* is safely secured. He'd still kill both of us if given the opportunity."

"I agree." Kane turned to see Eunis coming up behind him.

"I also agree." Eunis smiled at Kane.

"Nazar, I'd like you to meet Eunis, the woman who raised me, and has more than earned the right to be called mother."

Nazar bowed his head. "I'm honored to meet you."

"And I you. The last time I saw you was when I delivered you." Eunis hugged Nazar. "I'm glad to see you as an adult. I always wondered if Pakar would…"

"Kill me?" Nazar laughed. "He tried a few times, but I'm too stubborn to die."

"So is he." Eunis stared at Pakar on the ground. "I must ask you both if it's your heart's desire to Kill him?"

"It is, but we've both decided death is too easy. Real punishment is letting him live to see the respective sectors return to controlling themselves without interference from him."

Nazar nodded. "He should live to see his planned dictatorship fail. And he should face all those families who suffered at his hand. They deserve justice. I'd tell you everything he did to make his plan work, but the disastrous list of deeds is far too long."

"I understand." Kane gave Nazar a healthy pat on the back. "I'm with you, brother."

"Now isn't that *sweet*?" Pakar snickered while he stood. "Two little failures bonding together, thinking they have the upper hand on me, Pakar Moran, ruler of Okeron!"

Kane looked at Eunis, and she at him. Then he glanced at Nazar. "So, who wants to knock him out this time?"

"I heard that. I'll kill all of you if you come near me!"

Eunis smiled. "Let me."

He watched in amazement while Eunis took a deep breath then sent a bolt of white energy to Pakar, who gasped when it hit him. Pakar tried to maintain his stance, but was unable and fell backwards, landing on the cold stone floor. Not one muscle in his body moved. "Is he dead?"

"The thought is very tempting, but no, it's just a sleep spell." Eunis stared at Pakar and smiled. "I may have sent a little more spell than he needed."

"That's amazing, mother."

"Thank you, son." She leaned closer to Kane and gave him a hug. "It's time for me to go, before I…"

"Stay for good?" She nodded at him. "Before you leave, you have to tell me how you knew to arrive here, at the exact moment I needed you?"

"My dear boy," Eunis took several steps away from Kane, "A sorceress never reveals her secrets." She smiled. "You know that as well as you know I love you." She crossed her arms over her chest, closed her eyes, and instantly disappeared.

"You're right, she's amazing."

Kane grinned and cocked his head. "I couldn't agree more. But for now, let's get this evil bastard restrained." Nazar agreed and tilted his head toward Dobie.

"Let's get your friend down and put Pakar in his place."

"You read my mind." Kane chuckled. "Why didn't we ever notice we were more alike than different?" They each grabbed an arm and pulled, and together they drug Pakar's unconscious body to where Dobie hung.

"Better late than never." Nazar laughed. "By the way, how long will that sleep spell last?"

"If I know Eunis he'll probably be out for at least eight time-units."

"She did say she sent more than he needed, whatever that means."

"Then he'll be out for twelve to fifteen time-units."

Nazar looked into his brother's eyes. "Fantastic. Wish I'd had Eunis around during my childhood, it would have saved me a lot of heartache."

Kane nodded at Nazar and they both dropped Pakar a few feet from where Dobie hung. When Kane straightened he glanced toward the entrance and thought he saw someone leave. The lighting was subdued in that area, and the cavern was quiet, but he still sensed someone had been there watching them, and the feeling was familiar.

"What is it?"

"Is anyone else here with you?" Nazar shook his head. "Did you see someone just run out the entrance?"

"I sensed something, but I didn't see anything."

"I'll take a look when we're done here." Nazar unlocked Dobie's cuffs while he held his friend up so Nazar could free his feet. Dobie moaned and blinked several times.

"Chief?"

"It's me. I've come to your rescue...*again*." He had to chuckle at his friend, who tried to laugh, but then cringed due to the facial injuries he'd sustained.

"Yeah, but you're good at it."

"Glad you noticed." When Dobie was completely free he tried to take a step, but could not support his own weight and Kane kept him from falling down. "Are you all right?"

"As well as can be expected."

Nazar laid a hand on Dobie's shoulder. "I'm glad you're free. I apologize for stringing you up."

"Nazar, apologizing to me? That's a first."

"Here's another first," Kane glanced at Nazar, then back to Dobie. "Nazar is my brother." Dobie's eyes grew big and his eyebrows lifted in surprise. His friend's face always gave him away, even when it was bruised and swollen.

"You're what?"

"You heard me."

"Wow. When did this happen?"

"At birth." Kane laughed. "A few moments ago, but you were sleeping over here." They walked Dobie over to an old sofa and helped him to sit.

"Kane," Dobie took a deep breath, "you can't believe what Pakar says. Nazar may not be related to you."

Kane laughed. "I believe nothing that man says. It was Eunis who told me." He glanced at Nazar, "Or should I say, us?"

"Us. I had no idea. I never even suspected the selfish bastard had any more children." Nazar shook his head. "For the child's sake I say that. So at least you were spared his physical presence in your life."

"And for that, I'm grateful. You have my sympathy for having to put up with him. Now I know why you never went home during the holidays."

"Stupid me, I thought you stayed for the same reasons I did."

Kane laughed along with his brother. "We were quite a pair back then."

Dobie looked at Nazar. "If Kane accepts you, then so do I. Welcome to the family."

Nazar stepped closer to Dobie. "I know we've had our differences, but I hope you can understand where I was coming from back then." He shrugged his shoulders. "I give you both my word, I'm done with Pakar and everything he stands for."

"Are you sure?" Kane took a deep breath. "I mean, you've spent your lifetime with him. He's your father. He raised you, he--"

Nazar held up his hand. "First I spent very little time with him. He was either gone, or had no time for me. Second, it's only an accident of nature he's my father. Third, I wouldn't say he raised me, at least not like other fathers. He mainly ordered me around, and taught me how to do his dirty work like a professional. I was rarely allowed to call him father. So don't think for one moment that I care deeply for him, or that I would ever work to free him. He deserves whatever punishment the courts decide. If it's death, that suits me fine."

"You have my sympathy, brother. I can't imagine what kind of Diabolous you lived in with that man raising you." Kane turned and walked back toward Pakar's still body.

"I appreciate your sympathy, and I'm glad you didn't have to experience it. No one should have to have that man for a father. I was thrilled to go to Academy, because it meant time away from him. But for some reason, I did enjoy picking on you." Nazar laughed while he helped Kane pick up Pakar.

"We did have a competitive relationship, didn't we?" He smiled while vivid memories of the times they tried to kill each other ran through his mind. He held Pakar while Nazar secured the cuffs around his wrists and ankles. He released Pakar who now hung by himself the same as Dobie had.

"We have a lot of time to make up for." Nazar slapped Kane on the back. "I've always wanted a brother."

"So did I." And he meant it. "It was lonely growing up as an only child." Kane glanced at Dobie who sat on the sofa shaking his head.

"Nazar, just remember, I was his brother first, and I have far more seniority than you!"

"Got it, Dobie." Nazar looked at Kane. "You're lucky to have him."

"That I am." Kane turned and looked at the front entrance again. "Are you sure you didn't see anyone run out of here earlier?"

"No, but why don't you check it out while I make arrangements for a heavily guarded transport to pick up Pakar."

"Don't forget those other two guards in case they wake up."

"I'll secure them right now."

Nazar walked away with a big smile on his face. He'd had a brother for less than one time-unit, yet it seemed like a lifetime. What they say about twins must be true, they really do share a bond that defies explanation.

"I'll be right back."

"Be careful. I just gained a brother, and I don't want to lose one as quickly."

"Not a chance."

CHAPTER FORTY SEVEN

Jorell wiped her eyes and blew her nose for the thousandth time. How could she have been such a fool? She'd put all her trust into a man who cared nothing about her! He'd called her a whore, naïve and stupid, and to make matters worse, he is Pakar Moran's son! It couldn't get worse than that.

Never had she been so humiliated, especially by someone she'd paid a fortune to for...now she wasn't even sure. The credits were not the main sacrifice, it was her heart and soul. Kane made Rand look like a good catch, but now Rand was gone, killed in cold blood by Pakar. At least Kane had not lied about how evil the man was, but she'd always known that fact. He forgot to mention the man was his father.

There would be no more secrets to keep, or tell, because she'd never allow him that close again. He had his credits, Pakar's attempt to take over Okeron had been stopped, so she had no further use for the lying, conniving, womanizer. He'd told her what she wanted to hear, needed to believe, and like a fool, she'd taken the bait and allowed him access to everything.

Never again would she see him, nor would she get close to another man. First Rand used her for his personal gains, then Kane took over where he'd left off. Well, she may be a slow learner, but they taught her well. She'd learned men had no scruples or honesty, they took what they wanted without a thought about pain or deceit.

The only man who deserved her loyalty was her father, a man who had never let her down, not as a ruler, or a father. Her future would consist of serving her people and doing what was right for them. Her personal life was over, but that could be said for most dedicated government representatives.

She pulled herself together, went into the lav and washed her face with cold water, but it did little for swollen eyes. What did she care? There was no one to impress. After blotting her skin dry with the towel, she walked out of the lav, through her bedchamber and into the main living area of her private quarters where her two dear friends waited for her.

"Are you all right, Jorell?"

The twins both walked up to her, each taking one of her hands in theirs. "I'm...well, I'm..."

Alesa squeezed Jorell's hand. "Never mind. How about something to drink?"

Jorell nodded and tried to conjure a smile. "Make it something strong." She watched Ariel walk to the serving bar and pour three glasses of wine, put them on a tray, then head back to her.

"Let's sit." Alesa led Jorell to the couch and sat next to her. "Are you ready to talk about it?"

"It won't help."

"It always helps." Ariel handed Jorell a glass. "What did he do?"

"I didn't say anything about Kane, so how..."

"It's always about a man." Ariel laughed, and Alesa joined her. "You realize we're women too, don't you? Of course we've been in your shoes before." Ariel looked over at her sister. "But neither of us cried over such a muscular, handsome, time-traveling warrior as you have."

Alesa tapped her temple with her finger. "No, I can't think of any that nice." She smiled. "But I do like Kane's friend, Dobie. He's so cute and cuddly, and--"

"Stop! Can't you see it's the wrong time to bring up men?" Jorell wiped her eyes again. "I'm sorry, Alesa. I don't expect the world to stop because of my problems. You have a right to like anyone you want. Just don't try to convince me to give Kane a second chance. He betrayed me, now he pays. That's the way it is, understand?" Both twins nodded. "Good."

"We've been friends a long time Jorell, and we just thought you'd feel better if you talked about what happened."

Jorell took a long drink of her wine. Maybe they were right. How could she put it behind her if she didn't face the problem? "Okay, you win." She knew her friends only wanted to help, and they had nothing but understanding in their eyes.

"I followed Kane. You know me, I just couldn't stay behind and wait, I needed to know where he was going. It seemed he was always leaving me behind when something really important was going on. So, without his knowledge, I followed him to the Greggan Mountains, way out in the northern countryside."

"He didn't see you? How could that be? That man has eyes in the back of his head. He's careful, very careful."

"You're right, Ariel, but so was I. He didn't see me because he was focused on saving Dobie."

"Dobie? By the Gods! Is he all right?" A tear ran down Alesa's cheek. "Please, tell me."

"I'm sure he's fine now." Relief flooded Alesa's expression. "Pakar abducted Dobie, so Kane went to rescue him. Nazar and Rand were there, both were working with Pakar. Pakar and Rand got in an argument. Pakar did not like Rand's attitude, so he shot him with his laser." The vivid memory still brought tears to her eyes. Even if Rand had betrayed her, she once had real feelings for him and certainly did not want to see him killed.

"He's dead?" Alesa asked.

Jorell nodded while she wiped tears from her cheeks, still unable to verbalize his fate. Her emotions were so raw right now they would bleed if they could. Alesa picked up her hand and gave it a squeeze.

"I know this is difficult."

"I'm so conflicted I don't know what to feel. I've just learned that both men I've had feelings for betrayed me. Difficult is not the word."

"Okay, how about hurt and angry?"

"Better." Jorell stood and walked to the window. "Kane told Pakar how he used me, and how easy it was since I was naive and stupid." She turned and faced the twins. "He said he made me love him just to gain my trust and get what he wanted. He said a lot of devastating things about me. I've come to know him well, and he meant every word he said."

"How do you know that?" Alesa walked to where Jorell stood. "I've read some of his thoughts, and he's devoted to you. His intentions have always been sincere and honest. I never sensed anything complicit about him, or even the possibility."

"If you weren't my dearest friend I'd scream at you. Instead, I'll just say you're mistaken about him. I was there, I saw him, I heard him. You're wrong." She turned her gaze back to look across the city's skyline. The sun was setting and she'd always enjoyed the colors, along with the peace and tranquility the blanket of darkness promised. Except this was no ordinary sunset, it was the end of a relationship she never should have had.

She knew when Alesa walked away, relieved she hadn't persisted in talking about the hopeless situation. When she turned, both twins stood by the main entrance.

"We decided you need some time alone. The doctor is still with your father, so he's fine. Please, call us if you need us."

"Thank you. I will." She turned back toward the window and listened to the door open, then close. She'd never been so alone, and not because her best friends left. She'd given her heart and soul to the love of her life, and he'd thrown her away like unwanted trash. Had he ever existed in the way she'd thought?

Shock continued to rock her body and she began to shake. How could she ever have trusted a man so completely? Kane's words cut through her very soul because they sounded completely sincere. She had blindly trusted him, a mistake she'd never repeat. She'd believed everything Kane told her.

Blind trust happened out of necessity, but she'd believed Kane deserved it, along with the credits. The memory of Kane laughing along with Pakar made her stomach turn, especially since she had been the source of their sardonic, gloating, lust and gluttony.

How could Kane have turned into an uncaring monster so fast? Had she lost all sense of good judgment? She'd put trust and love into two men who were both blatant liars and womanizers. What a record, but as of now, there would never be another man to make that list. She was finished.

Spending the rest of her life as a single woman had great appeal. Her mother died when she was six annual-cycles, but she still remembered when her father swore to her there would never be another woman in his life because no one could take her mother's place.

All the vows on the planet could not stop the pain that ate her alive. How could she forget him holding her in his arms, making love to her in such a magical way? They'd mind-melded, and no connection was more intimate than that, especially in bed. When she'd seen his inner thoughts she'd sensed nothing but truth and love, so how had she misread him so badly?

She may not be able to read the men she'd been involved with, but her political readings for her father were excellent, so she would stick to her profession and nothing else. There was even real pain in her heart. Tears began to fall uncontrollably once again. Not one tiny bit of her mind, body, or soul felt normal. This grieving process was painful in ways she never imagined possible.

No man was worth the price.

****

"You have to go see her. Now!" Dobie adjusted the icepack on his eye. "Don't be a fool."

"Me, a fool?" Kane laughed. "Don't answer that."

"I still can't believe Nazar is your brother." Dobie shook his head. You and Nazar had all those fights in Academy, constantly competing with each other. I should have seen it since you two were so perfectly matched physically." Dobie lifted the ice pack and looked at Kane. "I'm still adjusting to Pakar Moran being your father."

"I told you about Pakar, but I had no clue about Nazar." Kane scratched his head while Dobie reclined on the sofa. He sat on the chair adjacent to his friend and studied the cuts and bruises on his swollen face and arms. Actually he could barely find a place that wasn't bruised, and he was sure there were more in places he could not see. The mistreatment Dobie suffered at the hands of Pakar had been extreme, and it was a wonder he was still alive.

"You know, I heard some of your conversation with Pakar, and I must say, Chief, you have a lot of explaining to do."

"Of all people, I thought you'd understand."

"Not to me ya big lout, to Jorell!" Dobie moved the icepack to glare at Kane. "No wonder you're in so much trouble. What were you thinking?"

"Evidently I wasn't."

"You got that right!" Dobie put the ice back in place. "You'd better talk to her as soon as possible. The longer she has to think about it, the worse it's going to get."

"Are you sure you saw her?"

"As sure as I could be with two swollen eyes burning from blood running down my face. Yeah, I believe it was her. Where she came from, I don't know, but I saw bright red hair bobbing behind the rocks."

"I thought I felt her, but--"

"Quit being a coward."

Kane groaned. "I've never been a coward."

"There's a first time for everything."

His friend was right. At this moment, Jorell terrified him. She had every right to be furious. What could he say that she'd believe? Could she ever forgive him? This would be the true test of their love.

"What are you waiting for? It's not going to get easier, ya know?" Dobie chuckled. "What's the worst that could happen?"

"She refuses to see or speak to me again."

"That's one thing. Is that all?"

"You're not making me feel any better if that's what you're trying to do."

"I don't know what I'm trying to do. Those pain meds the doc gave me are making me feel pretty good. Maybe you should try one, then you could just float in and nothing would make you lose your temper."

Dobie laughed like a child, uninhibited and carefree, something he always admired and wished he could do. "That is tempting, but would only make matters worse."

Kane stood and took a few steps toward the door then turned. "It's possible it wasn't Jorell. It could have been one of Pakar's men."

"Dream on, fool. Do you really think anyone else would have a reason to show up in a deserted cave in the middle of nowhere, and hide so they can listen to a conversation without being seen?"

"You're the one who's always telling me to think positive, you know, wishful thinking?"

Dobie shook his head. "Well, you're the one always stuck on facing reality. But I never told you to think stupid. Besides, if she were faithfully waiting for you she would have been here at the warehouse when you returned. Neither she nor Alextor, were here, plus the doctor, Alesa and her sister were also gone. Got a guess why?" He shook his head. "The only way Jorell would know it was safe to leave here is if she already knew what happened in the cave."

"I think the drugs are getting to you more than you thought." Damnation, Dobie was right. He'd had so much on his mind that he'd missed the obvious. With Jorell it was easy to do. He'd hurried back here to be alone with her, not to find himself alone.

"Is that you admitting I'm right?"

"Yeah. So, I'm out of here."

"Good luck, chief. You're gonna need it."

He walked to the door and waited for it to open, then he just stood contemplating the situation. He turned to give Dobie a piece of his mind, but his dear friend had suddenly drifted off to sleep. He'd been through a lot, and the doctor wanted him to rest, so the meds he'd given him were strong, and Dobie wasn't used to that, but it was for the best.

Dobie had gotten a call earlier from Alesa. They talked for quite a while, and the woman certainly brought a smile to his friend's face. He hoped Dobie could find a woman to love one day. They both knew if either of them settled down with one woman it would be the end of their partnership and travels.

The door closed and locked itself behind him. There was an even higher price he'd have to pay for life-mating outside of the Mageous sect. His father was a full-blood, but his mother was a *normal*, which is what the Mageous called anyone outside of their sect. Life-mating a normal happened all the time, but the sacrifice for a half-Mageous was their gift of powers, whatever specialty was theirs. For him, it was his ability to time travel and mind-meld. He did not care what abilities he lost, he still wanted Jorell.

If he never time traveled again it would be fine with him. Besides, he'd traveled more than any one person should have, and he'd seen more problems than he could solve in any time zone. He just wanted to be a human man who life-mated a human woman. That was all he wanted. It may have taken a strange turn of events to convince him, but he'd learned what was most important to him, and it was Jorell's love.

It was time he and Dobie found happiness in one time and place. They were both tired, and needed a break. They'd planned time off until Jorell needed their help. Once he laid eyes on Jorell, and held her in his arms, he knew he had to have her. It was an instant attraction that went far deeper than he could explain.

They were perfect together, they completed each other. His connection to Jorell superseded anything he'd ever experienced. She was one of a kind, and he did not want to face a future without her. He refused to take no for an answer, and he'd wait for her as long as it took.

The door opened and he hurried to his vehicle in the parking area of the warehouse. He'd brought Dobie back to their home where he could rest undisturbed. Safety was no longer an issue with Pakar in a secure prison cell with more guards than anyone could count. The evil man was not going anywhere until he was brought before the tri-sector court to receive his sentence, which without doubt, would be death.

He entered his transport, settled into the driver's seat and secured the hatch. The docking door opened and he eased out of the garage. When the vehicle was clear, he piloted up and entered traffic faster than usual. The capitol building was not far, but it seemed like the slowest, longest ride of his life. When he passed the large, public transport in front of him, the capitol was in view and he headed for his usual parking area.

Before he knew it he'd secured his transport, entered the building, traversed several long halls, and now stood at Jorell's door. Truth time. He rang the bell, his heart in his hands, ready to give it to her, if she'd have it. He'd survived many battles with fierce warriors, yet this fight felt like the toughest of his life. Fate was often funny, ironic, sad, and joyful, all rolled into one. The only truth that stood the test of time was that fate could not be avoided. He prayed she was his fate.

The door slid open and he stepped inside, his throat suddenly dry. Jorell stood at the far end of the living area looking out over the city from her vantage point in front of the window. "Jorell? Are you all right?"

"Don't pretend you care, when you don't. Just state your business. This will be our last meeting."

"How does your father fare?"

"Fine." Jorell turned to face Kane. "I must thank you for saving his life."

"I've been well paid. That's not why I'm here." She looked at him with pity in her eyes, and that was the last thing he wanted.

"Why *are* you here?"

"To explain." He stepped closer to her, but stopped when she held out a hand in warning. "I know you heard, and saw what happened at the cave." She turned her head away from him. "I sensed you. I felt you."

"You had nothing good to say about me."

"You must know I was playing into Pakar's hands. It was a bad attempt to bond with him."

Jorell abruptly turned to face Kane. "Why wouldn't you bond with your father? After all, you're just like him. I saw and heard the proof."

This was not going as he had planned. "I came to tell you how important you are to me. I don't want to live without you, Jorell. You must believe me."

"I must?" She laughed. "You're deluded." Jorell walked past Kane into the galley. She picked up a glass of water and took a drink.

"You're right. I'm deluded because you make me crazy. I need you Jorell. I want you." He put his hands on her shoulders and turned her to face him. "I want you now, and forever. Please, don't give up on us. I love you."

"Really? You have a strange way of showing it. I've already come to terms with what we are to each other." She turned her back to hm. "There is nothing that Pakar Moran's son could say that I'd believe." She shrugged out of his grasp and walked around the counter. "I believed you once, and once is all you get."

Kane's heart sank faster than an overturned ship. Under normal circumstances he would agree with her. He had to make her understand this was different. A few steps brought him to her side where he inhaled deeply of her sweet scent, and wished she were lying next to him, naked and willing. Right now that was truly a wish.

He touched her hair and ran his fingers down the silky strands. He needed her now more than ever. "I want your love, Jorell. Nothing else."

"You threw that away." She turned to face him. "You had it all once. I was willing to betray my father and Rand for you. I would have done anything you asked. I trusted you…completely. You violated that trust."

He tried to pull her into his arms, but she pushed him away. "Please, Jorell. Let me prove to you how—"

"No!" She walked toward the living area, but stopped at the entryway and pointed to the door as it slid open. "I did not become First Advisor by being played, and if I make a mistake reading someone, I never make the same mistake twice. Now, leave. Do *not* make me call security."

He walked out into the hall, then turned. "You know how to reach me if you change your mind. And I pray, you find it in your heart to do so." While her contemptuous gaze bore into him he left, and he heard the door automatically close behind him.

The dimly lit, deserted hall summed up his mood quite well--depressed. It seemed hopeless to convince Jorell she hadn't heard what she heard. How could he persuade her when it sounded ridiculous even to him? He'd solved some of the greatest mysteries of life, jumped from the past to the future, reunited lovers, and ended family feuds, yet he could not solve his own problems with one woman.

Maybe he should hire someone to work for him who could make matters right again. Who? Dobie? The thought made him smile. He knew his friend would move heaven and Okeron to bring him and Jorell back together. If only it were that easy.

There was one option left--cut his losses and accept the outcome. That rubbed him wrong. There was one person's opinion he'd accept, and that was Eunis'. The idea of counting on his mother again caused that same warm, fuzzy feeling he'd experienced as a child, the safety and understanding only a loving mother could provide. The truth was he did need her for the most important request of his life.

He hurried down the hall toward the parking area, exited the building and nearly ran to his transport. He boarded the craft, steeled into the pilot's seat, but he could not stop the memories that flooded his mind. How could one woman change his life in so many ways? He pulled from the garage into normal ground traffic. Flying when he was this mentally distracted was not a good idea, so it would be the long, safe route home.

This would not be the end of his love for Jorell. If he had his way, it would be the beginning of forever.

CHAPTER FORTY EIGHT

"Father, I heard him myself! I saw him with my own eyes!"

"That's not possible. Kane would never betray you, or me. It's just not possible."

"I'm no longer *taken* with Kane, if that's what you're worried about. He betrayed me. In fact, I have no desire for any man. Not today, or anytime in the future."

Alextor stepped closer to Jorell. "You've been a good daughter, and the best Advisor I've ever had. I only want the best for you, and I must admit, I don't know what that is right now."

"That makes two of us."

"I thought I'd chosen well with Rand. He convinced me he loved you deeply and would take good care of you. I believed the man. Why shouldn't I? He said all the right things, did all the right things, and appeared to be there whenever you or I needed him. Who would have thought?"

"We're both to blame. Trusting someone in the future will be far more difficult, and I won't be as quick to do so." Her father took her hand in his and gave it a reassuring squeeze. She smiled at his knowing wink she'd loved as a child, and appreciated even more as an adult. However, he couldn't know her feelings since he did not know how deeply she loved Kane, or how his devastating betrayal cut her to the bone.

"Kane saved my life. Without him I wouldn't be here, nor would Okeron's style of life be preserved. Instead we'd be under one evil dictator, Pakar Moran. So, no matter what you think of the man, he's done a great service. In fact," Alextor released Jorell's hand and stepped back, "the council has plans to honor him with our highest award."

"The Supreme Accommodation?" He nodded at her and her heart sank. She would have to play an important role in the ceremony, and she'd sworn never to see Kane again.

"What's wrong? You seemed troubled by that."

"I've already told you how I feel, and why, and you have the audacity to ask why I'm *troubled*?"

"I like the man. I can't help it, but I do. And I think he's good for you. Far better than Rand." Alextor laughed. "I must apologize again for that choice."

"As you should. You did cram him down my throat. But, I'll accept your apology only if you promise never to mention Kane to me again."

Alextor rubbed his chin with his right hand. "You drive a hard bargain, but I'll honor your request, only if you forgive me if I slip, and you can't hold it against me while planning and executing the mandated ceremony."

Jorell sighed loudly in an effort to show displeasure, for all the good it would do. Her father was stubborn, but she also knew she had no choice in the ceremony. "When is the award to be given?"

"Three sun-cycles from now. Is there a problem?"

"No, father. I will do as I'm required. Nothing more. The moment my services and duties are complete, I will leave. Agreed?"

"Yes. Thank you." Alextor reached out and hugged his daughter. "I know you've been through a lot recently." He eased her back, but kept his hands on her shoulders. "Why don't you take some time for yourself, until it's time for the ceremony to begin. You need some rest, my dear."

"You're right, I am tired." She kissed her father on the cheek, then walked away. When she reached the door she turned back toward her father. "Thank you for understanding."

"I try." Alextor smiled. "Just remember, fate has a way of working everything out for the best. The way it's supposed to be, even if it's hard to swallow."

"Right now I can't swallow, I'm still gagging." She laughed, then left her father's quarters as quickly as possible, before she threw herself on his mercy and cried her eyes out. His good-bye smile was suspicious. It seemed he knew better than she what the future held, but in this case, he was dead wrong. Kane belonged to her past now, and that is exactly where he would stay.

It was time to move on, and face life as a single woman, the way most politicians lived. She came close to life-mating Rand, a man she did not love, then fell in love with a man she should have stayed away from.

Now she would live the rest of her sun-cycles without love, but it beat the alternative of life-mating the wrong man.

The future lay ahead, and she planned to make the most of it by herself. She had dreamed of children, a home of her own, and a loving husband. Now that was a fairytale she had to bury deep inside.

Many said that to have loved and lost was better than not loving at all, but she fervently disagreed. Now that she knew how the right man could make her feel, nothing would ever be the same. The joy of pure love had turned into the pain of loss.

The sound of Kane laughing along with Pakar was still fresh in her mind, and each time it played out her stomach turned. She'd been the source of their sardonic, gloating, and she could never forgive Kane for his actions.

How could Kane have turned into an uncaring monster so fast? Had she lost all sense of good judgment? She'd put trust and love into two men who were both blatant liars. What a record. She was finished.

Spending the rest of her life as a single woman had great appeal once again. Her mother died when she was six annual-cycles, but she still remembered when her father swore to her there would never be another woman in his life because no one could take her mother's place. Now she fully understood why he'd said that to her.

She vowed never to allow another man intimate access to her mind, or body. That belonged to Kane alone. No matter what she'd heard in that cave, she still could not stop thinking about the tender moments, and the unequaled intimacy they'd shared. It went without saying she'd never have that opportunity again, and not simply because she was angry, rather that he was half-Mageous and able to meld with her in an extraordinary way.

Based on the way they melded, she would swear she too was half-Mageous. If she were, her father would have told her since there was no need to keep such a fact secret. Long ago the Mageous Sect was not well accepted, but currently they were quite accepted. Right now nothing made sense.

All she had to do was get past the ceremony with Kane and her life would fall back into order. She would concentrate on the reading she did for her father, and work to return all three Sectors to normal. What happened to her people was of great concern to her, and they needed her help.

The only question that remained was who would help her?

****

327

Thankful to be home, Kane burst into the living area, shocked to find someone with Dobie. Not just anyone, his head was in Jorell's friend, Alesa's lap.

"Hello, Chief." Dobie sat up straight right next to Alesa. "Wasn't it nice of Alesa to come take care of me?" He stood and walked over to Kane. "She even managed to take my pain away with some kind of magic."

"Magic?" Kane laughed. "I suppose that's about the only thing that would make you feel better."

Alesa stared at him as if she were waiting for a reprimand. Before this job he and Dobie were the only two people who knew about the warehouse. It was difficult for him to realize that it no longer mattered. His time travel days were over, so they no longer needed ultimate privacy. "Good to see you, Alesa. You've worked miracles on my friend here. When I left he was looking bad, now he looks..."

"Don't you dare say it."

Dobie had interrupted him, but it was for the best since it would not be appropriate to say, "Smitten."

Dobie stared at Kane. "Better?"

"Exactly what I was thinking. You really do look better, my friend. But I think you should sit back down with Alesa."

"Chief, what aren't you telling me?"

He watched Dobie return to his previous position beside Alesa. They did look great together, and they both had that look of love in their eyes. The same look he'd shared with Jorell once. "To complete our last job, I need to take one last trip to the past. There is one thing that needs to be cleared up before we can close out our obligation."

"I can only guess what you need to do," Dobie shook his head, "and I'm not sure it's a good idea."

"It's the only thing left for me to do."

Dobie stood and walked over to Kane. He glanced back at Alesa. "Would you mind getting us all something to drink, my dear?"

"Of course. I'd be happy to."

Kane and Dobie waited for Alesa to disappear into the galley. "What do you want to know, that you don't already?"

"Chief, my dearest friend on this planet, have you lost your mind? You're going to play with your own past again, aren't you?"

"Not exactly." Dobie looked at him with a lost look. "We discussed ending our little business before we took this last job. Are you still willing to do so?"

"I haven't changed my mind. I think we're playing with fire, and if we're ever to have a life, we need to concentrate on that."

"Exactly. And that's what I'm going to do. I just didn't want to proceed without your blessing, because if I'm successful, I'll never jump again. Are you sure you're ready for that?"

"As long as you are." Dobie scratched his head. "I can't say I won't miss it, but I *am* ready."

"I appreciate that."

Dobie looked over his shoulder, then back at Kane. "How did it go with Jorell?"

"Do I look like a happy man?"

"Not really. Come on, spill it before Alesa comes back."

"She wants nothing to do with me. Not this sun-cycle, or any other. She made that abundantly clear. The only hope I have is to show her what I'm willing to sacrifice for her. For her I'll give up my ability to time travel. I'm hoping that will make a difference."

"For your sake I hope it does. Just come back here, in one piece, in this time, okay?"

Kane put his hand on Dobie's shoulder. "I will, my friend. I will." He watched Dobie nod, then return to the sofa. Alesa returned with three glasses and a carafe of wine. One glass wouldn't hurt before the last jump of his life.

CHAPTER FORTY NINE

Eunis put her hand on Kane's arm to stop his pacing. "What did you just ask me to do?"

"I want you to remove the cuffs. I've used the powers you gave me to the best of my abilities, but I'm done with it all, and I want them off."

"You've time traveled and mind-melded your entire adult life, and you've made a very good living with your talents. Now you want to give it all up?"

"Yes." He saw pain well in his mother's eyes. "Please understand, this is not personal. I'm eternally grateful for what you did, and I've cherished your gift. Your sacrifice has been a part of me, the same as you have always been." He took Eunis' hand in his. "I love Jorell with all my heart, and I want to life-mate her. You know the rules as well as I do. Please, take these bands off."

"You just told me your relationship with her was over. Have I missed something?"

"I want her back, and I'm willing to make the ultimate sacrifice. I need to show her she means more to me than time travel, mind-melding, or anything else on Okeron, or in the universe. I mean it, mother. I appreciate what you did for me, and you said if I were to life-mate a mere mortal I'd lose all my powers."

"That's the code of the Mageous."

"I'm ready to abide by their rules. Take these cuffs off."

"Do you fully understand what you're asking?"

"I do. Believe me, I do. It's all I've thought about since I met Jorell. I have not come to this decision lightly, or without regret, but Jorell is worth the sacrifice. I promise."

"I've yet to meet her, but I trust your judgment. I'll do as you ask. I've only ever wanted your happiness, son."

"I know."

"Kane, before I do, there's something you should know."

He held up his hand. "There's nothing you can say to change my mind."

Eunis laughed. "You still don't have any patience, do you? I knew how impatient you were as a child, but I hoped you'd outgrow it." She put her hands on his cheeks. "Are you sure you don't want to know what I have to say?"

"Positive."

"Alright, but you must appear in front of the Mageous Council. I'm sure they'll agree to your request. They usually do, but there's always a small chance they could deny you."

"Point taken." The knowing smile his mother flashed him said she understood even more than he thought. She seemed to know exactly how he felt about Jorell, as well as his regret for surrendering the cuffs. They'd always shared a deep connection that defied explanation. "We won't lose our bond, will we?"

"I can't say for sure about mystical powers, but our love bond will never change."

For some reason his mother looked away. It was obvious this bothered her more than she'd admitted. He never wanted to hurt her, nor could he hurt Jorell. It was torture thinking about the last time they were together. He could feel her pain and he'd never forgive himself.

Eunis gazed up at Kane. "I must go to the council and set a hearing date." She moved closer and laid her hand on his arm. "This will not be easy."

"I didn't expect it to be." He watched his mother nod her agreement, then smile. She knew what he was thinking, she always read him perfectly. "Before you go, I want you to come with me to my time, I really want you to meet Dobie while you can."

"I'd love that."

"Since I'm still able to jump, allow me to take you there."

"I'd be honored."

He put his hands on Eunis' arms and she did the same. The moment he did, he felt a jolt of energy infuse him like he'd never before experienced. He was used to taking Dobie, who nearly drained him every time they traveled together.

Energy swirled and the light around them was so bright he had to close his eyes. Then the feeling of weightlessness took over and the jump progressed faster than usual, but then he'd never jumped with a full Mageous before. The sensation ended as abruptly as it began, and he found himself inside his warehouse.

Eunis released her hold on Kane. "Is this all yours?"

"It is, but I suppose I'll no longer need any of it. We've managed quite a collection. I like to be prepared."

"And so you are. You and Dobie have created quite a traveler's closet here."

Kane laughed. "This isn't our only warehouse."

"Let me guess, you have a couple in different time zones?"

"You know me well, mother."

Eunis reached out and cupped his cheek in her hand. "My dear son, what I wouldn't do to know you better, to stay with you here and now."

"There must be a way. You know I desperately want you to stay."

She sighed. "If I stay here, who would raise and protect ten-annual-cycle Kane? You need me more in the past, because the future Kane would also change. You know the ramifications of jumping, and what outcomes you can change, and what must remain the same."

All he could do was nod his understanding. "I also know that with a petition to the Mageous Council, they can grant a person permission to move their life permanently to the future or the past."

"Then you also know that has happened only a handful of times in over thousands of annual-cycles."

"I know the rules, but I don't like them." His mother laughed, and it was a delightful sound. "I know, I haven't changed. But, those few that were granted the permanent jump probably doubted they would receive a favorable judgment. Which proves, it could happen."

"True. However, I don't think you want to know how many were turned down."

"You are correct, as always. I much prefer to think positively. It's how I've survived."

"Are you ready to meet Dobie?"

"I'd love to."

He offered his mother his arm, then escorted her to the entrance to the living quarters. Before he could touch the hidden button to open the door, Dobie controlled it from the inside. At least the heat sensors in the warehouse still worked.

"Chief!"

Dobie rushed forward and gave him a bear hug, then paused in front of Eunis. "I'd like you to meet Eunis. Eunis, this is Dobie, my partner in about everything you can think of. He is more like a brother. And Dobie, this is the woman I call Mother."

"May I hug you?"

"Absolutely."

The affection Dobie gave Eunis was real and honest. As long he'd known his friend, he'd hugged very few people, so he knew Eunis was a special person to Dobie.

Dobie stepped back. "I'm thrilled to meet the woman who could put up with this man, especially as a child. I'll bet he challenged your patience constantly."

"He did. However, I was always one step ahead of him."

"Don't tell him, but that's my trick as well."

Eunis and Dobie both laughed long and hard. "I can't believe my own mother, and my best friend are laughing at me."

"We're just teasing, son. Don't tell me you've lost your sense of humor?"

"At the moment, I have." The looks he received were confused, and guilt sprang forward. "I'm sorry. I know you're teasing, it's just that I'm about to lose the only woman I've ever loved." He looked at Eunis. "Except for you, mother."

"Son, I understand more than you think." She laid her hand on his forearm, on top of the cuff. "You want to hurry up so you can lay the Vambrace Cuffs in Jorell's lap to prove your love. It's your way of asking her to life-mate you." She smiled. "How am I doing?"

Kane could not help the chuckle that escaped from deep within. "You're good. Very good."

"I'm glad I haven't lost my touch."

"Chief, you'll have to forgive me since I've never seen you in love before. I think it's new to both of us."

He laughed. "I thought I saw something sparking between you and Alesa, or should I say firing up?" Dobie's face turned red, and he almost felt sorry for his friend. He stepped over to stand beside Dobie, then put his arm over his shoulder. "Don't be embarrassed, love just happens, and it waits for no one, nor does it come easy." He looked Dobie in the eye. "I hope you find the love you're looking for."

"We deserve to find life-mates and settle down."

Kane shook his head. "Never thought I'd hear those words spoken by you."

Dobie punched Kane in the chest. "Me? What about you? Tough guy!"

"Boys, boys!" Eunis smiled.

"You've never been alone, *Traveler*. You just never realized it before."

"You're right. I never thought about it before."

Eunis looked around. "You must have had some very interesting jumps together."

"The only jumps I've ever done as myself are these last few. We've been successful because we've remained anonymous. No client could give our identity away since we looked different every time. Dobie kept track of where and when we used each identity."

"That's brilliant. I've known many professional jumpers who had multitudes of problems because everyone knew who they were, and what they did for a living." Eunis cleared her throat. "I'd better go to the council now. You need that hearing as soon as possible, right son?"

"Absolutely." Kane hugged his mother. "Thank you. I really appreciate what you're doing for me."

"Anything for you."

In an instant Eunis disappeared in a flash of light. He silently wished her luck since she was his only hope to win Jorell back. It had to work.

****

Kane took his seat next to Eunis at the table before the Mageous High Council. He still could not believe Eunis was able to set the hearing so soon, and she even convinced Alextor they needed to use his facility. So here they were in Sector-Three's Main Chamber.

He and Eunis stood in respect when the Mageous High Council entered and took their appropriate places on the dais. The six men and six women stared at him as if he were a criminal. Eunis said this would not be easy, and she was correct as usual.

The main speaker entered and took his place at the podium. He gestured for everyone to sit and waited for the group to settle before he spoke. When he began his welcome speech, Kane knew exactly why he was their speaker, his voice sounded clear, demanding and authoritative.

"Our business today is complex and difficult. A request has been submitted for a removal of power by Kane Sinue. He has also requested that Eunis Sinue be allowed to remain in this time and place."

The speaker paused and glanced around the chamber. "Before we continue with this hearing, the High Council has requested that Alextor Sutone and his daughter, First Advisor Jorell Sutone be in attendance. So at this time, please welcome Ruler Alextor Sutone and First Advisor Jorell Sutone."

Kane felt his jaw drop. The last thing he expected just happened. Why would the High Council ask the Sutones to attend his hearing? He wanted to be the one to tell Jorell about giving up his powers. His request just became public knowledge. So much for privacy.

He watched Jorell and her father take their seats at a small table next to the High Council on the dais. He did not have to look at her, he felt her gaze on him and his entire body turned warmer. She was still angry with him, that message came through loud and clear. He did not need a mind-meld to interpret her thoughts.

"Now that everyone is here, we will begin. Mageous Kane, please make your plea to the High Council."

Kane stood and moved to the platform in the center of the room where there was a pulpit complete with microphone. He clasped his hand in front of him and rested them on the polished wood surface. "High Council members, Speaker, Ruler Sutone, First Advisor Sutone, and honored guests. I have had the honor of being half-Mageous from birth."

He certainly had their attention since every eye was on him, and he felt the pressure. "I realize the High Council knows my complete story, from my birth to this day. Nothing escapes the High Council. You know my father, the erroneous Pakar Moran, is currently in custody and awaiting trial for his numerous crimes against society, and the Mageous Sect.

"What the High Council does not know, is that I am in love with First Advisor Jorell Sutone. It is for her that I willingly relinquish my powers. I would give anything for her, including my life. I wish to present her with my Vambrace cuffs, as a gift to prove my love for her, and that I will never leave her again, or put anything above her."

The silence in the room nearly overwhelmed him. He had no idea what anyone was thinking, but all he could do was continue his plea. "I ask you also to spare Eunis's life and allow her to remain here, in this time, with me. She has more than earned her due, as you are aware. She has led an exemplarily life, and does not deserve to be tortured and ultimately murdered by Pakar Moran. If not for her Ruler Sutone would be dead, and the entire planet would be embroiled in war.

"Eunis sits here today, knowing her fate, which I realize is a violation of The Mageous Code, but she has more than earned the right to survive." He paused and noticed some of the members on the dais looking at each other, and giving a slight nod here and there. Hopefully that was a good sign, but he knew better than to read anything into a few physical responses. Not one garnished a smile, or even a hint of a grin. They were a tough group. It was easier facing warriors and Pakar, at least with them he knew what to expect.

"Therefore, I beg the council for Eunis's life. She has much to contribute, and will continue to do so if given the opportunity. I also know how few of these requests are seriously considered, but I beg for your consideration and leniency.

"The Council will have no worries regarding me since my request is removal of all powers, a price I am more than willing to pay." He glanced at Jorell who stared down at the table in front of her and refused to look at him. He hoped to reach her with his request, but his chance of success appeared slim to none. "And with that statement, I shall close. I anxiously await your decisions."

The Speaker stepped back up to his podium. "Thank you, Mageous Kane Moran. The Council will adjourn for a brief consult. They ask that you, Eunis and the Sutones remain available. We will re-adjourn shortly. Thank you all for your attention."

Everyone stood while the High Council filed off the dais and retired to their meeting room. Both Sutones silently followed behind them without a glance back. Every muscle in his body rebelled and he nearly fell back onto his chair once everyone was gone. He felt a hand on his shoulder, relieved to know he still had one friend on the planet.

Dobie sat on the empty chair next to Kane. "What can I do?"

He looked into Dobie's loyal eyes. "I wish there were something you could do, my friend. It is now in the hands of the High Council. There's nothing anyone can do."

"That may be, but I could at least go talk to Jorell for you."

"No. Any decision she comes to must be her own. She heard what I said before the High Council. It's up to her now."

"What will you do if--"

Kane shook his head. "I refuse to think about that eventuality."

****

"Father? Are you all right?"

"I am." Ruler Sutone put his hands on his daughter's shoulders. "For the first time in a very long time, I am really all right. Thanks to you and Kane. I owe you both my life, and that is something I will never be able to repay."

Jorell hugged her father. "You never have to repay me, or anyone else. I'm just happy you're still here in one piece." She let go of him and took a step back. "I was so afraid this day would never come."

"You mean seeing Kane before the Mageous High Council?"

"No! Seeing you alive and well, mentally and physically."

"I think you protest too much." Alextor took a seat in a large upholstered chair by the window. "When are you going to be honest with me?" He smiled. "And yourself?"

She turned her back on him. "I don't know what you mean."

"Of course you do, so stop playing games and talk to me." He patted the arm of the chair next to him. "Please, sit by me. We need to talk." He cleared his throat. "A long overdue talk."

Jorell took a deep breath, then walked to where her father waited and sat in the chair beside him. "And what's so overdue about this talk?"

Alextor laughed. "Everything I suppose." He patted her hand for a moment. "First, you need to bring me up to date on several issues since I spent so many sun-cycles asleep. Second, but not least, I want to know about you and Kane." He cleared his throat. "All of it, every detail."

No way would she tell him about making love to Kane. No father wanted to hear that, and no daughter would tell all. He stared at her in silence and waited.

"Maybe every detail is not necessary. I shouldn't have said that, but as your father, and ruler, I must know where you stand."

"Why do my feelings for Kane make a difference on where I stand?" She shook her head. "My loyalty is with you and our people first and foremost. Always."

"I understand that, I really do. What I meant was..." Alextor stood and began to pace the floor in front of the chairs. "As your father I'm concerned about your mental state. If you're depressed it could interfere with your work."

"I would not let that happen. Is that what you think of me?" Jorell stood. "I am not mentally weak."

Alextor scratched his head. "This is not going well."

"You're right about that." She walked over to the table in the corner where there was a bottle of wine and several glasses and poured herself a glass. After several sips she turned and faced her father. "Care to explain yourself?"

"Only if you bring me a glass of wine. I need all the help I can get."

Her father was acting very strange. She had only seen him like this once before, and that was when he was trying to keep a secret from her. Did he have another one? She saw the worried look on his face and it seemed far more important than a simple secret.

She poured wine in a glass and carried it over to her father. When he took it from her his hand shook, and that was very odd. He was as steady as a boulder, nothing shook him. It was the main reason he made such a great leader.

"Please forgive me for what I'm about to tell you. I should have had this talk with you long ago, but I just couldn't bring myself to do it." He looked into his daughter's eyes. "Please, don't hate me, I...."

"Father, just tell me and stop this nonsense."

"No matter how I say it, it won't sound right, or make sense to you."

"In case you haven't noticed, I'm a big girl now, and I can handle about anything, so please, get on with it."

"It's about your mother." Alextor took a deep breath. "Before you were born, the Mageous Sect was not looked at in good favor, and your mother was a full-blooded Mageous."

Her heart began to race and she felt faint. She returned to her chair before she fell to the floor. Whatever she thought her father was hiding, this never occurred to her. "Go on." For the first time she heard her own voice quiver.

"We were young, and very in love. I'd just been elected to my first council term, and naturally feared for my career. I wanted to life-mate Felice, so I met with the Mageous Council and begged them to allow our union, and to keep her powers secret. It was agreed she would keep her name, but her records as a Mageous were erased, including her family history."

Jorell shook her head. The impact of realizing she was half-Mageous had not settled in her mind. No wonder she could read people, and it certainly explained how she and Kane could mind meld so perfectly. Of course. The possibility should have occurred to her before, but she believed her father. Of course he could not tell a child, but he should have told her before now.

"You look angry, my child."

"I am." She groaned in an effort to remove the fury she wanted to release on her father, but could not. He'd barely escaped death, and this was not the time for a fight.

"I well understand the sound of that groan, I've heard it all too many times before. As I said, I'm sorry for waiting so long. I guess I figured there was no reason to tell you, that it had no effect on your life. But that changed rather quickly, and I wasn't able to...well you know."

"I know all too well." Tears rolled down her cheeks. Could this get any worse? It could if she turned her back on her father. It was bad enough losing the one man she loved, why destroy her father when she fought so hard to save him? "I nearly lost you."

"I didn't mean it that way, I only meant I was not able to talk to you when you needed me to, so now is the moment for truth." He walked closer to Jorell then pulled her up from her chair and hugged her. "I love you more than you know. I'd do anything for you. You mean everything to me."

All she could do was nod her head against his shoulder. Life was strange, that was a fact, but she was not going to lose her father, not now. She pushed back from him, wiped the tears with her hands and took a deep breath. "All we have is each other. I may be upset about your secret, but I do forgive you."

"That is music to my ears, however, I believe you have more than just me. You have Kane. He loves you."

She looked deeply into her father's eyes. "You really do believe that, don't you?"

"I know that. I've seen the looks between the two of you, the same looks that your mother and I had."

"A look is all you need?"

"Of course not, Kane and I talked when you weren't around, and I also heard it from Dobie."

"Dobie is now an expert on love?"

"You'd be surprised what that man knows. He's very observant, plus he said if he's going to lose his best friend, he's glad it's to you because he's also seen the love you both share for each other."

"That may have been true once, but I heard firsthand how he really feels when I'm not around."

"And you don't think he was playing a part and saying what that evil man wanted to hear? Jorell, I thought I raised you better than that. Kane did what he had to do in order to bring down Pakar Moran, or Loran Narom, or whatever name he wants to go by. Evil is really his name, and I can't thank Kane enough for stopping a planet-wide war and a dictatorship. He did what no other man could have done."

She sighed deeply. He was right and she knew it, but Kane's words still tore at her heart. Hearing him speak about her like she was trash still resonated in her mind. How could she not hear him? The real question was did he mean what he said?

"Daughter? I know that look. You're thinking about what I said and you're realizing I'm right as always!"

Without thinking she gave her father a loving slap on the arm and he laughed, which made her smile. "I'm not going to say you're always right, but I will say you've given me something to think about." And she would think--long and hard about the man who mysteriously appeared in her life, took it over, and won her heart. How could she live without him?

CHAPTER FIFTY

"For the last time, sit down. Relax. Calm down. The council will reconvene soon, and there's nothing you can do to hurry them up."

"Dobie, what will I do if I give up my powers and Jorell refuses to forgive me?"

"Try again, chief. You're stubborn and she'll see your side if you plague her long enough."

"Grovel? Is that what you're saying?"

"If that's what it takes, yeah." He stared at his friend. "That's if you love her."

"You know I do, but she heard me say awful things about her, things I didn't mean."

"I know, and she'll figure it out. She's one smart lady. After all, she fell in love with you, didn't she?" Dobie laughed.

"I'm glad you think this is funny."

"Lost your sense of humor?" Dobie walked over to his friend and sat next to him. "Kane, you've always had the ability to be logical and level headed. You've planned way more difficult missions than this one, and you know it."

"I have to agree, but I was in charge, and this time I'm not. That bothers me."

"Have faith, my friend. Or has love caused you to totally lose your mind?" He laughed. "That's why I haven't gone over the edge for a woman."

"And what about Alesa?"

"I'm biding my time. If you and Jorell life-mate, then I'll consider

340

getting serious with Alesa."

"Well, you might be waiting a long time." He hung his head and exhaled. He wanted Jorell, and he wanted Dobie to be happy and settle down with a woman. Alesa was sweet on his friend, and they really were good together, but he was afraid Jorell would turn him down. He couldn't blame her, but he prayed she'd find it in her heart to forgive him.

He stood and began to pace around the large, elaborate waiting area. Dobie gave him the look but left him alone. Waiting was the worst. He was a man of action, yet he was at the beck and call of others, a situation he hated.

Had he known Jorell was in the cave he never would have said those terrible things about her. How was he supposed to know she'd followed him? It was too late for second thoughts. But was it too late for them?

The two large doors across from where he stood opened and a messenger stepped inside. He knew what the man would say. This was it, his life was about to be decided, and he could be left with nothing.

"The Mageous High Council requests your presence immediately in the hearing chamber."

The man turned on his heel and walked back out into the hall. He looked over and Dobie who stood and walked toward him with a worried expression on his face. "This is it my friend."

Dobie slapped Kane's back. "You're right, and I'm with you all the way. You know that."

"I do, and I'm grateful for your devotion. I'm not sure I've always deserved it, but I am appreciative beyond words."

"I accept your words. Now come on Chief, we don't want to be late."

He walked with Dobie to meet up with the messenger who led the way down the long hall. Why did he feel like he was walking to his own execution?

****

"Kane Sinue Moran, please stand and face the Mageous High Council."

The moment had finally arrived and he rose from the chair and stood before the Mageous High Council, who held his future in their hands. Jorell and her father sat in a place of honor on the podium next to the Council members. She refused to meet his gaze, but Alextor looked at him with an expression he did not know how to read.

The Head Mageous stepped up to the pedestal at the left-hand side of the general members. Of course he wanted to be sure everyone heard his words.

"Kane Sinue Moran, which is your full legal name. However, we have decided you have the choice of keeping the last name of Moran, or dropping it for all time. What is your decision?"

"Moran is a name that has brought pain and suffering to many, a name without respect or honor. I choose to drop that name as offered."

"Very well. The High Council agrees with your assessment of your biological father, and regrets everything concerning the man, including what you have had to endure due to his evil. Kane Sinue will be your official name of record from this sun-cycle forward. The Mageous High Council has ruled on your two requests." He cleared his throat. "To date, no living Mageous has ever made requests such as yours.

"First, your request for Eunis Sinue to remain in this time and not be returned to her eventual death is granted. We carefully considered all circumstances regarding the issues involved with the normally illegal practice of toying in life and death matters. That said, since you are a grown man, and already suffered the loss of your surrogate mother, and learned what you needed to know on your own. This most unusual request was granted due to the mitigating situation, and the previously discussed evil deeds of Pakar Moran.

"We *do not* want you, or any other Mageous to think this favorable decision will ever happen again. As all Mageouses know, life and death are *never* to be manipulated in a manner that will affect the outcome of any person's future. However, because Eunis Sinue did a superior job raising a son, who single-handedly saved the outbreak of global war on Okeron we made a special exception. Plus, all of the exemplary deeds performed by Eunis herself showed us she did not deserve the terrible, premature ending of her life."

Kane let out the breath he'd been holding. At least he was half-way through, and so far, so good. Jorell had still to meet his gaze, although he'd kept his focus mainly on the speaker as was expected. Would Jorell forgive him? Would it matter if he had powers or not? How would he ever know if she wouldn't even look at him?

"The Mageous High Council has kept an eye on you and your business since its conception, and you have always operated within the Mageous Laws. In fact, we must commend you on the amount of people you have helped."

Kane's heart raced. They respected him, and that in itself was a shock. Since they granted his request about Eunis, they would easily grant his request to remove all his powers. He would now have a chance with Jorell.

"As for your second request for us to remove all your powers, the vote was unanimous to deny your proposal. As we previously stated, your work is excellent and needs to continue. Any man who single handedly saves the life of a sector ruler and keeps Okeron from planetary war, or dictatorship, must be able to do more good deeds." The man took a deep breath.

"Plus, there is no barrier with you and Jorell having a relationship since she is half-Mageous. That brings this hearing to a close. Do you have anything further to say?"

Kane took a deep breath and tried to think after what the man just said about Jorell. First things first. "I want to thank the council for their decisions and kind words. My gratitude for your time and consideration." He bowed slightly to pay his respect even though blood pounded through his veins. He could not tell if it was anger or relief, but he'd be glad to sit down and let everything settle.

The Mageous High Council filed off the podium quickly, then the audience behind him made their way out through the open doors at the rear of the large room. He felt a familiar hand on his back and turned to greet Dobie.

"Chief, congratulations on Eunis, that's fantastic!" At that moment Eunis stepped in front of him and hugged him tightly. He returned the embrace. They did not need words to know how each other felt.

Eunis pulled away from her son. "I can't thank you enough, but right now I believe you have someone you need to speak to. Isn't that right, Dobie?"

"I uh..." Dobie stumbled backward when Eunis shoved him away from Kane. "He does, that's right. He does!"

"What are you two up to?"

"Nothing, son, we've been sitting in this chamber right behind you. What could we possibly have done?"

"I'm not sure, but--"

"But nothing. You need to listen to your mother now, and get your handsome self over to the back corner of this room where Alextor and Jorell are. You need to talk to her." Eunis grabbed his arm. "Use your head, son. Speak from a place of love and understanding only. This will work out. I'm sure of it."

"I hope you're right." He turned and walked toward his fate.

****

The closer Kane came to her the faster her heart raced. How could she, Jorell Sutone remain calm and collected when the most handsome man in the galaxy walked toward her. He was her love--her life. But first they had issues to work out.

"Ruler Sutone," Kane bowed slightly, "First Advisor Jorell Sutone, greetings. I thought, if Advisor Sutone agrees, we could have a private moment?"

Alextor reached out and patted Kane on the back. "Of course, my boy, of course." He turned to look at Jorell. "Be nice, daughter. Remember what we talked about."

She nodded at her father and smiled. "Of course. How could I forget? You beat it into me." She paused and took a deep breath. "I mean, I remember, father."

"That's better, my dear. Now, you two play nice, but I think you need to go into my private chamber behind the podium. You wouldn't want to be overheard."

"As always, wise advice." She looked at Kane. "Follow me." She turned and began to walk toward the front of the room. A tingle ran down her spine from the sense of Kane's eyes on her backside, watching her every step. She could almost hear him in her mind. At least he still seemed attracted to her.

It only took a moment to climb the side steps onto the podium, then walk past a tall curtain to the hidden door in the back. She looked into the iris scanner and the door slid open. Once inside she turned to face the man who meant the most to her. Hopefully he would understand.

"First, I need to expla--" Before she could say the full word his mouth covered hers and the kiss was deep and telling. He never tasted so good, or touched her soul the way he did at this very moment. She could kiss him like this forever, but he needed to sweat just a bit first. She pulled back and pushed him away. The look on his face was priceless, like a child with his hand caught in the candy jar.

"I'm sorry, Jorell. Please forgive me. I don't know why I did that." He cleared his throat. "To be honest, I couldn't help myself. It's been too long since I've been with you, alone."

"I understand, but we have some things to talk about before we take any further steps toward a reconciliation." She turned her back on him before she smiled and gave herself away. "First there is the issue of what you said about me to Pakar Moran, of all people. The man who is *your father*?"

"The fact that he is my father is a crude mistake of nature, nothing more. I hold nothing but contempt for the man."

She turned back around to face him, and to apply a bit more pressure. Although it appeared her plan was working quite well when he wiped his forehead with the back of his hand. "Many share that opinion."

"Be that as it may, I would have killed him with my own hands, but my brother and I decided it would be best to hold him publically responsible for his crimes against humanity."

"I understand. We'll discuss your "brother" later. Now, about your words."

"My sweet, I would give anything if you had never heard me say those things. But you must know what I said was to appeal to Pakar's evil side in an effort to show him we had something in common. At the time I was a bit outnumbered and had to appeal to him in some way."

"By calling *me* a whore?"

He smiled. "I admit that was a stretch since it's so opposite of you. In any other circumstances that word would never have occurred to me. Especially since it could *never* describe you in any way. My apologies." Kane fell to his knees and bowed his head. "I beg you for your forgiveness, my love. You mean the world to me, and I did not mean one word of what I said to Pakar on that fateful sun-cycle in the cave."

"I'm not sure exactly why I should forgive you, or why it even matters." She wanted to hear how he really felt, because her decision did rest on what he said next. Both of their futures rested on his next words, fair or not. She stared at him and waited. More sweat beaded on his forehead. Confusion was the only emotion she sensed, even though his mental wall had lowered.

Kane raised one leg and remained on one knee. He reached out, took Jorell's hand in his and gazed up into her eyes. "You are the one and only woman I have ever loved, or will love. I do not want to live without you. Please, Jorell, forgive me and become my life-mate so I can love you today and every day of our lives."

Tears welled in her eyes. "Your words are perfect. You passed the test." She knelt down to meet his gaze, and when she did he asked permission to mind-meld with her. Right now she could not deny him anything.

"My sweet, what is your answer?"

"How could I say no to a man who just confessed his love to me? Of course I'll life-mate you!" He leaned forward, wrapped his arms around her and kissed her. It wasn't the usual kiss, it was filled with gratitude, hope, and more love than anyone could imagine. *"Kane, your kiss says it all, but there is one more thing we need to verbally discuss."*

Kane reluctantly ended the kiss, pulled back and stared at her. He looked worried so she wanted to get this last thing straightened out. "Did you hear what was said about me during the reading of the verdict?"

He sighed. "They revealed you are half-Mageous."

"It was a secret my father withheld from me my entire life. He only told me moments before the council reconvened. I need to know how you feel about my undisclosed powers?"

"Part of me was totally shocked when I heard it announced. Part of me realized long ago when I took you and Dobie on a successful jump with me. I should not have been able to take two non-Mageouses at the same time."

"So, you were out of your mind when you tried it?" She laughed.

I've been out of my mind since the sun-cycle I first laid eyes on you, and will probably remain so as long as you're with me! Kane laughed. I'm getting quite used to the feeling. But only because I love you with every ounce of my being, and always will.

She placed her hands on his cheeks and soaked in the warmth and the love that radiated from him, inside and out. *I feel the same, but you still did not say what you think of my being half-Mageous.*

I think we shall make one fantastic baby, and I think it's time to start right now.

He lowered her to the floor and kissed her once again, sending unending love with his mind, the loving response of his body pressed against her. She could not argue with him. Never before had she thought about having a baby, but the time and the man were perfect. *I love you Traveler--now and forever.*

ABOUT THE AUTHOR

Kathleen Garnsey was born in Michigan, raised in California and has lived in the beautiful Missouri Ozarks since 1987. She lives with her husband and their Boxer named Ginger. Her son, his wife and three beautiful grandchildren live close and keep her busy.

She became serious about her writing over twenty-eight years ago and continues to plot new stories. Kathleen has written five futuristic romances which will all soon be available on Amazon. Since she has always loved sci-fi and romance, combining the two became her passion. She hopes you enjoy her stories of love and adventure in ***another time and place.***

www.ingramcontent.com/pod-product-compliance
Lightning Source LLC
Chambersburg PA
CBHW062012170626
46813CB00001B/123

* 9 780692 740422 *